DUDLEY PUBLIC LIBRARIES

The loan of this book may be renewed if not required by other readers, by contacting the library from which it was borrowed.

...loves ...r family and ...s: Visit her website at

...has devoted her life to an intensive study of charismatic heroes who cause the best kind of trouble in the lives of their heroines. As a sideline she researches locations for romance, from vibrant cities to desert encampments and fairytale castles. Annie lives in eastern Australia with her hero husband, between sandy beaches and gorgeous wine country. She finds writing the perfect excuse to postpone housework. To contact her or join her newsletter, visit annie-west.com

Maisey Yates is a *New York Times* bestselling author of over one hundred romance novels. Whether she's writing strong, hard working cowboys, dissolute princes or multigenerational family stories, she loves getting lost in fictional worlds. An avid knitter with a dangerous yarn addiction and an aversion to housework, Maisey lives with her husband and three kids in rural Oregon. Check out her website, maiseyyates.com or find her on Facebook.

Bachelor Bosses

Bachelor Bosses:
Calling the
Shots

LUCY MONROE

ANNIE WEST

MAISEY YATES

MIX
Paper from
responsible sources
FSC C007454

This book is produced from independently certified FSC™ paper
to ensure responsible forest management.

For more information visit www.harpercollins.co.uk/green

Printed and bound in Spain using 100% Renewable electricity at
CPI Black Print, Barcelona

MILLS & BOON

First Published in Great Britain 2022
By Mills & Boon, an imprint of HarperCollins*Publishers,* Ltd
1 London Bridge Street, London, SE1 9GF

www.harpercollins.co.uk

HarperCollins*Publishers*
1st Floor, Watermarque Building,
Ringsend Road, Dublin 4, Ireland

BACHELOR BOSSES: CALLING THE SHOTS
© 2022 Harlequin Enterprises ULC.

An Heiress for His Empire © 2014 Lucy Monroe
The Flaw in Raffaele's Revenge © 2016 Annie West
Want Me, Cowboy © 2018 Maisey Yates

ISBN: 978-0-263-30457-2

AN HEIRESS FOR
HIS EMPIRE

LUCY MONROE

For Judy Flohr, a very special reader who I have long considered an honest friend. It's sort of amazing to me that you've been reading and sharing your love of my books since the very first one, *The Greek Tycoon's Ultimatum*, back in 2003. When I'm doubting myself, or the story, I know I can re-read your emails or online reader reviews and remember why I write and that maybe I'm not so bad at this after all.

THANK YOU!!!

Hugs and blessings, Lucy

CHAPTER ONE

MADISON ARCHER SET her morning coffee down, hot liquid spilling over the rim, as she read her Google alerts with growing horror.

Madcap Madison Looking for New Master?
Archer Heiress into Heavy Kink
San Francisco Bad Boy Dumps Very Bad Girl

The articles made lurid claims about a lifestyle and relationship between Maddie and Perry Timwater. A completely nonexistent relationship.

The fact that Perry was the source caused the coffee to sour in Maddie's stomach.

His supposed exposé of their fictitious relationship claimed she was a submissive with a serious pain fetish and need for multiple partners. She gritted her teeth on the urge to swear as she read it was her inability to remain faithful that forced Perry to end things between them.

Maddie wouldn't mind ending Perry right that minute. Betrayal choked her.

How could he have done this?

He was her *friend*.

They'd met their freshman year at university. He'd made her laugh when she'd thought nothing could. Not after her epic fail trying to get Viktor Beck's attention. She'd started

university with a broken heart and Perry had helped her
paste over the cracks with friendship.

She'd helped him pass his accountancy courses. He'd
played platonic escort for her and she'd provided him entrée to Jeremy Archer's world—an echelon above his own.

But never, not once, had their friendship ever taken a
turn toward something heavier.

Pounding sounded on her front door. "Maddie! It's me,
don't freak." Then barely a second later, the double snick of
locks sliding back was followed by the door swinging wide.

Holding a bag from their favorite bakery aloft, her black
bob swirling around her pixie face, Romi Grayson kicked
the door shut behind her. "I come bearing the panacea for
all ills."

"I'm not sure even chocolate and flaky pastry can make
this situation better." Maddie slumped against the back of
her chair.

Eyes the same vibrant blue as Maddie's glittered with
anger. "So, Perry's lost his mind, right?"

"You saw the articles?"

"Only after reporters woke me from a dead sleep demanding my opinion of my best friend's darker sexual
proclivities." Romi's mouth twisted wryly. "Proclivities
I'm pretty sure you wouldn't have even if you *weren't*
still a virgin."

"You've got that right. I've never been able to trust one
man enough to have sex, much less multiple partners."

As ridiculous as that might seem at twenty-four, it
wasn't going to change anytime soon, either.

"If you ask me, it's got less to do with trust and more to
do with the fact you imprinted on Viktor Beck like a baby
bird when you were a teenager and you've never gotten
over him."

"Romi!" Maddie was in no mood to hash out her unrequited feelings for her father's dark-haired, dark-eyed, to-die-for-bodied golden boy.

"I'm just saying…"

"Nothing you haven't said before." Maddie's stomach grew queasier by the second.

Along with the rest of the world, Vik would see the articles, but she couldn't afford to think about that right now, or she really was going to lose it. "Father is going to kill me."

This new scandal was bound to crack even the San Francisco tycoon's icy demeanor. And not in the way Maddie had always craved.

He'd sent her away to boarding school months after her mother's death and Maddie had courted media attention in the hopes of gaining his. It had worked for her mother, Helene Archer, née Madison, the original Madcap Madison, but Maddie had come to realize the strategy had backfired pretty spectacularly for her.

In the nine years since Helene's death, Jeremy had developed a habit of thinking the worst of his daughter. When he wasn't ignoring her existence all together.

"If he doesn't die of a stress-related heart attack first." Romi put a chocolate-filled croissant in front of Maddie.

"Don't say that."

The other woman grimaced. "Sorry. Stuff just comes out. You know what I'm like. Your dad is wound pretty tight, though."

Maddie couldn't argue that.

"I think this time, Perry's diarrhea of the mouth has me beat anyway." Romi chewed her pastry militantly. "What was he thinking?"

Morose, Maddie stared at her friend. "That he wanted the money the tabloid paid him for the story?"

She'd had no idea that turning down his latest request for a loan would result in her utter humiliation. How could she? Friends didn't do that to each other.

"Jerk."

Maddie usually played peacemaker between her two closest friends, but she wasn't about to stand up for Perry this time. "What am I going to do?"

"You could threaten to sue and demand a retraction."

"Based on my word against his?"

Romi made a sound very close to a growl. "You two have never even kissed with tongue."

"But we have kissed, for the cameras." Perry had always made a joke of it.

He had been Maddie's go-to escort for years and more than one article speculating on their relationship had been run, often quoting anonymous sources and always accompanied by the joke kissing pictures.

"Do you think he's done this before?"

"Sold *confidential details* of your supposed relationship?" Romi asked.

"Yes."

"You know what I think."

Maddie sighed. "That he's a leech."

"Always has been."

"He was a good friend." Maddie couldn't make herself claim he *still* was.

Romi just gave Maddie a disbelieving look, no words necessary.

Ignoring it, Maddie said, "I probably can't prove we never had a relationship, but I can sue them for libel in the details."

"His word against yours."

"But he's lying."

"This is something new for the tabloids?"

Feeling hopeless, Maddie pushed her croissant away.

"You could always sic your dad's dogs on Perry. That media fixer of his could be cast in Shark Week on the Discovery Channel."

"I should." Even supposing her dad cared enough to assign his media fixer's precious time to helping Maddie.

Romi's expression turned knowing. "But you won't. Perry was your friend."

Maddie opened her mouth, but Romi put her hand up, forestalling words. "Don't you dare say he still is."

"No." Maddie swallowed back emotion. "No, it's pretty clear he's not my friend and maybe he never was."

"Oh, sweetie." Romi came around the table to hug her.

Maddie fought down stress-induced nausea. "I thought he was real."

"Instead, he turned out to be just another one of the plastic people." Romi's tone reflected her own experience with that. "All looks and no substance."

Maddie choked out a morbid laugh. "Yeah."

A bugler's reveille sounded from her smartphone.

With a snicker, Romi moved back to her seat. "Daddy's PA?"

"I thought it was appropriate." Maddie clicked into her text messages, unsurprised to see that there were dozens.

While she checked her phone periodically throughout the day, Maddie only had sound alerts set for certain people: Romi, Perry—who was going off the list today—Maddie's father, his personal assistant. Viktor Beck.

Not that her father's business heir apparent contacted Maddie these days. But still, if he did…she'd get an audible alert.

Ignoring the numerous messages from *friends*, acquaintances and the media jackals, Maddie clicked into the one from her father's PA.

Mtg w Mr. Archer @ 10:45—conf rm 2.

Mr. Archer. Not Mr. A, even though the PA had used text speak for the rest of the message. Not *your father*. That might have been too personal.

"He wants to meet this morning." Maddie bit her lip, considering what she'd have to change to make that happen.

Romi nodded. "Are you going to go?"

Maddie considered putting off her morning plans for the meeting with her father.

"No." It wasn't as if her showing up when he called was going to make Jeremy any less angry.

She shot a quick text back to the PA offering to come anytime after noon-thirty.

Fifteen minutes later, Romi was gone after a final pep talk when the strains of Michael Bublé's "Call Me Irresponsible" sounded from Maddie's smartphone.

Her father was *calling* her. Personally. Not texting.

Any other time, she would be thrilled. But right now? The crooner's smooth voice was as ominous as the sepulchre tones of a Halloween horror flick's sound track.

Maddie put the phone to her ear. "Hello, Father."

"Ten forty-five, Madison. You will not be late."

"You know I have a standing morning appointment." Not that he knew what it was.

Maddie had tried to tell him once, but Jeremy had mocked the very idea of his flighty daughter doing anything worthwhile. Worse, he'd made it clear how useless he thought it was to spend time volunteering at an underfunded public school predominantly populated by the children of poverty-level families.

Since then, Maddie had kept her two lives completely separate. Maddie Grace, nondescript twentysomething who loved children and volunteered a good chunk of her time, had nothing in common—not even hair and eye color—with Madison Archer, notorious socialite and heiress.

"Cancel." No give. No explanation. Just demand.

Typical.

"It's important."

"No. It is not." His tone was so cold it sent shivers along her extremities.

"It is to me." She wished she could be as unaffected by his displeasure as he was by hers. "Please."

"Ten-forty-five, Madison." Then he hung up.

She knew because the call dropped.

Wearing the armor of her socialite Madison Archer persona, Maddie got off the elevator at the twenty-ninth floor of her father's building in San Francisco's financial district.

None of the nerves wreaking havoc with her insides showed on her smooth face.

Makeup applied to highlight, not compete with, the blue of her eyes and gentle bow of her lips, she'd styled her chin-length red hair in perfectly placed curls around her oval face so like her mother's. No highlights had ever been necessary for the natural copper tones.

Her three-quarter-length-sleeved Valentino black-and-white suit wasn't this year's collection, but it was one of her favorites and fit the image she intended to convey. The wide black banded hem of the straight skirt brushed a proper two inches above her knees and the Jackie-O-style jacket with a statement bow was a galaxy away from slutty.

She'd opted for classic closed-toe black Jimmy Choo pumps that added a mere two inches to her five-foot-six-inch height. Maddie carried a simple leather Chanel bag, her accessories limited to her mother's favorite Cartier watch and diamond stud earrings.

Maddie didn't look anything like the woman described by Perry in his "breakup interview" with the press.

She walked into Conference Room Two without knocking, stopping for a strategic pause in the doorway to allow the other occupants a moment to look their fill.

She wasn't going to scurry in like a mouse trying to avoid the cat's attention.

The brief moment had the added benefit of allowing her to take her own *lay of the land*.

Seven people sat around the eight-person conference table. As to be expected, her father occupied one end. Maddie was equal parts relieved and worried to see his media fixer at the other end, but not happy at all to see the man seated to the right of her father.

Romi was right that Maddie had had a crush on the gorgeous Viktor Beck since he started working for Jeremy Archer ten years ago. The unrequited feelings had evolved from schoolgirl infatuation to something more, something that made it impossible for other men to measure up.

That first year, Maddie had still had her mother and Helene would tease Maddie for her blushes in the tycoon-in-the-making's presence.

Maddie had learned to control her blushes, but not the feelings the handsome third-generation Russian engendered in her.

Having him here to witness her humiliation tightened the knot of tension inside her until she wasn't sure it would ever come undone.

Less understandable, but not nearly as upsetting, was the presence of two of her father's other high-level managers in the remaining chairs on that side of the table. Her father's PA sat to his left, with an empty chair beside her.

The final man at the table had a powerful presence and a familiar face, but in her current state of highly guarded stress, Maddie couldn't place him.

Everyone had a stack of papers in front of them. It took only the briefest glance to see what they were: printed-out copies of the news stories Maddie had seen earlier on her smartphone. Underneath them was an individual copy for each person in the room of the actual tabloid the original story had run in.

Vik's pile was different. It had what looked like a contract on top. Looking around the table, Maddie realized everyone else had a copy of that as well, but on the bottom of their pile—the stapled corner was the only thing visible in the other piles.

She looked at her father and gave him the sardonic expression she'd been using for years to mask her vulnerability. "I don't suppose it occurred to you to discuss this with me privately before bringing in a think tank."

"Sit down, Madison." He didn't even bother to respond to her comment.

Which should neither surprise, nor hurt. So why did it do both?

She waited a count of three before obeying his brusque order, deliberately ignoring the stack of papers in front of her. "I assume we've already drafted a letter demanding a retraction?"

When her father didn't answer, she stared pointedly at his media fixer.

"Is it likely your ex-lover will recant his commentary?" the fixer asked in a flat tone.

"First, he was never my lover. Second, he doesn't have to recant his lies for us to sue the tabloid for libel." Though her chances of winning the suit weren't high without Perry's honesty.

"I am not in the habit of wasting time or resources on a hopeless endeavor," her father said.

"The story is out there and that can't be changed," she agreed. "But that doesn't mean we leave Perry's lies unchallenged."

Her father's eyes were chips of blue ice. "If you wish to challenge your ex-lover's *lies*, you may do so, but that is not my concern."

"You don't believe the stories?" she asked with a pained incredulity she couldn't quite hide.

"What I believe is not the issue at hand."

"It is for me." There were only two people in that room whose opinion Maddie cared about.

Her father's and Viktor Beck's, no matter how much she might wish that wasn't the case.

Her gaze shifted to Vik, but nothing from the stern set of his square jaw to the obscure depths of his espresso-brown eyes revealed his thoughts.

There had been a time when he might have tried to encourage her with a half smile or even a wink, but those days were gone. There'd been no softening in his demeanor toward her since her first trip home after going away to university.

And while that might be her own fault, she didn't have to like it.

Her father cleared his throat. "Those tawdry stories may have precipitated this meeting, but they are not the reason for it."

Maddie's attention snapped back to her only remaining family. "What do you mean?"

"The issue we are here to address is your unacceptable notoriety, Madison. I will not sit by while you attempt to rival other heiresses for worldwide infamy."

"I don't." Even when Maddie had tried to court her father's attention by gaining that of the media, she hadn't gone that far.

Okay, so she and Romi were known for their participation in political rallies of the liberal variety, which included a well-publicized sit-in protesting cuts in local school funding. That Maddie had gone further, bungee jumping from the Golden Gate Bridge with five others and unfurling a giant banner that read Go Green or Go Home, was beside the point.

There were videos online of her bungee jumping in less politically motivated and slightly more risky circumstances. The snowboarding had been a total failure, but she'd always loved downhill skiing and learning to jump had been fantastic. Of course, only her tumbles made it into the media.

But she hadn't done a thing to get herself in the papers in over six months. Not since hitting the headlines with a nighttime adventure in skydiving that had resulted in her hospitalization with a hairline fracture to her pelvis.

Her father had not only ignored her exploit, but he'd also ignored Maddie's injury. And not only had he refused to take her phone calls from the hospital, but he'd also made it clear, through his PA, that Maddie was not welcome at the family mansion for her recovery.

She'd been forced to hire a nurse to help during the weeks of her limited mobility. Romi had offered to stay with her, but Maddie refused to take advantage.

"Am I to understand you didn't read Madison in on the contents of this contract?" Vik asked, unexpected disapproval edging his deep tone. "Do you actually expect her to agree?"

"She'll agree." Her father gave her a stern glare. "Or I will cut her out of my life completely."

The words were painful enough to hear, but the absolute conviction in her father's voice stabbed straight through Maddie's carefully cultivated facade to the genuine and all-too-vulnerable emotions underneath.

"Over this?" she demanded, waving her hand toward the printed articles. "It's not true!"

"You will not continue to drag my name and that of my company through the mud, Madison."

"I don't *do* that." While she'd managed a certain level of media notoriety, it had never before been because of anything even remotely like the lies Perry had spewed to the tabloids.

Her father began reading the headlines out loud and weak tears burned the back of her eyes. Maddie refused to give in to them, wishing she could be as genuinely emotionless as the steel-gray-haired man flaying her with other people's words.

"I told you, *he lied*."

"Why would he?" the media fixer asked, sounding interested in an almost clinical way.

"For money. For revenge." Because she'd turned him down one too many times and compounded that by refusing his latest request for a loan. "I don't know, but he lied."

How many times did she have to say it?

"It is time for definitive measures to be taken," Jeremy said, as if she hadn't spoken.

"On that at least, we can agree, beginning with the demand for a retraction. I can do my own interview." Even though she hated that kind of direct contact with the media.

She considered offering the ultimate sacrifice of integrating her Maddie Grace life with that of socialite Madison Archer in order to combat the negative image that clearly concerned her father.

Jeremy dismissed her offer with a slicing gesture. "I believe I've made it clear that the current scandal is not my primary concern."

"What is your concern?" she asked, confused.

"The capricious lifestyle that has resulted in your unacceptable and notorious reputation."

"You want me to come work for AIH?" she asked with zero enthusiasm and even less belief.

The last time the issue of Archer International Holdings had come up, her father had made it clear he no longer harbored dreams of her one day taking over.

His harsh bark of laughter was all the answer she needed. "Absolutely not."

"You want me to get a job somewhere else?" She could do that.

She preferred using her education as a volunteer teacher's aide, but if it would help her relationship with her father, she would get a paying job—which hopefully wouldn't conflict with her volunteering schedule.

More derisive laughter fell from her father's lips. "Do you really think any reputable charity or business would hire you right now?"

Heat climbed up her neck, ending in a very rare blush. She'd become adept at hiding her emotions, even suppressing her blushes of embarrassment a long time ago.

But suddenly, she realized that if it *did* become known that Madison Archer was Maddie Grace, the school might be forced to disallow Maddie's volunteering. All because a man she'd thought was a friend had turned out to be a lying, manipulative, opportunistic user.

"He wants you to get married," Vik informed her, no indication in his tone or demeanor that he was joking.

Her father did not jump in with a denial, either.

For the first time, she looked around the room to see how the other occupants were reacting. Her father's media fixer and PA were both busy on their tablets, ignoring the conversation now, or giving a pretty good pretense of doing so.

One of his managers was looking at her with the type of speculation that left Madison feeling dirty, but the fact he had the articles about her spread out in front of him could have something to do with that, too.

The other manager was reading through the paperwork and the man who Maddie did not know was looking at her father, his expression assessing.

Vik's expression was enigmatic as always.

She met her father's gaze again, finding nothing there but implacable resolve. "You want me to get married."

"Yes."

"Who?" she asked, unhappily certain she already had an inkling.

"One of these four men." Her father indicated Vik, the two other managers and the man she did not know. "You know Viktor, of course, and I am sure you remember Steven Whitley." Jeremy nodded toward a manager she was fairly certain had been divorced once already and was nearly twice her age.

Maddie found herself acknowledging both men with a tip of her own head in some bizarre ritual of polite behavior. Or maybe it was just the situation that was so bizarre.

He indicated the manager whose look had given her the willies. "Brian Jones."

His expression was benign now, almost pitying.

"I thought you were engaged," she said, her voice almost as tight as her throat. But that couldn't be helped.

Hadn't Maddie met his fiancée at the last Christmas party?

"Are you?" her father asked, annoyance clear in his tone. "Miss Priest?"

His PA looked up from her tablet with a frown. "Yes, sir?"

"Jones is engaged."

"Is he?" Miss Priest didn't sound concerned. "He is not married."

"But I will be." Brian stood. "I don't believe I'll be needed for the rest of this meeting, if you'll excuse me, sir?"

"Did you read the contract?" her father demanded.

"I did."

"And you are still leaving?"

"Yes, sir."

A measure of respect shone in her father's eyes even as he frowned. "Then go." He nodded toward the stranger on the other side of Maddie as if the introductions had not been interrupted by the defection of one of his candidates. "Maxwell Black, CEO of BIT."

Maxwell smiled at her, magnetism that might actually rival Vik's exuding from him. "Hello, Madison. It's good to see you again."

He wasn't overtly sexual, but there was a vibe to him that made Maddie wrap her arms protectively around herself. This man carried power around him the same way Vik did, but with a predatory edge she hadn't experienced from her father's heir apparent.

Then, she'd never been his business rival.

"I don't believe we've met?" She forced her arms to fall to her sides.

"I saw you at the Red Ball last February."

She remembered going to the charity event that raised money for research into heart disease, but she didn't remember seeing him.

"I would have remembered."

"I'm glad to hear you say so." His teeth flashed in a blinding white smile. "But I meant what I said. I saw you there. We were not introduced."

"Oh."

Her father cleared his throat in that disapproving way he had, but if he expected Maddie to say it was a pleasure to meet the man—under these circumstances—he didn't know her very well.

But then that had been her problem most of her life, hadn't it?

CHAPTER TWO

THE MORNING HAD gone according to Viktor's plans so far, but the spark of temper in Madison's brilliant blue eyes threatened to derail it.

If Jeremy had evinced even one iota of the concern Viktor knew the older man felt for his daughter's current predicament, she would be reacting very differently. But then if father and daughter got along perfectly, or even very well, Viktor's own plans would by necessity be very different.

"You know, I never even entertained the fantasy that you called me to help me, to take *my side* for once, to protect me because I mattered to you." The beautiful redhead offered the emotionally laden words in a flat tone Viktor almost envied.

She would be one hell of a poker player.

She was lying, though. Madison wouldn't have shown up if she didn't think her father would help her.

"You never were a child taken with fairy tales," Jeremy said.

Viktor could have reined in the older man's prideful idiocy, but that wouldn't further his own agenda. However, he felt an unexpected pang of guilt at Madison's barely there flinch and flash of pain in the azure depths of her eyes.

She recovered quickly, her expression smooth—almost

bored. "No, that was always Mom's department. She lived under the fallacy that you cared about us. I know better."

It was Jeremy's turn to flinch and he wasn't as fast at hiding his reaction as his daughter, but then he had to be in shock. Madison didn't go for the jugular like that. In fact, in all the arguments between the tycoon and his daughter Viktor had been privy to, he'd never heard Madison use her mother's memory against her father before.

No triumph at the emotional bloodletting showed on Madison's porcelain features.

Instead, she looked like she wanted nothing more than to get up and walk away. The fact she stayed in her seat was proof the heiress might be criminally flagrant in her personal life, but she wasn't stupid.

She knew her father well enough to be aware that Jeremy's arsenal of threats wasn't empty.

"You have five minutes." Madison's words verified she did indeed realize her father had more *encouragement* to lay on the table, but also that she had little patience in waiting to find out what it was.

Color washed over Jeremy's face. "Excuse me?"

"She wants the other two prongs to the pitchfork," Viktor informed his boss.

Jeremy's scowl said he knew that's what she'd meant, but he didn't like the time limit or implied ultimatum that Madison would get up and leave if it wasn't met.

"Pitchfork?" Black asked.

Viktor could have answered, but he didn't. Giving Maxwell Black any kind of information wasn't on his agenda for the day. Viktor had ignored the presence of the other *candidates* at the table as superfluous, and planned to continue to do so.

Madison wasn't so reticent. "Jeremy never enters a fight he isn't sure he can win. To that end, he stacks the deck.

He'll have three scenarios in the offing, none of which will I want to eventuate."

"You call your father by his first name?" Black asked.

Madison flicked a meaning-laden glance in the tycoon's direction. "As he pointed out, I'm the not the one in the family to wallow in sentimental fantasy."

What she didn't say was that until that morning, Madison had called Jeremy Archer *Father* and sometimes even *Dad*. That she would no longer do so could be taken from her words as a given.

No question that the company president had seriously messed up in his approach to his daughter.

Viktor might have suggested the current course to protect AIH's interests and future, but he would not have blindsided Madison with it during a meeting with strangers.

He'd been angry when he realized Jeremy hadn't even bothered to brief his daughter about the meeting's agenda before her arrival. She might be flighty and prone to inauspicious, risky behavior, but she deserved more respect than that.

Viktor had no doubts that Jeremy would ultimately get what he wanted, not least of which because Viktor would make it happen.

However he had a nascent suspicion that the personal cost for that success might be higher for Jeremy than the president of Archer International Holdings anticipated.

Madison flicked a glance at the Cartier watch on her wrist. "Your time starts now, Jeremy."

"Golden Chances Charter School."

"What about it?" Madison asked with caution, the barest crack in her calm facade finally showing.

"Over the last three years, you have donated tens of thousands of dollars from your Madison Trust income to school improvements and projects."

"I am aware."

But Viktor hadn't been. He began to wonder what else he didn't know about Madison.

Jeremy's eyes, the only feature truly like his daughter's, reflected subtle triumph. "The school's zoning is under scrutiny."

"It wasn't as of yesterday."

"Things change."

"I see." Madison glanced pointedly down at her watch.

"Are you pretending that does not matter to you?"

"No. You have two more minutes."

Viktor was impressed. Madison would have done a better job negotiating a recent deal with a Japanese conglomerate than the project manager they'd sent to Asia.

Jeremy frowned. "Ramona Grayson."

"What about her?"

Viktor would be crossing his legs protectively if that tone and look had been directed at him.

"Her father is a drunk," Jeremy pointed out with well-known derision toward a man Madison had made no bones about considering a second father.

"And mine is a conscienceless bastard. I guess we both lost in the masculine parent lottery, though given a choice I'd pick Harry Grayson. His emotions might be pickled with alcohol, but at least he has them."

Viktor had seen Madison angry. He'd seen her hurt, embarrassed and even seriously disappointed. He had never seen her this coldly furious.

The Madison that Viktor had known for ten years was in no way reflected in the harshly dismissive woman in front of them.

Despite the implication of her words, she loved her father. In the past, she hadn't been able to hide her need for his attention and approval. Her mistake had always been how she went about getting it.

She'd followed in her mother's footsteps, not realizing

Jeremy Archer had been too traumatized by the loss of his wife to want to see her audacious nature reflected in their only child.

"Do you think Ramona sees it that way?" Jeremy asked. "Or perhaps she would prefer a father not lost in a bottle."

Madison shrugged. "It's not something we discuss."

"Nevertheless, the destruction of her father's business, followed by him losing everything to bankruptcy, would hurt her a great deal. Don't you think?"

Madison pulled her phone from her purse with an almost negligent move belied by the blue fire in her gaze. "You have exactly fifteen seconds to take that tactic for coercion off the table."

"Or what?"

"Ten."

And for the first time in Viktor's memory, infallible businessman Jeremy Archer made a mistake in negotiating. He silently called his daughter's bluff.

He believed that because she had no interest in business, Madison was not capable of the same level of ruthlessness as he was.

Viktor knew from personal experience that just because a parent and child lived very different lives, it did not mean that they shared no common personality traits.

Madison pressed her phone to her ear.

"Don't," Viktor said.

Madison just shook her head. "I'm sorry, Viktor."

There would be only one reason for her to apologize to him. Whatever she had planned would have a detrimental effect on AIH and, by default, Viktor's job and livelihood.

The possible implications were still firming in his brain as she made contact with the lawyer in charge of the Madison Trust. "Hello, Mr. Bellingham. I need you to draw some papers up for me. I'm texting you the instructions now."

Seconds later the lawyer's agitated tones came through her phone.

Madison listened for a moment in silence and then replied. "Yes, he knows. He's sitting right here. In fact, he's the one who put this in motion."

The fact the unflappable Bellingham was still speaking loudly enough for Viktor to almost make out his words said something about the nature of Madison's instructions.

"I am absolutely certain, and Mr. Bellingham? If your firm wishes to keep the Madison Trust as a client in sixty-five days when it falls under my control, I suggest you have those papers ready for me to sign when I stop by your office later this afternoon."

Another spate of conversation, this time quieter.

"Thank you, Mr. Bellingham."

Madison tucked her phone back into her purse and faced her father, her expression daring him to ask what she'd done.

Jeremy remained stubbornly silent, or maybe he was in too much shock to react. He had to realize the likely content of those papers, or maybe he didn't.

Maybe Jeremy Archer was under the mistaken impression that Archer International Holdings was important enough to his daughter that she would not do what Viktor was almost positive she had done.

"What do the papers say?" Viktor asked, unwilling to make decisions based on assumptions.

"As you know, because of the financial deal Grandfather Madison made with Jeremy upon his marriage to my mother, the Madison Trust holds twenty-five percent of the privately held shares in Archer International Holdings."

"Those shares are your heritage," Jeremy said.

"Romi is my friend."

"So you gave her some of your shares?" Viktor asked with no real hope it could be that simple.

"If Mr. Grayson's company is under threat from AIH or any company remotely affiliated with it, at one minute past midnight on my twenty-fifth birthday, all of those shares will be signed over to Harry Grayson personally. Not his company."

"You cannot do that!"

"I can." Madison looked more like her father in that moment than at any other time Viktor had known her.

"And if his company is not under threat?" Viktor asked, suspecting that Jeremy's calling his daughter's threat had precipitated some kind of permanent action on her part.

"Half of my shares will be signed over to Romi."

Jeremy stood up, his face flushing with color, his eyes narrowed in fury. "You will not sign those papers."

"I will." Conversely, Madison relaxed back into her chair. "You had your chance to take my friend's happiness off the table as a negotiating point, but you refused to take it."

"That's insane," Steven Whitley said, speaking up for the first time since his introduction to Madison. "Even half of your shares are valued at tens of millions."

"Romi won't have to worry about her drunk of a father ruining *her* life, will she?" Madison asked her father, as if he'd been the one to bring up the point of the shares' value.

Jeremy slammed his hand on the table. "I am not ruining your life, Madison, you've done a fair job of that yourself."

"No, I haven't, but I don't expect you to believe me."

"You are not giving away twelve and a half percent of my company!"

Viktor didn't know if Jeremy realized he'd just effectively taken the third prong of his threats off the table. No way was he going to allow Harry Grayson Sr. to own twenty-five percent of AIH.

Jeremy and Madison were too much alike. Both would

go to extreme measures for what was most important to them. The problem was that while Madison was very important to Jeremy, she did not believe it and Jeremy was willfully blind to what Madison needed from him.

Beyond that Archer International Holdings came first with Jeremy, and the people she cared about came first with Madison. Right now, those two priorities were in direct conflict.

Things were going to go completely pear-shaped if Viktor didn't take control.

"Sit down, Jeremy," Viktor instructed the older man in a tone that was respectful, but firm.

With a glare for his daughter, Jeremy returned to his seat.

"This meeting has derailed and I believe it is time to regroup."

Jeremy nodded.

Viktor stood and straightened his suit jacket before walking around the table and offering his hand to Madison. "Come with me."

"What are you doing, Viktor?" Jeremy asked, his expression considering.

The man knew that AIH sat near the top of Viktor's priority list, too. The company was the conduit for his own plans and no chance was he starting over because of the father-daughter issues of its owner.

"Madison and I have some things to discuss."

Steven frowned at him. "You are not the only candidate, you know. This contract was offered to four of us."

"I am the only one who matters."

An infinitesimal quirk of his boss's mouth said he knew that was true, but he said, "I believe that is up to Madison."

The lady in question made a sound of disparagement. "Right. If the decision is mine to make, I assume it's to be from the men you included in this meeting. One of whom was already engaged, another is old enough to be my father with a history of failed marriages and the other a complete stranger. And then there is Viktor."

"Maxwell Black is a man worth knowing."

While it might be true, Viktor didn't appreciate Jeremy pointing it out. Two half-Russian boys, raised to appreciate a culture not fully American, Maxwell and Viktor had grown up together, their families close, their goals similar.

Friends of a sort, but too alike for comfort, both men were determined to make their mark on the world, to be at the top of the food chain.

Because of the different paths they took to dominant positions in the business world, Viktor's and Maxwell's interests had not conflicted before today.

Thankfully, Madison didn't look impressed by her father's words.

She shifted so she could make eye contact with the CEO of BIT. "Mr. Black, do not be fooled by Jeremy's mistaken ignorance. Those articles are lies made up by a man I believed was my friend. Perry and I never had any sort of sexual relationship, much less a BDSM one."

The pain underlying her measured tones prompted Viktor to make some plans in regard Perry Timwater.

"I believe you." Maxwell's assurance proved he was every bit as intelligent as Viktor had always known him to be.

Madison relaxed infinitesimally. "Good."

"Regardless of the reason for our meeting, I would like to get to know you, Miss Archer." Maxwell, damn his hide, smiled charmingly at Madison. "You seem like an interesting person."

She inclined her head. "Thank you, but—"

"Don't dismiss the possibility of our compatibility out of hand," Maxwell interrupted her with another of his lady-killer smiles. "I bet I could teach you to like some of the things you've been accused of needing."

Madison's gasp said she was shocked by Maxwell's words.

Whether the words themselves or where he chose to speak them, Viktor didn't know and it didn't matter. *He* wasn't surprised. Maxwell played to his strengths and exploited the weakness of others.

Turning the lurid headlines into something forbidden but potentially exciting was a solid tactic for handling the current situation and the humiliation Madison had to be experiencing. Though she'd done nothing to let it show.

Unfortunately for Maxwell, Viktor wasn't going to let the ploy succeed.

Nothing was standing between Viktor and control of AIH. Not even Madison herself, but particularly not Maxwell Black.

Clearly upset with Maxwell's words, Jeremy made a sound of protest.

Before the older man could say anything Viktor was in front of Black, blocking his line of sight with Madison. "That is not something you are going to discuss here, or with Madison at all."

"You think not?" Black challenged back.

"I know not."

"I don't need your protection, Viktor," Madison said quietly from behind him.

He turned to face her, but didn't move so Black would have to stand and sidestep to see her. "Nevertheless, you have it."

She shook her head, whether in denial, or frustration, he didn't know.

"I'm nowhere near taking him up on his offer. I'm pretty sure even the mildest form of that kind of relationship requires trust and I don't have any. Not for men, particularly men with the same priorities as Jeremy Archer. *Businessmen.*"

She made the word sound like a slur.

Viktor didn't believe her regardless. Madison trusted *him*. She always had; even if she no longer realized it.

And while Maxwell's words hadn't surprised him, Madison's willingness to meet them head-on did. But then maybe it shouldn't have. She'd already shown her willingness to stand against her father.

Maxwell got up, his pose too damned relaxed for Viktor's liking. Even less did he like the way the other man moved around him to face Madison. "I see."

"Good."

"Nothing in the contract states we must share a bedroom."

Madison's eyes flared with...was it interest?

Viktor cursed under his breath. "In order to receive the shares stipulated, Madison and her husband must provide an heir for Archer International Holdings."

Madison gasped, anger shimmering around her like electric currents.

Before she could say anything, Maxwell shrugged. "There is always artificial insemination."

"While we live two entirely separate lives?" Madison asked in a tone Viktor recognized, but from the reaction of both Maxwell and her father, they did not.

Jeremy puffed up with renewed anger while the other Russian-American nodded with smug complacency. "Exactly."

"We would be married in name only?" she asked, the disgust levels rising enough that the others should have recognized them.

They didn't.

"No." Viktor was done with the verbal games.

Madison gave him a look like she was questioning his right to make the pronouncement.

"That sort of relationship would be too uncertain for the health of Archer International Holdings," Viktor pointed out.

Disappointment dulled the blue of Madison's azure gaze, but she masked the emotion almost immediately. Viktor cursed silently.

Her father, however, nodded vigorously. "Precisely."

"I think your daughter has already proven she is more than capable of her own decisions." Maxwell's admiration was annoyingly apparent.

"I won't sign the contract," Jeremy said in implacable tones.

The BIT CEO didn't look worried.

Madison's features had gone smooth with a lack of emotion once again as she stared at her father. "You believe I would agree to that kind of marriage?"

For once Jeremy seemed incapable of speech, perhaps realizing finally how little interest Madison would ever have in such a cold-blooded bargain.

"But then you believed the lies Perry spewed, didn't you?"

"I never said that." Jeremy's voice had an alien quality.

Realization of his colossal error in judgment in the handling of his daughter must be settling in, but being who he was, Viktor's boss wasn't going to back down, either.

Madison pulled her copy of the contract from the stack of papers in front of her and stood. "I assume you aren't going to do anything to mitigate Perry's lies."

"I have done it. Do you think this agreement is only about AIH? This is as important for you as it is the reputation of my company." Jeremy clearly believed what he said, but then Viktor had made sure his company's president saw things exactly that way. "Once you are married to a powerful man with an impeccable reputation, you can begin to live down your youthful excesses."

"My life has nothing to do with your company."

Viktor wasn't about to let the conversation degenerate further and there was only one direction it was headed if the two kept talking. Down.

"Conrad will put out a press release categorically denying all of Timwater's allegations," Viktor inserted before another word could be said.

The media fixer looked up from his tablet. "I will?"

Severely unimpressed with the man's lack of dedication to the protection of the company president's daughter, Viktor let Conrad see his displeasure. "You will do a hell of a lot more than that. If you'd been doing your job properly to begin with, this situation would not have happened."

"Protecting Miss Archer from her own excessive behaviors has never been in my job's purview," Conrad claimed in snide tones.

"Did you notice the loss of confidence in AIH articles in the online press this morning?" Viktor asked. "The first of which went live within thirty minutes of that tabloid hitting newsstands. Or did you think that was just a coincidence?"

The media fixer swallowed audibly and shook his head.

Jeremy didn't look too happy, either. He'd been too focused on using the current situation to bring his daughter into line, and had ignored the bigger picture. Something that was anathema to him.

"Your job is to protect the image of this company and anyone affiliated closely enough with it to impact our reputation in the financial community," Viktor reminded Conrad in a hard voice.

"Yes, sir."

"Maybe it's too much for you. Perhaps you'd prefer to move to a PR position working for a nursing home?" Viktor allowed the implication that was the only type of job Conrad would be able to get to hang in the air between them.

The usually unflappable media fixer paled, showing the man still had some of the intelligence he had originally been hired for. "I'm on it."

"You should have been on it at four-fifteen this morning after the scandal sheet went on sale."

Conrad didn't argue. He'd screwed up.

"I don't know what you spent this meeting doing on your tablet, but whatever it was, it wasn't as important as getting ahead of Madison's situation."

"I was writing the engagement announcement."

"I see. Not nursing homes then. Maybe you should be writing puff pieces for online dating sites," Viktor opined.

Nervous laughter filled the room and Jeremy made a sarcastic sound of approval, but it was Madison's genuine amusement that Viktor enjoyed the most.

"I'll need your signature on a civil suit against Perry Timwater," Conrad told Madison.

"No."

Viktor wasn't surprised by Madison's answer and forestalled any arguments from the media fixer or Jeremy. "The man was her friend. She's not going to sue him."

"Some friend." Conrad snorted.

The tiny wounded sound that Madison made infuriated Viktor. "We have other avenues of influence to bring to bear. I want a retraction from Perry in time for this evening's news. Play it off as a joke perpetrated by one friend on another."

Viktor turned to Madison. "For real damage control, you are going to have to do an in-person interview for one of the big celebrity news shows and meet with a journalist with a wider readership than the original article."

"Whatever I can do," she said with more conviction and none of the disagreement he expected.

Viktor's brow wrinkled in thought. Something about this scandal concerned Madison enough that she'd come to her father to ask for help.

While Jeremy might not see Madison showing up for this meeting as that, Viktor was certain of the truth.

Unlike her other escapades, Madison wanted this one cleaned up and her father's refusal to take it seriously had bothered her. A lot.

Viktor needed to figure out why it meant so much to her.

He put his hand out to her again. "Come with me, we'll talk your father's plan through and make some decisions from there."

She looked ready to argue.

He smiled at her. "Is that really too much to ask? I've got Conrad working on fixing this for you."

"Are you going to tell him to stop if I refuse?"

"No." Madison needed an act of good will.

It was important she realized that she could trust Viktor to watch out for her. He had to be the only candidate for her fiancé that she seriously considered.

Because her husband was going to take over AIH eventually and Viktor had every intention of that man being him.

Madison tucked her purse under her arm. "Okay."

"Just a minute," Jeremy said.

Viktor turned to face him. "I know what you want."

"But—"

"Have I ever neglected your interests in a negotiation?"

"No." Jeremy got that implacable look he was known for on his face. "Just remember that Madison's cooperation isn't the only thing on the line right now."

Viktor wasn't surprised by the threat, or even bothered by it.

He'd spent ten years working for this man and his ultimate goal was finally in reach. Viktor wasn't about to let it pass him by.

CHAPTER THREE

MADDIE FOLLOWED VIK into Le Mason, not at all surprised when the maître d' found them a table in a quiet corner in the perpetually busy restaurant, popular with tourists and locals alike.

"Did you eat breakfast?" he asked.

She shook her head, not even pretending to herself that shredding Romi's offering of chocolate pastries counted as actually ingesting calories.

He ordered the restaurant's specialty pancakes for her and coffee for himself.

"Did you bring me here to remind me of friendlier days?" she asked, sure she knew the answer.

"I brought you here because you used to crave their banana pancakes and I hoped to tempt you to eat." His six-foot-four-inch frame should have looked awkward in the medium-sized dining chair, but he didn't.

With his dark hair brushed back in a businessman's cut, his square jaw shaved smooth of dark stubble and a body most athletes would be jealous of covered in a tailored Italian suit, nothing about Viktor Beck could be described as awkward.

Doing her best to ignore his sheer masculine perfection, Maddie adjusted her napkin over her lap. "How did you know I hadn't already?"

"I guessed."

"I used to stop eating when I was stressed." She was surprised he remembered.

"Are you saying that's changed?"

"No." Too much was the same, but she wasn't about to tell him that.

She had to remember that Vik's interests here were aligned squarely with her father's. Not Maddie's. He'd made that clear six years ago and nothing had changed since.

Yes, Vik had gotten Conrad focused on curtailing the media frenzy around Perry's supposed breakup interview, but he'd done it for the sake of the company. Again...not Maddie.

Whatever his agenda now, it had the welfare of AIH as the end goal, she was sure of it. And if she got swept along with the tide, so be it.

"Give me the bullet points of the contract." She was morbidly curious about what her father had done to entice a man like Viktor Beck, or Maxwell Black for that matter, to marry her.

Vik's dark brows rose. "You trust me to tell you everything important?"

Answering honestly wouldn't just make a lie of her earlier words, but it would make her a fool. "I'll read it later to make sure."

"Your father accepts that you will not be his successor."

"What was his first clue?" She'd refused to get a degree in business and had fended off every request, demand and even plea for her to take a job at the company.

"Do you really need me to enumerate them for you?"

"No."

"Suffice it to say, Jeremy has finally accepted you are never going to be CEO of Archer International Holdings." Vik's deep tones were tinged with more satisfaction than disappointment at that pronouncement.

"It would certainly set a roadblock in your own career path if I were."

His espresso eyes flared with quickly suppressed surprise.

She smiled, pleased that he hadn't realized she knew. "You don't seriously think your desire for that office is a secret?"

"It's a family-owned company."

"That you plan to run one day and if Jeremy doesn't realize it, he's being willfully blind."

"That is one of his failings."

"You think?"

"He does not see you for who you are or what you need from him."

"You tried to tell him, once." The year before her clumsy attempt at seduction.

She'd thought Vik standing up for her meant he cared. But looking back, she had to conclude the friendship he'd offered her had been in pursuit of his own goals. Gaining Jeremy Archer's unmitigated trust.

She could have told Vik befriending her wouldn't do anything for him. Her father would have had to care about her for that to be the case. And he didn't.

The only thing that mattered to Jeremy Archer was the company. He'd married her mother to gain the necessary infusion of capital to make AIH a dominant player in the world market. His only interest in Maddie had been as a potential successor.

"He's given up on me personally because he realizes I'm never going to be his *business* heir." As much as it hurt, it also made sense of how unconcerned he'd seemed to be by "Perrygate."

"The only thing Jeremy has given up is his plan to try to lure you into the business."

Maddie shook her head, not buying it for a second. "You

heard him. He had no intention of having Conrad help me until you stepped in."

"Your father can get tunnel vision."

"And all he could see was the endgame." He hadn't even noticed that her scandal had adversely impacted AIH's reputation.

"Yes."

Maddie waited for the waitress to place her pancakes on the table and walk away. "Which is?"

"You married to a man who can and will be groomed to take over as Jeremy's successor."

"If my father can't get what he wants out of me, he'll use me to get it, is that right?"

"That's a very simplified view and not entirely accurate."

She wasn't going to argue something she knew to be true, as did Vik, even if he was too loyal to admit it.

"Jeremy wants his successor to be family." Hence the marriage. "How old-fashioned."

"It ensures his grandchildren will inherit his legacy intact."

"And that's important."

"To him."

The smell of pancakes, fresh bananas and syrup had her mouth watering. "What about you?"

"You need to ask?"

"AIH is your life." As much as it had always been her father's.

"Say rather AIH is the vehicle for my own dreams."

"I didn't know men like you dreamed."

"Without visionaries at the helm, companies like AIH would atrophy and eventually die."

"So, you think my father is just a very dedicated dreamer." Sarcasm hanging thick from her words, she took a bite of her pancakes and hummed with pleasure.

Vik laughed. "That is one way to put it."

"And your personal dreams include being president of AIH one day."

"Yes."

His easy honesty surprised her and charmed her in a way. She'd always thought of men like him as having goals. Solid, steady, unemotional stepping stones that marked their success.

"Wow. I guess the heart of a Russian really does beat under that American-businessman veneer."

"My grandparents like to think so."

She offered him a bite of pancake with a slice of banana. "And your parents?"

Vik took the bite just like he used to and memories of a time when they'd been friends, and all *her* dreams had centered on this man, assailed Maddie.

"My mother has been out of the picture for all of my memory. My dad is like a computer virus. He keeps coming back."

She smiled. "I should say I'm sorry, but having a father who drives you nuts makes you more human."

Vik shrugged, but she couldn't help wondering if he'd told her about his dad on purpose. To build rapport. She thought Vik had outclassed her dad a long time ago in the manipulation department.

After all, Jeremy Archer still thought he ran AIH. However anyone with a brain—not blinkered by willful blindness—and access to the company would realize it was actually Vik's show and had been for a few years.

"Whose idea was it to offer Steven Whitley and Brian Jones up on the chopping block?"

"It's hardly a sacrifice to be offered this kind of opportunity." Vik drank his coffee, his expression sincere if she could believe it.

But then what was to say she couldn't?

"Marriage to the prodigal daughter for an eventual company presidency?" That might well be worth it to a man like Vik.

"You don't exactly fit the distinction of prodigal."

"Don't I?"

"You haven't blown through your inheritance. In fact, you are surprisingly fiscally responsible."

"Thank you, I think."

"You haven't abandoned your family to see the world."

"I moved out of the family home."

He winked at her. "But stayed in the city."

"What can I say? I love San Francisco."

"And your father."

"I'd rather not talk about that."

"Understood." He smiled and her nerve endings went *twang*. "Your media notoriety isn't even of the truly scandalous variety."

"Until Perrygate."

Vik waved his hand, dismissing the importance of Perry's lies. "That will be handled."

"Thank you for that." The thought of being forced to give up her volunteerism because of an unsavory reputation hurt deeply, compounding her pain at Perry's betrayal.

He knew how important working with the children was to her.

"But seriously?" she asked, refocusing. "Whitley and Jones?"

Vik shrugged, but his lips firmed in a telling line. "They're the most likely men within the company to do the job."

"Marrying me?"

"Becoming the next president."

"Besides you."

"Besides me," he agreed.

"You're the only *real* candidate."

"I would like to think so."

"And then there is Maxwell Black."

Vik's eyes narrowed, the brown depths darkening to almost black. "Your father is never going to approve the kind of marriage Black suggested."

"And if that is the only kind of marriage I'm willing to agree to?" she taunted.

"Jeremy will hire a surrogate and have his own child in hopes of succeeding with him where he failed with you."

Wholly unprepared for that answer, several seconds passed before Maddie felt like she could breathe again. "He's not a young man any longer."

"He is fifty-seven."

"He would not be so cruel." And she did not mean to her.

No child deserved to be born merely as a player on the chessboard. She should know.

She'd taken herself out of play, but she'd had the strength of the memory of her mother's love to bolster her own courage.

This child would only have Jeremy Archer.

Maddie shivered at the prospect. "I'm not having a child simply for him or her to be put in the same position."

"You want children." There was no doubt in Vik's voice.

"Someday."

"Whenever you have them, or whoever you have your children with, Jeremy will want the company to ultimately pass on to them."

"I know." Her father's role in her life and that of any children she might have was something she'd already spent several hours talking to her therapist, Dr. MacKenzie, about.

"That is not a bad thing."

She'd come to realize that. While Maddie's feelings about AIH were too antagonistic for her to ever want to be a part of it, as she'd always seen it as the entity that kept her father from her, it did not automatically follow that her children would feel the same way.

"You said something about me having a child being necessary for the man I marry to take over AIH."

"Upon the birth of our first child, my succession to the presidency will be announced. Your father will shift into a less active role as chairman of the board on his sixtieth birthday."

"And if I haven't had a child by then?"

"My becoming company president will not happen until we have had our first child."

"What if we can't have children?"

"We can."

"You sound very certain."

"I am."

She remembered the ultrasound her doctor had ordered as part of her last physical, at the company's request. She'd thought it was odd, but since her medical insurance was through AIH, Maddie hadn't demurred.

"Jeremy had them run fertility tests on me."

"Just preliminaries, but enough to know that aside from something well outside the norm, you should have no trouble conceiving."

"That's so intrusive!"

Vik didn't reply and, honestly, Maddie didn't know what she wanted him to say. She wasn't entirely sure the test had been all her dad's idea. If Vik had suggested them, she wasn't sure knowing would be of any benefit to her.

"What else?"

"The contract gives five percent of the company to me on our five-year anniversary. Another five percent on the birth of each child, not to exceed ten percent."

"How generous, he'll allow me to have two children." She'd always dreamed of having, or adopting, at least four and creating a home filled with love and joy.

"The contract does not limit the number of children you have, only the stock incentive to me for fathering them."

She ignored the way Vik continued to assume he was her only option. "What else?"

"On your father's death, if we have been married for ten years, or more, I will get another five percent of the company. The remaining fifty percent of the company will be placed in trust for our children with voting proxy passing only to our children actively involved in the executive level of running the company. I will hold all outstanding family-voting proxies."

"But the other children will receive the income from the shares."

"Yes."

"It sounds complicated." But then her father wasn't a simple man, not by any stretch.

Vik took a sip of his coffee. "Jeremy wants a legacy and you've made it clear you won't be part of it."

"So he wrote me out of the will."

"Only insofar as his ownership of Archer International Holdings is concerned."

"I see." Honestly, she didn't care.

The Madison Trust provided all the income she needed to live on. That income would decrease once half of her shares in the company transferred to Romi, but Maddie didn't mind.

The biggest expense she had was keeping up her appearance as Madison Archer, socialite. As far as she was concerned, that part of her life could go hang. If her father wanted her to keep up appearances, he could pay for the designer wardrobe and charity event tickets.

"Is there anything else pertinent to me in the contract?"

"Your father would like us to live in Parean Hall."

The Madison family mansion, named for the pristine white marble used for flooring in the oversized foyer and the risers on the grand staircase, had stood empty since the death of Maddie's grandfather from a massive coronary upon hearing of his daughter's accidental death nine years ago.

"I have plans for the house." It was part of the trust and would come to her when she turned twenty-five.

"What plans?"

"That is none of your business."

"Indulge me."

Maddie didn't answer, but concentrated on finishing her pancakes. Vik didn't press.

His patient silence finally convinced her to tell him.

She said, "I want to start a charter school, this one with boarders from the foster-care system."

"An orphanage."

"No, a school for gifted children in difficult family circumstances." A place the children could be safe and thrive.

Vik sipped at his coffee pensively for several moments.

"How will you fund it?"

"A large portion of my trust income will go to it annually, but I also plan to raise funds amidst the heavy coffers of this city. I've learned a lot about fund-raising since my first volunteer assignment on the mayoral campaign when I was a teenager."

"Your father has no idea how full your life is."

"No, he doesn't." And Vik had barely an inkling as well.

She'd stopped telling him about her plans and activities when he'd rejected her so summarily six years ago.

Vik relaxed back in his chair. "The Madison family estate is a large house, even by the elite of San Francisco standards, but hardly the ideal location for a school. Either in building architecture or location."

"Oh, you don't think poor children should live among the wealthy?" she challenged.

He didn't appear offended at her accusation. "I think it will cost more than it's worth to get zoning approval."

"That section was zoned for the inclusion of a local school, but none was ever built."

"And you think that zoning will remain once your neighbors learn of your plans?" he asked in a tone that said he didn't.

"I don't intend to advertise them."

One corner of his lips tilted just the tiniest bit. "A fait accompli?"

"Yes."

"You have to apply for permits, hire staff…it's not going to stay a secret long."

"And then the fight begins, you are saying?"

"Yes."

"But why should the residents care if there's a school in their neighborhood? The city planners clearly intended there to be one."

"And the fact there isn't should tell you something."

"But—"

"I can find you a better building."

She didn't want to sell her grandparents' home. Her memories there weren't the greatest. Her Grandfather Madison had often made Jeremy Archer look warm and cuddly by comparison, but Maddie's mother's stories of her own childhood had been filled with delight.

Maddie always wished she'd had a chance to know her grandmother, Grace Madison.

"I'll have to sell the mansion to finance another purchase." No matter how much she might not want to do it.

The school was too important to give up and Vik was right, as he so often was—the opposition to a boarding school in that neighborhood for the underprivileged was bound to be stiff.

Vik shook his head decisively. "I'll buy the other building."

"In exchange for what?"

"Consider it my wedding gift to you."

"Presumptuous."

"I'm the only man I will allow you to consider." Dark brown eyes fixed on her with unmistakable purpose.

She ignored the way his words sent shivers through her insides. "You're assuming I'll agree to marry."

"Your father doesn't realize it, but I know he didn't need anything beyond his first threat to convince you to fall in with his plans."

"You don't think so?"

"Are you in another relationship?" Vik asked, the words clipped, something like anger smoldering in the depth of his gaze.

"No." Maddie saw no reason to hedge.

"Dating anyone?" he pressed.

"No." She frowned. "Why are you asking about this now?"

"Because if you were in a relationship with someone who mattered to you, no pressure your father brought to bear would sway you into marrying someone else."

He was right, but it rankled. "You think you know me so well."

"I know that your dad means more to you than you want him to believe."

"It's not a matter of what I want." Her father didn't think he mattered to Maddie because she wasn't all that important to *him*. Not in a personal way.

"Jeremy isn't going to back off on this."

"Why now?"

"You need to ask?"

"Yes." Her father had been too unconcerned about

Perry's scandal for it to be what tipped him into must-get-my-wayward-daughter-married mode.

"Jeremy has been worried about what will happen when you come into your majority for the Madison Trust for a while."

"Now he knows."

"I don't believe he saw that one coming."

"No. It wouldn't have occurred to him that I would purposefully put Archer International Holdings at risk."

"No."

"But apparently the idea that I might marry someone who might do that had already occurred to Jeremy."

"Yes." Something about the quality of Vik's stillness said he might have had more to do with that than her own father's paranoia.

"So, he was already considering how to get me to marry the man of his choice?" Maddie surmised. "He's using Perrygate as a vehicle for his own agenda."

She wasn't surprised by her father's mercenary motives, but she didn't have to like them.

"You would have to ask him." Vik indicated to the waitress to bring their bill. "I think the reality is more that he is afraid you'll end up with Mr. Timwater. Your father will do anything to prevent that."

"To protect the reputation and future of the company." Considering Perry's poor luck with his own business ventures, she could understand her father not wanting him to get even shallow hooks into any part of AIH.

"Sometimes, I think you are as willfully blind as your father." Vik shook his head. "He wants to stop you from marrying a man who would go public with the kind of claims Perry made in his interview."

"And Jeremy believes you're a huge improvement."

"You don't?" Vik asked, his tone more than a little sardonic.

She wasn't about to answer that. "Perry has never been in the running."

"Several articles in the media over the past six years would suggest otherwise."

"And the media *never* gets it wrong."

"You've never denied it, not publicly and not to your father."

"That's where you are wrong." And she had no satisfaction in that truth. "I told my father that Perry was just a friend, but he never believed me. He's always been more interested in his own interpretations and those of the media than anything I might have to say."

"I don't think that's true, but he is stubborn."

"So are you, in the way you defend him."

"Would you respect me if I had no loyalty for *my* friends?"

"Is my father your friend?"

"Yes." The single word wouldn't let her doubt his sincerity.

She used to think Vik was her friend, too.

Then things changed.

Now, she was facing the reality that it wasn't just that her father wanted her to marry Vik, but so did the man himself. Both had their reasons, but while different those reasons all centered around AIH, not Maddie.

She wasn't sure where, if anywhere at all, she came into the picture, other than as a minor piece on the chessboard. She certainly didn't feel like the queen.

CHAPTER FOUR

"I'LL BE BACK at three to take you to the lawyer's office," Vik informed Maddie as she unlocked her door and stepped inside.

"Are you sure that's not a conflict of interest?"

"Would you rather go alone?" he asked, a mocking twist on the masculine lips she'd spent far too much time studying as a teenager.

"No." Especially not after witnessing the media circus outside her building.

The paparazzi had always found her interesting, but it had never been like this.

And it was only getting worse as the morning wore on.

She'd managed to sneak out of the back entrance earlier, but the story and her location had spread in just that amount of time. There were almost as many media leeches haunting the other entrances to the building as in front now.

Even the parking garage hadn't been free of their presence.

She'd expected Vik to have his driver drop her off, but she could only be grateful he had insisted on getting out of the car and escorting her all the way to her apartment door.

He'd kept his body positioned protectively between her and the reporters stalking her. Vik was also very good at remaining silent no matter what was thrown at them and Maddie found it easier not to react with him as a buffer.

"Security will have the parking garage cleared," Vik said after a short text conversation on the elevator.

"Thank you."

They stepped off the elevator into a thankfully empty hallway.

Vik looked both ways before leading her toward her door anyway. "You need a security detail."

She shrugged, not wanting to get in to this argument right now, and not at all sure she would win it.

"When was the last time you had this lock changed?" he asked as she opened the door.

She looked up at him, wishing it didn't feel like all the oxygen got sucked out of the air every time she did that. "Why would I have it changed?"

"At least tell me you had new locks installed when you moved in."

"Why would I?" she asked again. "I'm sure the building management took care of it when the previous tenants moved out."

His expression said he didn't share her confidence. "You don't own the apartment?"

"No." She'd always planned to move into the mansion once she'd turned it into a school after she got control of her Madison Trust inheritance.

"Who has a key to this door, besides any previous tenant?" he asked with sarcastic emphasis on his last words.

Maddie leaned against the doorjamb when he showed no signs of following her inside. "Romi." She grimaced. "Perry, but he's not going to show his face."

Vik just shook his head before pulling his phone out and making a call. "Get the building access cards affiliated with Madison Archer's apartment deactivated and new cards issued for her, Ramona Grayson and myself."

He listened in silence for a moment. "Yes, have Ms. Grayson's delivered to her and the others to my office. I will pass Miss Archer's on when I see her later this afternoon. I want a security system installed, along with high-grade safety locks while we are gone."

The day before, Vik's high-handedness would have made Maddie livid. Today? It just felt like someone was watching out for her.

"You know, for a corporate shark, you're pretty good at this white-knight stuff," she observed as he tucked his phone away.

"I make a good ally."

"But a terrifying enemy, I bet."

"You'll never have to find out."

"Even if I refuse my father's ultimatum?" She didn't bother to point out that if she did agree, she could still choose to marry a different man.

They both knew how unlikely that was.

Her youthful affections notwithstanding, she wasn't about to marry a stranger or a man who had multiple divorces under his belt.

Vik reached out and cupped her nape, stepping forward until mere centimeters separated their bodies, the heat from his surrounding her in a strangely protective cocoon. He didn't say anything, just caught her gaze, his dark eyes compelling her to some sort of belief.

Her breath escaped in a whoosh, unexpected and instant physical reaction crackling along her nerve endings while her heart started a *precipitando*. "Viktor?"

"You will never be my enemy, Madison."

"You're so confident I'll do what you want?"

"I'm confident *in* you, there's a difference."

There so was. He couldn't have said anything more guaranteed to get to her. People who believed *in* Maddie were a premium in her life. And less by one after this morning.

Dark espresso eyes continued to trap her even more effectively than his hand on her neck. "Trust me."

"Do I have a choice?" she asked with an attempt at sarcasm.

"No." His reply held no responding humor. Tilting his head, he stopped only when their lips almost touched. "You don't, and do you know why?"

"Tell me," she said in a voice that barely registered above a whisper.

"You already do." Then his mouth pressed against hers and the drumbeat in her chest went to the faster paced *stretto,* while electric pleasure sparked from his lips to hers.

A sensation she'd only known once before despite the fact she'd tried kissing other men. Six years ago when she'd thought the best way to celebrate becoming an adult would be to tell the man she'd been infatuated with for years that she loved him.

Even the memory of that old humiliation could not diminish the feelings of ecstasy washing over her from this elemental connection.

The kiss didn't last long, just a matter of seconds, but it could have been hours for the impact it had on her. When Vik pulled away and stepped back, Maddie had to stop herself from following him.

"Three o'clock. Turn your phone ringer off. I'll text."

She nodded, her mind blown by a simple kiss. Which did not bode well for her emotional equilibrium.

She fought acknowledging the possibility that tycoon Viktor Beck might well be more dangerous to the almost twenty-five-year-old Maddie as Archer business protégé Vik had been to her as a teenager.

"Go inside and lock the door, Madison."

She nodded again, but didn't move as she tried to reconcile the present with the past.

He shook his head, a curve flirting at the corner of the usually serious lines of his mouth. "You're going to be trouble."

"That's what my father says."

"I was thinking of a very different kind of trouble." Vik traced her bottom lip. "Believe me."

"Oh, really." Her lip tingling from his touch, warmth infused her that corresponded to the heat in his voice.

His smile became fully realized, and it was almost as good as the kiss.

She wasn't the one who was going to be *trouble*.

"Oh," she said again, this time without intending to, her body reacting to that warm expression in ways she just *didn't* with other men.

Vik waited in silence, no sense of impatience in evidence, but Maddie knew every minute he spent with her cost his tightly packed schedule.

She nodded to herself this time. "See you later."

Maddie stepped back into her apartment. Closing the door on him was a lot harder than it should have been.

She threw the dead bolt and a second later there was a double tap on the door. Vik's goodbye.

Using the pay-as-you-go cell phone she'd bought to provide Maddie Grace, volunteer, with a contact number, she called the school and let them know she wouldn't be in for at least a couple of days. She couldn't risk being caught in her Maddie Grace persona and having the best part of her life exposed to the media furor.

The next call she made was to Romi, who started cursing in French when Maddie told her friend that Jeremy Archer was using Perrygate to try to push Maddie into an *approved* marriage.

Maddie didn't tell Romi about the threat to her own

father's company or Maddie's response to it. Romi would demand her friend not sign the papers.

"Are you going to do it? Are you going to marry the man you've been crushing on for the last ten years?"

"That was a schoolgirl crush. I'm twenty-four years old now."

"And still a virgin. Still avoiding relationships."

"I'm not exactly alone in that."

Romi's silence was as good as a verbal acknowledgment.

"Besides, I *could* marry one of the others."

"Right."

"Maxwell Black offered a marriage of convenience with children by artificial insemination." She couldn't help a small smile at the memory of her father's reaction to that offer.

She knew Romi would get a kick out of it as well.

"Max was part of your father's deal?" Romi demanded in a tone a couple of registers above her normal one.

All of Maddie's humor fled. "You know Maxwell."

Silence. "A little."

"More than a little if you call him *Max*."

"We went out a few times."

"You never told me."

"It's no big deal." But, threaded with vulnerability, Romi's tone said otherwise.

Maddie warned, "I think he found Perry's claims about our supposed sex life *intriguing*."

"I know."

"You what?" Maddie practically screeched, her own problems forgotten for the moment. "How do you know that?"

"Do you really need me to spell it out for you?"

"You're still a virgin."

Romi had said so and the woman might be a hyperactive, borderline political anarchist and more than a little eclectic in her dress style, but she never lied.

"Technically, that is true."

"Technically?" Maddie drew the word out.

"Look, Maddie, I don't want to talk about it." Vulnerability now saturated Romi's voice, defenselessness that Maddie could not ignore.

"Okay, sweetie. But I'm here for you. You know that, right?"

"Always. SBC."

"SBC." Sisters by choice.

Maddie's mom had called them that the first time when she was explaining to the elementary school principal why the girls would do better with the same kindergarten teacher.

He'd refused to change their assignments and Helene Archer had called in the big guns.

It was the only time Maddie could remember her father stepping foot in her grade school. Mr. Grayson had come down, too, threatening to withdraw his company's support from the prestigious private school.

Romi and Maddie had never been assigned different classrooms again.

They had shared everything, including their grief at the loss of the only mother either girl had ever known when Helene Archer's speedboat had crashed into rocks invisible under the moonless sky.

Maddie hadn't gotten her propensity for risky behavior from nowhere.

She understood now that her mother's increasingly erratic behavior had been Helene's way of crying out for help. Help neither Maddie, nor her father, realized Helene needed.

It was a failure Maddie was still coming to terms with.

Vik's text came in at ten minutes to three.

He was on a conference call he could not reschedule,

but two bodyguards would be at her door in a few minutes. They had AIH indigo-level security IDs and she was not to open the door unless she saw the familiar badges through her peephole.

Specially trained for protecting people rather than corporate property and secrets, the indigo team was her father's personal security detail. It used to be hers, too. Wanting to live as normal a life as possible, Maddie had refused to be assigned bodyguards when she moved out of the family mansion.

Her father had argued, but ultimately given in.

She didn't think Vik would be as easily swayed. If he thought Maddie needed a bodyguard for her security, she'd have one.

The same way the company's on-site security system had been upgraded because Vik deemed it necessary. Her father had been all for it, though.

Nothing was too good for Archer International Holdings.

The limo was waiting in front of the elevator bank in the parking garage. Thankfully, no enterprising reporter had managed to keep vigil. Which probably had less to do with the parking garage guards than the two additional indigo-badge bodyguards standing at attention on either side of the elevator doors.

One of them stepped forward to open the door to the limo and she stepped inside, only then realizing that Vik had taken the conference call on his mobile.

Every dark hair perfectly in place, his designer suit immaculate, he nodded at her while carrying on a conversation in Japanese.

His words did not falter, his Japanese smooth and unhesitating, and yet she felt the weight of his full regard. Like his attention was fully on her.

Like she mattered.

Succumbing to the desire to sit beside him, Maddie settled onto the smooth leather seat across from AIH's media fixer. Relieved that none of the bodyguards had instructions to join them in the back of the limo, she was still grateful the other occupant gave her an excuse to give in to the irresistible urge.

The need to be near Vik was verging on ungovernable, just like it had been six years ago.

Maddie wanted to chalk it up to the exceptional circumstances. She just wasn't sure she could.

Which was not enough of a caution to move to the other seat. There was simply no comparison between Vik and Conrad, who until that morning she had found slightly annoying but now considered flat-out obnoxious.

The PR guru took a break from typing madly on his tablet to silently acknowledge her. If his smile looked more like a grimace, she wasn't interested enough in interacting with him to call him on it.

Besides, Perry's fake exposé had triggered an ugly media frenzy beyond anything Maddie had ever experienced for her far more innocent escapades.

There was even speculation now that some of her riskier endeavors had been the result of orders from her *master*. That wasn't even the worst of it. Maddie did not know how a virgin could be labeled a sex addict with obvious intimacy issues, but she'd stopped reading her Google alerts after that headline.

The limo had exited the parking garage and pulled away from her building when Vik ended his phone call.

"Are you okay?" he asked Maddie.

Honesty would reveal a level of vulnerability she wasn't comfortable sharing with Vik, much less Conrad. She had no idea how her life had spun out of control so fast.

And Perrygate was only part of it. Her father's ultimatum and the realization their relationship would never be what she wanted had been followed too closely by the equally alarming, if for different reasons, acknowledgment that she was actually considering marrying her girlhood crush.

"I'm fine."

"Good," Conrad said, as if he'd asked the question. "Containing this media bloodbath is going to take serious effort and you need to be on your top game."

He didn't have to tell her. Maddie had spent the time since Vik had dropped her off earlier worrying about what would happen if she couldn't reclaim her reputation.

The all too real prospect of losing her dreams of opening a small charter school tightened Maddie's throat, so she just nodded.

Once the media started looking more closely at Maddie's life, her alter ego was bound to come to light and the probability of losing her volunteer position was pretty much guaranteed.

While she enjoyed the anonymity of her Maddie Grace persona, she'd only taken rudimentary steps to keep her two lives separate. She wasn't James Bond, after all, just a socialite who craved time contributing as a *normal* person.

The only reason no one had cottoned on to Maddie Grace and Madison Archer being the same person before was that the news simply wasn't all that interesting. Or it hadn't been.

Her notoriety as Madcap Madison had been of the innocent variety, good for filler pieces in the social columns, but not salacious enough to really impact circulation numbers. Therefore *she* had not been interesting enough to be targeted by any serious digging.

She'd no doubt reporters were getting out their sharpest spades now. Perrygate was all that and a bag of chips for the gossipmongers.

The most painful part of Maddie's predicament was

that it wasn't just her dreams on the line here; Romi was equally invested in the charter school.

Vik sent a text and then pocketed his phone. "Our lack of an immediate response opened the door to other spurious claims from supposed former lovers."

Vik gave Conrad a look that left no doubt exactly who the VP of Operations for AIH blamed for that mistake.

Maddie felt no smugness at the media fixer being so obviously in the doghouse with Vik. Her life was too out of control to harbor even a hint of that, but she couldn't help the small thrill of pleasure at him taking her side.

From the moment he'd stepped in and ordered Conrad's cooperation that morning, Maddie had known she wasn't alone in facing the painful consequences of her onetime friend's betrayal.

Conrad tugged at the collar of his shirt. "We're working on retractions, but the best strategy for solidifying the prank angle is to give the media hounds another story."

"What do you mean? Like a two-headed baby from outer space, or something?" Maddie asked as her phone chimed to indicate a text from one of her select group.

Thinking it was Romi, she pulled out her phone and checked the message. It wasn't from her SBC; it was from Vik and said, You are not fine. We will talk. Later.

She texted back. If you say so.

Vik pulled his phone out and replied to her text while speaking. "Or something. A glossy celebrity gossip magazine has already offered a two-page spread announcing our formal engagement in exchange for exclusive photos of a lavish, well-attended wedding reception."

"We're engaged now?" Had she missed something between the text convo and their in-person discussion?

Vik didn't answer, but waited in silence for her to come to her own conclusion.

"It's the best way to stop any more dirty snow falling in this avalanche," Conrad said unctuously.

"Dirty snow? Really?" she asked sarcastically.

"Do you have a better word for it?"

"Perrygate."

"Appropriate, but don't use it on your social networks," Conrad instructed her. "It implies a negative rift between you and Mr. Timwater. We're dismissing all this as a joke gone wrong."

"Then you can play it off as the bad joke that ruined a friendship. I won't play nice with Perry." She couldn't.

Conrad frowned thoughtfully. "It would be better for you to be seen as the forgiving friend. Waiting a few months to cut the man from your life will increase your popularity."

"I don't care."

"Timwater isn't coming within a hundred feet of Madison, not even to apologize." Vik's voice brooked no argument.

And Conrad proved he was more intelligent than other evidence to the contrary because he didn't make one. "Fine. Fine." He started taking notes. "'The Prank That Ended a Friendship.' I can use that. We can spin the angle even. 'The Bad Joke That Almost Ended an Engagement.'"

Maddie looked at Vik. "Is he for real?"

Part of her knew this was the way things had to be, that Conrad was just doing his job, but having her life reduced to clichés and headlines was not fun.

"It's going to be okay, Madison." Vik pulled her cold hand into his own. "Trust me."

He had never hesitated to invade her personal space, or to touch her, though she'd never noticed him being so free with others. It was one of the reasons she'd convinced her eighteen-year-old self that Vik might return her feelings. She'd realized later that the small touches were probably the result of the way his Russian grandparents had raised him. Maddie had figured she hadn't seen him behave that way with others because he had so few personal relationships.

None but his grandparents and her father that she'd ever actually come into contact with.

That was one thing she and Vik had in common.

A very small inner circle.

She didn't comment on this now, just gave thanks for the fact he was willing to offer her the kind of comfort she needed and had never been able to ask for.

Vik squeezed her fingers. "Conrad is one of the best in the business. Before this morning I would have said *the* best."

Conrad flinched, proving he'd been listening even as he typed.

"And our engagement is the only way to restore my reputation?" she asked almost rhetorically.

She didn't see another way out, either.

Her father had more leverage for his plan than he could possibly comprehend. The realization of Maddie and Romi's dreams relied on a reputation Maddie could not afford to lose.

Vik frowned. "I'm sorry, Madison, but nothing is going to make the story go away completely."

"Why not?" Media fixers worked miracles.

Isn't that what everyone said? If they couldn't fix this, her and Romi's dreams were going to crash and burn. There was no way Maddie was going to let that happen.

Conrad looked up from his tablet. "Some people will always believe that where there is or was smoke, there had to be some ember of fire."

"But there isn't one."

The twist of Conrad's lips said he was probably one of *those* people.

Vik's hand moved to Maddie's thigh, bringing her attention careening back to him and him alone. "I believe you."

"No matter what the press has claimed, I've never even had a serious boyfriend," she admitted painfully.

Something flared in Vik's eyes, but he just nodded. "You've been too busy getting into trouble."

"Not *this* kind of trouble."

"I know."

"And not even my usual in the last six months."

Conrad's head snapped up. "Is that true?"

"I haven't done anything zany or even remotely newsworthy since I broke my pelvis in that botched skydiving landing."

Conrad narrowed his gaze. "What about parties? Random hookups?"

"Did you not hear her, Conrad?" Vik asked, dropping the temperature in the limo with the ice in his tone. "Madison does not do random hookups."

"She said she hasn't had a serious relationship, that the men claiming to have engaged in BDSM encounters are lying. Miss Archer never claimed to be celibate." Okay, so Conrad *had* been listening.

Vik didn't thaw even a little. "You can take *no random hookups* as a given."

"Can I?" Conrad asked Maddie, surprising her with his tenacity.

"Yes," she replied firmly. "I haven't been out in the evening except to attend charity events since my accident."

"With Perry as your escort?" Conrad asked, sounding unhappy by the possibility.

Which she could understand, in light of recent events. She wouldn't call the emotion she was feeling right now unfettered joy, either.

"A couple of times."

Vik's jaw hardened.

"Most events, Romi and I go together. Perry isn't all that interested in helping others." Maddie felt disloyal admitting that truth, but Romi had always said it.

Perry had never been as interested in the causes Maddie supported as the A-listers and potential business contacts he could meet at certain events.

"You've been at most of them, yourself," she offered to Vik.

He frequently represented AIH at that sort of thing, being an expert at making connections Perry only aspired to. Maddie knew that Vik also supported the causes in very tangible ways, both on behalf of the corporation and personally.

The gorgeous, corporate white knight nodded.

"That could work in our favor, unless you were photographed with your date for the evening," Conrad mused. "Even then, we could make it work."

"Vik hasn't had a date with him at one of these events in over a year." Knowledge that revealed how much attention Maddie paid to Vik.

A fact she'd done her best to hide even from herself, darn it.

His raised brow and knowing look said he realized that, too.

"That's good. We can back-engineer a budding relationship you've taken pains to keep out of the media spotlight." Conrad took more notes on his tablet. "This works."

Maddie turned toward Vik. "We're really getting married?"

"You tell me."

"Only it doesn't seem possible." Everything since her nearly spilled cup of coffee that morning felt like a dream, at times odd, unpleasant and bordering unbelievable.

"Believe it," Vik said, unconsciously answering her silent thoughts.

She narrowed her eyes, trying to read him. "How can you take this so calmly?"

"What am I supposed to be upset about?"

"Yesterday you were a free agent. Today you are engaged." Didn't that bother him, even a little?

Or was it something Vik had planned all along? Somehow, she couldn't quite dismiss that possibility.

"We are not engaged yet."

Something went tight in her chest. "But—"

"We will finish this discussion after you meet with the lawyer."

What did that mean? Did he think they were engaged, or not? *Were* they engaged? Had she said *yes?* She was pretty sure she hadn't. And she might know her choices were very limited, but did Vik? Really?

He returned his attention to his phone and sent a text.

This time she had no doubts it was to her.

Sure enough a few seconds later, her phone chimed. Trust me.

Trust him. Right. He thought it was that easy? "You aren't going to try to talk me out of signing the paperwork?"

"I told Jeremy threatening Romi could boomerang on him."

"He didn't believe you."

"He has a hard time backing off once he's set a thing in motion."

"Are you saying he's already started the wheels of destruction for Mr. Grayson's company? They used to be good friends."

Vik shrugged noncommittally. "He's done the research on how to make it happen."

"And he didn't want to waste his efforts?" Her dad could be so cold, but then that wasn't breaking news.

"You and I have agreed Jeremy could have no idea how spectacularly it would come back to bite him on the ass."

"But you aren't trying to change my mind."

Conrad stopped typing and listened as if he, too, was curious about what was motivating Vik's behavior.

Vik ignored the other man, his focus entirely on Maddie. "Those shares ultimately belong to you."

"My father doesn't see it that way."

"It never occurred to Jeremy that any child of his would consider AIH as a means to an end rather than the end itself."

What did he know? Did Vik realize she had always intended to use her income from the shares to run the school?

It wouldn't be a long stretch from what she'd told him that morning.

What he couldn't know was that Romi would do the same. She wanted the school as much as Maddie.

Vik's dream was something quite different, but obviously just as important to him. "You want the company."

"Like your father, I want to leave a legacy for my children." Some might think the lack of emotion in Vik's deep tones belied his words.

Maddie knew better.

His dark brown eyes burned with certainty. "Archer International Holdings will be that legacy."

"But we're not engaged." She couldn't help the small bit of sarcasm.

Maddie was unsurprised by Vik's lack of response.

CHAPTER FIVE

MADDIE'S TIME IN the lawyer's office went quickly, though the elderly man did ask if she was sure she knew what she was doing.

Maddie had no doubts.

Vik stood when she came back into the anteroom, no sign he was in any way upset about what she'd been doing. "All finished?"

"Yes."

"Do you have any plans for the rest of today?"

"No."

Vik put his hand on the small of her back and walked with her out of the law office. "Good."

"Why?"

"We have a photo shoot with the magazine photographer this evening. He'll join us for dinner at your father's mansion. My grandparents will be there."

"Playing happy families? Is that really necessary?"

"Yes."

When they reached the parking garage, he led her to his car, the limo and SUV full of bodyguards nowhere in evidence.

"Conrad is in the limo with a redheaded decoy." Vik opened the passenger door of the black amethyst Jaguar XJL for Maddie.

She settled into the luxury car. "Better her than me. I would have made a lousy celebrity."

"You think?" he asked. "Your father thinks you've been doing your best to become the next reality TV star."

"Just Madcap Madison, version two-point-oh."

Vik's expression went from smile to grimace, reflecting Maddie's own conflicting feelings about her mom's escapades in the light of adulthood. "In many ways Helene Madison Archer was an amazing woman and she raised a strong and impressive daughter, but the way she chose to cope with the things she didn't like in her life wasn't healthy. You must see that."

"I do." It had taken some time, but Maddie had come to that conclusion a while ago. The *Madcap* was something Maddie was doing her best to drop from her name. "Believe it, or not, I've always been very careful what part of my life I allow the media into."

"Perry isn't so choosy."

Vik was in the driver's seat, their identity obscured behind the Jaguar's tinted windows, when she replied. "Perry is an idiot who relied on our friendship to protect him from the consequences of his lies."

"It is."

"You think so?" She indulged in an old favorite secret pastime as he drove out of the financial district and through Chinatown toward Van Ness.

Watching Viktor Beck.

Memories of their recent kiss played over in her mind, a mental movie she could not seem to turn off and that caused a visceral reaction in her body. A reaction she wasn't sure if she should try to suppress, or not.

If they were getting married, reacting to his kiss was a good thing, right?

Thankfully, she didn't have to answer the disturbing question of whether she would marry him for the sake of her dreams if she *wasn't* attracted to him. How much of her father's ruthlessness colored Maddie's spirit?

She was sure Jeremy Archer would say the papers she'd just signed answered that question, but that wasn't how she saw it.

Vik shifted down, his car purring as it climbed the hills of San Francisco's streets. "You refuse to sue Perry despite his defamation of your character."

"Our friendship is over." Ultimately that would cost Perry more than any settlement she might get in court.

"Is it?"

"Yes."

"You sound very certain." Vik didn't.

"I am."

Vik turned onto Highway 101. "Good."

"And even if for no other reason than that he'll never get another loan from me, that's a serious consequence for Perry." One she really didn't think the other man had foreseen. He would have counted on her loyalty, but had made the egregious error of not giving her any. "He'll also never again be able to use being my escort as a way into events his own connections won't provide entrée."

"It sounds like it was a pretty one-sided friendship."

"That's what Romi always said, but it wasn't true."

"Yes?" Vik sounded genuinely curious, if doubtful.

"Letting people in isn't easy for me."

The business tycoon who had spurred more fantasies than any teenage heartthrob in her adolescent breast made a disbelieving sound. "You have a huge social network."

"And a total of two people I called friends, now only one."

"I think two still." Vik flicked her a glance with meaning. "Just not the same two."

Unexpected and not wholly welcome warmth unfurled

inside Maddie at the claim. Nevertheless, she admitted, "I'm glad to hear that."

She just hoped it was true. Chances were good. Viktor Beck might be a bastard in the business world, but he was no liar.

"He made me laugh," she admitted, falling back on old habits of sharing her uncensored thoughts with Vik.

"You have an infectious laugh," Vik offered. "I missed it."

It was weird to think of Vik missing anything about her. "You decided our friendship was over."

"Not over, just truncated."

"If you say so." But six years on, she could maybe share his point of view.

"I thought it for the best."

It was entirely possible it had been, no matter how much his rejection and subsequent pulling away had hurt. She hadn't thought so at the time, the combined loss of her mom, then her grandfather, what little attention she'd had from her father and then Vik's friendship had left Maddie with real intimacy issues. But if she and Vik had maintained their close friendship, she never would have gotten over him.

Nor would she have made her own way in life, building dreams completely independent of AIH.

"Looking back on it, it's kind of surprising I let Perry get so close." But then she'd needed a replacement for Vik at least.

"You loaned him money."

Which had taken their friendship into a different realm, she now realized—a realm where Perry saw Maddie as a resource rather than a friend. "In the interest of accuracy, we'll have to call them gifts, not loans."

"And that makes it better?"

She shrugged, though Vik's attention was on the road as

they joined the heavy traffic over the Golden Gate Bridge. "Perry's business ventures never seemed to work out."

"Selling this story to the tabloids is pretty stupid as a long-term plan if you were already bankrolling him."

"I wasn't. I turned him down the last time he asked for money." It had been a hard decision, but she'd had her own dreams to bankroll. "I'd come to the conclusion there were better places I could sink my money than down the rabbit hole of another one of Perry's unlikely business ventures."

"So, he betrayed you."

"Yes." She sighed sadly. "I had no idea my friendship was only worth a few dollars."

"Fifty thousand."

"That's how much he got paid?" She wasn't surprised Vik knew.

The man made it a habit to know everything of even peripheral importance to him. Maddie figured it would be a matter of days, if not hours, before he learned of her anonymous volunteering and even her therapist.

Uncertainty about his reaction to her secrets was the only thing stopping her from telling him herself.

"For the initial tabloid article. He planned to leverage the scandal into more paid interviews and even a book deal." Vik's voice was laced with disgust.

"That's ridiculous. I'm not exactly a celebrity." She hated this.

"No, but you are the Madcap Heiress."

"Madcap Madison. It's what they called my mother." She could still remember the first time one of the tabloids had used the moniker for Maddie.

It had made Maddie feel like maybe Helene was still with her in some small way. Only later had her own maturity and help from her therapist helped Maddie to see how distorted that thinking was.

"You share her penchant for making it into the press,"

Vik agreed. "Perry's book wouldn't have made him a million dollars, but someone would have paid him a hefty advance for it."

"That's just stupid."

"That's our reality-television, celebrity-drama-obsessed society." Vik shifted into the higher gear as they finally made it over the bridge.

San Francisco's gridlock could get really ugly, though it was better than the freeways that became parking lots during high commute times in and around L.A.

"I suppose. You talk about the book deal like it's in the past."

"It is." Definite satisfaction colored Vik's two-word answer.

She shouldn't be surprised Vik had worked so quickly, but she couldn't deny being impressed and only a little apprehensive. "What were Perry's terms?"

"Timwater didn't set the terms, trust me."

She had no trouble believing that, not when Vik was involved. Perry had no hope with the power of AIH brought to bear against him at the instructions of its VP. "What did Conrad get him to agree to?"

"Do you think, after his screwup this morning, I would trust this negotiation with Conrad?"

"*You* met with Perry? Wasn't that overkill?" Putting Vik and Perry in the same room was like pitting an alley cat against the heavyweight champ.

The cat might be wily and street smart, but he was still going to get pulverized.

And she wasn't entirely convinced of Perry's street smarts.

"From now on, anything to do with you goes through me personally." Vik exited the freeway, downshifting the powerful Jaguar.

"That's not how my father operates."

They were headed toward the Marin Headlands. Maddie recognized the route, though she hadn't been there since her school days, on the obligatory field trip to the Golden Gate Bridge and to view the city vista.

"I am not your father."

"But you're a lot alike."

"In how we do business? Yes. But you share more personality traits with your father than I do."

"You're kidding."

"No."

"I know we're both stubborn, but…"

"It does not stop there, believe me."

"So you say." She was *nothing* like her father.

"I do."

Typical. Vik felt no need to explain himself, or convince her, which only made her want to hear his justifications all the more. She wasn't going to ask, though.

Not right now.

Right now, she was far more interested in what they were doing in the parking area near Battery Spencer. "Is the magazine photographer here to get some color shots, or something?"

"No."

Vik pulled neatly into a parking spot and turned off the car, but made no move to get out.

He unbuckled his seat belt and turned to face her. "It is a good thing the friendship is over from your side. Timwater signed a nondisclosure agreement that covers every aspect of his association with you. The penalties for breaking it are severe."

"But he's going to talk about our friendship." It had spanned the same six years as the dearth of Vik in her life.

"No, he is not."

She had no desire to see the man again, but she wasn't sure how she felt about their friendship disappearing as if it had never been, either. "It isn't going to help with what he's already done."

Vik's eyes bored into hers. "He's signed a retraction, admitting everything he told the tabloid was a lie."

"Won't that leave him open to a lawsuit from them?" And why was she worried about someone who had so very blatantly not been worried about her?

"They don't get a copy of the confession…unless he screws up again." The threat in Vik's words would have been spelled out to her ex-friend in no uncertain terms.

"And that will protect him?"

"Do you care?"

"I probably shouldn't."

"You would not be you if you didn't," Vik said with something like indulgence and no evidence of judgment.

"I'm not a pushover."

"No one witnessing you facing your father down in the conference room this morning would ever question that."

"Okay."

Vik smiled. "You are a strong woman whose strength is tempered by compassion. My grandmother Ana is such a woman."

"And you love her."

"Yes."

Did that mean he might love Maddie one day? She did her best to quash that line of fantasy thought. Like she'd told her father earlier, Maddie wasn't the fairy-tale believer her mom had been. She had no expectations of marrying for undying love and irresistible passion.

So, she couldn't understand where the tiny ember of hope burning deep in her heart despite Maddie's strictest self-talk came from.

Unaware of the war going on inside of Maddie from that simple admission, Vik added, "Timwater will make a public apology for his prank after our engagement is announced."

Even though they *weren't* engaged, according to Vik.

It suddenly occurred to her that they hadn't come to the overlook for privacy to discuss Perry.

Even so, she needed to know one thing. "How much?"

"Did we pay him?"

"Yes."

"The way his apology will play, he'll get to keep his fifty thousand from the tabloid." Vik didn't sound particularly happy about that fact.

"And?"

"The only thing I gave Timwater was my word not to destroy his name in the business world. The nondisclosure agreement guarantees we will not sue him in civil court, either—so long as he keeps his side of it."

"He never would have believed I would do that."

"I would. Regardless of if it was on behalf of the company rather than you, Timwater would be just as screwed."

"You're ruthless."

"It's not just an Archer family trait. We do what we need to get what is important to us."

"Like marrying the owner's daughter to take control of a Fortune 500 company."

"Yes."

"Thank you."

"For?"

"Not trying to pretend this is something else." No matter what her heart wanted.

"What exactly do you think this is?"

"Necessary."

He nodded. "Yes, but it will be a marriage in every sense of the word. You do realize that?"

"You mean…"

"Sex. We will not be living celibate lives."

"No affairs?" Not that she would be willing to take this step if she thought he was a womanizer, if she herself had plans to look outside the marriage for that kind of companionship.

"No affairs," he repeated, making no attempt to suppress how disgusting he considered the idea.

Vik wasn't that guy.

He *was* the grandson of a very traditional Russian man. Vik would never do anything that would disappoint the old man. He thought his father had done enough of that.

He'd shared that, and a lot more she hadn't expected him to, when they were friends during her teen years. He'd never been like a brother, but he had been one of the few people she'd believed she could rely on back then.

Could she rely on him now?

"Be very sure you understand what I am saying here, Madison." Vik reached across the console and cupped her nape in a move that was becoming familiar. "I am not Maxwell Black. My children will not be conceived in a test tube."

"Of course not." Whatever their feelings for each other, this situation was very personal for him.

He nodded like that had settled everything still left unsaid between them. She wasn't so sure she agreed, but she didn't hesitate to get out of the car with him.

They took the path to the overlook, Maddie grateful she'd worn the sensible pumps and that the ground was dry. Neither of them spoke while they walked, but he kept his hand on the small of her back, moving it to her elbow in the uneven patches of terrain.

When they stopped, they were at one of the favorite overlooks that gave a view of both the famous bridge and the San Francisco skyline. A few tourists dotted the area, but none near enough to hear any discussion she and Vik might have.

Vik maneuvered them so he stood only a few inches from her, his body acting as a barrier against the incessant winds off the harbor. The close and clearly protective positioning felt significant.

"My grandfather gave my grandmother her first view of San Francisco in this very spot," Vik said after a moment of silent contemplation of the vista before them. "He promised her a future with food to put on the table for their family. A future without oppression for their Orthodox beliefs."

"He kept his promise."

"Yes." Vik went silent for several seconds of contemplation. "Grandfather brought my dad up here as a child. Misha told Frank he could be anything he wanted to, a true American with no accent, his name just like all the other boys'."

"Your grandfather gave your father the freedom to be anything he wanted to."

"Even a failure."

She couldn't argue that assessment, not when she knew Frank Beck had spent his adulthood running from responsibility. Unless something had changed in the last six years, Frank only contacted Vik when he wanted something. Usually money.

Placing her hand on his forearm, Maddie said, "He didn't fail when he fathered you."

"Misha and Ana raised me to be who I am."

"An undisputable success."

Vik turned to face her. "You believe that?"

"I do."

"That is good."

She smiled, not sure why she felt the need to reassure Viktor Beck, but determined to do it anyway.

"*Deda* brought me up here, too, when I was boy. Frank could not be bothered, but I made promises to myself, commitments to the children I would one day father. Promises *I* will keep."

"I have no doubt."

Vik's gaze warmed, his expression filled with unmistakable determination. "My grandparents were not in love when they married, but theirs is one of the strongest marriages I have ever witnessed."

"They are devoted to each other."

"And to their family, even my dad."

"I believe it."

Vik nodded, his dark eyes reflecting approval of her words. "That kind of dedication runs in my veins right along with the ruthlessness."

"I know."

Vik laid his big hands on her shoulders, creating a private world of two for them. "I believe our children will share those traits."

"No doubt." There was nothing she could do about how breathless her voice had become.

He was touching her, and even through the fabric of her Valentino suit jacket and the shell she wore under it, she felt the connection intimately.

"Considering it will come from both their mother and their father, our children have little hope otherwise."

"I'm not ruthless," she said, shocked by the accusation.

"The paperwork you signed today would say otherwise."

"You know that isn't the way I usually do things." It just had been…necessary.

"Ruthlessness does not have to be the dominant trait in your nature for you to have it."

"And it doesn't bother you?"

"That you'll fight for those who deserve your loyalty, even those who do not? No."

"You expect to deserve my loyalty."

"Yes."

"And will I get yours?"

His expression said her question surprised him. "Do you doubt it?"

"Six years ago…"

"You kissed me and I pushed you away."

"That's a simplified way of looking at it and not entirely accurate."

"No?"

"No. I told you I loved you. You told me I was too young and you didn't just push me away, you pushed me out of your life completely. Our friendship ended with one kiss."

"It was necessary."

"We could have stayed friends."

"No."

"Why not?"

"You were an eighteen-year-old, barely a woman."

"But I was a woman."

"I know." There was a message in his voice she couldn't decipher.

"You were also the daughter of a man I admired and who trusted me with you."

"Not to mention he was your boss," she reminded him a little snidely.

"Yes, my boss. The president and owner of a company I intended to run one day."

"A relationship with me would hardly have gotten in the way of *that* goal."

"It would have. Six years ago."

"But not now." No, *now* it was the opposite.

Marriage to her would give Vik exactly what he wanted.

"No, not now."

"I loved you." She wouldn't call it a crush; it hadn't been by then. She'd gotten over it, but at one time she *had* loved him. "Your rejection hurt me."

"I am sorry."

But he wouldn't change his past actions, even if he could. She knew him.

"Look on the bright side," he said almost teasingly.

She didn't remember anything bright about that time. "What?"

He smiled like a shark. "It should be easy for you to learn to love me again."

"Emotion doesn't work like that." And she was pretty sure falling in love with this man, even if she married him, wouldn't be the smartest thing she could ever do.

"Doesn't it?" He pulled something out of the inside pocket of his coat. A small lacquer box that fit in his palm. "My grandmother brought this *Palekh* over from Russia when she and my grandfather defected during the Cold War."

"It's beautiful."

"It is a reminder."

"Of what?"

"The beauty they left behind and the life they hoped to build. *Deda* always said *Babulya* was his frog princess."

The top of the box was decorated with an image from the Russian fairy tale where Prince Ivan ended up married to an industrious and lovely princess who had once been a frog. The magical princess outdid her aristocratic counterparts set to marry Ivan's brothers in every way.

Maddie thought maybe she understood why Vik's grandmother Ana had told Maddie the story of the frog princess the first time they'd met.

"Does this make you my frog prince?" she asked tongue in cheek.

Vik traced the rich image painted in egg tempera on black. "Perhaps it does."

"You know I don't believe in fairy tales."

"Maybe you should."

Now, *that* was definitely *not* something her father ever would have said to her.

"Your grandfather's promises seem to fly in the face of Russian pessimism." But then Misha Beck had never struck her as a pessimist.

The man who had changed his last name to reflect his new country and life had a decidedly forward-thinking attitude.

Maddie had only met Vik's grandparents a few times, but she liked them.

A lot.

Despite the fact Misha and Ana had raised their grandson, Maddie had always considered them the epitome of a *normal* family. The kind of family she'd always wanted.

The kind she wasn't sure Vik was offering with whatever was in that small lacquer box.

"*Deda* never believed the old adage that to speak of success cursed it." Though his shoulders didn't move, there was a shrug in Vik's voice.

"His life and yours prove his skepticism."

"That is one way to look at it."

"The other?"

"*Deda* gave up being a Russian and embraced the way of his new homeland."

"The American ideology does tend toward the positive."

"Remember that."

"You think I have to be a dreamer because of where I was born and raised?" she demanded.

"No. You have your dreams. I have mine. It is not about where you were born, but who you were born to be. I want you to believe in both of our dreams."

"And that takes some of the idealism this country is known for."

"Yes."

He wanted her to believe in his dreams.

It might be love between them, but this was more than a business proposal—no matter what had prompted it.

CHAPTER SIX

"AND THIS?" SHE pointed to the *Palekh* that had to be at least fifty years old. "Is it a reminder for *me* now?"

No matter how unmoved she tried to appear about that possibility, it touched her deeply.

"Yes."

Her breath hitched. "Of the successful legacy you promised your unborn children?"

"Among other things."

"That kind of success is more important to you than it is to me." Maddie wanted promises of other things.

She wasn't naive. She wasn't looking for undying love, despite the odd feelings deep in her heart she was doing her best not to acknowledge. Even Helene Archer had been too pragmatic to promise her princess a knight in shining armor that would *love* Maddie. But there was more to life than building a company that dominated the world market.

"You think so?" he asked, sounding amused.

Though she didn't understand why. Maddie could only nod.

"It will take the *significant* results of that type of success to make your school a reality."

She couldn't deny it.

"You think money means little to you, but then you have never lived in fear of want." If he had sounded even a little condescending, she would have been angry.

He didn't.

"And you have?" she asked, wondering if there was something about his past she didn't know.

"Not like my grandparents, but let's just say the year between my mother's death and *Deda* deciding I would come to live with him and *Babulya* was not one I would ever allow my own child to endure."

"I'm sorry."

"Frank's inability to make anyone's needs as important as his own, including the basic need to eat of his six-year-old son, taught me as much about who I did not wish to be as *Deda* taught me about the man I would become."

"Your grandfather is a good man."

"He and *Babulya* raised me with an appreciation for the difference between working to provide and working an angle."

"Like your dad."

Vik grimaced. "Frank is very good at angles."

"You want your life to matter."

"It already does."

She couldn't argue that. Didn't want to. "I want my life to matter, too—we just have a different way of going about it."

"Yes, we do." He didn't sound bothered by that fact. Why was she?

She wanted to tell him about Maddie Grace, but wasn't sure how she would handle it if Vik had the same attitude about her efforts as Jeremy had had.

"I have already promised to help you see your dream of a charter school realized," Vik pointed out.

Yes, he had, which put Vik miles ahead of her father in that regard already. Maybe their differences would make both of their lives better, rather than tearing them apart.

"What kind of promises are you making with that box,

Vik?" she asked, almost ready to believe in the possibility of the complete family she'd never had.

His handsome lips tilted a little at the nickname she hadn't uttered in six years, keeping it strictly private to her thoughts. Something she had not been able to let go of, but would not share with others, either.

"If you accept my proposal, I promise fidelity."

She nodded.

"I will expect the same," he said, as if there was any chance she didn't already realize it.

Interesting that he'd led with that one, though. Was that because he thought she needed it after Perry's betrayal, or was it more personal for Vik?

Either way, she said, "That's a given."

"I am glad to hear that."

When he said nothing else, but looked down at her with an expression that seemed to see into her soul, Maddie prompted, "And?"

"I promise to continue to grow AIH, leaving our children a legacy worthy of both my family and yours."

It was a promise meant more for and to himself and their future children, but she didn't dismiss it is as unimportant. Not after he pointed out her own dreams required money just like his did, if not on the same scale. "All of our children?"

"Yes." His brow furrowed. "Why would I distinguish?"

He could be one of those men who considered their eldest their only important child, or only their sons. But she knew he wasn't.

Her concerns were a lot more unpredictable.

"I am willing to have two children with you, but I want more and they will be adopted." This wasn't a deal breaker for her.

Not if she could have her school, but it was something she desperately wanted to do. Be open to the possibility of bringing children into her life that they could offer a family, not just support, encouragement and help.

Vik's brows drew together in thought, not a frown. "You want to adopt?"

"Yes."

"Babies or children?" he asked.

"Does it matter?"

"No."

Happy with that answer and the speed of it, she offered, "Most likely children."

"All right."

"That's it? You agree?" Shock coursed through her.

"I assume we will make any decisions in regard to bringing more children into our lives—both those born to us and adopted by us—together."

"Of course, but you're open to it?"

"Nothing would delight Misha and Ana more than a house full of grandchildren to spoil."

"There are a lot of bedrooms in Parean Hall." Which was her acquiescence to living there as a married couple.

His satisfied smile said he recognized that as well. "I do not anticipate filling them all with children, but have no objections to our family inhabiting half of them."

It was a ten-bedroom mansion.

Could it really be this easy? "You'll put that in the prenup?"

"If you insist, but I assure you it is not necessary." He placed the antique Russian keepsake against her palm. "Any promises I make you here will not be broken."

"So long as it is within your power."

"Yes." His tone and expression implied Viktor Beck considered very little outside his power and influence.

"And you will be a father to our children, not just the man with that title." He wasn't the only one with memories of neglect after the death of a mother.

Hers might not have been to her physical needs, but Jeremy Archer had let Maddie starve emotionally.

"I cannot promise to make every Little League game or sit-in your daughters organize, but I will make our children a priority."

"*My* daughters?"

"Mine will be too busy trying to take over the corporate world for social activism."

Tickled, she laughed like she hadn't with him in too long, but grew serious again quickly enough. "I won't have my child forced into dedicating his or her life to AIH. That has to be a personal decision."

"Agreed." But clearly Vik had no problem believing his children would be as dedicated to AIH as he was.

Who knew? Maddie herself might have wanted a career in AIH, at least in some capacity, if she'd had a different relationship with her father.

"I think we will have to accept that our children will be influenced by both of us," she told him.

"I can think of much worse things."

"I'm glad you said so," she replied cheekily, secretly touched by his sincerity.

"Open the box," Vik instructed.

"Are you done making promises?"

"Any other commitment I make to you would fall under the three I've already made."

"Three?"

"Fidelity. Dedication. Family."

Inexplicable emotion clogged her throat, but he was right. He'd promised the things that mattered most to her. With a few words he'd committed to building a *family* with her and all that entailed.

She took the lid off the box, incapable of hiding the way her fingers trembled.

Inside, nestled in a bed of black silk, were two rings.

One she recognized as a traditionally inspired Russian three-strand wedding band. Each diamond-encrusted ring interwoven with the others was a different shade of gold: yellow, white and rose.

It was beautiful, but not ostentatious. Perfect for her. Beside it rested a diamond engagement ring set in the pink-tinted gold that would sit flush against the curved wedding band when he put it on her hand.

She didn't ask how he knew the rose tint that used to be known as Russian gold was her favorite. Vik was scary like that.

She didn't ask if she would be able to wear the ring beside the wedding ring after they were married. She could see the curve in the band that would make that possible.

He'd melded the traditions of his homeland with that of his grandparents and taken her own preferences into consideration. It was so Vik. She might not still be in love with him, but it was no wonder she'd never been able to accept a substitute.

"It's beautiful," she breathed, the moment feeling unexpectedly profound.

"As is the woman it was designed for."

"You didn't have this designed for me." He couldn't possibly have.

This kind of custom work wasn't done in a few hours.

He cupped her hands with his own. "You will have to accept that my plans for the future have included you for much longer than you considered me in the same regard."

"I sincerely doubt that." He'd been *it* for her since she'd had her first real thought about boys and girls and how their lives came together.

Even when she hadn't realized she was still comparing every man to Viktor Beck. Darn Romi being right all these years anyway.

He shook his head. "You had a schoolgirl crush, but have not thought of me in that way for six years."

So, he *wasn't* all-knowing. "That shows how much you know. Romi always says I hold other men up to your example and they pale in comparison."

"And what do you say?"

"I always denied it."

"See, I told you."

"I've begun to realize she might have been right." No other man had a chance with Maddie.

Not Perry, not anyone.

Vik's expression dismissed her words as an exaggeration.

"I never forgot you." He'd been too deeply embedded in her psyche, if not her heart.

Maddie had honestly believed her issues with trust had prevented intimacy with another man, but now realized memories of *that guy* had been enough to keep others at bay.

"You avoided me like the plague."

"You did your own avoidance."

"For about a year," he acknowledged. "I missed our friendship. I thought enough time had passed that we'd gotten past the awkward incident."

And he'd approached her. She'd rebuffed him, doing her best to never be put in a position where they could speak privately again. She'd stopped coming home unless her father demanded her attendance and that happened rarely enough.

For at least two years, Maddie had turned down every invite that might put her and Vik in the same sphere.

"I wasn't on the same page." What had been awkward for him had been humiliating for her.

"You made that unmistakable."

"I was angry with you." She'd felt betrayed.

Perry's treachery hurt; Vik's rejection had devastated her.

"And now?" Vik asked.

What did he want her to say? She'd stopped avoiding him at social functions before she graduated from university, but she'd still made sure there was no opportunity for them to renew the old friendship.

"The world looks like a different place from twenty-four than eighteen." It was the best she could do.

"You will forgive me for hurting you?" he asked, like it really mattered.

So, she told him the truth. "I forgave you a long time ago, Vik."

"It did not feel like it."

She looked up into his espresso-brown eyes. "Do you forgive me?"

"For kissing me?" he asked, sounding genuinely confused.

Not a usual circumstance for him. She would take a moment to savor it and even tease him if the discussion wasn't so important.

She explained, "For mistaking your kindness for something more and making our friendship impossible."

"I never held it against you." His tone implied something else altogether.

"You thought you should have known I was falling in love with you," she realized.

"That wasn't the way I termed it, but yes."

Right. He'd thought her love was a crush. But if it had been only a crush, it would have taken months, not years, to get over.

"You're not omniscient, Vik."

"If I'd been paying better attention, I could have headed you off gently."

She wasn't sure that was true. Vik was right that she

and her father shared a stubbornness that resulted in a tenacity of purpose almost impossible to derail.

"If we'd remained friends, Perry would never have gotten the hold on you he did."

"You think you would have stopped us becoming friends."

"I would have prevented him from using you as his personal bank and he would have known that you had people looking out for you."

"People scary enough to abandon his plans for the phony exposé before he ever put feelers out for the first reporter?" she asked with a smile.

"You think I'm scary."

"To men like Perry? Oh, yes, definitely."

"But not to you."

"No, Vik, you don't scare me."

"Good."

He frowned. "Perhaps you would not have taken the chances you have in the past years if you'd had the stability of my presence in your life."

"You're pretty arrogant."

"Do you deny it?"

"Actually yes," she said firmly. "My actions are not your fault, or your responsibility."

He shrugged, clearly disagreeing.

"You really have a God complex."

"No, but I know my responsibilities."

"And I'm one of them?" she demanded, frustrated more with herself for seeing that as romantic than Vik for his arrogance.

His smile sent heat through her, reminding her of that lack-of-celibacy thing he'd taken pains to make clear. "I hope more than that."

"Friends again?"

"Yes, definitely."

"But you want more." Maybe not passionately and personally, though she was beginning to see that Vik *did* desire her, but to make his dreams come true, Vik was going to marry her.

"Yes."

"Okay."

"To?"

"Everything."

His expression turned even more heated and predatory. "Be careful what you promise."

"This is a special place. Promises made here stick, right?"

"Yes." No doubts.

"Then I promise to do my best to make both our dreams come true."

"I make this promise as well."

That was way better than him promising to build AIH into some world superpower, in her opinion. "Thank you."

His kiss took her by surprise. It shouldn't have. Wasn't it natural to kiss to seal an engagement?

But the kiss did surprise her. And then it overwhelmed her, his lips coaxing a response that radiated throughout her body. They took possession of hers, no longer coaxing, but insisting on the two things she'd said only that morning she wasn't capable of.

Submission and trust.

But then, like with so many other things in her life, the rules did not apply to Viktor Beck.

She found herself melting into him, no thoughts for self-preservation or holding anything back.

And he accepted her surrender with a forceful masculine desire that belied any claim for a lack of passion between them.

He devoured her mouth, his arms coming around her,

his hands pressing her body against his, one thigh pressing between her legs as far as her skirt would allow.

Maddie's knees would have given out, but Vik's hold on her was too tight.

She'd thought the kiss this morning had been hot, but it was nothing like Viktor Beck staking claim to the woman who promised to marry him and give him his dreams.

Viktor knocked impatiently on Madison's door thirty minutes before they needed to be at Jeremy's ostentatious home in Presidio Heights.

Viktor had not given himself time for a drink or idle chitchat on purpose. After the kiss at the overlook, he did not want to risk his self-control before the dinner.

If his grandparents weren't going to be there, as well as the photographer from the magazine, he would never have left Madison that afternoon. But she deserved to show up to her engagement dinner on time and *not* looking like she'd spent the hours before in bed.

He'd told her the truth earlier. Six years ago he'd seen her as barely a woman when she'd kissed him.

He'd been shocked by his own body's response to her overtures, realizing for the first time that she was an adult and *not* a child. Not that he'd given that revelation much credence.

Not at first, but after a year of avoiding her and indulging in more liaisons than his workaholic regime usually allowed for, two things had become obvious.

He missed Madison and she was the only woman he wanted sharing his bed. She was still too young and Viktor's plans didn't include marriage for at least a few more years.

Anything else with the daughter of AIH's president and owner was out of the question. And not just because Viktor considered the older, driven businessman a friend.

Viktor wasn't sure when he realized his own business ambitions included marrying Madison, but it was well before he broached the subject in any oblique way with Jeremy. The older man's concern regarding what would happen when Madison inherited full control of the trust gave Viktor the traction he needed for Jeremy's approval of his own future plans.

He'd had the rings commissioned and intended to launch his courtship of Madison in the coming weeks when Timwater sent a spanner into the works with his "breakup interview."

If Viktor had started his pursuit of Madison earlier, the opportunistic man would not have had a chance to hurt her with his lies. It was unacceptable bad timing that had left Madison vulnerable.

It angered him. Viktor did not do bad timing. And he did not get caught by surprise. But he had not anticipated Timwater's betrayal of his long-standing friendship with the heiress.

While it had not precipitated long-term action on Viktor's part that he wasn't already planning, the intolerable situation had brought things to a head before he intended. *And* it had forced him to work around Jeremy's knee-jerk response to his daughter's misadventure.

While that might have ended up working in Viktor's favor, it had come with additional emotional cost to Madison.

He might be ruthless, but that was not okay with him. Her well-being was his responsibility now.

The door opened and Viktor's thoughts scattered.

Madison's copper curls flirted around her face, her blue eyes vibrant and flashing with a response to his presence that found a corresponding reaction in his body.

Lips entirely too kissable despite the dark color staining them in a perfect scarlet bow curved in a smile of welcome. "Hi, Vik. Are you coming in?"

She'd encased her tempting body in a 1950s-inspired couture cocktail dress in a shiny dark blue that rustled as she moved.

The skirt was full, nipping in at the waist, and the bodice fitted, the artistically cut neckline dipping to reveal the hint of cleavage he found more sexually alluring than any woman he'd seen in a dress that revealed most of her breasts.

"You…" He cleared his throat, finding it unaccountably dry. "You look beautiful."

Only after he spoke did it occur to him that he had not answered her question.

"Thank you." She blushed, something she rarely did anymore. "It works?" The nerves that slipped in to tinge her smile were something else she didn't show others. "Only I wanted your grandparents to see *me,* not the…"

She didn't have to finish. "It will be all right. *Deda* and *Babulya* are eager to see you and welcome you into our family."

"They know we are engaged? Have they seen the articles?"

Ignoring his own best intentions, he pushed into the apartment and right into Madison's personal space.

She gasped and looked up at him, eyes wide, breath hitching. "Vik? What?"

He curved his hands around her waist, enjoying the soft slide of the fabric and the heat of her skin under it even more. "They know we are engaged and they are delighted."

"Oh."

"They know about the stories and they are furious with Timwater."

"They don't believe them? You told them he lied, didn't you?"

"I did and they don't." Viktor reveled in the implicit trust in his ability to make things right that could be read into her questions.

"Thank you."

Mindful of the crimson color on her lips, he bent down and pressed a soft kiss to the side of her neck, staying to inhale the subtle fragrance of honeysuckle mixed with orange and a hint of vanilla and her own unique scent. "You smell good."

"It's my perfume."

"It's you. Rosewater would smell just as delicious against your skin."

She trembled against him, her hands pressing into his chest. "Vik."

That was all she said. Just his name. But it was a plea, whether to step back or to do something about the electricity arcing between them, he did not let himself contemplate.

He stepped back. "We need to go. Everyone is waiting."

"Including the photographer."

"He has his instructions to be as unobtrusive as possible."

Madison grimaced, her opinion of how unobtrusive that could actually be very clear.

He looked around and spied her coat over the back of an armchair. Viktor had always enjoyed Madison's efficiency and was glad to see that she had not developed the habit of keeping a man waiting that he always found more irritating than intriguing.

Grabbing the coat, he offered it to her. "We need to head out."

"You cut it a little close." But she didn't hesitate to let him help her into the fitted wool trench coat the same crimson red as her lips.

He saw no reason to hide the truth. "Protecting us both from how much I want you."

"What are you talking about?" she asked, sounding genuinely confused as she did up the oversized black buttons and tied the belt on her coat.

"You must realize the prospect of having you in my bed has my libido in overdrive." The truth of that was never more blatant to him than in how hard he found it to lead her out of the apartment without once mussing the color of her lipstick.

However, nothing said he had to curb his desire to touch her completely. They made their way to the elevators with his arm around her waist.

"But why would it?" Could she sound more innocent? He didn't think so.

"You are an incredibly beautiful woman." But more importantly, she was the one woman who sparked desire hot enough to do his ancestors proud.

"You didn't want me before."

"We discussed this. You were barely more than a child." And he *had* wanted her.

"You're right," she said distractedly. "But—"

"Nothing. Trust me. I want you. Six years ago, the timing was wrong, but I will gladly offer you all the proof you desire later tonight, *after* dinner with our respective families."

"You want to come back to my apartment tonight?" she squeaked, charming him.

The elevator doors closed, giving a false sense of privacy he had to once again fight taking advantage of.

"You have no reason to be nervous," he assured her. "I am not an animal in the bedroom."

Even if he wanted her with heretofore untapped primal mating instincts.

"Vik…" She blinked up at him, her lips parted slightly. "I told you, I'm a virgin."

"What?" The elevator doors opened but he didn't step out, his brain short-circuiting.

"I told you—"

"That you hadn't been in a serious relationship." But that didn't mean she hadn't had sex. Things happened. She was twenty-four. This was not possible.

"No random hookups."

"Ever?" he asked in disbelief.

"I told you I had no experience."

"In BDSM."

"In anything."

"That will change." Viktor was not above using whatever means necessary to ensure the future he planned. Including being Madison's first lover.

The fact he wanted her more than any woman he had ever known was beside the point.

She stepped off the elevator into the parking garage. "I don't think being engaged to you is going to be anything like I was imagining."

"If you thought it was going to be without sexual intimacy, I'd have to say you are right," he said as he helped her buckle into the passenger seat of his car.

He gave in to the urge that had been riding him since the moment she'd opened her door and kissed her. He reined in his desire. Barely. And stepped back.

He closed her door and took several deep breaths before moving around the car to slide into the driver's seat.

Her eyes glowing with blue fire, she asked, "No pretense of waiting for our wedding night?"

"We made our vows at the overlook this afternoon. Nothing said later between us will be any more profound." He started the engine, but didn't back out of the parking spot, waiting with an odd feeling in his chest for her reply.

"I thought it felt that way…like it was profound."

"It was." He put the car in gear.

"So what? You consider us married now?" She sounded like she didn't believe her own words and yet he knew she had felt the weight of the promises they'd made earlier.

"As good as, yes."

"You make your own rules, don't you?"

"You are just now figuring this out?"

CHAPTER SEVEN

THE ENGAGEMENT DINNER was a lot more enjoyable than Maddie had expected it to be.

Especially considering the fact the guest list had grown to include some Archer second cousins, a Madison great-aunt, one of Misha's nephews and his wife, who just happened to be visiting friends who owned a vineyard outside of Napa, and Romi.

Maddie's father was all smiles, though underlying his bonhomie was an unfamiliar reticence with her that gave Maddie a certain level of comfort. He had not escaped this morning's debacle in the conference room unscathed.

Small winces indicated he did not like her new habit of calling him by his first name, either, but if he wanted her to stop, he'd have to ask. Nicely. And behave like a father. Somehow.

She hadn't started calling him Jeremy to hurt him, but because it simply hurt *her* too much to refer to a man who treated her like a stranger more often than not as Father.

Vik acted as a buffer between them, not exactly a new role for him, but one he hadn't played with any consistency in six years.

Taking it a step further than he used to, Vik actually physically stood between her and others in unconscious protection whenever she felt herself growing uneasy. While no one had the bad taste to actually mention the articles spawned by Perry's lies, family could manage intrusive-ness in subtle ways strangers never could.

Thankfully, Vik seemed to recognize her moods—sometimes even before she did—and took steps to make sure the questions didn't get a chance to edge into being blatantly intrusive.

Tellingly, no one seemed to find it hard to believe they'd been carrying on a relationship outside the media's radar for months now. Not even Misha's nephew evinced sur-prise at the engagement.

Everyone was happy to congratulate Maddie and Vik, making her feel like maybe this thing could really work.

Regardless of what had precipitated the engagement, their friends and family considered them a good match. A big part of her agreed.

She only hoped she wasn't making a huge mistake... that Vik was the man she was discovering. More the white knight in Armani than the heartless tycoon following in her father's footsteps that she'd seen him as for the past six years.

Vik's grandparents were wonderful, as always.

Misha was a gray-haired, slightly stooped version of Vik with an exuberant warmth very unlike his more re-served grandson. A retired scientist, Ana was both highly intelligent and gently affectionate by nature. She wasn't as overt as her husband, but she would make a wonderful great-grandmother for Maddie and Vik's children.

The magazine photographer turned out to be extremely good at fading into the background and Maddie found her-self relaxing and enjoying the first real family dinner she remembered since her mother's death.

"Your grandparents are such nice people." Maddie allowed Vik to remove her coat and his own before taking both of them and hanging them in the hall closet.

Such a simple thing to do. She'd done it hundreds of times for other guests, but never with the same homey feeling—or sense of irrevocability that washed over her as she closed the closet door.

Vik was staying the night.

And Maddie's heart was pounding in her chest like a bass drum.

Not from fear, though. No, nothing like it, though that surprised her. Shouldn't there be at least a little anxiety?

She'd never done this before, after all.

But all she felt was excitement.

Maybe it was because she knew Vik would leave if she asked him to. Only she didn't want him to leave.

She wanted him to follow through on the promise of passion in their kisses earlier. Besides, if they weren't compatible in bed, that could be a real problem.

Right?

Only what were the chances when his kisses turned her inside out. Self-justification much?

She made a sound of self-deprecating humor.

"Liking my family is a source of amusement for you?" Vik's hands landed on her shoulders before he turned her to face him.

His expression wasn't mocking or judging, just inquisitive.

She smiled up at the beloved handsome face as she shook her head. "No, I was thinking about the things we tell ourselves to justify doing what we want to do."

His look promised things she'd never experienced but was pretty darn sure she wanted to. "What *things* do you want to do?"

"Like you don't know."

He shook his head. "I'm still a little stunned you've never done them before."

"Pretty pathetic, huh?"

"In what way were you pathetic?" Vik asked in a tone that didn't bode well for anyone who might have used that word to describe her.

Including herself.

She liked the feelings his instant protectiveness engendered in her despite the fact she thrived on her independence.

Feeling a little odd about that, she moved away from him and crossed the living room, which was decorated in her favorite shabby chic. While she loved the perfect blend of distressed wood furniture, floral damasks, life-like silk bouquets set in epoxy to look like water, the pristine whites and abundance of feminine styling screamed "single woman living alone" to her.

And while there was *nothing* bad about that, she wasn't as pleased by the fact she'd never even had a short-term relationship. She'd be happier if something in her home indicated the need to take someone else's preferences, or even needs, into account.

"What would you call a twenty-four-year-old virgin?" she asked, turning back to face him.

"Picky." His smile melted her.

She grinned up at him. "That's one word for it."

"You were waiting for me." She could tell by his tone he thought he was joking.

A sudden revelation hit her. Romi had definitely been right all along. "I was."

She might have been able to get over her first love, but Maddie had never moved on from thinking that Viktor Beck would be the ideal lover. And so she had turned down every other man.

Yes, trust was an issue for her, but right along with her lack of trust in other men had been a primal certainty of whom she wanted to share her body with.

A certainty she'd been consciously denying but living under for the past six years.

Espresso eyes darkened with unmistakable lust, blowing her mind. He wanted her. He'd said he did. He'd kissed her like he did, but that look?

It was imbued with the same primitive passion she'd acknowledged in herself. So predatory. It sent shivers chasing along her nerve endings.

"You were made for me," he said, confirming it wasn't her imagination.

The driving force between them was very mutual.

"A pity you didn't realize that six years ago." She regretted the words as soon as she said them and shook her head. "Forget I said that."

Maddie got why Vik had turned her down before. Wishing they'd already taken this step so she wouldn't be dealing with her public humiliation right now was both futile and borderline ridiculous. Because even if they'd gotten together then, there was no guarantee they would still be together now.

His jaw firm, his lips set in a determined line, Vik moved toward her with intent. "I was not ready for marriage and you were not ready for me."

"I—"

His finger pressing against her lips stopped the argument. "We both had living to do."

"You were really thinking about *this* then?" she asked with surprise she couldn't hide.

"Yes."

"But you weren't happy about it." Wasn't happy about the memory if his current expression was anything to go by.

"You were eighteen. I was still used to thinking of you as a child. It felt wrong."

"I was an adult, a grown woman." But even as she made

the claim, she knew that compared to Vik she *had* been a child.

"You could vote, join the armed forces and take on your own debt. That didn't mean you were ready for a relationship with a man like me."

"A relationship, or sex?"

"Same thing when it comes to you and me."

"Is it?"

"It has always been marriage or nothing between us, Madison." Vik reached out and traced the line of her bodice, his fingertip never straying from the sapphire-blue taffeta of her dress to the skin of her bosom.

Her breath hitched, but she didn't move away. "Because of AIH."

"Because my grandfather raised me to be a man with a sense of honor." The "unlike Frank Beck" went unsaid, but she heard it anyway.

Vik would never be like the father that had caused both him and his grandparents so much grief and disappointment.

"You may be a shark, Vik, but you're an honest one."

He smiled wryly, his fingertip resting on the point of the V dipping between her breasts. "And I don't eat guppies for breakfast."

"Am I a guppy?" she asked breathlessly.

"No." Satisfaction burned in his dark gaze. "You are a twenty-four-year-old woman."

The emphasis he placed on the word *woman* was a conversation all in itself.

"You planned to marry me before Perrygate ever happened."

"I did." Vik looked with significance down at the custom ring on her finger and she caught on.

There was no denying the truth in front of her eyes. "You really did have the rings made for me."

"I do not lie."

"No, but…" The scope of what he was saying left her grasping for words that would not come.

"Timwater forced me to move my plans forward, but only by a couple of weeks."

"You were going to ask me to marry you?"

"I planned to date you first," he said with some wry humor, almost self-deprecatingly. "We needed to rebuild the rapport we once had."

His thinking made him a different man than her father in ways she didn't feel like enumerating, but wouldn't deny. "You recognized before Jeremy did that the only way my father would have an heir to leave in charge of the business is if I married him."

"Yes."

"So, you made plans to play on my father's desire to leave his legacy to *family*." It was brilliant. And manipulative.

But he'd already shown that as important as his own plans for AIH were to Vik, he would not ignore Maddie's happiness. He'd offered to buy her a building for her dream as a wedding gift.

Calculated? Maybe, but *for* her benefit, not to her detriment.

Vik's silence was answer enough. Not only had he strategized, but he'd also started working on her father already. Jeremy had come to the whole "his daughter must marry to save herself and the company's reputation" pretty darn quickly otherwise.

"I'm not sure how I feel about this," she admitted.

She understood. To an extent.

But it still felt like she'd been maneuvered.

Vik's touch finally strayed entirely from her dress to the upper swell of her breasts, tracing the same path as before, only along her skin this time. "While you are deciding, take into account that if you had been a different woman, my plans would have taken a different direction."

She shivered, her breath quavering in her chest until another thought came to her. "You would have taken AIH out from under my father?"

Horrified because as much as she didn't get her father, she loved him, and she was certain Vik would have done exactly that. Rather than allow a stranger to come in and take over what he considered to be his.

Vik shrugged, neither confirming, nor denying. "It was not necessary."

"You said Jeremy is your friend."

"He is."

"But you would still take his company."

"I would not have betrayed him."

No. That wasn't Vik's style. "You still would have figured out a way."

"Does that upset you?"

"I said before that you're ruthless."

"This is not news."

No, it really wasn't. "My mind doesn't work like yours."

"Make no mistake, you have your own brand of ruthlessness, but if you were too much like me, we would not fit so well together." Both his hands moved to settle on her waist.

She was distracted by the sensation of his thumbs brushing up and down against her lower ribs. "You think we fit?"

"I know we do."

"So, you're saying you don't just want the company. You want me, too." Not just sex with her, but Maddie as a complete person.

At least the Madison Archer he knew about. What would Vik think of Maddie Grace?

"You will support my dreams in a way a woman of less strength could not do."

"Your plans would have been really messed up if I'd picked one of the other candidates Jeremy put forward." She gave in to the irresistible urge to poke at the bear.

Vik's gorgeous mouth twisted in disdain. "You were never going to choose another man."

"You don't think so?"

"I know."

"Another word for excessive confidence is arrogance."

"I prefer honest."

She laughed softly and then had a revelation. "You manipulated the choice of candidates."

"I was not expecting Maxwell Black."

"Neither was I." And she still wanted to know what the man had done to Romi. "He's intense."

"He's a good businessman."

"Is he honorable?"

"Yes."

"As honorable as you?"

Vik considered his answer for a second. "I would do business with him on a handshake."

"Good to know."

"Why? Considering your options?" He didn't sound too worried by the prospect.

"According to you, there are no other options."

"True." Vik looked like he was considering what he was going to say next. "We grew up together."

"What? Like in the same neighborhood?"

"Same Russian-American-dominated street, same school, same afternoons spent in activities sponsored by the Russian cultural center."

"Were you friends?"

"We still are...of a sort."

"You're too alike to be really close."

"We jockeyed for the top place in class until we went to different universities."

"No one else had a chance."

"No."

Maddie bit her lip, but finally decided she would be honest about her concerns. "Romi dated him."

Vik's gaze flared. "I see."

"He's intense," Maddie repeated.

"Are they still dating?"

"No."

"Then…"

"I don't need to be worried?"

"He is a good man."

When it was Viktor Beck making the claim, Maddie believed him.

"Are you really spending the night?" she asked, focusing on what mattered most in the present moment.

"Yes."

"After a single day." One day in which they had decided to get married, made that decision public and negotiated a future they could both live with.

"In one respect, but between us?" He pulled her body close so they shared heat. "Tonight is the culmination of ten years."

"We've barely spoken in six."

"When was the last time Frank was in town?" Vik asked her, like she'd know.

And she did. "Three months ago. He was in San Francisco for Christmas." Vik's father had attended Jeremy's holiday party along with Misha and Ana.

Vik nodded, his expression dour. "*Babulya* was pleased."

"But you couldn't wait for him to leave."

"You are the only person who knew that."

She found that hard to believe, but then…maybe not. Vik didn't wear his emotions on his sleeve.

But that wasn't the point, was it? "Just because I saw

your father at my father's home and knew he was in town doesn't mean you and I communicated in any meaningful way."

"Didn't we?"

Okay, so in the past two years, they'd had increasing numbers and depths of conversations. And it struck her. She'd thought she was just being grown-up about the past, but he'd been working on rebuilding that rapport he had mentioned earlier.

The man made Machiavelli look like a preschooler in the art of the deep play.

"Still." Not a brilliant comeback, but what she had.

Vik smiled that shark's smile. "When was the last time I took a date to an event?"

So, she knew the answer. She'd revealed earlier in the car with Conrad how closely she watched Vik without meaning to watch him at all. "That doesn't mean anything."

"Doesn't it?"

"Vik…"

"I believe both the fact that I have not had another woman on my arm in over a year *and the fact you know that* is significant."

"Really?" she drawled sarcastically even as she couldn't help wondering if he was right.

"I know that you haven't dated, either. I wasn't entirely sure about Timwater, but the way you two are together doesn't imply sexual intimacy."

"I should hope not."

"Besides, he was sleeping with other women."

She'd suspected, though Perry had always tried to play it like he didn't sleep around. She wasn't sure why. It wouldn't have mattered to her either way.

Vik knowing however, meant he'd been paying attention. "You have a file on him, don't you?"

"Naturally."

"And Romi?"

"Romi has been your friend for longer than me."

"You're saying you don't have a file."

Vik leaned down and spoke softly, right into Maddie's ear. "I'm saying I don't need one."

It wasn't exactly sweet nothings, but she still shivered from the sensation of his breath gently blowing across her ear.

"You know her well, too," Maddie said, not even sure why she was trying to keep the conversation going.

"Yes."

Curiosity and concern prompted her to ask, "Did you know she'd dated Maxwell?"

"No."

"Good. I don't feel like I was so oblivious."

Vik straightened, but didn't move back. "I'm sure if you did not know, they both took pains to keep it private."

"You're right." While Maddie was still worried, she didn't feel like a bad friend anymore.

She let herself fall into his deep coffee gaze, even as she relaxed more completely into his body. "I want to kiss you."

Bad friend, or good one, Maddie didn't want to think about anyone except her and Vik right now.

"What is stopping you?" He leaned down so their lips were a fraction of an inch apart, taking away the only barrier that mattered.

She moved toward him, speaking in a breath against his lips. "Nothing."

The first brush of her lips against his electrified her. It was the barest of caresses, but near unbearable in its intimacy. She was staking a claim with the featherlight touch and he was accepting that claim as surely as she'd accepted his promises earlier.

They were distinctly different, one set of lips masculine, the other feminine, and yet they fit with the perfection of molds aligned and cast simultaneously.

Vik's response was full-on alpha man, accepting her mouth with his and then turning it around and moving his lips against hers, driving the kiss to greater sensation and closeness.

Nipping oh-so-gently with his teeth on her lower lip, he demanded entrance. With no thought but to give it, she let her lips fall open.

His tongue swept into her mouth and just that fast Maddie was drowning in a sexual response only this man had ever brought out in her, thoughts and emotions overwhelmed by the onslaught of devastating sensuality.

Vik's hold on her tightened as he pulled her body completely flush with his, his big hands roving over her back and up to knead her scalp.

Her own hands slid of their own volition up his pecs, over his shoulders and to the back of his neck, pulling her body around so her breasts were crushed against his chest. Sparks of delicious sensation pricked her nipples nearly to the point of pain in their intensity.

It felt so incredible still dressed, she could not fathom what it would be like once they were naked skin pressed to naked skin.

Vik made a rumbling sound of approval in his throat before his body shifted and then she was being lifted into his arms as he stood.

The man was strong. Following on that thought came another.

They were really going to do this.

For the first time, Maddie was glad she was a twenty-four-year-old virgin.

She wanted no past experiences shadowing this moment with him. No memories of hands on her flesh but his.

Vik carried her unerringly into to her bedroom, lowering her back to her feet and pulling his mouth from hers. She didn't want to stop and used her hold on his neck to lift herself back up so the kiss could continue.

It was only natural to swing her legs up and around his waist, locking her ankles behind his back.

Something about her actions flipped a switch in Vik and the kiss went nuclear. His mouth devoured hers as he cupped her bottom through the rustling silk of her dress's full skirt.

Overwhelmed by sensation, Maddie lost her connection to anything but the kiss. She did not know how long their mouths ate at each other. Nothing registered but the sparks of pleasure he ignited in her rapidly fanning into a conflagration that consumed.

She wasn't even aware he'd moved them to the bed until he broke away from her and she didn't fall to the floor.

She mewled with her need to reconnect to his lips, a sound that would have mortified her if she was not too lost to desire to care.

"Vik!" she demanded, no other word coming to the forefront of her mind.

His smile was feral and hot. But the wink that came with it was hotter. "Clothes."

CHAPTER EIGHT

ONE WORD BUT it was all Maddie needed.

She sat up and reached back to unzip her dress. It was tricky at the best of times, the top of the zipper hitting her in the center of her back.

With her hands trembling from need, it was impossible. So frustrated she could almost cry, she struggled to unzip it.

All the while, she couldn't pull her eyes from Vik. He'd ripped his Armani sweater off and tossed it on the floor, the black T-shirt he wore under it joining the pile of cashmere a second later.

His belt made a whoosh as he pulled it out of his trousers and the buckle clunked against the wall when he tossed it. His tailored slacks were next, dropping to reveal a straining bulge behind dark designer briefs.

"Your body is beautiful," she breathed in awe.

Every muscle of his six-foot-four-inch frame was honed. Dark hair covered his chest, narrowing to a trail that disappeared into the waistband of his briefs.

She didn't know if it was the dark, clingy fabric or reality, or even her oversensitized emotions, but Vik looked huge.

Maddie's thighs clenched even as her fingers itched to touch. And she hadn't seen the actual package yet.

Vik looked back, his own expression filled with desire. "You're still dressed," he accused.

"I know," she said with pure frustration.

He winked again, the expression just as mind-bogglingly sexy this time as the first. "Need some help there?"

"Yes."

He stalked toward the bed like a big sleek cat, climbing on with the same grace. He reached around her and let his fingers trail down the shallow V of her dress to the top of the zipper. "Is this your problem?"

"I can't reach it."

"How did you get dressed then?"

"I wasn't hampered then."

"By what?"

"What do you think?" she asked, wanting to sound annoyed and only succeeding in revealing the need inside her.

"Me?"

"Desire," she clarified.

"Desire for me."

"Yes," she admitted, no real reason to pretend otherwise, but annoyed all the same at having to say it out loud.

"Good." He lowered the zipper inch by inch. "I like this dress."

"I'm never wearing it again."

"Please do."

"Why?"

"I have always enjoyed unwrapping my gifts. Just ask my grandparents."

"I'm not a Christmas package."

"No, you are something far more valuable." He kissed the corner of her mouth and then brushed her lips with his lightly. "You are the woman who will share my life."

"You're awfully good at romance for a corporate shark."

He wasn't kidding about enjoying the process of unwrapping. Time moved by in increments measured by her rising passion as he took off first her dress, removing it to reveal her body one slow inch at a time. His desire-filled gaze burned her with sensual appreciation.

The silk foundations she wore under the dress came next, but he took even more time with those than the blue taffeta, kissing bits of her flesh as it was revealed, sensitizing her body in ways she'd no idea he could do.

When he was done, she was a naked, quivering mass of sexual need.

And he still had his briefs on.

She tugged at the waistband, her voice husky with passion when she managed to force the words past the tightness in her throat. "Take them off."

"Not yet."

"Why?" she demanded, patience in another universe.

"You are a virgin."

"So?" He was going to change that, wasn't he?

"So, you need preparation and I'm on a hair trigger where you are concerned."

"You have to take your underwear off to make love to me," she spelled out slowly, like she wasn't sure he got it.

He bared his teeth in a smile that had no humor. "And before that happens I will make sure you are ready to receive me."

"But—"

"You will have to trust me on this." His eyes demanded her acquiescence.

She didn't know if she could give it. "I want you!"

"And you will have me."

Vik's hand slipped between her legs right then, fingers delving in the moist heat no other man had ever touched, and she cried out. He touched her in ways she'd only ever dreamed of being touched, caressed her to her first shattering climax before she even realized what that desperate feeling inside her was leading to.

She'd touched herself, but it had never felt like this. She was still trembling with spent pleasure when a single long masculine finger slipped inside her. Something shifted in her heart at the intimate intrusion.

He was not inside her, not the way she'd always imagined, but they were connected on a level that corresponded to a place inside her soul.

He pressed upward and she winced with pain.

"Hurt?" he asked, his own tone strained.

"A little."

"It will sting."

"Why?"

"I am going to break your hymen with my finger. It will make the actual penetration of my sex easier on you." The words were clinical, but his tone and the concern in his expression was not.

He'd thought this through and that touched her in the same place in her soul his intimate intrusion had.

He pressed a little harder.

A sharp shard of pain stabbed her. "It more than stings!"

"I am sorry." He grimaced. "It will be worth it."

She wasn't so sure about that, but trusted him enough to give him the benefit of the doubt.

That trust was sorely tested a moment later when the pain increased to the point that she felt like he was invading her with a hot poker, not his finger. She gasped and tried to pull away, surprised when she succeeded in dislodging his hand.

He leaned back on his haunches, the telltale traces of blood on his finger a testament to his success.

Grateful that the pain was already morphing to a low-level throbbing rather than stabbing, she asked, "Now?"

"Not yet. There is more to do."

The more included him stripping naked finally. In the bathroom, where he ran a very hot bath.

He looked even bigger jutting out from his body than he had with his erection tucked behind black silk knit.

He smiled at her with gentle humor. "Your eyes are as wide as saucers."

"You're as big as a baseball bat."

That startled a laugh out of him. "Not even close."

"Right."

"Your eyes are playing tricks on you."

Unsure where it came from, annoyance drove her stomping across the tiled floor and gave her the boldness to grope him in her fist. "My fingers are not touching."

The sound he made was not a word.

Viscous drops formed on the tip of the flesh in her hand. She touched it with her fingertip and brought it to her mouth, licking it cautiously.

Surprisingly it was almost sweet, with only a hint of the salty bitterness she'd heard about. "I like it."

He groaned and then jerked his body backward so his hard flesh slipped from her hand. "Bath. Now."

"Why?"

"Can't you just trust me?"

"I trust you more than any other man on this planet." He might be the only man on the planet she *did* trust. He had to know that.

"It will make it better for you," he explained.

"How do you know?" she demanded. "Have you had sex with many virgins?"

She found that possibility seriously disturbing.

"None," he practically snarled as he lifted her up and set her in the bathtub with surprisingly gentle movements, considering his apparent irritation. "I read up on it."

"Because you're a planner."

"Yes." He still sounded like a man ready to take someone's head off.

"Why are you mad?" she asked plaintively.

"I'm not angry!"

"You're snarling at me."

"I'm turned on." The low growl rumbled through her.

"So am I. The bath was your idea!"

"For your benefit."

Oh, man. "I'm sorry. This isn't easy for you, is it?"

"Waiting?" He stepped into the bath behind her, pulling her into his lap, his hands settling on her possessively. "No, my sexy little redhead, it is not easy, but you are worth it."

Another white-knight moment. "If you aren't careful, you're going to have me believing in fairy tales."

His only answer was one languid touch to her thigh. That caress was followed by another and another and another, all over her body and each touch accompanied by the ever-present presence of his hardness pressed against the small of her back.

Her nipples were aching and sensitive, her clitoris vibrating with pleasure, and her entire body melted over his by the time his hands stilled their insidious movements.

There were no words left in her brain when he drained the tub and lifted her back to the tile floor. They dried off in silence, bodies aware and straining toward each other.

She and Vik stripped the bedding back without acknowledging that was what they were going to do, and then together they fell to the mattress covered by the single sheet.

The lovemaking was everything she had ever dreamed it would be, his sex filling her so deeply she felt like they'd really bonded into one entity in that moment.

There was still some pain, but nothing stabbing and dark, and the pleasure pushed any lingering discomfort to the bottom register of Maddie's awareness.

This time when she climaxed, she screamed until her throat protested the strain. Vik grew impossibly hard inside her, his body going rigid just before he shouted his own release in the form of a single word.

"Mine."

She didn't even think about birth control until the next morning.

Viktor came to awareness in the dark, two things at the forefront of his mind. The woman he'd craved for years was now in his arms and they hadn't used birth control the first time they made love.

The former gave him satisfaction and the latter a twinge of regret. In a perfect world, they would have a couple years of marriage to enjoy their time together as a couple, to solidify their relationship.

In the real world, Madison had been forced into marriage by the actions of that bastard who had called himself her friend, and Viktor's grandparents were getting on in years. If his children were to have the time to enjoy them as Viktor had, they would have to come along sooner than later.

Viktor had taken advantage of Timwater's idiocy. He could deal with the consequences of other realities, too.

For him, family was everything.

It was the reason he'd been driven to succeed. The one thing that drove him most intensely was the desire to not only make his grandparents proud, but to also provide for his own family as his own father had not done.

Viktor had determined early in his life never to walk a single step in his own father's shoes.

When he'd first met Jeremy Archer, Viktor had believed he'd found the mentor he sought. And he had, but he had also come to the realization that as wrapped up in AIH as Jeremy was, his vision was still too limited.

Both in a business sense and when it came to family.

Jeremy had never understood that all of AIH's success

meant nothing in the face of his spectacular failure with his daughter.

Madison was Viktor's match in every way. They were not just sexually compatible, they were combustible. Just as he'd known they would be.

But equally important, they were friends with compatible, if very different, goals for the future.

Viktor felt an unfamiliar sense of having dodged a bullet with Maxwell Black's presence in the conference room that morning. Jeremy bringing in Maxwell—of all men— had precipitated actions on Viktor's part he hadn't intended to take until later.

But he couldn't complain about the outcome.

He in no way regretted making love to Madison and had every intention of showing her that no other man would be her match as Viktor was.

He wasn't just the perfect successor for AIH, he was perfect for Madison.

With that thought, he brushed his hand down her flank, leaning over to kiss the side of her neck and bring her to wakefulness for another example of how very well they meshed in bed.

For the first time in her life, Maddie had woken in another person's arms.

She lay, warm and secure as half of Vik's body covered hers, his breath still even and slow in sleep.

And she thought of babies and the possibility of family. Had he done it on purpose? Or had he been as lost to the final satiation of years' worth of unfulfilled desire that the idea of birth control hadn't even entered the picture?

Before she'd been made love to by a man who never seemed to get enough, she would have written the latter off as a complete improbability.

But Vik had woken her several times in the night and

pushed the boundaries of pleasure and her body on each occasion, his hunger for her something she would never again be able to doubt. There'd been no question when they *were* sleeping that they would do so skin-to-skin.

The one time she'd tried donning her sleep pants and tank top, he'd gotten this look in his eyes. Really intense, feral and determined. Her pajamas had been in a puddle on the floor moments later and her body humming the music of the Viktor Beck pleasure symphony.

Even now, his oversized sex…

No, she didn't believe him that he was no bigger than most men. She'd heard on one of those talk shows hosted by a group of interesting and mostly famous women that the average length was just about five inches erect. Well, she knew from five inches and his was nearly twice that. Average? She did not think so.

Right now, that not-at-all-average hardness was pressing against her hip, telling her that when he woke he'd be ready for more physical intimacy. Despite the twinges of soreness making her aware of muscles she hadn't known she had, nipples that ached from all the stimulation they'd enjoyed and a tender feeling in the flesh between her legs, she knew she wouldn't hesitate to respond.

Except…they hadn't used any form of birth control in the long night of passion. Not once.

"I can hear you thinking." Vik's early morning voice rumbled above her head.

"You said we would make any decision about children together."

Tension seeped into his big body, but he did not move away. "Yes?"

"We did not use birth control last night."

Oddly, he relaxed. "No, we did not."

"Vik," she said in warning.

He sat up, somehow getting pillows propped against

the headboard behind him and her sideways in his lap with a minimum of movement. It was a position he apparently enjoyed.

He tilted her chin up, bringing their gazes into alignment. "We made that decision together."

"I didn't make a decision at all. I didn't even think of it."

His eyebrows rose. "Neither did I."

She narrowed her eyes, trying to gauge the truth of his statement. She might be blind, but Maddie couldn't see the smallest flicker of deceit in the espresso orbs.

"It never once occurred to you that a condom might be a good idea?" she asked.

It was his turn for his eyes to narrow, but they glittered with anger not concentration. "You believe I would lie to you?"

"No, but you're ruthless enough to take advantage of an expedient situation."

He agreed, no sign of embarrassment at the truth. "Yes, but to what end would I ignore birth control?"

"You get five percent of the company when I give birth to our first child." Did she really have to remind him of that fact?

"Did you plan to wait to start a family?"

"No." She couldn't even claim not to have thought of it.

Dreams were something even a woman who didn't believe in fairy tales could indulge in. And Maddie's dreams included building the kind of family she'd always wanted to have.

"I did not think you did." Therefore, he had no need to take advantage of circumstance.

"Okay."

"Okay, what?"

"I believe you."

He kissed the tip of her nose. "As you should."

She wrinkled her nose. "It might be old-fashioned, but

I would still like to wait until we are married to conceive our first child." Though if she *was* pregnant, she would accept that as the gift she believed it to be.

"Agreed."

"So, from now on, birth control," she insisted.

"Agreed."

"You're being awfully compliant."

"The truth? I would prefer to wait a couple of years before having children."

"Oh." She hadn't considered he wasn't keen on starting a family right away.

"But my grandparents are in their seventies," Vik continued. "If my children are to have the benefit of *Deda* and *Babulya's* presence in their lives, we cannot indulge me."

"I see." Wow.

Once again, she was reminded that while she and Vik might be motivated by different hopes for the future, they both had them. And lucky for her, they dovetailed, as surprising as that might be.

"I hesitate to point this out," Vik said. "Because I *do* want to gift my grandparents with the next generation of our family."

"What?" Maddie couldn't believe how comfortable she was having this discussion naked and sitting in his lap on the bed.

"Won't it be difficult to start your school if we have a baby right away?" he asked.

She gave him a self-deprecating grimace. "I say all the time that money doesn't matter to me, but the truth is, I'm counting on it to be able to 'have it all,' as they say."

"You plan to have a nanny?" He sounded almost shocked.

And she loved him all the more for it. "Probably, but not to *raise* our children. However, if we are ever going to be able to leave the house, we have to have someone besides your grandparents we can trust to care for our children."

"Yes."

"So, we'll have a nanny, someone who fits into our family, preferably matronly in both appearance and age." So, sue her if Maddie didn't want a beautiful young woman living under Vik's nose in their house.

"What do you mean about the money then?"

"I have every intention of hiring qualified staff who share mine and Romi's vision to run the school."

Vik's dark brow furrowed. "But you will both still give a great deal of time to the school. You will have to."

"Yes, but we'll make it work. Romi and I already discussed what would happen in the event one or both of us had a family."

"I'm not surprised."

"My father would be." He'd always assumed she had no business sense if she didn't want to be part of *his* business.

"Jeremy only sees part of the picture when he looks at you," Vik agreed pragmatically.

"That's all he's interested in." Jeremy Archer had never wanted to give the time necessary to get to know who Maddie was, not before Helene's death and definitely not after.

"He *can* break out of his tunnel vision."

"So you say. I've witnessed no evidence."

Vik shook his head, clearly done with the topic. "You'll need an efficient and knowledgeable personal assistant."

"Exactly." A nanny for convenience, not necessity, but a PA? That Maddie would *need* to make sure things got done.

Vik's phone rang before they could continue their discussion. It was Conrad, excited about the opportunity for a live interview with the newly engaged couple on an evening celebrity-news show.

And so it began.

* * *

The next weeks passed in a whirl of activity. Interviews as a couple, interviews by herself. The media furor around Maddie and Vik's engagement was even bigger than the initial craziness Perrygate had spawned.

Vik slept at her apartment every night while decorators and contractors worked overtime getting Parean Hall habitable for them. Maddie interviewed domestic staff while overseeing the changes to the main rooms and the master suite. She did her best to make sure both her and Vik's design aesthetic was incorporated in their new home.

And could hear his voice saying "I told you so" when she realized she knew enough about his preferences to do that.

Maddie went back to her secret volunteering in her brown wig and contacts, dressed in clothes from the local superstore. Every minute spent with the children cemented her determination to do more.

She also scheduled a visit with the therapist she'd seen in the immediate months after her skydiving accident, when Maddie had realized the time had come to break away from her past. Dr. MacKenzie was vocal in her praise for how far Maddie had come in dealing with both her mom's death and her father's emotional neglect.

However the therapist evinced some concern about the marriage that Vik said he intended to be *real* and yet was connected to a very lucrative contract for him. Dr. MacKenzie asked Maddie to consider carefully her reasons for agreeing to the engagement.

So Maddie did and, even more importantly, she talked to Vik about it.

"Yes, the contract your father offered is beneficial to me, but getting married right now is important for you, too."

"You think I said yes to the whole marriage thing because of the school, don't you?" Had she?

She'd told herself on that crazy, surrealistic day that was exactly why she needed to consider the idea seriously.

But Vik just shrugged. "Even if the scandal had blown up like it could have, you would not have given up on the school. Romi would have been the public face to run it and you would have been the silent partner as I now will be."

She loved his confidence in her. The pleasure of it masked the full import of his words for a moment, but then it settled in.

"*You* will?" When had Vik offered to partner with her and Romi in founding the school?

"We made promises to see one another's dreams fulfilled. Marriage to you will give me AIH. I've told you that I will ensure it provides for your dreams as well."

Maybe she should have expected something like this, but she hadn't. "You really are my white knight."

"I thought you did not believe in fairy tales." His voice and expression were teasing, but something told her he liked her claim.

"Maybe I just believe in you." He had always been the exception, the one man she trusted—even when she hadn't thought she had a reason to.

Refusing to admit it didn't make it any less true.

"You do," he said with a mix of implacability and smugness that should have annoyed her.

It didn't. She liked it. "So certain."

"Of you? Yes."

Ultimately, it all came down to that simple truth. *She* trusted Vik to keep the promises he'd made at the Marin Headlands overlook.

The fact that she was falling in love with Viktor Beck all over again? Well, that was something she didn't bring up even to Romi.

How could she help it? The man spent more time masquerading as a white knight than a business tycoon.

The wedding was going forward. And soon.

For the ceremony itself, they planned a very small gathering, but the reception would be huge and attended by the cream of society, the scions of the business world and even a few celebrities.

When Maddie's follow-up therapy appointment conflicted with a meeting with the caterers for their wedding reception, she told Vik she didn't want to reschedule her time with Dr. MacKenzie.

"You are seeing a therapist?" Vik asked. "Why didn't I know this?" The latter clearly the only thing that bothered him about her revelation.

"Because I didn't tell you?"

He made a scoffing sound.

"No one knows except Romi."

"When did you start seeing him?"

"Her. And right after the skydiving incident." Maddie had realized she was taking the same self-destructive path as her mother and she wasn't going to do that. "I saw her weekly for a couple of months and then a few more times after that."

"I'm impressed."

"You are?" She had worried a little he would think she was weak for needing to see someone.

"You realized you couldn't help children if you didn't deal with your own childhood issues."

That had been exactly it. "How do you know me so well?" she asked, falling a little more in love with him right then.

"You know the answer to that."

"You make it a point to get to know everything about the people and businesses you plan to partner with, or take over."

"Our partnership will supersede all others. Of course, I will know everything about you."

She liked hearing that, even if it wasn't exactly true. "But you didn't know I was seeing Dr. MacKenzie."

"No." He sounded chagrined.

Maddie laughed. "Even you are not infallible, Vik."

"Miss Grayson knew."

"She's my best friend."

"What am I?"

"The man I'm going to marry. The man I'm falling in love with all over again." There, she'd said it.

What he did with that knowledge was up to him. But one thing she knew, it was time he met Maddie Grace.

Silence stretched between them.

"Vik?"

"I am…honored."

"Good." That was better than thinking she was a fool for believing in the emotion.

"You…I…" For the first time in memory, Vik didn't sound in complete control of his words or his thoughts.

"I don't expect you to say it back."

"Good." The relief in his tone was not complimentary, but she wasn't surprised by it, either.

"You'll never lie to me," she said, as if just making that revelation.

But maybe she understood the depth of his commitment to honesty between them fully for the first time.

"No, I will not."

That included not claiming to love her when he didn't, but it also meant that his promises? Were written in concrete as far as Viktor Beck was concerned.

CHAPTER NINE

MADDIE WAS SHOCKED when her father called and asked her to come to dinner. Alone.

They ate in the formal dining room. Even with the leaves removed from the table, it would easily seat six.

Maddie sat to her father's left and swirled her soup with her spoon, pretending to eat.

Her father didn't seem any more at ease than she felt.

Finally she gave in and asked, "Why am I here?"

"It's been a long time since we had a family dinner."

"There's a two-page magazine spread to prove otherwise."

He shook his head, an expression she couldn't quite decipher on his familiar features. "That is not the same."

"I'm not sure what you mean then."

"You and me. Family."

"We stopped being a family when Mom died." She didn't say it with accusation, or even anger.

He could thank the therapist he didn't know about for that, but it was still the truth.

"It was never my intention for that to happen."

She couldn't hold back a small scoffing sound. "You sent me to boarding school within months of her death. I'd say your intentions were pretty clear."

"That was a mistake."

Something inside Maddie cracked at that admission,

but she merely shrugged. What could she say? *Yes, it had been a huge, painful mistake.*

Somehow agreeing didn't seem like the thing to do, though. Not least of which because no acknowledgment now could change the consequences of his choice when she was fifteen.

"I didn't know what to do," he admitted with a candidness rare for Jeremy Archer. "I failed your mother and I was terrified of failing you, so I sent you away, hoping they could do for you at school what I was so clearly not qualified to do at home."

Maddie stared at him as an emotional maelstrom swirled inside her. "Who are you and what have you done with my father?"

It was an old joke, but *man,* was it appropriate.

Her dad barked out a laugh. "I told Viktor this wouldn't be easy."

"He wanted you to talk to me?" Why wasn't she surprised?

"Yes." Jeremy sighed. "Viktor thinks our relationship is salvageable."

"He's an optimist."

"He is."

Giving up on the pretense of eating, she set her spoon down. "You sound surprised by that fact."

"It's not a side of him I noticed before."

"You don't think his business world-domination plans take optimism?" she asked, only partially tongue in cheek.

Her dad laughed again, this time longer and with more real humor. "I suppose they do."

"I guess that makes you something of an optimist, too." Which wasn't something she'd ever acknowledged before.

"Enough of one to believe things could be different for you than Helene." He sounded like he meant it.

"We all have our demons. I'm learning to cope with

mine without jumping out of airplanes." Maddie could give him that at least.

Her father took a ruminative sip of his wine. "I used to think Helene got into trouble just to get my attention. She seemed to take a perverse pleasure in being written up in the media."

"She did."

He looked startled at Maddie's agreement. "But she was a risk taker before we ever met. You know that, don't you?"

"She used to tell me stories over her scrapbooks." It had all sounded so thrilling to a young girl.

Jeremy nodded. "It was one of the things I admired about her."

"You weren't the first important man in her life to ignore her." That was one of the things Maddie had come to realize.

Helene Madison had craved her own father's attention and only managed to get it when she acted out. By the time she married Jeremy Archer, the attention-seeking behavior was an already established coping mechanism.

"You're saying Helene wasn't adventurous by nature, but because her exploits got her father's attention."

"Oh, I think Mom was definitely adventurous, she just discovered that in giving in to that side of her personality, she got something she craved."

"She always said she understood the amount of time I had to give to my company."

"Would you have listened if she said she didn't?" He certainly hadn't responded to Maddie's verbal pleas for his time, or to return home from boarding school.

"Probably not," her father admitted with more honesty than she expected.

"Her death wasn't your fault." It was a truth that had been very hard come by for Maddie.

She'd blamed her dad for so long, but one of the first

breakthroughs she'd made with her therapist was the realization that Helene Archer had been responsible for her own choices.

"Wasn't it?"

"No."

He didn't look like he agreed.

"Do you think Mom went racing because she didn't love me enough to want to be around to raise me?" Maddie asked.

Her dad went pale with shock, his eyes dilating, his mouth going slack for a second before he nearly shouted, "No, of course not. She adored you, Madison. You must know that."

"But she still went racing on the water at night."

"Not because of you."

"And not because of you, either."

"But—"

"Mom was an adult woman who suppressed normal caution for the adrenaline spikes that made her feel alive." The fact it had the side effect of gaining her the attention she craved only made her mom's adventures doubly irresistible to her.

"You sound like a psychologist."

"A degree in early childhood development has its share of psych courses." Maddie wasn't telling Jeremy about her sessions with a therapist.

She wasn't ashamed of seeing Dr. MacKenzie, but Maddie didn't trust her father enough to share the more private parts of her life with him. Not even this *new and improved* Jeremy. She didn't know how deep the changes went or how long they would last.

Her dad's eyes—the same shade as her own, but without the vulnerability she saw in the mirror when she was alone—flickered with something between speculation and curiosity.

"Speaking of your mother," he said in a more familiar tone that revealed no emotion.

"Yes?"

"You and Viktor have chosen her birthday for your wedding date."

"Yes." A month before Maddie turned twenty-five, it had just felt right to speak their vows on a date connected in such a special way to her mom.

"Viktor said you wanted to honor her memory with the date."

"We do." Did her dad find that uncomfortable?

Neither she nor Vik had considered that possibility.

Her father smiled, the expression appearing genuine. "I was hoping you would be willing to honor her memory in another way as well."

"How?" she asked warily.

"Do not worry, I am not going to use your mother's memory to try to guilt you into withdrawing the paperwork giving company shares to Ramona Grayson upon your twenty-fifth birthday."

But he hadn't forgotten it, either.

"It wouldn't work anyway. Mom loved Romi and I personally wouldn't have survived boarding school if her father hadn't sent her there, too."

Maddie had desperately wanted her SBC to come to the school once she'd realized her father wouldn't budge about her going there. However she'd never asked. It wouldn't have been fair. Just like Maddie, Romi had a life in San Francisco.

But Romi had begged her dad to send her and he'd done so.

Jeremy nodded. "He sent her because I offered to pay the tuition and dorm fees."

"No." Wouldn't her father have told her that before this?

"Yes. He told me when Romi came to him and asked to

follow you. He didn't want to send her, but I thought you would both be better off with each other than your fathers."

Maddie's dad was sounding more and more human by the minute. She wasn't sure how she felt about that, but she thought it might be hope.

However, she felt compelled to say, "Mr. Grayson always loved Romi."

"But he was already drinking heavily by then. Do you think he was any more aware of his daughter's needs than I was of yours?"

No, the man who had fallen asleep drunk most nights had not been aware of what Romi needed.

"If she hadn't gone to boarding school, she would have become her dad's caregiver." Jeremy sounded very certain of that. "Romi needed to get away and Gray needed to pour *himself* into bed at night."

"You used to be his friend."

"I still am, as much as you can befriend a man intent on drinking himself into an early grave and his own business into bankruptcy."

Worry creased Maddie's brow. "It's not that bad."

"Yet. But it will be."

"Don't pretend threatening to take his company over was a favor you would do him."

"No, it wouldn't be a favor to Grayson, but it would be to Romi." Her dad sounded very sure of that assertion.

"So you say."

"You don't trust me at all, do you?"

"Not really, no." She couldn't even say that if she thought the welfare of AIH was a given that her dad would put hers next.

She wasn't convinced of that.

Rather than appear upset by her denial, her dad shrugged. "Maybe you are right not to."

"That's not a comforting thing for you to say."

He shrugged. "Would you rather I lied?"

"No, but you would, if you thought it would get you what you wanted."

"That's one of the primary differences between Viktor and I. Our business peers know it, too. If I want another company president to believe something, I make sure he hears it from Viktor."

"Has he ever lied for you unknowingly?" she asked, not sure she wanted to know the answer.

"No. I'm not saying I haven't been tempted, but while I may not feel the same compunction for truth that my successor does, I do recognize that if I did that and Viktor found out about it, he would find another vehicle for his ambition than AIH."

Well, she'd never considered her father to be stupid. "I think you're right."

"I know I am."

"So, about Mom's memory…" Maddie said, ready to get back to the reason for her presence at her father's dinner table.

"She always said she wanted you to wear her wedding dress when you married."

"You still have it?" Maddie couldn't hide the eagerness in her tone.

If she'd been with Vik, she wouldn't have even felt the need to try.

"Of course."

"But you got rid of all her things." Maddie would never forget coming home for the first time from boarding school to find most of the house redecorated and her mother's things gone.

"I kept her wedding dress and her jewelry for you." Her father's tone implied he didn't understand why Maddie wouldn't know that.

"Why? When you got rid of everything else?"

"The dress is a piece of history."

"Not business history." So, why would her dad care?

"Family history. A famous designer created it for your great-grandmother in 1957, the year after he did a similar dress for an actress in one of her more famous roles." Jeremy cleared his throat almost as if talking about this was making him emotional. "Every generation in her direct line has worn it since."

"I know."

"Oh, I thought maybe you'd forgotten. You didn't mention wearing it."

"I thought you'd gotten rid of it."

"I didn't."

"I'm so glad." It was a dream she'd thought would have to die with her mother.

"You're very much of a size with your mother. I doubt it will require much tailoring."

The beautiful ivory strapless gown with embroidery in champagne silk thread around the full skirt and on the bodice required no altering at all.

Though she and Romi agreed Maddie should wear a corset under the embroidered bodice for smooth lines. The champagne lining flipped over the hem as a contrast lay exactly as it was supposed to.

"You look so beautiful," Romi said with suspiciously shiny eyes.

The dress hugged Maddie's breasts and torso, nipping in at her natural waist and then flaring in a full skirt shorter in the front than the back, which had an understated train that swept the floor elegantly behind her.

"I look like my mom."

"But you have your dad's eyes." Romi twisted her mouth comically. "I can't believe he paid for me to attend boarding school with you."

"Me, either." But Mr. Grayson had confirmed Jeremy's claim.

"He loves you, I always said so."

"In his own way," Maddie agreed. "Just not the way I needed."

"Maybe he just didn't know how. From what you've told me about his parents, it doesn't sound like the Archers were a warm family."

Maddie had only a few memories of grandparents who were both dead by the time she turned five, but none of them included a hug, or a kiss, or any other sign of affection.

"You could be right, but Jeremy admitted he'd lie if it got him what he wanted."

"Well, you knew that."

"I did. It was just weird having him admit it. I guess he has his own personal brand of honesty, too."

Romi adjusted the folds of Maddie's skirt just so. "I suppose. I prefer Viktor's."

"Me, too," Maddie said fervently.

Both women laughed, and it felt good.

But then most things felt pretty amazing right now. Maddie was marrying the man she loved and even if he didn't love her, he'd promised a *real* family.

And Vik kept his promises.

Viktor walked down the elementary school's hallway behind an office aide who had agreed to escort him to Miss Jewett's first-grade classroom.

Unlike Madison, Viktor and Maxwell had attended public school, but in an area more affluent than this one. The mix of children and teachers here reflected San Francisco's varied population like the rarified social strata of the Archers did not.

Viktor wasn't sure why Madison had asked him to meet

her here. She'd said something about wanting to talk to him with the help of a visual aid.

He didn't know what that meant. He couldn't see how an overcrowded public school would work as inspiration for her charter school. Unless it was the success they had with their volunteer program.

He'd done a little research before leaving the office on this grade school and discovered that they had a significantly higher than usual rate of parent participation in the classroom as well as other volunteerism.

When he'd arrived at the office, it was to discover that he was expected. So, he was definitely in the right place.

Whatever Madison's reasons for having him there.

He noticed two things immediately after the aide opened the classroom's door—Madison looking very unlike herself and the absolute silence he did not associate with a roomful of children.

Wearing a mousy brown wig, contacts that obscured the Mediterranean blue of her eyes with brown and clothes clearly bought off the rack at a box store, his fiancée sat at a small desk in a circle with six students.

Tattered books with brightly colored pictures, large print and few words were open on the desks in front of the children. Madison held her own copy, a smile frozen on her face as she met his gaze.

Vik allowed one brow to rise in query. "Hello, Madison. It appears you have some friends I haven't met."

Her fixed smile morphed into a genuine grin as she jumped to her feet. "You're early."

He couldn't help noticing the cheap cotton top and denim jeans she wore showed off her curves in ways that affected his libido as surely as her designer dresses.

He didn't like the wig or colored contacts, though.

He shrugged away her comment about his timing. "Introduce me."

"Of course."

Not wanting to intimidate the children with his size, Viktor dropped to one knee and reached to shake hands with each child as Maddie introduced them.

A few returned his greeting with charming politeness. One small girl, clearly Madison's favorite from the way the small girl tucked herself behind his fiancée's legs, ducked her head, but wiggled her fingers in a shy hello.

Viktor met the teacher and the parent volunteer as well.

"Very nice to meet you," he said to Miss Jewett.

"The pleasure is all ours." She smiled, her eyes warm as they lit on Madison. "Your fiancée is a fantastic volunteer. She's so good with the children and could be a teacher with her credentials."

"I am aware." He just hadn't been aware that she volunteered in the public school system.

Did her father know?

Madison clearly didn't want to leave right away, so Viktor stayed, enjoying the time helping six-year-olds with their reading.

They were in his Jaguar and headed toward the other side of the city when she finally pulled off the offensive wig, exposing her red curls crushed in a messy pile. It reminded him of the way she looked after sex, the only time she was completely disheveled—Madison woke looking more tempting than ever.

She rubbed at her scalp and ran her fingers through her hair, causing some curls to bounce up again. "It's always such a relief to get that thing off."

"Why do you wear it?"

"Because *Maddie Grace* is a normal woman with a degree and desire to volunteer with children. She doesn't get written up in the tabloids or followed by the paparazzi."

"And that's important to you?"

"To be normal? It was when I started. Now, it's just

easier. Can you imagine what the media would make of the billionaire heiress as a volunteer teacher's aide?"

"I have a feeling we're going to find out."

"That's what I thought. With our marriage and the vestiges of Perrygate, I kind of figured it was only a matter of time before my secret got exposed."

"Some secret." She was even more wonderful than he'd always known. "How long have you been volunteering like this?"

"It started as a dare with Romi. Trying to attend a political rally incognito. It worked and I got the idea to volunteer at a soup kitchen the next weekend *dressed up*."

"Don't you mean dressed down?"

She laughed, the sound soft and more enticing than he was sure she meant it to be. "I guess."

"It might be a good idea to come clean before some enterprising reporter does it for you."

"I guess," she said again, not sounding nearly as amused or enthusiastic.

"As much as you enjoy being Maddie Grace, Madison Beck will be able to effect more widespread change and influence." Just giving Madison his last name verbally was satisfying in a way Viktor didn't understand or analyze.

"But will she get to teach a first-grader how to read?"

"Yes. That's what the charter school is about, right? Helping children one-on-one."

"It is." He could hear the smile in Madison's voice.

"So Grace for Romi Grayson?"

"No, my grandmother Madison."

"That's right." He'd forgotten.

"You don't mind?"

He pulled into a parking spot on the side of the road, wanting to have this conversation face-to-face. Cutting the engine, he turned to face her.

Brown eyes stared back at him and he frowned. "Can you take those out?"

"What? Oh…" Comprehension dawned.

She pulled a small case from her backpack, so different than the trendy designer bags he usually saw her wear, and proceeded to take out and store away the contacts.

"This persona, she's more you than the famous designer wedding dress?"

"Sometimes. Sometimes I just really love my Chanel, you know?" Madison's pretty bow lips twisted in a wry grimace. "I like to pretend that I couldn't care less about the latest fashions and keep up with them just to be Madison *Archer*, but the truth is? I like both."

He nodded. Not because he understood. He wore tailored designer suits as a sign of power, not because he thought about how they looked. But because he was glad Madison Archer, soon to be Madison Beck, wasn't someone she didn't want to be.

"So, the question was *do I mind?* Yes?"

Madison's beautiful blue eyes shone at him. "Yes."

"Do I mind that I am going to marry a woman who cares so much about helping others she has created an alternate persona so she can do it? No, Madison. I do not mind at all."

Giving in to the urge that seemed to grow with each passing day, Viktor leaned across the console and kissed Madison.

He lifted his mouth to say, "In fact, I think it's amazing."

Madison sighed and leaned back into the kiss, delight radiating off of her and twisting its way around Viktor's heart.

Viktor's *deda* and *babulya* had them over for dinner a couple of days later and dropped their own bombshell.

Stunned at his grandparents' request, Viktor could only ask, "You want us to what?"

"When we moved here, we gave up all the old ways," Misha said. "We changed our last name from Bezukladnikov to Beck—we even changed our baby boy's name from Ivan to Frank. Very American."

"I know all this." It was family history he had shared with Madison years ago.

Her lovely face expressed memory of the event too. Viktor just didn't understand why his *deda* felt the need to rehash those realities now.

"We did not speak Russian in our home. We encouraged our little Ivan to become fully American." *Babulya's* voice broke on his father's original name. "Frank, who spoke without an accent and did all the things the other children at school did."

"You wanted him to embrace and be embraced by his new homeland," Madison offered in understanding while Viktor reeled with alien confusion.

His grandmother smiled appreciatively. "Exactly, but we gave away too much and he became the man he is today."

"A flake. You can say it, *Babulya*." Vik frowned with frustration, really not liking the idea his beloved grandparents were trying to take responsibility for his father's lifetime of selfish and poor choices. "My dad is a deadbeat."

"Do not speak of your father that way," Misha said, but with little heat.

Viktor didn't argue, but he didn't promise not to, either. He couldn't.

Madison looked at him with something far more attractive than compassion. Her eyes glowed that way they did when she called him her white knight. Viktor had no clue what in this particular situation would put that look on her face, but he would not question the obvious lack of the one emotion he hated above all others.

Pity.

His *babulya's* eyes usually filled with a tranquility he'd always relied on, but now shimmered with regret. "We think we let go of too many traditions and he felt himself cast adrift."

"Oh, for…" Viktor clenched his jaw to bite back the first words that came to his mind. "Dad did not become a con artist because he didn't have a traditional Russian wedding. The one right and good thing he did in his life was his marriage to my mom."

"That is not true," Misha said in a deep voice so like Viktor's own. "He fathered you."

Viktor opened his mouth and shut it again without a word.

Madison grinned, a smug glint in her azure eyes. "I told him the same thing."

"You are a very good match for our grandson." His grandmother's answering smile was blinding. "It pleases Misha and me very much that you appreciate our Viktor as we do."

"He's easy to love."

Once again Viktor did not know how to respond to those words, though he liked hearing them. Very much.

But love was not something he had ever considered in the equation of his marriage to Madison and the life they would build together. Was it enough that she felt the emotion, or did she expect him to reciprocate one day?

Could he? Did he even know how?

He had never been in love before. The affection between his grandparents had grown over time and did not look on the surface anything like the passion that burned between Viktor and Madison.

The silence had stretched and it should have been awkward, but the three most important people in the world to him simply observed Viktor with varying degrees of understanding.

It was a strange experience, but not unpleasant.

"Thank you," he finally said to Madison, hoping that once again it was enough.

His grandfather winced, but patted Viktor on the shoulder. Misha didn't say anything, though.

Madison's smile turned soft in a way Viktor did not understand, but liked nonetheless.

His grandmother rolled her eyes. "Viktor, my dear grandson, you have much to learn about romance."

Viktor could not deny it.

She didn't seem to expect an answer. "Is it so much to ask you follow a few of our family's traditions?"

"I'm not answering before you tell me exactly which ones you're talking about." His caution was necessary.

Russian wedding preparations and celebrations could become extremely complicated and involved.

But his grandparents' requests weren't unreasonable, even if they did mean Madison had to spend the night before her wedding at Jeremy's home instead of Viktor's bed.

Five weeks after Perry's exposé, Maddie waited in the drawing room of her father's mansion the morning of her wedding.

She was wearing the gown her mother had worn, and her mother before that and *her* mother before that in 1957.

Her full-length Victorian-era veil of Brussels lace was even older than the dress. Romi had shown up with it a week ago. And it was the exact same ivory as the gown.

Romi adjusted the veil around Maddie's face now. "You are so beautiful."

Maddie couldn't answer. If she tried to talk, her emotions were going to get the best of her.

"Viktor is going to be here any minute. Are you ready?"

Maddie indicated herself with a wave of her hand and forced an even tone. "What do you think?"

"I already told you, beautiful. But, sweetie, that's not what I'm talking about. Are *you* ready?"

"According to Vik, we got married that day we made promises overlooking San Francisco's skyline."

"Pffft." Romi shook her head. "Men."

"Those promises were vows." Of that Maddie was very certain.

"So are the words you're going to speak today."

Maddie nodded. "I'm ready."

"You love him."

"I do." There was no point in denying it. Besides Romi could always tell when Maddie was lying.

"You always have."

Maddie wasn't so sure about that, but she couldn't deny she'd never fallen in love with anyone else.

"Perry didn't stand a chance."

"He didn't want one." Their friendship had never been like that.

"I'm not so sure about that."

"It doesn't matter."

"No," Romi said with finality. "It doesn't."

Maddie grinned at her sister-by-choice. "I'm getting married today."

"You are." Romi grinned back.

Their hug was fierce enough to crush silk and neither of them cared.

The sound of the doorbell came faintly from the hall. Then Vik's voice and Misha's laugh.

Oh, this was real. It was happening. Now.

More laughter and then the door to the drawing room swung in and bounced against the wall.

Her six-foot-two distant cousin James, wearing a distinctly masculine tuxedo and tulle veil, stumbled in first. "He figured out I wasn't you, cuz."

Maddie found herself laughing along with the others as they came in behind him. The first tradition had been observed. Her father had pretended to offer an alternate "bride" and Vik had shown his determination to only wed one.

Misha, looking dapper in his own tux, and Ana, beautiful in her rose-pink suit, came in behind James. Maddie's father wore a traditional morning coat and ascot, but Vik was in breath-stealing Armani.

James's parents were there, too, along with the second cousins who had been at the family engagement dinner. Vik's aunt, his father's younger sister by ten years, and her two teenagers had flown in from New York. Frank hadn't made it.

The cousins from Russia had extended their stay in California, though, so they were here as well.

Enough family to please Misha and Ana's need for traditions to be observed, Maddie hoped.

But really? As far as she was concerned, no one else mattered, not when Vik came to stand in front of her, his expression hungry, approving and supremely satisfied all at once.

"Ti takAya krasIvaya." Vik reached out to touch her, but his hand hovered in the air between them, not quite connecting.

"He is telling you that you are beautiful," Misha informed her.

Maddie nodded her understanding, but couldn't look away from the intensity in Vik's espresso gaze.

"I have come to ransom my bride," he said in formal tones clearly meant for her father, but Vik's attention never strayed from Maddie.

"Your father tried pawning this one off on us," Misha

said, pointing at James. "But my grandson is too observant to be fooled."

Because anyone would have mistaken her tall, *male* cousin for her.

But Maddie laughed because it was supposed to be in fun and she found she enjoyed this Russian tradition very much.

Vik offered an open Tiffany box with a sapphire-studded tiepin and cuff links resting on the cream satin.

Her father accepted it with what sounded like genuine thanks, but then he shook his head. "This is not enough."

And she knew that was part of the ritual Misha and Ana wanted to see observed.

Misha made a production of arguing the merits of the gentlemen's jewelry, but Vik never even cracked a smile. His powerful focus was entirely on Maddie and she felt a connection to him that was more spiritual than humorous.

Finally, Misha came between them, offering her another Tiffany box. This one contained a five-strand pearl necklace and perfectly matched pearl studs in a vintage inspired gold setting.

Her gaze flicked between the pearls and Vik and then to Romi, because Maddie's SBC had convinced her to go without a necklace. "You knew."

Romi nodded, her brilliant smile watery.

Maddie reached up and removed her mother's diamond earrings and handed them to Romi, who she now realized had left her own ears bare just for this. It was right that Romi would be wearing something of Helene's at Maddie's wedding.

Vik helped Maddie put on the earrings and the necklace, the moment unbearably intimate. When he was done, he bent down and placed a barely there kiss against her lips before carefully dropping her veil back into place.

"Now, there can be a wedding," Misha said with hearty satisfaction.

CHAPTER TEN

THEY TOOK TWO limos to the church.

Maddie didn't pay attention to who went where except that she had Vik on one side of her and Romi on the other.

The Holy Virgin Cathedral looked like it had been transplanted right out of Russia, with its cross-topped triple-domed spires and white facade. The inside was awe-inspiring, with its domed ceilings decorated with iconography and the ornate public altar area.

She lost herself in the beauty of the service, but nothing was as moving as the moment before the crowning ceremony when Vik sidestepped tradition and lifted her veil to kiss her again and whisper that now even God knew she was his.

The words might be considered irreverent by some, but they settled in Maddie's soul. He left her veil folded back so that when the crown was placed on her head signifying the sacrament, Maddie felt both bound and freed at the same time.

They skipped the civil ceremony that would have been required to make the wedding legal in Russia because it wasn't necessary in America. Consequently, they broke crystal glasses at the reception in front of a few hundred of her father and Vik's nearest and dearest.

Both glasses shattered into rubble, though there could

be no doubt that Vik threw his with an impressive force beyond what Maddie used. Everyone cheered.

"It will be a long and blessed union," Misha announced loudly.

She was a little surprised to discover the man hired to be toastmaster was a well-known Shakespearean actor, and one of her favorite up-and-coming performers sang for the guest's enjoyment.

They ate, cut the cake and toast after toast was made to the happy couple.

It was all sort of overwhelming and amazing. Nothing about this wedding felt like a business arrangement. When she mentioned that to Vik, he smiled.

"Because this marriage is *not* a business arrangement," he said firmly.

"But—"

"It's a marriage of dreams. Accept that for what it is."

Happier than she had ever been, Maddie nodded and did just that. She wasn't at all surprised when Romi caught her bouquet.

Maddie had been aiming after all.

What was surprising and even a little worrisome, was that Maxwell Black caught the garter. The look he gave Romi would have had Maddie running for the hills, but her friend just blushed. And looked more than a little interested.

Huh. That was something to think about.

After Maddie's own honeymoon.

She smiled so much during the reception that her cheeks hurt by the time the white Rolls-Royce arrived to take them away.

Maddie was surprised when the car pulled up in front of the Ritz-Carlton instead of Parean Hall.

She turned to Vik. "I thought we were going home."

"I like the sound of that."

"Going home?" she asked, confused and not minding a bit.

"Home. *Our home*," he emphasized.

Heat she did not understand crept into Maddie's cheeks. "But we aren't there."

"No, we are here. And this moment the only three people who know that are you, me and the driver." Vik sounded very proud of that fact.

"What about security?"

"Not even them. Not tonight. No friends. No family. No security. *No press.*"

Delight suffused her. "Tonight is ours."

"Yes."

"I like it."

"Good."

He carried her over the threshold of Suite 919, one of the two most luxurious sets of rooms on the club level.

Its beauty was lost on Maddie, though. She was way too focused on Vik to pay attention to marble floors and Chippendale furniture.

"Champagne?" he asked without putting her down.

She shook her head.

"Snack?"

A smile flirted at her mouth as she said primly, "No thank you."

His eyes darkened with primal intent. "Bed then?"

"Oh, yes."

He carried her into the bedroom and lowered her to her feet. "Did I tell you how lovely you are today?"

"You may have mentioned it, yes."

He nodded, as if in serious contemplation. "I can only imagine one circumstance in which you could be more breathtaking."

"Yes?" she asked.

"Let me show you."

"Okay," she breathed out.

He removed her crown and veil with careful, deliberate movements. Then he took off the jewelry he'd helped her put on earlier.

"I don't think I told you. The pearls are exquisite. Thank you."

"They are just little white beads until you are wearing them."

"Oh, wow…I don't know even know how to take some of the things you say."

"As truth. We've established I do not lie to you." He brushed his lips over the back of her neck.

She did nothing to suppress the shiver the small touch elicited. "Or at all, according to Jeremy."

Vik came around and faced her, and then leaned down to press their mouths together softly for only a brief moment. "Or at all." He kissed down her neck and along her bare shoulder.

Each caress of his lips left a trail of goose bumps in its wake and she was trembling with desire by the time he made it around to the back of her dress.

He undid the bodice, trailing kisses down her spine as he did so.

The silk of her corset was no barrier between his lips and her skin. He helped her step out of the dress and then took the time to carry it into the dining room and lay it on the table.

When he came back into the bedroom, she said, "Thank you."

He looked at her questioningly.

"For caring about my dress."

He shrugged as if his consideration wasn't important, or maybe rather that it should be taken for granted. "It is a living memory for your family."

She hoped she never stopped appreciating the big, but especially little things he did to take care of her.

"So, is this what you were talking about?" she asked with a sweeping gesture toward herself with her hand.

Maddie stood before Vik in her corset, panties, sheer silk thigh highs and glittery Jimmy Choo heels, but nothing else.

His smile was predatory when he shook his head. "Almost, but not quite."

She stepped out of her heels.

"Closer." Sensuality oozed through his voice.

She swallowed. They'd made love every night for the past five weeks, so nothing about this one should make her nervous.

But as much as he'd claimed to consider their promises at the Marin Headlands overlook to be enough to bind them, the look of possession in his eyes was about ten times more intense than it had been the past weeks.

She reached down to unhook her stockings, but he put a staying hand. "Let me."

"Okay." She straightened and waited.

With no consideration for the expensive fabric of his tuxedo trousers, Vik knelt in front of her. But rather than undoing the slide button holding her stocking in place, he settled his big hands on her hips and leaned forward to press a kiss between her breasts.

Her breath caught and her knees went weak. "Vik, please."

"Please what?" he asked, his voice dark with passion. "This?"

He nuzzled the slopes of her breasts, his tongue flicking out to taste her skin. Little sparks of pleasure chased the path he took with his mouth.

His hands slid around to cup her bottom and then fingertips teased the exposed skin between the bottom of her panties and the tops of her stockings.

She only realized he'd undone the hooks when the soft silk slid down first one thigh and then another—with a little help from Vik.

Over a month ago, she'd never been touched like this, but now her body knew the delight to be had. She felt empty inside in a way she never had before she'd known what it was like to be filled up.

Her thighs quivered with brush of his fingertips while part of her craved even more. Firmer touch, more intimate caresses.

Her nipples had already drawn tight in anticipation of his attention.

Images of what he'd done before melded with the present to intensify every brush of skin against skin.

Vik reached behind her to undo the corset and she was grateful she'd gone for one with a zipper rather than laces. It parted and came away from her overheated skin in a matter of seconds.

"Mmmm…" he hummed, his expression both pleased and predatory. "Almost there."

There was no surprise when he hooked his fingers in the waistband of her panties and tugged them down. Only a sense of breathless anticipation.

With one final kiss on each of her nipples, he stood. "Now, that is the most beautiful sight I could ever imagine."

Heat suffused her body; she'd lost her ability to suppress her blushes around this man.

None of her defense mechanisms came naturally around Vik anymore.

"You're still dressed." Her voice sounded like a croaking frog.

"Would you like to change that?" he asked, his tone filled with sensual challenge.

In answer, she stepped forward and undid his bow tie.

"I'm starting to understand how you feel about unwrapping gifts," she said as she pulled the tie slowly from the starched collar of his shirt.

"Yes?"

"Oh, yes." She took her time on the buttons as well, leaning forward to inhale his masculine scent and nuzzle the chest hair not covered by his white silk undershirt.

Maddie reveled in each new inch of golden skin revealed, taking her time to touch and kiss as he had done.

Funny how quickly she'd gained the confidence to do this, but then he'd never reacted with anything but all-out enthusiasm to any sexual overture she made. No matter how small.

When she had him completely naked, she stepped forward so their bodies were flush. He was so much bigger than her and yet they fit together like they'd been created as adjoining pieces of a puzzle.

They kissed for several very satisfying minutes, no sense of urgency, just pleasure as they connected as intimately as when he was inside her.

But there was something she wanted to do, something she hadn't yet tried, something that intrigued, but also intimidated her.

What better time to take the plunge but on her wedding night?

She pulled back to break the kiss, but he drew her back in. This happened a few more times before she finally managed to separate their lips and bodies.

"I want to taste you," she told him.

A supernova flared in his eyes. "I'm not about to tell you no."

"I didn't think you would." She dropped to her knees in front of him.

"Wouldn't you be more comfortable on the bed?" he asked, sounding like it really mattered to him.

And she knew it did.

She took his large erection in her hand and caressed up and down. "Maybe, but not yet." Maddie stroked him a second time.

Groaning, Vik swayed.

She loved the velvety smoothness of his skin here and knowing that small touch affected him in such a primal way.

Leaning forward, Maddie took her first real taste of Vik's straining sex. The skin should taste like any other skin on his body, but it was even more addictive to her taste buds.

Drops of preejaculate burst with flavor on her tongue and she thought how she would be the only one who got to experience this. Never again would another woman know him in this way.

Only Maddie.

Vik was hers.

She swirled her tongue around the spongy skin of his head and he made a sound between a growl and a groan. "Please, *milaya moya*."

He could deny it, but the wedding made a difference to Vik. He'd never spoken in Russian to, or around her, before today. He was bringing her into his inner sanctum.

And that was as alluring as the naked man in front of her.

"What does that mean?" she asked, tipping her head back to see his face.

Their gazes locked, his dark eyes filled with passion.

"My sweet." His hips canted forward, seemingly of their own accord, and the tip of his erection brushed her lips.

She took him into her mouth, bringing forth another deep sound of pleasure from Vik. Hollowing her cheeks, Maddie sucked, moving her mouth forward and backward, but never so far forward she choked.

His hands settled softly against her head, but he made no effort to hold her in place or guide her movements. It was like he was giving her silent approval, as if he thought maybe his sounds of pleasure weren't enough.

It was wonderful, but her jaw got sore faster than she expected and she had to pull back.

"That was amazing," he said with apparent sincerity.

She smiled up at him. "Short, you mean."

He laughed, the sound husky. "Much longer and I would have come."

"You're easy."

"For you? Definitely." Vik pulled her to her feet and right into a mind-numbing kiss.

Not just easy, but *hungry*.

She hadn't known that missing a single night of lovemaking would make him so impatient, so ravenous for her and the pleasure they created together.

But Vik lost no time backing her up to the bed. He ripped the coverlet and top sheet off with a single, powerful yank and then maneuvered them onto the center of the king-sized mattress.

He guided her legs apart, her knees bent and she expected immediate penetration. What she got was his mouth against her most intimate flesh.

In moments, she was writhing with the need to climax, but an even stronger desire to have him inside her.

"Please, Vik. Make love to me now."

His head came up, eyes nearly black with passion meeting hers. "What do you think I am doing?"

"Not like that."

"Oh, yes, like this."

"But I'm going to come." Desperation overrode her every inhibition.

"Yes, you will," he promised in a sexy growl.

"But—"

"At least once."

Then he went back to what he was doing, taking her to the edge and over, her cries echoing around them in the luxurious bedroom. His tongue laved her gently through aftershocks until her body went boneless, her legs flopping down to the bed.

He pulled the sheet from its tangle with the comforter and wiped his mouth on it before surging up and over her. "Condom, or no condom?" he asked.

They'd been lucky and their first time without protection hadn't resulted in pregnancy. He'd been very careful to use condoms since.

But they were married now and had agreed to start a family right away. Equally important to her, she wanted the intimacy of no barrier between them.

"No birth control."

He nodded, if anything, his expression turning even more feral with a voracious sexual need. His desire came off him in waves and he still managed to enter her carefully, giving her most sensitive flesh a chance to adjust to his granite-hard erection filling her.

After her recent explosive climax and the way he incited aftershocks until she simply couldn't respond anymore, she'd been prepared to share the intimacy with him and revel in the emotional connection. But not much more.

Maddie was not prepared for the way her body reacted to their joining. The physical ecstasy ignited again, as if it had never been banked, burning hotter with every movement of his body in hers. Pleasure that she should be too sated to feel rolled through her, making her womb spasm and the muscles around his hardness contract.

He set a slow, but thoroughly penetrating rhythm that built the ecstasy inside her until she was on the verge of another inconceivable orgasm.

As if he could read her mind, or maybe it was just the clues her body was giving him, Vik sped up, pounding into her, jolts of pleasure going through her on every thrust.

He stared down at her, his face a rictus of sexual ecstasy, his coffee-brown eyes burning with demand. "Come now, *milaya moya*."

And improbably...she did, screaming as rapture sent her body into tremors that could have toppled cities.

He went completely rigid and joined her in the ultimate sexual pleasure, their gazes as connected and intimate as the most passionate kiss.

"If that didn't make a baby..." she said breathlessly.

He pulled her close into his body. "We will keep trying with great delight."

Which they did for the rest of the night, falling into exhausted slumber after the sun lit the morning fog.

He woke her to shower at noon. Not alone. Showering together was one of her recently discovered perks to sharing physical intimacy with Vik.

They came out of the bathroom to find clothing lying across the freshly made bed.

A familiar black-and-white polka-dot set of hard-sided luggage was sitting against the wall beside a black fold over garment bag and matching leather duffel as well.

"How long are we staying here?" she asked as she donned her bra and then tugged on a black silk shell over it.

Vik flicked the suitcases a glance and then met her eyes. "We are checking out in an hour."

"Where are we going?" Not home.

Both their personal possessions had been moved to Parean Hall the day before the wedding. So, there would be no need for luggage.

He pulled on his briefs and then a pair of dark indigo designer jeans. "Palm Springs."

"Why?"

"Our honeymoon."

She stilled in her own efforts to get dressed. "But I thought we weren't going on a honeymoon."

"I do not recall agreeing to that."

"We never talked about it," she pointed out.

He pulled on a black-and-white Armani X polo. "It is traditional."

"Our marriage isn't exactly." The jeans she stepped into were a pair of her favorites.

"I disagree."

She shook her head, knowing he wouldn't budge on his outlook. Vik saw nothing odd in marrying a woman he didn't love so he could build a legacy for the children he most certainly would.

"So, Palm Springs."

His grin was knowing. "I saw little point in an exotic location when we are likely to spend most of our time in the bedroom."

Blushing, she ignored his assertion and shrugged into the burgundy-and-black color-blocked jacket someone had left out for her to wear. "I like Palm Springs."

In fact, the small resort city nestled in the California desert was one of Maddie's all-time favorite places. She used to visit with her mother every winter. There were enough celebrities that vacationed there, the Archers of the world were barely a blip on the media's radar.

Maddie had continued to travel to the desert when she needed to get away from being Madison Archer, notorious heiress.

Somehow, she thought Vik knew that.

He smiled. "It is a good thing you are as intelligent as you are, or the amount of school you missed traveling with your mother would have been a real problem."

"She always brought a tutor along and got my assignments."

Vik's expression turned heated. "I'll be the only tutor you'll need this week."

"After the last five weeks, and particularly last night, I'm pretty sure there isn't much for you to teach me."

"You'll be surprised."

Not "you could be" or "you might be," but "you will be" surprised. The man had no shortage of confidence.

And the following eight days proved how justified he was in that regard.

True to his word, they spent *a lot* of time in the bedroom of their suite at an oasis-style resort outside of the city. However, Vik also insisted on visiting Maddie's favorite spots, taking her to dine at some of the best restaurants in and around the city as well as shopping in the exclusive boutiques of top designers.

Maddie, who had always considered her socialite side something of a necessary evil, enjoyed herself in ways she hadn't in Palm Springs since Helene's death.

Vik was flatteringly enthusiastic about almost every article of clothing Maddie tried on, and even the growls that particularly revealing pieces elicited were flattering in their own way.

They returned to San Francisco to a list of possible properties for the charter school that Vik had his real estate agent compile.

Vik had too many things on his desk no one else could handle after a week's absence to accompany Maddie and Romi when they toured the properties. But he asked detailed questions each evening about what Maddie had seen, proving the sincerity of his interest in the project.

* * *

Friday morning, Maddie got a text from her father's assistant requesting she come to a meeting in his office that afternoon.

She was supposed to do another tour of the property she and Romi had pretty much decided was *the one* for the school. Feeling magnanimous toward the world in general, even her father, Maddie called and rescheduled the tour before texting the PA that she would be at the meeting.

Maddie was shown into her father's office by his secretary, who surprisingly did not stay to take notes. So, it was a personal meeting?

Only, why at his office?

Her dad stood and came around from behind his desk. "Madison. I would like you to meet Dr. Wilson, the director for…" Jeremy named a well-known institution that specialized in psychiatric studies.

It was then she noticed the other man in the room.

Gray-haired and distinguished-looking in a suit of good quality, if not an Italian designer label, Dr. Wilson was sitting in one of the armchairs that sat opposite a matching leather sofa on the other side of her father's office.

He rose now and walked to Maddie, putting his hand out for Maddie to shake. "Madison. It's a pleasure to meet you."

"Thank you. I hope I can say the same." Though she did not have a good feeling about this.

Why did her father have a psychiatrist in his office for their meeting?

"Let's all sit down and get comfortable," Dr. Wilson said, indicating he considered himself a key player in the meeting to come.

The fact that her father followed the doctor's lead without comment indicated he agreed.

Maddie wasn't feeling quite so acquiescent. She remained standing as her father took a position at one end of the sofa and the doctor returned to his leather armchair. "What is this about?"

"Sit down, Madison, so we can discuss this like civilized people."

"Tell me what we are discussing first," she demanded in a chilly tone she hadn't used in weeks.

Her father frowned. "You are being rude."

"And you are being cagey." When it came to her father? Cagey was way worse than rude.

"Do you see what I mean?" Jeremy asked the doctor. "Unreasonably intractable."

"You've asked Dr. Wilson here to evaluate me?" Maddie demanded, emotion cracking through the facade of cool before she reined it in.

Surprisingly, her dad winced, but he nodded. "It has come to my attention that you've been seeing a therapist."

"I did for a few weeks, yes. Half of America has at one time or another." And her choice to do so was a good thing, not a weakness.

"That is actually a bit of an exaggeration," Dr. Wilson said, like he was making note of Maddie's tendency to overstate things. "The number is closer to twenty percent."

"Who told you I was seeing someone?" she asked Jeremy, ignoring the doctor.

Vik wouldn't have told him. He might not love Maddie, but he was her white knight. Vik would never sacrifice her to the king.

"Does Vik know about this meeting?" she demanded.

Her father gave her his game face. "What do you think?"

"That you don't want to answer my question." She pulled out her phone.

"Who are you calling?" Dr. Wilson asked, his tone overly patient.

"My husband."

"You see? Shades of codependency and paranoia," her father said.

Maddie wanted to throw her phone at his head, but didn't want to know what the psychiatrist would make of that. Vik's phone sent her to voice mail.

He must have been in a meeting.

She left a message. "It's me. Jeremy called me in for a meeting with a psychiatrist. I need to talk to you. Call me."

Dr. Wilson was watching her with an indecipherable expression. Her dad's eyes were narrowed, but she wasn't sure if it was with worry or annoyance.

"So, you know I saw a therapist and you've brought Dr. Wilson here to observe me. Why?"

"No one said I was here to observe you," the doctor said.

"No one said you weren't."

Neither the doctor nor her father answered that.

Finally, Jeremy said, "I've told Dr. Wilson my concerns about your increasingly erratic behavior over the years."

"And while I applaud your positive action in seeking help," Dr. Wilson said, as if speaking to a child, or an adult whose reasoning ability was compromised, "I must concur with your father that your actions since your mother's death indicate a spiraling condition."

"I do not have a condition." What she did have was a brain and it was starting to work. "You aren't going to prove me mentally incompetent to sign the paperwork giving Romi half of my shares in AIH. It's not going to work."

Her father's expression said he disagreed.

Even more ominously, the doctor shook his head. "Signing such a document as the one your father described to me in and of itself is hardly a rational action."

"You think not?"

"You think it is?"

"I know it is and I also know what I do with my money

and assets is not your business, Dr. Wilson, or for that matter, Jeremy Archer's."

"You call your father by his first name. That indicates a level of dissociation to those closest to you."

Who was this guy? Popping off with psychobabble on the basis of nothing but her father's obviously biased assertions and a few seconds conversation was not in any way professional.

"I'm closer to my cleaning lady than my father. In fact, I'm closer to *his* housekeeper than I am to him." And that might have been an exaggeration, but she defied either of them to prove differently.

The psychiatrist gave her a concerned look. "Your lack of emotional intimacy with your one remaining parent is certainly something we can explore together."

"Dr. Wilson, you are not and never will be *my* doctor. Now, if you two will excuse me." She turned to leave the office.

"Madison!" her father barked.

She didn't stop. He could leave whatever threat he wanted to make on her voice mail.

CHAPTER ELEVEN

MADDIE WAS IN the parking garage when her phone rang. Vik's ringtone.

She answered. "My father found out I was seeing a therapist."

"I didn't tell him."

"I didn't think you did."

"Good."

"I'm just…" Frustrated. Confused. Upset. "He wants to prove me incompetent to sign the papers giving Romi half my AIH shares."

"I had n—"

"There's something he didn't think of, I bet," she interrupted, not really hearing Vik.

"What is that?" Vik asked, sounding both cautious and concerned.

"If he gets a judge to say I wasn't competent to sign those papers. I wasn't competent to say my vows, either, and *we* aren't married. What will that do his precious plans to marry me off to his heir?" she demanded.

Vik made a sound like a growl. "That is not going to happen."

"I thought things were getting better with him."

"They are."

"If anyone has lost their mind it is him."

"I agree."

She nodded.

"Madison?"

"You're on my side, right?" Vik wouldn't support his mentor and friend in this, would he?

"Of course. You are my wife and you are staying that way."

Because he wanted control of AIH. Because he wanted the future he planned with her. Right that second, Maddie wished desperately there was another, more emotionally compelling reason for Vik to insist their marriage stood in validity.

Love.

She needed her husband's love. More than she wanted her father's acceptance. A lot more.

She couldn't really care less about Jeremy sliding back into old habits. However, suddenly the knowledge that the man she loved more than her own life appreciated her feelings but didn't share them hurt in a way she couldn't ignore.

"I need some time to think."

"What? Madison, where are you? I will come to you."

"No. I just…give me some time, Vik." She ended the call and then turned off her phone.

She didn't want to talk to anyone. Not even Romi.

Maddie got into her hybrid car—not exactly what an heiress might be expected to drive, but it was environmentally responsible—and drove to her favorite coffee shop/bookstore.

How was she going to live the rest of her life in love with her husband and knowing he didn't reciprocate her feelings. She didn't know if it was *couldn't* or *wouldn't*, but it didn't matter.

Maddie hadn't been to the coffee shop since before Perrygate, but she needed time to think and a place to do it in that Vik wouldn't think to look.

She got her usual order and took it to her favorite table positioned between a book stack and the window. Since the lower half of the window was painted with a mural that looked like old leather volumes on bookshelves, no one would see her from the outside.

Not unless they got right up to the window and looked down.

Her thoughts whirled in a mass of contradicting voices and images as her coffee cooled in its cup, but one idea rose to the surface again and again.

Vik *acted* like a man in love.

He couldn't get enough of her sexually. Maddie's happiness was very important to him. Given a choice, he *always* opted to spend time with her rather than away from her. He wanted her to be the mother of his children.

Did the words really matter?

She'd been doing fine without them to this point. But being thrown back into Ruthlessville by her father had undercut Maddie's sense of emotional security.

Did she really need Vik to admit he loved her for her to feel secure in her happiness with him?

She still had no answer to that question when she heard her name spoken in a masculine tone she'd never planned to hear again.

She looked up and frowned. "Go away, Perry."

"You don't take my calls or respond to my texts."

He was surprised? "I blocked your number."

"I figured that out."

"You aren't supposed to be talking to me."

"Nothing in the agreement that bastard you married got me to sign said I couldn't talk *to* you, only about you." Perry sounded really annoyed by that.

"What did you expect?"

He put on the wounded expression that had always gotten to her in the past. "I didn't expect you to dump six years of friendship over one little mistake."

"It wasn't the first time you lied to the media about us." And that sad look wasn't tugging at her heartstrings anymore.

Perry jerked, like he hadn't expected her to have worked that out. "It was all harmless. I needed the money. We aren't all born with the silver spoon of Archer International Holdings to feed off of."

"Telling people I was a sexual addict who couldn't be satisfied with a single partner wasn't harmless. You destroyed my reputation."

"For exactly twenty-four hours. Viktor Beck saw to that."

"Conrad is good at what he does."

"Your dad's media fixer? Yeah, I kind of expected him to get involved, but he's a cuddly kitten compared to that vicious shark you married."

"Vik protected me when *you* fed me to the wolves. I'm not sure I'd label *him* the vicious one."

"You know I didn't mean it." Perry sounded like he really expected her to believe that.

What a jerk. And this man had been one of her dearest friends for *six* years. "I knew you were lying, that's not the same thing as knowing you didn't mean it."

"I needed the money. You knew I did."

"And I refused to give it to you." Which was what it all came down to, wasn't it?

"I asked for a loan. From a *friend*."

"When have you ever paid back even a single dollar of all the money you *borrowed* from me, Perry?" she demanded, the confrontation with her ex-friend unexpectedly bringing her current situation into clear and certain focus.

Perry was that guy. The user. The manipulator. The prevaricator.

Vik was her white knight. Full stop.

He might never say the three little words she most wanted to hear, but she wasn't going to spend the rest of her life lamenting that fact. Not when he gave her so much to rejoice about instead.

"You can't guarantee business investments."

"So now they were business investments." She narrowed her eyes at Perry. "Where are my contracts showing the percentage ownership I had in those business ventures?"

"We don't need contracts between us."

She thought of the agreement Vik had forced Perry to sign. "Apparently, we do."

"Come on, Maddie. Call off your attack dog."

"Vik?"

"Who else?" Perry did his best to look beseeching.

"We aren't friends anymore and we never will be again," she spelled out very carefully.

"This is because of Romi, isn't it? She finally turned you against me."

"*You* turned me against you, Perry. You lied about me and did your best to destroy my reputation."

He'd gone back to looking wounded. "No."

"Yes. And if you'd succeeded, my dreams of starting a charter school would have been dust." At least with her name on any of the paperwork.

Perry shrugged. "San Francisco doesn't need another school."

His ability to dismiss the dreams of her heart so easily took her breath away. "I don't agree."

"Well, it didn't happen."

"No thanks to you."

"Hey, I went public with an apology and a confession that it was all a joke."

Did he expect her to thank him? "But it wasn't a joke.

It was a big ugly lie. Nothing even a tiny bit amusing about that."

"Come on, Maddie. You have to forgive me."

"Yes, for my own sake. I have to let it go."

Triumph flashed in Perry's washed-out blue eyes. "We can be friends again and forget about that agreement Viktor forced me to sign."

"No."

"But—"

"No one forced you to sign anything. You signed that agreement of your own volition because you didn't want to risk being sued by both AIH and the tabloid you sold that story to."

Maddie's head snapped up at Vik's voice. What was he doing here? How had he found her?

He stood like an avenging angel over Perry. "You are not my wife's friend. She's convinced you were at one time, but that time passed long before this latest incident."

"Who do you think you are to—"

"I am the man who will *ruin* you if you come near *my* wife again." His jaw hewn from granite, Vik's eyes burned with dark fury.

Perry put his hands up. "No problem. Look, I just thought we could still be friends, but I can see you're not comfortable with that."

"I'm not comfortable with it," Maddie inserted. "Stop blaming other people for your screwup, Perry. You destroyed our friendship and Vik is right, that started a long time ago."

"But, Maddie…"

She shook her head. "No. We're over. If you see me at a function, walk the other way because I don't want to talk to you anymore."

"We aren't going to be at the same functions," he said bitterly.

Maddie didn't bother to reply. That was Perry's problem, not hers.

"Are you going to leave, or will you force me to call the police to enforce the restraining order we have against you?"

"I'm leaving," Perry said quickly, backing out of the alcove.

"We have a restraining order?" Maddie asked Vik.

"Yes."

"Didn't I have to sign something for it?"

"No. His malicious intent was in the papers for the world to see. We filed for it on behalf of AIH and its primaries, of which you are one."

"Oh."

He looked down at her untouched coffee. "You're not drinking that."

She shook her head. "How did you find me?"

"Are you sure you want to know?"

"Yes."

"The 'find me' function on your phone."

"I turned it off."

"As long as the battery is in it and holds any charge, the GPS function works."

"So, if I want privacy, I have to take out the battery. Good to know."

He had to have looked up her GPS signal right away to have gotten to the coffee shop so quickly. More evidence that she mattered to him in the ways that were truly important.

Her father never would have just dumped his schedule to go running after her mother, or Maddie, certainly.

Vik inhaled, opened his mouth to speak, closed it again and then said, "I would prefer you not do that."

"Okay." It was a matter of safety as well, as much as she might prefer to forget that fact. "You came after me."

"Of course. You were upset. What Jeremy did to you…"

She coughed out a laugh at the rare vulgarity that came out of her husband's mouth.

Vik put his hand out to her. "Will you come *with* me now?"

Maddie didn't hesitate. "Yes."

"Don't you want to know where?" Vik asked as she took his hand and let him lead her from the coffee shop.

"I guess I assumed we'd go someplace private."

Vik's expression turned hard. "Actually, we're going back to AIH to confront your father."

"Together."

"Yes."

Implying Vik and Maddie were on one side and Jeremy Archer the other. Nice. If she'd needed proof that she came first with Vik, her father couldn't have provided a better opportunity.

Which, okay, maybe having the proof *was* nice, but she wasn't about to thank Jeremy.

Her father was in his office when they arrived, Dr. Wilson gone. The PA tried to tell them that Jeremy was in a meeting, but Vik just walked through.

He reached across Jeremy's desk and ended the call, sending Maddie's father surging to his feet as he spluttered with annoyance.

Vik waited until her father had gone silent to speak. "Have you ever known me to lie to you?"

Jeremy shook his head, his expression instantly wary.

"Do I bluff?" Vik asked.

"No," Jeremy said shortly.

"Then you will know I mean every word I say when I tell you that if you attempt to prove Madison incompetent to forestall her giving half her shares to Romi Grayson, I will destroy Archer International Holdings until the very building we are standing in is leveled to the ground."

"You don't mean that," Jeremy said, his voice warbling with emotion for the first time in Maddie's memory.

She hadn't even seen him appear this distraught at her mother's funeral.

There was no give in Vik. Not in his expression. Not in the way he stood, towering over Jeremy's desk. "We have just established that I do."

Definitely not in his tone.

Her dad said something else, but Maddie wasn't listening. Everything inside her had gone still as she had her second major revelation for the day.

"You *do* love me," she said to Vik, ignoring her father completely.

That oh-so-serious espresso gaze fixed on her. "You are mine to protect."

"And to love." Giddy with joy that could not be tempered even by her father's machinations, she could hardly help the delight surfing every syllable.

She didn't even want to try.

Maddie beamed up at the man she'd crushed on since she was fourteen and loved since she was sixteen. "I love you, too, but you know that."

"Do you?" Vik asked. "Even now?"

"Especially now." He wasn't even remotely responsible for her father's actions.

"I meant what I said to your father." He said it like it was a warning.

"I know."

"I am utterly ruthless and without remorse."

She might argue that point, but understood that Vik believed it. And that was okay with her.

He used his powers for good, even if he didn't see it.

She smiled at him, letting her love show in her eyes.

"Your sense of honor is the shiniest and clearest facet of your nature. Everything else about you is filtered through the light it casts."

"I am not a nice guy."

"You just threatened to destroy my company," her dad said with feeling. "You sure as hell are *not* a nice guy."

Maddie's smile morphed into a full grin. "It's all a matter of perspective. I love that you would pull out every stop to slay my dragons."

"I'm not a dragon. I'm your father, damn it."

She flicked him a disgusted glance. "Who threatened to have me declared mentally incompetent."

"You can't believe I wanted things to go down that way, but you're giving away my company." Vik might claim to be remorseless, but Jeremy's expression and tone were soaked with regret.

"Don't exaggerate," she said, dismissing her father's words. "Twelve and a half percent with the voting proxy assigned to Vik and any successor he should formally appoint."

Vik jolted beside her. "I didn't know that."

"I trust you."

His gaze turned soft like she'd never expected to see. "You do."

"You knew that."

"I told myself you did."

"And me." He'd told her when she'd still been denying it to herself.

"Apparently it is different coming from you."

Her dad sighed. "You know, your mother and I never felt the need to talk our emotions to death."

Finally, Maddie gave Jeremy her attention. "Maybe if you had, things would have been different."

"I cannot change the past," he said with a pained expression.

"You spend enough time screwing up with your daughter in the present, the past is hardly what you need to be worried about," Vik told her father.

"I am sorry for ambushing you with Dr. Wilson, Madison." Jeremy looked at her with appeal. "It probably makes no difference to you, but I told Dr. Wilson I wouldn't be needing his services immediately after you left my office."

"That's hard to believe." Her father didn't back down once he'd set a course of action in motion.

He just didn't. And he *did* lie.

Jeremy said, "Call him. He'll tell you."

Bluffing or truth?

"He's telling the truth," Vik told her.

Maddie looked up at her husband. "How can you tell?"

"His eyes shift to the left when he's lying about something important."

"And this is important to him?" she asked with suspicion.

"It involves you and his company. There is nothing more important to him."

That she believed. At least the part about the company.

"Why did you tell Dr. Wilson to back off?" she asked.

Jeremy shifted uncomfortably in his chair. "I knew that if I followed through with my plan, you would never forgive me."

"Are you sure it wasn't because you realized that my marriage to Vik would be invalidated if I was deemed unfit to make legal decisions?"

Her father's eyes widened, his skin going pale. A reaction he could not fake. He *hadn't* thought of that. "No wonder Vik pulled out the rocket launchers."

"He wants to be married to me more than he wants to be president of AIH." Just saying the words gave her emotional satisfaction to the very depths of her being.

Jeremy nodded, his expression more vulnerable than

she'd ever seen it. "I hope you've worked out that I want to be your dad more than I want control of those shares."

It was her turn to nod, but maybe with not as much conviction.

"It might benefit you both if your father attended some sessions with you and Dr. MacKenzie," Vik said.

Maddie waited to see her father's reaction to that piece of advice before offering her own.

Jeremy Archer shocked her to the very marrow of his bones when he said, "I would like that very much. Are you willing, Madison?"

"I don't know." What if he used the time they had together with the therapist to compile ammunition against her?

"Do you believe Vik will destroy Archer International Holdings if I attempt to have you declared mentally incompetent?"

"Yes." There was not a single atom in her body that did not trust Vik to do just that.

"Then you have nothing to fear," her father said, showing he'd guessed correctly what had her hesitating.

"I'll talk to Dr. MacKenzie. If she thinks it's a good idea, we'll arrange the sessions."

Her dad startled her again, getting up from his desk and coming around to kiss her on the cheek and shake Vik's hand. "Thank you for watching out for her better than I ever have."

"I always will." It was another Viktor Beck promise.

And the places still cold inside from Maddie's unexpected meetings with her father, the psychiatrist and then Perry, warmed. "And I will watch out for Vik."

Starting with taking him home and teaching him how to say three all-important words.

"I believe you. You have your mother's loyalty and my stubbornness. He couldn't be in better hands."

Maddie surprised herself, accepting the compliment with the warmth it was intended. "Thank you."

Vik slid his arm around her waist. "It's time for us to go home, I think."

"What about your afternoon meetings?" she asked, not really wanting him to go back to work.

But now that she knew he loved her, Maddie could wait for the evening to hear him say it. Maybe.

"I canceled everything after your phone call."

"Because nothing is more important to you than I am," she said with satisfaction.

Vik could have shrugged. He could have tried to deny it. He could have grimaced in unhappy acknowledgment.

He did none of those things.

What he did was turn his big body to face her, blocking out her view of her dad and his office.

Vik cupped Maddie's cheeks, his hands trembling against her skin. "Exactly."

Oh, man. She was going to melt right there.

"Take me home, please," she said, her voice low with fervency.

Vik made a sound like something had broken inside him and then leaned down and kissed her. His mouth claimed hers with undeniable need. She gave in to it without hesitation.

Maddie didn't know how long the kiss lasted, but when her father's voice finally penetrated, she was pressed against Vik, his arms tight bands around her.

"Sheesh, you two need to go home."

"Kicking us out?" Vik asked with no evidence of embarrassment at what they were doing.

Her dad, on the other hand, had a definite ruddy cast to his cheeks. "What's coming next is not going to happen in my office."

Maddie's own cheeks heated at the implication of his words. He was absolutely right. It was time to leave.

The trip home happened in a haze for her and Maddie was glad Vik drove.

He surprised her by pulling her into the morning room, the shabby chic so like her former apartment and cheery lemon-yellow accents barely registering as he pulled her to sit with him on the deep sofa.

"I thought we were going upstairs." To make love.

That's certainly where their kiss in her father's office had been leading.

"We're going to talk." Vik winced as if the words pained him. "About the emotional stuff."

"Can't we do that later?" Knowing he loved her was making her desire for the physical proof overwhelming.

"No."

"Why not?" She wasn't whining.

She wasn't, but so far, her day had sort of sucked. Making love with her husband? Now, after learning he was in love with her, that would take this one into the "best days ever" category.

"Because maybe things would have been different for Helene and Jeremy if they had," Vik said, quoting her own words back at her.

"That was them. We aren't my parents."

"No, we aren't." Vik took a deep breath and let it out, his complexion just a little green. "I love you, Madison."

She didn't tease him for nearly being sick with stress over the admission, though the temptation was great. But she appreciated how hard this had to be for her usually single-minded, alpha business tycoon.

"Maddie."

"What?" he asked, like she'd strayed from the script.

"You love me. I love you. You call me Maddie, like Romi does."

"Perry, too." And Vik didn't appear happy about that.

"Not anymore. Perry doesn't get to call me anything. You saw to that."

"The restraining order lasts two years, but we'll renew it."

She shook her head. "I don't need the restraining order. Trust me, you're enough, Vik."

"He approached you."

"So, I'll stop going to that coffee shop."

"That won't be necessary. I'll buy it and have him banned."

"Can you say overkill here, Vik?"

"Nothing is too much to protect you."

"Oh, man." She saw a lifetime ahead of her of reining in Vik's impulses to keep even the hint of harm from her and the children they would have.

Honestly? The image had a pretty rosy glow.

"Do you want me to leave AIH?" he asked.

"What? No!" It was her turn to reach out and cup his face, meeting his eyes with an expression as sincere as she could make it. "I do not need you to give up your dreams to believe you love me."

Though knowing he was willing to heal wounds in her heart from twenty-four years as Jeremy Archer's daughter.

"I do. I did six years ago, but…"

"You didn't recognize what the feeling was," she guessed.

"No. I'd never been in love."

"I'm glad." The thought she could have lost him before she ever had the chance to catch his eye sent cold tremors through her.

"I didn't think I needed love."

"We all need love."

Vik frowned. "I'm not sure that is true."

He sounded so uncertain, so very unlike the man she was used to. But this was not his area of expertise.

Emotions were almost as foreign to Vik as they were to her dad.

"It's okay, Vik. We love each other and we are going to be very happy."

"Aren't we happy right now?"

Giving in to the urge, she threw herself into his arms with a laugh. "Yes, my darling, wonderful husband. We are very happy."

He caught her to him, responding to her kiss and holding her tight.

Oh, yes, *very* happy.

They made love, right there on the sofa, and practiced saying those three little words to each other.

EPILOGUE

VIK AGREED WITH Maddie and Romi on the property they picked out for the charter school. Declaring it the perfect location, he insisted on putting an offer in on it immediately.

Afterward, he took her and Romi out for champagne to celebrate.

"Isn't this a bit premature?" Romi asked as they clinked glasses. "The offer hasn't been accepted yet."

Maddie just laughed. "The sellers could be a business consortium of questionable pedigree and they wouldn't have a chance against Vik."

"We'll get the property," Vik said as if there simply wasn't another option.

Maddie was pretty sure with her tycoon on the case, there wasn't.

Romi grinned, lifting her glass toward Vik. "To business shark negotiators and dreams coming true."

They didn't go straight home after, but Vik took Maddie back up to the overlook at Marin Headlands. She didn't ask what they were doing there.

Maddie just held his hand as they traversed the path to what many considered the best place for viewing San Francisco's skyline.

He stopped in the same spot he'd proposed. "We forgot some promises when we were here before."

"Did we?"

He nodded. "You forgot to promise not to leave your security detail behind anymore."

That wasn't what she was expecting him to say, but it was so in line with Vik and his priorities that she grinned. "Duly noted."

"Promise."

She put her hand over her heart. "I promise to keep my security detail with me."

"Your days of volunteering anonymously are over." He leaned down and kissed her. "I'm sorry."

"It's okay. You'll just have to find me a detail that likes children."

"I think that can be arranged."

Suddenly she realized why they were dealing with this now. "If my detail had been with me when I went to the coffee shop, Perry wouldn't have gotten within ten feet of me."

"If that."

"Right."

Vik shrugged. "Do you think Romi would allow me to assign a detail to her as well?"

"What? Why?"

"She is your sister-by-choice."

"I didn't know you were aware of that."

"Your mother considered her another daughter."

"She did." Maddie smiled in memory. "But I'm not sure Romi needs security because I consider her my sister."

"In a few weeks, she will own twelve and a half percent of a multibillion-dollar company."

"No one but us will know that."

"You know better than that."

She did. "I don't know if we can convince her."

"Tell her security comes with the shares."

"She's not going to be happy."

Vik didn't look too worried about that reality. "She's part of my family now. She'll get used to it."

Maddie wasn't sure she agreed, but she loved the sentiment.

Vik pulled Maddie close, but kept eye contact. "I love you."

It didn't matter that he'd said it before, that she knew it to be true—saying the words here made them a vow for him.

Maddie's throat constricted, moisture burning hot behind her eyes and all she could do was nod.

"I will love you always," he promised.

She took a steadying breath. "Me, too."

"We *will* say the important stuff."

"Yes."

"We'll talk about the emotional stuff often." He still looked a little green around the gills at the idea, but he was making the promise.

And Maddie knew Vik would keep it.

"With our children, too," Maddie vowed.

Vik nodded. "When I forget, you'll remind me."

"Yes." Not that she was convinced he would ever forget the important things.

When Vik set his mind to something, he succeeded.

He looked like he had something he wanted to say, so she waited for him to say it. "Your father…"

"Yes?"

"I could have been him."

"No. You're different."

"I am, but I could have been. He never got that love and family made having the power and the business matter, not the other way around."

"But you do."

"I do." The absolute conviction in Vik's tone touched her to the core.

"Perry really played into your hands, didn't he?"

Vik shrugged. "We would have married, one way, or another."

"Because you loved me and could not imagine your life without me."

Vik's smile was brighter than the sun in the height of summer. "Exactly."

"Ditto."

Their shared laughter floated over the bay as their bodies pressed together in the most basic promise of all.

Shared love for a lifetime.

* * * * *

THE FLAW IN
RAFFAELE'S REVENGE

ANNIE WEST

An enormous thank you to dear Abby Green, who heard my plot ideas then asked why I didn't combine them.

I loved our rare chance to talk stories!

And a huge thank you to Franca Poli for your support and patient assistance with your lovely language.

Any errors are mine.

PROLOGUE

RAFFAELE PETRI POCKETED his credit card and left the water-front restaurant. Ignoring the stares, he nodded his thanks to the waiter. The service had been excellent, attentive but not fawning, the tip well-earned.

Raffaele hadn't forgotten how it felt to depend on the goodwill of rich foreigners.

He paused, his eyes adjusting to the sunshine. The sea glittered as it slapped the whiter-than-white yachts. The salt tang was strong on the air and he breathed deep, relishing it after the overpowering perfume of the women who'd tried to catch his attention from the next table.

He sauntered past huge yachts and motor cruisers. The Marmaris waterfront was packed with ostentatious displays of wealth. Just the place to invest, if his research was right, which it always was. This trip to Turkey would be profitable and—

A bray of laughter froze his footsteps. The hoarse, distinctive sound ran up his spine like dancing skeletal fingers, pinching his skin.

Raffaele's breath rushed in like the snap of a spinnaker in a stiff breeze. The laugh came again, yanking his attention to a towering multistorey cruiser. Sunlight polished the chestnut hair of the man leaning from the upper deck, shouting encouragement at two women on the promenade.

The ground beneath Raffaele's feet seemed to heave and buckle, mirroring the tumble of his constricting gut. His hands rolled tight as he stared at the florid man waving a champagne glass at the women.

'Come on up. The bubbly's on ice.'

Raffaele knew that voice.

Even after twenty-one years he recognised it.

That smug tone, that hoarse laugh, had crept through his nightmares since he was twelve.

He'd given up hope of finding him. He'd never known the man's name and the slimy villain had disappeared from Genoa faster than a rat leaving a scuttled ship. No one had listened to a skinny twelve-year-old who'd insisted the foreigner with hair the colour of *castagne* was to blame for Gabriella's death.

Gabriella...

Fury ignited. The wrath of thwarted retribution, of loathing and grief.

The blast of emotion stunned him.

He'd spent his life perfecting the art of not feeling, not caring for anyone, not *trusting,* since Gabriella. But now... It took everything he had merely to stand still and take in the scene.

Keenly he catalogued everything, from the guy's features, grown pudgy with age and self-indulgence, to the name of the cruiser and the fact his staff, neat in white shorts and shirts, spoke English as only natives could. One of them offered to help the women aboard.

Girls, Raffaele amended, not women. Both blonde, both in their teens, though one was made up to look ten years older. Raffa was an expert on make-up and on women.

The Englishman's tastes hadn't changed. He still liked them young and blonde.

Bile rose. Raffa's heart thrashed with the need to climb aboard and deliver justice for Gabriella with his fists. There was no doubt this was the same man.

But Raffa was no longer an impulsive, grieving kid.

Now he had the power to do more than beat the man to a bloody pulp. That thought alone held him back. Even so, it was a battle to rein in his need for instant vengeance.

'Ciao, bella.' He strolled forward, curling his mouth in a half smile the camera, and millions of women the world

over, loved. Not for a second did he lift his gaze to the middle-aged man above them.

'Lucy—' The taller one nudged her companion. 'Quick. Turn around. He looks like… He couldn't be…could he?'

Two pairs of eyes widened as he approached. Twin gasps of excitement. The one who'd spoken smiled wide while her companion looked dazed.

Raffa was used to dealing with besotted fans. But instead of a nod of acknowledgement before moving on, he increased the wattage of his smile in an invitation that had never once failed.

The taller girl stepped closer, pulling her friend along, the boat and its owner forgotten. They didn't even blink as the man above them called agitated instructions for them to come aboard.

'You look just like Raffaele Petri. I suppose people say that all the time.' Her voice was breathless and young. Too young for the man on the boat. Or for Raffa. The difference was that with him she'd be safe.

'That's because I *am* Raffaele Petri.'

Twin gasps met the announcement and the smaller girl looked as if she might faint.

'Are you all right?'

She nodded, goggle-eyed, while her friend dragged out her phone. 'Do you mind?'

'Of course not.' The world was full of amateur photos of him. 'I was going to get a coffee.' He gestured to a street leading away from the waterfront. 'Care to join me?'

The girls were so busy chattering as they walked that only Raffa heard the Englishman's abusive yells. He'd been deprived of his afternoon's amusement.

Soon he'd be deprived of everything that mattered to him.

The Englishman wouldn't escape again. Justice would be sweet.

This time Raffa's smile was genuine.

CHAPTER ONE

'STOP PULLING MY LEG, Pete.' Lily leaned back from the desk and shifted her grip on the phone. 'It's been a long day. You might be just waking up in New York but it's bedtime in Australia.'

Looking towards the window, she saw the reflection of her office in the glass. Her house was too far from town for street lights and the stars wouldn't show till she switched off her lamp. She rubbed her stiff neck. Completing this project within deadline and to her own exacting standards had been tough.

'No joke.' Pete's usually laid-back voice with its Canadian accent sounded excited. 'The boss wants you here and he never jokes about business.'

Lily straightened in her seat, her pulse thudding. 'You're serious?'

'Absolutely. And what the boss wants, the boss makes a policy of getting. You know that.'

'Except Raffaele Petri isn't my boss.' Even saying his name aloud seemed somehow ridiculous. What could she, ordinary Lily Nolan, living in a rundown farmhouse an hour south of Sydney, have in common with Raffaele Petri? 'He doesn't know I exist.'

Petri inhabited a stellar plane ordinary mortals only dreamed of or read about in gossip magazines, while she...

Lily dropped the hand she'd lifted to her cheek. She hated that old, nervous gesture.

'Of course he knows. Why do you think you've had so much work from us? He was impressed with your report for the Tahiti deal and asked for you on every one since.'

Lily blinked. She'd never imagined Signor Petri himself

reading her research reports. She'd assumed he had other things to do with his time, like indulging himself at the world's most luxurious fleshpots.

'That's fantastic, Pete. I can't tell you how pleased I am.' Despite her recent success, the size of the loan she'd taken to buy this house and expand the business kept her awake at night. But after years feeling like an outsider she'd been driven by the need to establish her own place in the world, something *she'd* achieved and could be proud of. Even though it meant moving across the continent from her anxious family. She needed this to turn her life around.

Tight muscles eased. If Signor Petri had personally commented on her work—

'Excellent. You'll find the contract in your inbox. It will be great finally putting a face to the voice once you're working here.'

'Whoa. Wait a minute.' Lily shot to her feet. 'I meant I'm pleased to have what I do valued. That's all.' She drove herself to excel and knew her service was first class, but it was reassuring having it confirmed by her most influential customer, especially now she had this mortgage.

'You *don't* want to accept the boss's offer to work here?' Pete's hushed tone made it sound as if she'd refused mankind's only chance to find a cure for cancer.

'That's right.' The thought of being in a city, surrounded by millions of people, being *seen* by strangers every day, made her flesh crawl as if she were breaking into hives. She even avoided driving into her small town when possible, opting to have her groceries delivered. Working in New York, constantly facing curious stares, would be a nightmare. It was one thing to be confident about your work and your worth, quite another to run the gauntlet of constant public interest.

'You're joking. Who wouldn't want to work for Raffaele Petri?'

Lily threaded her fingers through her long hair, pushing

it from her face. 'I already work for him, off and on.' Her contract work for his company had been so lucrative it had made her enormous mortgage possible. The prestige of his name on those regular contracts had convinced even the cautious loans officer. 'But I'm my own boss. Why would I want to change that?'

Her independence, her ability to *control* her life, meant everything. Perhaps because her world had been impacted irrevocably by a single, senseless event that had robbed her of so much.

A moment's silence told her how bizarre her attitude seemed.

'Let's see. The kudos for a start. Work for him and you can walk into any job you like. He only employs the best. Then there's the salary. Read the contract before you reject it, Lily. Chances like this don't just come along.'

His tone was urgent. But Lily knew what was right for her.

'Thanks for your interest, Pete. I appreciate it, really I do. But it's not possible.' She forked her hand through her hair again, for a millisecond wondering what opportunities she might have pursued if her life had been different. If *she* were different.

She dropped her hand, disgusted with herself. She couldn't change the past. Everything she wanted, everything she aspired to, was within her grasp. All she had to do was work towards her goals. Success, security, self-sufficiency. *That* was what she wanted. Not jostling with commuters or being a drone in a corporation. Or hankering after places she'd never visit.

'Lily, you can't have considered. At least think about it.'

'I have, Pete, but the answer is no. I'm happy here.'

At first she thought the chirruping noise was the dawn chorus. Each morning magpies and cockatoos greeted the first light. But this was too monotone, too persistent. Groaning, Lily opened her eyes. It was still night.

Pulse thundering, she groped for the phone. No one rang at this time unless it was an emergency.

'Hello?' She struggled to sit up, shoving her pillow behind her back.

'Ms Lily Nolan?'

The pulse that an instant ago had sprinted in her arteries gave a single mighty thump. The deep male voice was foreign, rich and dark like a shot of espresso.

She groped for the bedside light and squinted at her watch. Minutes to midnight. No wonder she felt groggy. She'd only slept half an hour.

'Who's speaking?'

'Raffaele Petri.'

Raffaele Petri!

To her sleep-addled senses that voice sounded like liquid seduction. She frowned and pulled the neck of her sleep shirt closed. Male voices didn't affect her that way. But then how many sounded like this?

'Are you still there?'

'Of course I'm here. I've just woken up.'

'*Mi dispiace.*' *I'm sorry.*

He didn't sound sorry. He sounded…

Lily shook her head. If it *was* Raffaele Petri this was business. She couldn't afford to think about how potently male he sounded. Even if her hormones were dancing at the sound of that deliciously accented voice.

'Signor Petri—' She raked her hair from her face, shuffling higher in the bed. 'What can I do for you?'

'Sign the contract and get here *subito*.'

Lily choked down her instinctive response. The only place she was going *subito*, immediately, was back to sleep.

'That's impossible.'

'Nonsense. It's the only sensible course of action.'

Lily breathed deep, letting the chilly night air fill her

lungs as she sought calm. He wasn't only her client, he was her most important client.

'Did you hear me?'

'Yes.'

'Good. When you've arranged your flight give my assistant the details. He'll organise for you to be met at the airport.'

This must be how Renaissance Italian princes had sounded. As if every word they spoke was law. Imagine having such confidence you'd always get what you desired.

'Thank you, but I won't be contacting Pete.' She cleared her throat, her voice still husky from sleep. 'I was very flattered by your offer, Signor Petri, but I prefer working for myself.'

'You're turning me down?' His soft voice raised the hairs on the back of her neck.

Had anyone ever denied Raffaele Petri what he wanted?

Lily's heart thudded. She was on dangerous ground.

Widely touted as the most beautiful man in the world, he'd become famous as the golden-haired, outrageously handsome face, and body, that had turned designer casual into a style men around the globe aspired to emulate. No doubt he'd had women saying yes all his life.

But he had far more than looks. After leaving modelling he'd defied the critics and proven himself über-successful in business. Wealthy and powerful, Raffaele Petri was clearly used to instant compliance.

'I'm very flattered by the offer—'

'But?' That purr of enquiry barely concealed a razor-sharp edge.

Lily drew in a slow breath. 'Unfortunately I'm not in a position to accept.'

Silence. Long enough for her to wonder if she'd burned her bridges. Fear skated through her. She needed the work his company sent.

'What would have to change so you'd be in a position to accept?'

Damn the man. Why couldn't he just accept no?

'May I ask instead why you want me?' For a nanosecond heat surged at the unintentional double meaning of her words. But the idea of Raffaele Petri wanting her for anything other than work was so utterly unbelievable it rapidly faded. 'I was told you were happy with my research and our current arrangement.'

'If I were unhappy with your work I wouldn't offer you a job, Ms Nolan.' His clipped tones twisted her tension higher. 'I want you here on my team because you're the best at what you do. Simple as that.'

The heat suffusing her this time came from gratification.

'Thank you, Signor Petri. I appreciate your good opinion.' She'd love to ask about a testimonial but the throbbing silence told her this wasn't the time. 'Please know I'll continue to offer the best possible service.' She wriggled back against the pillow.

'That's not enough.'

'Sorry?' What more could he want than her best?

'I'm starting a significant project.' He paused. 'I need my team on hand and bound by the utmost confidentiality.'

Lily stiffened. 'I hope you're not implying I'm a security risk. Every contract I accept is completed in strictest confidence. I safeguard my research and my clients.' She never shared details of clients without permission. Which was why it would have been a coup to have a testimonial from him on her website.

She'd begun as a researcher for a private enquiry firm but the cases got her down. She'd found her niche when she widened her horizons—from staff checks to analyses of businesses and commercial trends. Lately it had been the viability of new ventures or businesses ripe for takeover.

That was where Raffaele Petri came in. The man was like a shark scenting blood before his competitors. Every time she investigated a business for him she'd discovered vulnerabilities and problems. It was the magic of the man that, once he acquired them, he turned those businesses into some of the most successful in the leisure industry, from a glamorous resort in Tahiti to a marina and yacht-building company in Turkey.

'If I doubted your ability to keep a secret I wouldn't hire you.'

Lily released a breath, relief rising.

'But,' he added, 'I can't afford risks. This team will be the best of the best. And it will be in New York. I need you here.'

Pride swelled. Lily had never been *needed*. Never stood out. Looks, school grades, sport, she'd always been average, never in the limelight until—

Lily shook her head in self-disgust at that old neediness. It was a spill over from her teenage years when she'd felt no one really wanted her, that to her family she was only a burden and a worry. And to her friends an embarrassing, constant reminder of a disaster they'd rather forget. She'd hated that awareness of being included out of duty rather than because her peers wanted her around.

His words made her long to say, *Yes, of course, I'll be in New York tomorrow.*

Imagine exploring the Big Apple. Imagine...

She swallowed hard. It wasn't possible. Facing the curious eyes of all those strangers, seeing them stare in fascination or hurriedly turn away. She wouldn't put herself through that anymore.

'I'm used to working with your staff from a distance. I'm sure—'

'That's not the way this project will proceed, Ms Nolan.' His words were staccato, tiny darts pricking her skin. 'I won't tolerate failure on this one.'

Lily opened her mouth to say that if his project failed it wouldn't be down to her.

'Yes, Ms Nolan? You were saying?'

'I'm sorry I can't accommodate you, Signor Petri.'

'I'll double the salary. And the bonus on completion.'

Lily's eyes widened. She'd been curious enough to check the contract and the salary had staggered her. It was more than she'd earn in two years. The thought of four years' income in one hit was so tempting. It would solve her financial worries...

'Changing your tune, Ms Nolan? I thought you might.' That voice was smug now, making her want to hiss her displeasure. At him for thinking she could be bought? Or at herself for being tempted despite knowing it couldn't happen?

Part of her still hankered after adventure, travel, excitement. But she'd had to push those dreams aside when her life had derailed at fourteen. She'd been robbed of her best friend, her carefree youth, her 'normal' life. She'd even missed out on things everyone else took for granted like flirting with boys and dating.

She shook her head, long tresses slipping over her cheeks. Curse the man for stirring longings she'd put behind her years before.

She loved her home, was proud she'd saved enough to be buying it. But it was more than that. Lily *needed* the security and peace it provided. The sense of refuge.

'No, Signor Petri. That was the sound of surprise but not agreement.'

'Interesting, Ms Nolan. Most people would jump at this opportunity. Why aren't you? A family, is that it? You have a husband and children perhaps?'

'No! I don't—' Lily clamped her lips shut before she blurted out anything else. Instinctively she felt safer keeping her private life private from this man.

'No family? I thought you sounded a little young for one.'

Lily's eyebrows arched. At twenty-eight she wasn't so young. Or was he implying she didn't sound professional?

Or maybe he's just winding you up. This man enjoyed playing with her, like a cat with a trapped mouse.

Like a bully wielding his superior power.

Lily's chin shot up. 'I suppose age becomes important when one reaches…*mature* years.'

A little huff of sound reached her over the long distance. A gasp of irritation or, could it be, stifled laughter?

She shouldn't have said it. The veiled reference to his age, five years her senior, was indiscreet and possibly ruinous. But she refused to sit like a pincushion to be needled.

'Fortunately I'm not quite in my dotage, Ms Nolan.'

No, he wasn't. She kept seeing photos of him at glamorous functions. Always with a sophisticated woman on his arm, but never the same one.

'So if you don't have a family to tie you there it must be a lover.' His voice dipped low, like dark treacle rolling through her veins to eddy in her belly. Lily drew her knees up, pressing them to her chest, trying to kill the unsettling sensation.

'My private life is no concern of yours, Signor Petri.' Did he hear the wobble of fury in her voice?

'But it is, Ms Nolan, when it comes between me and what I want.'

'Then it's time you discovered you can't always get what you want.' The words poured out. 'I decide when and where I sell my services.'

Lily scrubbed a shaky hand over her face, her chest heaving. This was going from bad to worse. Anger and anxiety curdled her insides. And self-disgust. She needed to stay calm, no matter what the provocation.

'I assume you don't normally speak to your clients in that suggestively sexy voice.' His own voice was far too sultry. 'It would give them the wrong idea about what services you sell.'

Lily almost dropped the phone.

Suggestively sexy?

He had to be kidding! No man had ever called her sexy.

Of course he's kidding. He's playing with you, searching for your weak spots.

And finding them!

Curiously, the realisation calmed her, despite the burn of annoyance.

'There are reasons I can't work for you in New York, Signor Petri, but—'

'Name three.'

'Sorry?'

'I want to know why you reject my offer. Come on, three sound reasons.' The words shot out, quick and demanding, and before she knew it, Lily was answering.

'I don't have a passport for a start.' She winced. That made her sound like some country hick to a man who travelled the world as easily as she travelled it vicariously via the internet.

'That's one. What else?'

'I can't afford to rent a place in New York.'

'Not even with the bonus I'm offering?'

'I have commitments here. Any money I earn goes to those.'

'And the third? What's your third reason?'

Because she couldn't stand the thought of working in an office with other people? Because she wouldn't put herself through all that again?

Because she preferred solitude? She had a good life and an exciting business plan and no bullying magnate was going to disrupt those on a whim.

'You don't answer, Ms Nolan, which makes me think it's the most important reason of all. Or you don't have one.'

Sheer strength of will stopped Lily from blurting a response. He wasn't going to goad her again.

'Is it a lover holding you back?'

'You have no right to quiz me like this.'

'I have every right when it stymies my most important deal.'

Despite his monumental arrogance, Lily's ears pricked up. She was fascinated by this man's business acumen, his ability to see opportunities before anyone else. She'd love to know what this secret project was.

'You want my advice?' She was in the process of saying 'No' when he spoke over top of her. 'Ditch him, Ms Nolan. Find yourself a man who won't obstruct such a brilliant opportunity. You've got real talent. You shouldn't let him stand in the way of it.'

For a second Lily gawped. Raffaele Petri was beyond belief. If she had a partner she'd never leave him on the say-so of some self-important stranger.

'I wasn't aware you were an expert on relationships, Signor Petri. Aren't your girlfriends famous for being short-term?'

Lily gasped as she heard her thoughts slip out. She'd just scuttled her future with his company. But his behaviour, his whole attitude, was offensive.

A crack of laughter sounded on the line, resolving into a warm chuckle that did strange things to her insides.

Lily stiffened as fire tongued her sensitive flesh. A hot shiver ripped through her as if a warm masculine hand, rather than a disembodied voice, caressed her. She swallowed hard, horrified at her instantaneous response.

Wasn't it enough that the man looked like a Greek god come to life? Did he have to sound irresistible too? Lily pressed the heel of her palm to her sternum, trying to ease her heart's wild pounding.

She detested bullies. Her response was inexplicable.

Except it wasn't. She was a young, healthy woman, with the physical urges that went with that. Her hormones didn't care if he was a saint or the devil incarnate. All they cared about was that they'd been deprived of anything like excitement or satisfaction for far too long.

'Don't laugh at me!' Her words rapped out, too short, too sharp.

In the sudden silence she realised what she'd revealed. He knew he'd got to her.

Raffaele Petri might be a bully but he was clever. All the world knew he came from the backstreets of some large Italian city. His business success was a commercial miracle.

'What if I'm laughing at myself? Finally being called on my defects.' His voice held an edge but she couldn't tell if it was amusement or banked fury. 'My decrepit age. My lack of emotional staying power. What else, I wonder?' He paused. 'Have you been investigating me, Ms Nolan?'

Despite the rich cadence of his voice, Lily heard the threat in that low purr of sound.

'I haven't, Signor Petri. Your business, yes, before I agreed to work for it. But as for a personal profile...' She shook her head, her hair swirling. 'That wasn't necessary.'

'Because the paparazzi do such a thorough job of portraying someone's life, don't they?'

Lily frowned. Was that emotion? Had she hit a nerve?

'The passport can be fast-tracked. I'll get my people onto it. Accommodation will be arranged. Plus I'll have the contract altered to include the increased salary and bonus.' He paused, which was as well, because her head was spinning. His abrupt change of subject left her floundering. 'Appealing enough for you?'

The silence that followed was thick with expectation. He was waiting for her to agree before he hung up and dealt with whatever issue was next on his list.

Except Lily wasn't some problem to be fixed.

'I appreciate the offer, the very handsome offer,' she choked out, her fingers clamping the phone. 'But it won't work for me. I'm happy to do whatever I can from here—'

'But that won't work for *me*.' His voice sent a trickle of foreboding down her backbone.

For ten seconds there was silence. For twenty. But Lily

refused to back down. What he asked was impossible for her and she had too much pride to explain why.

'You leave me no choice, Ms Nolan. We'll find someone else to be principal researcher.'

Lily eased back against her pillow, shaky as the tension gripping her body finally began to abate.

'And my company won't hire you again.'

Lily couldn't stifle a hiss of shock. Air locked somewhere between her throat and her lungs as her body froze. Stars scattered her vision, dimming to pinpricks till, with a sagging release, her lungs began pumping again.

Without his business, hers was dead in the water. Four months ago she'd have weathered the setback but not now. Not since the loan and the expansion.

If she couldn't meet the repayments she'd lose everything—her work and her home. The life she'd so painstakingly built.

'Did you say something, Ms Nolan?'

Lily gulped to clear her throat but couldn't think of a thing to say.

'It won't take long for my dissatisfaction with your service to get out, either. You'd be surprised how fast news spreads. Continental boundaries don't mean anything and I have contacts around the world. From Melbourne to Mumbai, London to Los Angeles.'

Again that lethal pause, allowing her time to process the bleak scenario he'd painted. Her name would be mud with the really big enterprises, the internationals she'd set her sights on to make her expanded business a success.

'You'll go out of your way to blacken my name?' Her voice was a thin scratch of sound but at least it was steady. Unlike the rest of her. She shook as if with fever.

'I'll be sure to mention it whenever appropriate.' In other words he'd take delight in savaging her reputation.

Hatred coiled, tightening in her belly. Hatred as she'd only ever felt once before, for the guy who'd changed her life in an instant—from carefree to a grim round of medical treatments. Her hand lifted to her face.

Swallowing hard, Lily turned the nervous gesture into a defiant flick of the wrist, sending her long hair flying back from her face. Deliberately she set her chin, staring at her face reflected in the window.

One thing Raffaele Petri didn't know—she was a fighter. She'd survived far worse than he could dish out and emerged stronger as a result.

She lowered her hand, smoothing the quilt as she dragged in aching breaths. She opened her mouth to speak but he beat her to it.

'Of course if you were to change your mind…'

Fury swamped her. He knew she had no choice.

Even so, part of her brain noted that the snake in the Garden of Eden must have sounded like this. No hissing, no sharpness. Just a lush, seductive roll of sound that invited her to go against everything she knew and trusted. To take the plunge, even though it must end in disaster.

'You're nothing if not predictable, Signor Petri.' She pressed the phone to her ear but heard no response. 'Textbook bullying, in fact.'

Still nothing. His silence infuriated her but she refused to give him the satisfaction of hearing her rant. She looked at her hand, fisted so tight in her lap it was hard to prise open. When she did she saw scarlet crescents where her nails had scored.

'Very well, Signor Petri. I'll work for you.' Her lungs ached as she released the breath crammed in her chest. 'But you can change the contract to three times the original salary. Ditto with the bonus. Have it in my inbox tomorrow and if it's satisfactory I'll sign.' She paused, trying to control her sharp, shallow breaths.

To her astonishment he didn't disagree.

'I'll see you in New York, Ms Nolan.'

Not if I see you first.

She might be stuck working for him but she had no illusions he'd be part of the project team. He'd be sunning himself in the Bahamas or skiing in Switzerland or whatever the wealthy did when they weren't harassing ordinary people. Somehow she'd deal with the travel and all those people. She'd do the job, take his money and come back to build her future here as she'd planned.

She'd get through this.

'Goodbye, Signor Petri.'

'Not goodbye. *Arrivederci*, Ms Nolan.'

CHAPTER TWO

RAFFA GOT TO the office after a breakfast meeting.

Across the large room he saw an unfamiliar figure—long hair, loose shirt, loose trousers and flat shoes. The clothes were resolutely unfeminine but the body beneath all that unflattering drabness wasn't. Femininity was there in the way she moved, despite her rigid back and high shoulders.

It had to be Lily Nolan. The area was off-limits to all but his hand-picked team.

She'd been tense on the phone that night too. Uptight and angry, yet that husky, just-awake voice had done things to him no woman had in years.

He frowned at the unwanted memory.

Raffa's eyes narrowed on the rhythmic swish of hair down her narrow back as she walked away. It all but reached her waist. Not blonde or black or even dark but simply brown. A brown so ordinary and unremarkable it looked uncompromising, as if she spurned most women's desire to improve on nature with eye-catching colour.

He turned into his private office and took a seat, gesturing for his assistant to do the same. Through the glass walls he saw Lily Nolan talking with someone by the door to the conference room. Her body language radiated stress, right down to the fist clenching at her side.

Had he made a mistake bringing her here? He'd wanted her because of her talents, her often brilliant insights and her professionalism. He knew she'd go the extra mile to meet his needs.

But that night on the phone her obstinacy, the way she challenged him as no one else dared, had piqued his interest. He'd accepted her outrageous terms because every refusal she gave made him more determined to win.

The knowledge he'd acted on a whim had annoyed him ever since. He never allowed himself to be sidetracked. He'd got where he was by grabbing every opportunity to build his wealth and success. Even if some of those opportunities were unpalatable, they'd been necessary. He was never impulsive.

'How's our newest staff member fitting in? Any problems?'

'No, nothing like that.'

Was that a flush on Pete's boyish face? Raffa felt his eyebrows cinch together. The woman had been here less than a day. Surely she hadn't seduced his PA already?

'She's hit the ground running. She must be jet-lagged but she's already got acquainted with our set up here. Now she's meeting the rest of the team.' Pete swivelled his head towards the conference room, his gaze fixed.

Raffa realised it wasn't adoration on his assistant's face but something he couldn't read.

'Yet she makes you uncomfortable?'

Pete's face mottled red. Embarrassment? Lust?

'Of course not.' The words tumbled out too quickly. 'She's very professional.'

Professional. It sounded like faint praise. Especially since in the past he'd overheard Pete laughing with the woman over a long-distance connection.

'But?' Raffa fixed him with a stern gaze. His policy was to remove problems the instant they arose. If this woman disrupted the smoothly oiled workings of his team he'd take action immediately.

Pete shrugged. 'You know how it is when you know someone only from a distance. You build up a picture in your mind. The reality can be…different.' He gestured abruptly to the tablet he carried. 'About the review of the

Hawaiian hotel. Will I bring that forward? You'd mentioned a snap inspection to keep them on their toes.'

Raffa surveyed his PA, reading his discomfort. It was probably as Pete said—the deflating reality of the first face-to-face meeting. But Raffa never left anything to chance.

He'd planned to leave the rebellious Australian alone today to get on with the job for which he was paying such an exorbitant salary. And he would—after he'd checked her out.

'We're busy wrapping up some other projects but anything you need on the legal side, let me know.' Consuela Flores gave a brisk nod and smile from the end of the conference table and Lily felt herself sink back in her seat, a grateful answering smile on her face.

Among the group she'd be working with, the middle-aged lawyer had proved the easiest to deal with. Her severe demeanour, magenta power suit, expensive pearls and stiffly lacquered hair had made Lily wary. Here was an imposing woman for whom appearance as well as performance was important. Yet after a millisecond of silence when they met and that brief, predictable widening of the eyes, Ms Flores had treated Lily like everyone else around the table.

Lily had wanted to hug her for that.

This morning had been tough, every bit as difficult as she'd feared. Her hands were clammy, her chest weighted and her pulse still too fast. Forcing herself into the office had been a major test of nerves already strung out from the stress of travelling.

'Thanks, I appreciate that. For now, though, I suspect it won't be legal expertise I need. There'll be a lot of digging first.'

Consuela nodded. 'I'm glad it's you doing the digging. Your reports for the Turkish deal made our work much easier. There's nothing like heading into negotiations well-prepared, with no lurking pitfalls. Now you're onsite we can touch base as anything arises.'

Lily's smile grew, the clamp on her chest easing a little.

Only the knowledge she was up to this job, more than up to it, had got her across the Pacific, across the United States and into this building, when all she wanted was to lock herself inside her home and not budge.

She could do this, no matter how horribly far out of her comfort zone she felt.

No, she wouldn't just do the job. She'd excel! Her work meant everything. It was the one part of her world where she had complete control, complete confidence.

Which made it all the more infuriating that she'd been nauseous with nerves today. Fronting up at the office was the most difficult thing she'd done in years.

See what happens when you lock yourself away all the time?

Now it's you with the problem, not them.

Lily banished the voice in her head. She didn't have time for self-doubt.

'I'm looking forward to working with you too, Consuela.'

She darted a glance around the table. The woman from finance in retro-trendy glasses quickly turned her head as if she'd been watching the lawyer, not Lily. But she was too slow. Besides, the distressed twist of her lips, as if she felt ill, betrayed her.

Further down the table the guy from acquisitions flushed as Lily turned to him. Like Pete, Raffaele Petri's PA, he found looking at her embarrassing. Beside him the older man from systems management didn't even try, instead staring past her shoulder.

Lily sat straighter, determined not to be daunted.

Yet that didn't stop the sick feeling in her stomach, or the churning memories of her previous forays into office work. Each one a disaster. Eventually she'd given up trying and decided to work from the seclusion of home.

The fingers of her right hand twitched but she repressed the urge to raise her hand to her face. It had taken years to cure herself of the habit and she wasn't starting again now. No matter how exposed she felt before these strangers.

'I appreciate you all making time to meet me on my first day. I'll look forward to working with you.'

Liar!

'I have a question, though.' Lily looked to Consuela. 'We all have different areas of responsibility, but is there a team leader? Without coordination we'll have problems.'

'That would be me.' The masculine voice curled around her like warm smoke.

Her heart jolted and a prickling spread across her skin.

She'd only heard that voice once but its echo had lurked in her subconscious since, visiting in those moments between waking and sleep when she was most vulnerable.

Was that heat flushing her cheeks?

It couldn't be. She'd spent half her life being gawked at. She'd lost the ability to blush in her teens.

Reluctantly she turned her head.

It was a good thing she was sitting.

Raffaele Petri's face was known around the globe. Yet the photos hadn't prepared her. Tall, taller than she'd expected with his Italian heritage. Wide shoulders, slim hips, long legs—the epitome of masculinity in its prime. Oddly his casual jacket and open-necked shirt emphasised rather than detracted from the power she sensed in him. He didn't need a three-piece suit to stamp his authority.

Chiselled features that looked too close to perfection to be true. She'd assumed those photos had been airbrushed. Yes, there were crinkles around his eyes, as if from time in the sun, but perversely that only made him more attractive. Hair the colour of dark old gold, tidy but hinting at tousled. Enough to make her fingers twitch at the thought of touching. The hooded cast of his eyes looked languorous until you met that piercing blue stare.

Lily swallowed over a ball of sandpaper in her throat. Meeting his gaze was a palpable experience, as if he'd reached out and taken her hand. Sizzling heat ran through her as those eyes held hers—compelling, electric.

It wasn't just that he was ridiculously handsome, she realised as she forced a slow breath out. He was…*more*. Even from the other side of the conference table she felt the crackle of energy, the sense he was a man who made things happen.

Unhurriedly he surveyed her, cataloguing everything from the hair brushing her cheeks to her face, her throat and down as far as was visible above the table.

The old resentment rose, that he should scrutinise her like some animal in a cage. Till she realised she'd done the same—taking in his appearance in minute detail.

The knowledge sapped her anger, leaving her winded as his gaze lifted.

'At last we meet, Ms Nolan.'

So that explained it.

Realisation slammed into Raffa like a fist to the chest, so strong it felt like recognition. An unexpected hit of adrenaline.

But recognition implied a link with the woman on the far side of the table. That was nonsense, even if the memory of her husky voice and feisty attitude had intruded at the oddest times these past weeks. The pulse of energy he felt could only be satisfaction at getting to the bottom of his PA's discomfort.

Lily Nolan's long hair framed an oval face that should have been, at best, ordinary. Brown eyes, a mouth neither thin-lipped nor lush, an unremarkable nose. Beautiful she wasn't, but she might have been pretty if it weren't for the wide swathe of tight, shiny skin that ran from her temple down one cheek to her jaw.

Scars faded with time. How long had she had this? The colour wasn't livid and she'd had plastic surgery. It must have been a hell of a sight before that.

Not a knife wound. He'd seen enough in his youth to realise no knife marked like this.

A burn? Some other trauma?

'Signor Petri.' That familiar voice stirred something un-accustomed that for a heartbeat distracted him.

He circled the table, arm extended.

She hesitated then pushed her chair back to stand. Her long, buttoned-up shirt fell loose around her slim frame. Again her choice of clothes hit him. A deliberate attempt not to fit in? To make the point she was here under suffer-ance? As if he cared what his staff wore so long as they did their work.

Her hand clasped his. Smooth and cool and small.

She just topped his shoulder in her flat shoes, tilting her head to meet his eyes. At the movement her hair slid back off her cheek, revealing more of that shiny, scarred flesh. But it wasn't the blemish that drew his attention, it was the bright challenge in her eyes.

'I believe this is where I'm supposed to say it's a plea-sure to meet you, Signor Petri.'

A gasp from the other side of the room reminded him of the staff still there.

Raffa held her hand in an easy grasp, not ready to let go.

'That's right,' he murmured, bestowing a small smile. He'd won their little contest of wills and could afford to be gracious.

Yet he saw no softening in that stern expression, no easing in her rigidity. Not even a hint of response in those serious eyes.

Surprise flickered. It was rare to find someone genu-inely unresponsive to his charm.

Lily Nolan grew more interesting by the moment.

'It's definitely a pleasure to meet you, Lily.' He widened his smile just a fraction, lingering on her name. 'I've been looking forward to having you here as part of the team.'

Silence for just a moment too long. 'So I gather, since you went to such lengths to get me here.'

Another muffled sound came from nearby but Raffa didn't turn. He didn't care what anyone thought.

'You were certainly elusive.'

He waited, expecting her to pull her hand from his. Instead she stood, unmoving but for the fine vibration coursing from her hand to his. She was wound up tight, bottling in strong emotion.

Yet her eyes met his directly, nothing but challenge to be read there.

This woman would make a hell of a poker player. She betrayed no hint of weakness or discomfort.

His gaze zeroed in on a minuscule movement at the corner of her mouth. For a moment he wondered if it could be the scar pulling at her mouth, till he remembered there'd been no distortion of her lips when she spoke. The tiny flicker of movement was what then? Her biting her cheek?

'Did you want me for something now?' She looked pointedly at their joined hands and Raffa felt amusement bubble. She was so patently determined to be unimpressed. So ostentatiously unaffected by his looks or position. Perversely he liked it.

How long since he'd done anything, gone anywhere, and been treated like an average Joe?

It was a novelty he hadn't known he craved till a slip of a woman with muddy brown eyes looked at him as if he wasn't anything special.

'As a matter of fact, now is the perfect time to brief you in more detail about my expectations.' He turned and nodded to Pete. Moments later his stalwart PA had emptied the room and closed the door on them.

If Lily Nolan was intimidated she didn't show it. Her hand lay unresisting in his, as if making the point his touch was immaterial to her.

Who was this woman? She'd intrigued him from their first contact.

Raffa's world and the people in it were predictable. Mostly they wanted something from him—reflected fame, an 'in' to the best circles, business opportunities, sex. Everyone wanted something.

Except this woman who didn't want him at all.

Was that why she fascinated him? Because he'd grown bored?

Raffa released his hold. He had more significant things to concentrate on than the novelty of an employee who resented his authority.

Yet he admired the way she slowly slid her hand away, not snatching it, though he'd touched her far too long. Nor did she move back, but stood, taking stock as he did.

His eyes dipped to her loose, unattractive clothing. She'd gone too far with the dressing down, the not being just another cog in his corporate wheel.

Unless she dressed that way because the scar on her face wasn't the only one. Did she have other injuries that made it uncomfortable to wear fitted clothes? The thought stirred discomfort.

Because he'd brought her here against her wishes? The idea was ludicrous. Whatever her problems, he wasn't responsible for them. He employed her at an outrageously high salary and hitherto unheard of bonuses.

'Take a seat.' He gestured to the chair she'd vacated and sank into one beside it. He was determined to understand this woman. Then he could push her from his thoughts and get on with business.

She sat watching him, feet flat on the floor, hands clasped loosely. For all the world as if he, not she, was the one whose work had to impress.

Raffa felt his lips twitch. If ever he needed another negotiator on his acquisitions team he could do far worse than Lily Nolan.

Lily read that quirk of his sculpted lips and knew she amused him.

An icicle of frozen rage jabbed her side. She wanted to cry out but kept her mouth closed and her face calm. She'd weathered enough pity, horror, revulsion and sympathy to last a lifetime. A self-important tycoon who laughed at her because she wasn't a perfectly tailored, respectful employee hardly mattered.

Or was he amused by how unfeminine she looked? His inspection had raked her from head to toe.

Remarkably, though he'd surveyed her damaged face his gaze hadn't lingered longer there than anywhere else. Almost as if her scar were no more significant than the shape of her nose or the comfy shoes she'd grabbed rather than teeter in the unaccustomed heels she'd bought in a moment of weakness. As if a pair of shoes would transform her into just another office worker!

Not with her face.

Was that what amused him? The difference between his bronzed beauty and her marred features?

She swallowed hard, tasting sharp bitterness. She was jumping to conclusions. Raffaele Petri was selfish and ruthless. She had no proof he was shallow and cruel.

But the day was young.

It wouldn't be the first time someone had used her as a foil for their own beauty. In her final year at school a couple of new girls had befriended her, both beautiful, blonde and bubbly. For the first time in years Lily had felt accepted and valued. Till she overheard them discussing how letting her hang out with them made people see them as sympathetic and even prettier than they were.

Lily shoved the memories away, drawing back her shoulders, imagining strength streaming through her spine and lifted chin. Whatever his game, she was his match. She might not be much to look at but she'd developed a strength of purpose few could equal.

Silence stretched but she refused to fill it. If this was a test of willpower he'd be disappointed.

Eyes the colour of the Pacific Ocean met hers, piercing as if reading her thoughts.

'You're settled into your office?'

She nodded. 'Yes, thank you. Pete showed me around.'

To her horror she'd discovered the floor full, not of little rabbit-hutch cubicles where workers could hide from public view, but of spacious glassed-in offices that reduced noise levels but left everyone on show.

Worse was the fact her office was beside Pete and Raffaele Petri. The idea of working with this man watching her made something shrivel inside.

'And your accommodation? It's comfortable?'

Lily nodded. The size and luxury had overwhelmed her, reminding her she was a country girl, out of her depth in sophisticated New York. Fortunately jet lag had got the better of her last night before she'd had a chance to explore properly and feel like too much of a misfit. This morning she'd overslept and had to rush to get ready. All she'd really seen was the sybaritic black marble bathroom and the inside of her suitcase as she hunted for clothes.

'Yes, thank you. It's quite sufficient.'

'Sufficient?' His mouth kicked up in a smile that did strange things to her pulse, turning it from steady to riotous. It was bad enough when he'd smiled before. He'd looked so compellingly handsome he'd stolen her breath. But this was different—genuine, and more powerful for it.

'What's so amusing?' She sat straighter.

His eyes zeroed in on hers and a fizzle of heat zapped her bones. 'I've never heard my penthouse described as merely *sufficient*.'

CHAPTER THREE

'YOUR PENTHOUSE?' LILY COULDN'T hide the shock in her voice. 'I'm staying in your *penthouse*?' Her fingers dug at her chair's leather arms.

'No other floor has a roof garden or swimming pool.' He surveyed her as if analysing a curious specimen.

For the second time that day she felt almost like she were blushing.

'I didn't open the blinds. It was late and I was jet-lagged and—' She snapped her mouth shut before she blurted out any more. She'd had a vague impression of a spacious sitting room, of stylish furnishings, but she'd never dreamed...

'Never mind, you'll see the roof garden later.'

Lily shook her head. 'There won't be a later. I can't stay there.'

'But you said the accommodation was perfectly adequate.' This time his mouth didn't curl in a smile but she knew he was laughing at her. How could he not be when she was too thick to realise she'd spent the night in a Manhattan penthouse?

'It's your home. It wouldn't be appropriate.'

Raffa couldn't imagine any of the women he'd dated turning down an opportunity to move into his apartment, even if just the guest quarters. They'd see it as a stepping stone to more.

He'd known Lily Nolan was different from the moment she picked up the phone and spoke in that sultry midnight voice. It had evoked a fragile tendril of something—not quite arousal, but definite interest.

She continued to pique his interest. She was…refreshing. Intriguing. Not because of her damaged face or appalling clothes. He, of all people, was the last person to judge on looks.

How many years since he'd found any woman interesting?

He leaned closer, registering her subtle shift as she compensated by pressing back into her chair.

Did she dislike men or just him?

The fact he wondered pulled him up short.

He wouldn't be distracted into musing on Lily Nolan's likes and dislikes. But he *did* need to ensure he'd made the right decision, bringing her here. Too much rode on this.

'If I think the arrangement appropriate then who's to say otherwise?'

'Are you perverse with everyone or just me?' She spoke slowly, enunciating each syllable with clipped precision. 'I can't live in your home.'

'Is it your privacy you're concerned about? Are you worried I'll invade your space?'

The paparazzi labelled him a playboy because he wasn't seen with the same woman twice. No one knew that was due to boredom and a dislike of being the object of any greedy woman's avarice. These days his reputation for carnal pleasure owed everything to the fantasies of those he *hadn't* taken to bed. He hadn't desired a woman in years.

They always wanted something from him. Always had.

He hated how that made him feel.

Surely Lily Nolan didn't think he was so desperate he'd sexually harass his staff?

'The guest wing is separate, with its own entrance. There's a lock on the door connecting to the rest of the penthouse so you'll be quite alone.' In light of experience, *he* should be worried about *her* intruding.

Yet she remained silent. Indignation rose.

The sensation made him pause. Raffa couldn't remember the last time he'd felt it.

Because he always got his own way?

Or because there was little except business that he cared about, including what people thought of him?

'The arrangement is temporary. My PA had organised accommodation but there was trouble with burst pipes yesterday. The place is badly water damaged.'

'I could stay at a hotel.'

'You could, but you said you couldn't afford that. Something about spending your salary on other things.'

Her eyebrows lifted as if she recognised his curiosity and was surprised by it.

Dannazione! He was surprised by it!

'You couldn't have put me up somewhere else?'

'Because I'm rolling in cash?' She had a point. It would have been the work of a moment for Pete to make alternative arrangements. But Raffa was already financing her New York stay in style. Besides, having her close meant a chance to satisfy his curiosity.

'I didn't get rich by wasting money, Ms Nolan. The guest suite is empty and convenient for your work here. I can be sure you'll be on hand, doing what I want you to do, not off sightseeing.'

For a moment her eyes glowed and he could have sworn the temperature in the room rose a couple of degrees. But her temper didn't ignite. She really had phenomenal control.

Raffa refused to consider why he enjoyed testing it.

'You may recall I didn't want to come to New York. If you're concerned I'll get distracted I could go home and work there.'

He shook his head. 'You'll stay where you are till the other apartment is ready. I'm paying top dollar for your services. I want to be sure I get my money's worth.'

'You don't trust me?' Her head angled as if to view him better.

'I don't trust anyone till they prove themselves.'

Her gaze sharpened. 'You were the one eager to have me here.'

He shrugged and steepled his hands, elbows on the arms of his chair.

'Based on past performance, I judge you to be the person I need. But this project is more important than any you've done. Nothing will be left to chance.'

Lily looked into those bright blue eyes, felt the intensity of that searing stare and knew they'd reached the heart of things.

She felt the change in him. The quickening, the sizzle of energy.

Their conversation up to now had been skirmishes. Maybe he kept all new staff on their toes till he was convinced of their worth. Though why he'd take such a personal interest in her she couldn't fathom.

'Why is it so important?'

The furrow on his tanned brow disappeared as he leaned back. 'I won't brook failure on this.'

As far as Lily knew he never failed. Raffaele Petri had a nose for a good deal and a reputation for success. He also had an unerring instinct for what would appeal to the wealthiest clientele. That was how he'd built his fortune, with elite resorts, clubs and now marinas servicing those who demanded the best in everything. The rich always had enough to spend on themselves despite economic downturns that affected people like her, struggling to make a go of things.

'This man I'm to focus on, Robert Bradshaw...'

'Yes?'

'Can you tell me about him?'

'That's your job. I want a full report—his business interests, friends and connections. Everything.' Raffaele

Petri's expression didn't alter but Lily heard something in his voice that made the hair at her nape rise.

She had the disquieting certainty she was venturing into dangerous waters. Once more instinct yelled at her to back out. But she had no choice. He'd destroy her reputation if she reneged on this job.

'It would help if you told me something about the project.'

He regarded her, unblinking, and she shivered. It was said Raffaele Petri could seduce a woman with a glance from those stunning ocean-blue eyes. Not that he'd ever turn his fabled seduction skills on her. But what she read there now was hard calculation. Shrewdness as if he assessed her, deciding how much to share.

Not much, if the firm set of his sculpted jaw was an indication.

Lily stared back, trying to ignore the tremor of feminine response fluttering through her belly and the teasing trickle of heat in her blood.

What a time for her hormones to wake up from hibernation!

She breathed deep, corralling her thoughts. 'My other commissions for you have been to research companies or commercial trends, even localities.' They had been to determine if a site or company would be a good investment. 'This time it's about a man.'

Still he said nothing, as if waiting to see how far she could go connecting the dots.

Exasperation rose. 'Is there a particular angle I'm to focus on?'

'I told you. Everything. The size and nature of his income. His business associates. His interests, his weaknesses and habits. Who he sleeps with. The lot.'

Was it imagination, or did that stare harden?

She didn't imagine it. His voice when he'd said 'who he sleeps with' was different, his Italian accent stronger, like rich chocolate coating a lethal stiletto blade. She fought to repress a shiver. Whoever Robert Bradshaw was, whatever he'd done, she'd hate to be in his shoes.

In that instant Lily felt what she'd understood only intellectually before: Raffaele Petri would be a dangerous enemy.

Just as well she was too insignificant to be his enemy.

'I see.' She didn't, but clearly he wasn't going to enlighten her. 'Okay. I'll do the best I can.'

'That's not good enough. I need to know you'll deliver the goods.'

'You'll get your report, Signor Petri. But it will take time. This is a broad brief.' She waved one hand, trying to look brisk and organised, despite the chill sinking between her shoulder blades. 'His commercial interests and associates I can uncover. I'll do a thorough check on all those. His property and lifestyle, ditto. But there are limits.'

'Limits?' Dark eyebrows rose as if he'd never heard the word.

'I'm a researcher, Signor Petri, not a private detective. If you want information on this man's personal life, you'd do better hiring one of those. They can stake out his residence and give you an account of his comings and goings.'

He was already shaking his head. 'I learned long ago not to trust them. I want results, not excuses.'

Surprised, Lily leaned forward, then froze as she registered a warm, spicy scent. It teased her nostrils, sending shockwaves of delight to her belly.

It made her think of photos she'd seen of this man years ago. He'd lain half naked on a rumpled bed, jaw shadowed and his arms raised behind his head in a pose that accentuated the impressive musculature of his chest and arms. The sight had coaxed millions of women to buy decadently expensive aftershave for their men.

Was that what she smelled now? Lily inhaled, wondering at the art of producing a fragrance that seemed so purely natural, like hot male flesh and forbidden longing.

Abruptly she pulled back, trying to remember her train of thought.

That was it. When had he used private detectives in the past, and why didn't he like them?

His expression made it clear he wouldn't answer.

She shrugged. 'It's up to you. I'm just warning you that there are limits to my capabilities.'

'Yet you once worked in a private detection firm, even received some training.'

Lily stared. He knew *that* about her? She tried to recall how much detail she'd included on her résumé, but what really surprised her was that he'd read it personally.

'It was a long time ago and I didn't qualify as a private investigator. The work didn't suit me.' She'd got sick of grubbing around in people's personal lives. Commercial research was much less seedy.

'But you have the skills. I want everything, from Bradshaw's finances to his phone records.'

Lily laid her hands in her lap, maintaining her aura of calm despite the alarm bells going off in her head.

'Unless you have a warrant, phone records are protected.' She paused, breathing deep. 'Obviously you're not talking about hacking into phone company records.'

Those straight, decisive eyebrows rose. 'Aren't I? But I understood you included hacking in your skill set.'

Lily reared back, her seat sliding away from the conference table. 'How did you know that? It was years ago.'

Her breath came in staccato bursts. It had been years since anyone had mentioned her one brush with the law. She'd been just a kid, bored from being alone so much, cut off from her friends by the regime of medical treatment and surgery she'd undergone. And by the fact that to a lot of her schoolmates she'd become a freak. Not just because of her scars, but because she'd been the one to survive. She'd wondered if they felt guilty because secretly they'd have preferred it if her popular friend Rachel had lived, not her.

Emotion tugged at her like an ocean current, threatening to pull her under.

Instead she focused on Raffaele Petri—so strong and arrogant and utterly in control. She'd bet he'd never felt overwhelmed or insecure. Surprisingly, that worked. Her racing pulse slowed.

'I chose the best for this project team, with the best skill set. Your short-lived career as a hacker was impressive. It's a wonder you got off so lightly.'

Lily crossed her arms over her chest. 'I was underage. And I did no damage.'

'No, just managed to break into one of the best protected and encrypted government databases in the world.'

'If you hired me to break the law, think again, Signor Petri. I won't do that for any client.' She sprang to her feet and paced away.

That was better. At last he read something definite in Lily Nolan. Not just anger but indignation and surely a little fear?

He didn't want to scare her. But she'd sparred with him for so long he'd begun to wonder what it would take to probe past her control. Even when she was angry she'd been coolly poised, a challenge, a mystery he couldn't resist prodding.

Not now. Now Raffa saw the woman behind the mask of calm self-sufficiency.

What he saw heightened his interest.

Lily Nolan's eyes flashed fire as she turned to face him. Her lips moved in what he was sure was an unconscious pout of defiance. A pout any red-blooded man would respond to.

Except he was her boss.

He never harassed his staff.

Besides, he wasn't into kissing. He'd perfected the art from necessity but never really enjoyed it. It was a tool like any other to get what he wanted.

Raffa stilled, surprised at his blurring thoughts. He didn't want to kiss Lily Nolan. The idea was farcical.

He wanted to understand her. Label and catalogue her so she no longer took up even a scintilla of his brain space. Then he'd move on to more important things.

Yet now he'd provoked a reaction he wanted more. Contempt welled. Had he turned into what he'd always abhorred? A wealthy man so self-absorbed his only delight was toying with others?

'You have scruples, Ms Nolan.'

She strode back to stand close, hands on her hips.

'There are lines I won't cross, Signor Petri. Breaking the law is one.'

Spoken like a woman who'd never experienced real need. Raffa's mouth tightened. He knew precisely the depths to which poverty and desperation could drive people.

Or was that the excuse he used to justify his past?

'Not even for money?'

Those eyes weren't muddy brown now. They looked almost pure amber, rimmed with honey brown, and they met his with quiet certainty. 'Not even for money.'

Slowly he nodded. 'Good. Then presumably you can't be bought by a competitor to betray confidential information.'

A furrow appeared on her forehead. 'Was all this some elaborate test of my honesty?'

Raffa shrugged. Easier to let her believe his interest was so straightforward than try to explain something he didn't understand himself.

If her report was insufficient, he'd have to ignore his prejudice and hire a detective. At least now he wouldn't be sucked in by nebulous 'promising leads' that required just a little more time to produce results.

Years ago, when he'd begun making decent money, he'd

spent lavishly on fruitless investigations. Older than his years in most ways, his desperation to find the man responsible for his sister's death had made him gullible in this one area.

Now he knew better. He didn't trust investigators.

He didn't trust anyone.

Raffa pushed his chair back and stood. 'We'll meet when you've completed your initial report.'

By that time this fascination would have worn off. She'd be just another employee.

CHAPTER FOUR

THERE WAS NO SOUND, no disturbance, but suddenly Lily knew she was no longer alone.

Her spine tingled from her scalp to her tailbone. Her skin drew tight and she realised she'd frozen, fingers on the keyboard, waiting.

Slowly she lifted her head.

There he was, one shoulder propped against the door-jamb, legs casually crossed at the ankles. The only man whose presence she could sense with unerring accuracy.

Every time.

Even before he looked at her.

Even when he never looked at her.

It was a sixth sense, something primitive, buried so deep in her animal instinct as to be inexplicable. Yet it happened whenever Raffaele Petri got near. Lily was always the first to notice his presence. Her senses were on alert when he was nearby, even if he wasn't talking to her.

Now he watched her with a heavy-lidded look that made her blood surge.

She'd thought him stunning in the casual trousers and jackets he wore in the office. But in formal clothes… Her eyes widened. He looked like some sinfully gorgeous fallen angel wearing a tuxedo and a lazy half smile. The bow tie loose around his collar added a decadently raffish air.

'Working late again?'

Lily nodded and cleared her throat. Ridiculous that he had this effect after more than a month, but there was no mistaking the excited pump of her heart or that sudden breathlessness.

It did no good to tell herself millions of other women

had the same reaction. Or that she made a fool of herself. All she could do was ensure no one, most especially the man before her, guessed.

'But obviously not to impress the boss.' He crossed his arms but Lily kept her eyes on his face, refusing to dwell on the way the gesture emphasised the impressive symmetry of his broad-shouldered, slim-hipped frame.

'You think not?' Her voice worked after all.

What she'd give for an interruption! These days other members of staff were in and out of her office regularly. To her surprise, after their initial shock they'd accepted her as one of the team—so different from her other work experiences. Maybe because she'd been so focused on this project she hadn't had the leisure to stress about their reactions?

Yet a frantic glance through the glass walls told her they were alone. Everyone had gone home long ago.

'I know not.' He straightened and, to her alarm, stepped into her office.

'You're a mind-reader now too?' The words blurted out.

'In addition to what?' He stopped a couple of paces from her desk, sucking all the oxygen out of her office. 'No, don't tell me. I'll enjoy the challenge of working it out.'

Lily sat back, letting her hands drop to her lap. His words were light, as if he viewed their interactions as some sort of game.

Well, she wasn't playing.

Especially since his light tone didn't match that assessing scrutiny.

'How do you know I'm not trying to impress you with my diligence?' Better to stick to concrete issues than try to guess what was going on in that brilliant, convoluted mind.

He shrugged, the fluid movement innately Italian.

'You never look to me for approval. You don't hang about my office asking questions or showing off your success with what you've unearthed about Bradshaw.'

Lily's mouth twitched, a smile hovering at the implication he'd been impressed. But she was too much on edge to allow her lips to curve up. If she let down her guard with this man, she sensed she might never be able to resurrect it.

No matter how charming he could be, Raffaele Petri was dangerous. He'd forced her here. He'd unleashed a sexual awareness in her that terrified her. Every day and every night he'd loomed in her thoughts, a forbidden temptation when she should have been focusing on work or sleep or anything but mortifyingly sensual imaginings.

'You see the end results anyway.' Carefully she laced her fingers together as if relaxed. 'What would be the point of hanging around your office showing off every little success?'

Those sculpted lips stretched in a smile that tugged a sexy crease down one tanned cheek.

Heat drilled from Lily's lungs to her belly, cramping her abdominal muscles and stirring sexual arousal, instant and unmistakable.

That was why she needed to be vigilant. Raffaele Petri didn't just have the power to make or break her. He made her crave things that were impossible.

'You're paying for the best.' It had taken her a long time to develop self-confidence about her work and she refused to play coy about something that meant so much. 'I'm not so needy I require a pat on the head every time I do well.'

If she'd aimed to deflect his attention she'd erred. Instead of backing off, he surveyed her through narrowed eyes.

'Sometimes it's not about a pat on the head,' he murmured. 'Sometimes people just want my attention.'

Lily looked up into that bright, deliberate gaze, sifting his words.

Seeking attention.

From him.

Why? As soon as she asked the question she had the answer. Because they were attracted to him. Because they wanted him to notice them, respond to them. Just as a tiny, unstoppable part of her had fantasised he might—

She moved so abruptly her chair slid back from the desk, rolling till it crashed into the wall.

Lily found herself standing, her stomach churning so hard she tasted bile. He'd touched too close to her own secret desires and made them seem all the more pathetic. As if he suspected the attraction she couldn't quell.

Her right hand lifted in that old, compulsive gesture she'd taken years to vanquish. At the last moment, just before her fingers reached her scarred face, she remembered, forcing it back down, planting both palms on her desk. Her hands were damp against the wood, her throat jammed with distress.

It wasn't just that Raffaele Petri would never find her attractive. *No* man would.

She was experienced enough to accept that, after several painful experiences where she'd tentatively reached out to a man and had to endure horrified, embarrassed rejection. Yet some foolish part of her still fantasised.

It wasn't him she was angry with, but herself.

'You mean they want you to notice them because they're attracted to you?' Her voice was raw, stretched tight.

'It's been known to happen.' Again that fluid shrug, but she was beyond noticing how appealing it was. She was too caught up with the burn of shame and self-consciousness.

'You're annoyed I haven't fallen over myself to get your attention?' She almost choked on the words. Pride was her only lifeline and she clung to it tenaciously. 'You do realise there are some people who aren't bowled over by your beauty, Signor Petri?' Her tone made it clear she was one of them.

If only that were true! Daily exposure to Raffaele Petri had done nothing to inoculate her against his golden good looks. Instead it had given her a respect for his incisive decision-making and his ability to get the best out of his team. She'd discerned fairness and even a self-deprecating humour she found far too appealing.

The sound of laughter sliced her thoughts. Rich and warm, it encircled her like a caress. There was nothing calculated about it, or about his expression, and Lily had the impression that for a moment she saw Raffaele Petri as few did. For, despite his approachability to his staff, he usually exuded a sense of being utterly self-contained.

'You're absolutely right, Lily.' Her pulse gave a throb of pleasure at the sound of her name in that deep, lush voice. 'And an antidote to my overblown ego. Not everyone finds me attractive. It's good to know you're one of them. It makes working together much simpler.'

Lily breathed out slowly. Had she really fooled him? Maybe all those years masking her feelings and learning not to show vulnerability had stood her in good stead.

'What is it you want from me?' He hadn't singled her out again since her first day in the office, yet she hadn't been able to shake the feeling he noticed her almost as much as she did him. That he was aware of her, even when his attention was on something else. Not that he was attracted to her, of course, just assessing.

'Honestly?' Eyes of searing blue met hers and heat feathered her skin. 'I find you…interesting. Different.'

She snorted. This time she didn't stop her hand as it rose to her face. But, instead of touching scarred flesh, she deliberately pushed her hair back, tucking it behind her ear, revealing the whole marred side of her face.

Her chin angled higher as her gaze challenged his, defiant. 'Oh, I'm definitely different.'

'You think I'm talking about looks?' His eyebrows flattened in something close to a scowl.

It was her turn to shrug stiff shoulders. The movement had none of his beautiful fluidity. 'What else?'

He shook his head. 'I don't know.' For a moment he

looked almost perplexed. 'But it's got nothing to do with the way you look.'

Lily didn't know whether to be relieved or ridiculously hurt.

'Perhaps it's because I don't beat a path to your door.'

His eyebrows rose. 'If you had your way we'd be a hemisphere apart.'

Lily crossed her arms, projecting an ease she didn't feel. 'You're too used to people chasing you.'

'You think this is about ego?' He paused as if considering. 'Perhaps. But it's more too. I like the lateral way you think. The combination of solid, thorough research and inspired leaps of imagination. I saw it in your report on the Tahitian project and the ones since.'

Lily felt her strain ease, her muscles loosening. Professional accolades she'd accept gratefully. It was when they veered off work that discomfort grabbed her.

'I like that you're not afraid to voice your opinions.'

'I don't see any yes-men on your team.'

'Ah, but you take your independence to a fascinating new level. It's obviously a point of honour.'

'There's nothing special about me, Signor Petri. I'm merely a professional, used to being self-employed rather than having a boss.'

For too long he regarded her with that steady gaze she suspected saw too much.

'Maybe you're right.' He lifted his hands, closing the collar of his formal shirt then deftly tying the black satin bow tie.

Lily watched, fascinated to realise such a process could be so enthralling. Not just the fact he managed a bow tie with impressive ease and without a mirror, but that the action should be almost…arousing.

'Lily?'

She blinked. 'Yes?'

'I asked if it's straight.'

'Almost, just at a slight angle.'

'This way?' He twitched the black silk and she shook her head. 'Well?' An expressive eyebrow lifted. 'Can you help?'

She looked at the tie, askew against snowy linen and golden flesh, and felt something drop in her belly. She didn't want to touch Raffaele Petri. She didn't want to go near him.

But refusing wasn't an option. Briskly she stepped around the desk. She was close enough to inhale his signature scent of rich spices and warm male skin. That warmth enveloped her as she reached out and twitched his bow tie into place.

'There.' She kept her gaze fixed below his chin, ignoring her wobbly knees and the curious hollow sensation in her chest as if someone had scooped out all the air. 'Enjoy your evening out.' Then she turned back to her seat and her work.

It was only eleven-thirty when Raffa got home. Tonight's function had been more cloying than usual. His companion had pretended there was more to their night out than the mutual convenience of being seen with a suitable partner.

He strode through the living room, not bothering with lights. Moonlight streaming in made it easy to see the single bottle on the bar. Moments later he tossed back a mouthful of grappa, its heat punching through his impatience.

He was sick of the posturing and pretence, being part of the same well-heeled crew trying so hard to enjoy themselves. But he'd hoped to see Robert Bradshaw so he'd forced himself, pretending he gave a damn for 'society.'

Since he'd identified the man responsible for Gabriella's death he itched to bring him down. He had no hope of proving Bradshaw's guilt in court after all this time, but he'd see the man who'd seduced and discarded his sister utterly ruined.

But Bradshaw hadn't been there, probably nervous about facing so many creditors. Given the information Lily had unearthed, Raffa suspected he'd gone to ground on his private island, the one his family had owned since they'd traded in slaves and sugar. His homes in London and Cannes had been sold to pay debts and the New York apartment was next. No doubt he was licking his wounds, scheming how to recoup the fortune he'd inherited and squandered.

Raffa's fingers tightened on his glass as anticipation rose. It was time to take the game to Bradshaw. The decision lightened Raffa's mood. He'd grind Bradshaw into the dirt and enjoy every moment.

Discarding tie, shoes and socks, then yanking the top buttons of his shirt undone, he slid open the door to his roof terrace and stepped out. Raffa turned his face to the light breeze and stalled mid-step.

He wasn't alone.

Someone sat on a sun lounger by the pool. Someone staring not at the garden, or the Manhattan view, but the glowing screen of a laptop.

What was *she* doing here?

It had to be Lily Nolan. No one could get past security to his private space, except the woman in his guest suite. The woman who drew the curtains as soon as she got in each night to shut herself off. He'd wondered if she was agoraphobic. That might have explained her reluctance to come to New York. But here she was, with the city laid out before her, relaxed as if her eyrie position didn't bother her in the least.

So it wasn't the view she'd been shutting out, but him— her only neighbour on the penthouse level.

Intriguing.

A now familiar trickle of heat spilled through his veins. A sensation he felt whenever Lily Nolan interrupted his thoughts. He still hadn't found a name for it. Not arousal or excitement. Nor mere curiosity. More a charged awareness, as if he waited for...

Raffa shook his head. He wasn't waiting for anything from Ms Nolan, except another report, this time detailing Bradshaw's Caribbean island resort built around an old plantation estate.

She didn't hear him approach—was too absorbed in what she was doing. Surely not work at this time?

What he saw fascinated him. For the first time she didn't wear loose trousers and a shirt buttoned to the throat. Her feet and legs were bare. His gaze travelled along lissom thighs and shapely calves as she sat with legs bent to support her laptop. Her arms and shoulders were bare too and free of scar tissue.

He'd wondered if she carried more scars under her long sleeves and trousers. The thump of his pulse felt like relief that her injuries weren't worse.

Her swathe of long hair was tucked back. She wore a tank top and shorts and looked potently alluring.

Every woman he met projected an image—sophisticated, provocative, flirtatious, or brisk and professional. Raffa halted, enjoying the silvery light on her naked limbs, relishing the tantalising charm of a sexy woman who wasn't deliberately projecting anything.

Raffa felt a sharp, unmistakable tug of response low in his groin.

It was almost eclipsed by the quake of shock that ripped through him an instant later, making his eyes widen and his belly clench.

How long since he'd felt sexual arousal?

It seemed a lifetime since the thought of sex made him feel anything but impatient or...tainted. For all its transient pleasure, and Raffa had known plenty of that, sex was a transaction, intimacy a calculated risk.

He frowned, his gaze stuck on Lily Nolan and the innocent simplicity of her sex appeal.

Even when he was young there'd never been anything innocent about sex. Simple, yes. But never innocent.

His gaze swept from her hair, dark in the moonlight, to her marred cheek, delicate throat and long limbs. The tug of awareness sharpened to coiling, gut-grabbing tension.

He'd thought he didn't give a damn what Lily Nolan looked like. He'd been wrong.

It was true her scar meant nothing to him. What difference could that make when even the most glamorous beauty failed to stir him? Yet the sight of Lily's supple bare limbs, her ripe breasts and delicate collarbone...

But it wasn't merely that she had a sexy body. He'd seen more than his share of those.

His response was as much to do with the fact that this was Lily Nolan. The woman who'd defied, intrigued and surprised him for six weeks. Even before that, when they'd spoken on the phone, there'd been something, a fizz of energy in his veins that made him feel different—more *alive.* More *real.*

Raffa's frown became a scowl. He didn't do flights of fancy or self-doubt.

Yet he'd always been honest with himself. It had been the only way to keep his head on the tumultuous ride from poverty to success, from obscurity to being one of the most recognisable men on the planet.

Which was why he accepted that it was, remarkably, desire weighting his lower body, sexual interest spiking for the first time in years. More important—it wasn't a reaction merely to an appealing body but specifically to Lily Nolan.

He drew a sharp breath as heat stabbed, keen as a blade.

She must have heard his indrawn breath, swinging her head around and stiffening, hands grabbing the computer.

'You!'

Raffa's mouth twisted wryly. 'Don't sound so pleased to see me.'

Lily Nolan was guaranteed to keep him grounded. Far

from falling at his feet, she viewed him as a necessary encumbrance.

If he believed in good triumphing over evil, in redemption, he'd be tempted to think she'd come into his life to save him, from his ego if nothing else.

But it was a lifetime since Raffa had believed in anything but himself.

'It *is* my home.' His gesture encompassed the garden and penthouse.

'But you went out.' She snapped her mouth shut as if to prevent more words bursting free.

'I see. That's why you sneaked out here. You thought I'd be out of the way.'

Predictably her jaw angled up. 'I didn't sneak anywhere. You told me I had access to the garden.'

'A privilege you've never used unless you believed me safely gone.' He paused, watching her compose her face, wiping away the signs of shock and replacing them with her habitual mask of composure. It annoyed him to realise how much he wanted to peer beyond that facade.

'I thought you'd appreciate privacy. Especially in the evening when you might be…entertaining.' She looked beyond him towards the door to the penthouse.

'Thoughtful of you,' he murmured, 'but unnecessary.' He didn't explain that he never *entertained* at home. He valued his privacy too much.

Besides, the memory of the permanently drawn curtains in the guest wing spoke not so much of giving him privacy but herself. Why did Lily Nolan conceal herself? What secret did she protect?

How hard would it be to unravel that protective web she'd woven around herself? To discover the Lily Nolan who warded him off with her fierce concentration on work? He hadn't missed how she removed herself from his company when possible. How she kept her distance, calling him *Signor Petri* when others used first names.

Tonight he'd get answers.

'What are you working on?' Maybe she'd surprise him and reveal she spent her evenings playing online games.

Her hand went out as if to close her laptop, but his hand shot out, covering hers.

Raffa's pulse throbbed hard. He'd only touched her once, the day they'd shaken hands, but strangely there was a beckoning familiarity to her smooth flesh beneath his.

A second later her fingers slid away and she sat, cradling her hand as if stung.

Interesting.

And far more convenient to concentrate on her reaction than his own.

Raffa angled the screen to see it better. 'Consumer buying patterns in Brisbane? What's that got to do with Bradshaw? I wasn't aware he had interests there.'

'He doesn't.' The screen was pulled from his grip and closed. 'This work isn't for you.'

'You're moonlighting?' She was so close he inhaled that delicate scent he'd noticed before. Subtle yet sweet. It reminded him of crisp, cool days and…pears? That was it—ripe, luscious pears.

She shifted away, further down the lounge seat. Did she somehow register the abrupt spike of adrenaline flooding his bloodstream? The sharpening of his senses now she was within touching distance.

Raffa applauded her good sense in moving.

Yet he grabbed another chair and hauled it over, sitting so he faced her, knee to knee.

Playing safe had never been his style.

CHAPTER FIVE

LILY FOLDED THE laptop on her knees as if it might protect her from his keen gaze.

She felt vulnerable out here, away from the office. Away from her clothes! With that thought her nipples tightened into needy pebbles against the cotton of her sleep top.

How long before her body stopped responding to this man as a virile, spectacular male? She longed for the day she could relegate him to a mere colleague like the ones she worked with daily. The ones who, to her surprise, were becoming friends.

Lily swallowed a groan. Caught half naked by Raffaele Petri. Thankfully he hadn't turned on the lights.

Not that he needed lights. The moon was bright. Enough for her to have difficulty keeping her gaze off the tantalising V of skin revealed by his partly unbuttoned shirt. The combination of formal clothes and rumpled hair, bare feet and open shirt made him look even more potently masculine than usual. Every nerve centre relayed shock waves of pleasure at the sight.

How could her body betray her so?

'Moonlighting implies I'm going behind your back,' she snapped, stress tightening her vocal chords. 'That I'm cutting corners on my work for you. That's not so.' Better to focus on that than her body's tingling excitement.

'So what *are* you doing?'

She drew a deep breath, marshalling her thoughts, and was surprised to intercept a flicker of movement as his gaze dropped to her chest. Instantly her nipples budded tighter as if trying to push closer to him.

Lily told herself it was a reaction to the breeze.

'I told you I had responsibilities that meant I couldn't come to New York, but you forced my hand. This—' she waved a hand at the laptop '—is one of them. A job for a business looking to expand in Brisbane. I was checking a draft report from my assistant.'

'Assistant? I thought you worked alone?'

Once more Lily was unsettled that Raffaele Petri had taken time to learn about her.

'I recently expanded my business. There's a good market for high-quality research.' He said nothing and she felt compelled to fill the silence. 'I'm not cutting corners on your work. I'm doing this in my own time.'

'At midnight? That's no way to run a business.'

It stung that he of all people should lecture on her gruelling work schedule. As if her exhaustion didn't remind her every day when she dragged herself out of bed, almost drip-feeding coffee to keep going.

'You think I don't know that?' She shook her head, finally breaking free of his gaze and turning to look over the diamond-sprinkled velvet of the city at night. Even now, with Raffaele Petri evoking desires she had no business feeling, she couldn't quite get over the fact she was *here*, in New York, the city she'd never believed she'd visit. What wouldn't she give for a chance to explore? To wander and be part of the anonymous crowd? Yet, despite her growing ease with her colleagues, that was a step too far.

'I don't have a choice. Not since I was blackmailed into coming here despite my other work commitments.'

'*That's* why you were reluctant to leave? Not because of a man?'

Lily almost snorted in derision. A man? That was a laugh. There'd been no men in her life. They weren't exactly lining up outside her door, besotted by her looks and charm. Not even when she'd been fourteen and fresh-faced had she been that popular with boys. She'd been too ordinary, too easily overlooked. And later she was noticed for the wrong reasons. She'd learned the hard way not to confuse sympathy for interest.

'Several men, actually.' She watched, surprised, as he stiffened. Was it imagination or did his eyes narrow? 'That retailer in Brisbane. The HR manager of a security firm wanting checks on potential staff. The head of a planning authority—'

'Clients, you mean.'

'Yes. And all important. Which is why I use my spare time working for them.'

'But none are as important as me.'

True. None had the same power to make or break her business.

'*All* my clients are important. They expect results and I'd already promised to deliver. I don't take on work I can't complete to the best possible standard.'

'Even if the projects bring in a pittance compared with what you're doing for me?'

Lily tried not to grind her teeth. Good thing he was so arrogant. It would counteract this powerful attraction.

Shame it hadn't worked yet.

'You'd be surprised. Some of my clients even rival you.' She'd recently done work for a man who could reasonably be called Raffaele Petri's rival. Luca De Laurentis was another entrepreneur providing vacation services to the rich. 'For my business to expand it makes sense to cultivate as many sources of income as possible.'

Slowly—perhaps reluctantly?—he nodded.

'When you say expand, what do you mean? There's only so much you can do, even if you go without sleep.'

'Is it so hard to take me seriously as a businesswoman? To see me as an employer?' Umbrage thickened her voice. Her work, her professional success, meant everything. They were all she had. She'd long ago realised she'd never have a family of her own.

He shook his head. 'You're the most serious-minded

person I know, Lily.' Inevitably there it was again, the tiny thrill of delight as he turned her name into something exotic with that mellow voice and mouthwatering accent. 'It's just that you obviously prefer to work alone.'

'You mean I'm not a team player?' She read criticism in his words.

'No, not that. I've seen how meticulous you are about sharing information, making sure everyone's up-to-date. More that you prefer to be alone.'

Lily swallowed, her throat tight. He was right. Over the years she'd developed a taste for her own company. Surely he could understand that.

Or maybe not. People stared at him all the time, but it was in admiration, not horror at how he looked.

'Well, you'll be interested to know I employ two other people.' Albeit part-time, and both still learning the ropes. But for Lily this was a major step forward.

'Why?'

She frowned. Hadn't he listened? 'You said yourself there's a limit to the work I can do alone.'

'Why expand? Why build up a company rather than accept a permanent job here, for instance?' His voice resonated with genuine curiosity.

Lily stared into that gorgeous fallen-angel face. No one else, not her family or friends or even her bank manager, had bothered to ask.

Something faltered inside her. She found herself on her feet, staring at the beautifully lit pool. Yet she couldn't distract herself from stirring disquiet. Her heart thumped high in her chest and she knew it was because his interest made a difference. What he thought mattered.

Despite their differences she respected him—his business acumen, his drive, even his sometimes brutal honesty. And the fact he'd never once seemed fazed by her looks. He treated her not as scarred Lily Nolan but, she realised in shock, as someone strong enough to stand up to him. As an equal, despite their imbalance of power.

She should end this conversation. It bordered on the intimate. Yet their isolation in this moon-washed garden and the sense of familiarity made it seem almost normal.

It struck her how far she'd cut herself off from those who cared about her. In Australia she'd crossed a continent to get away from her family's loving but claustrophobic over-protectiveness, moving from Fremantle, on the west coast, to the east. Since then she'd focused on work. She had no bosom buddy, no confidante. No one close to share her hopes and dreams.

'I want to build something for myself.' The words tumbled out.

To her surprise he nodded. Only a tiny inclination of the head but it seemed to bridge the distance between them.

'I want…' How did she put it into words? 'Security, the safety that comes from success, but more too. I want…'

'Recognition.'

Lily's eyes widened. 'How did you know?'

His shoulders lifted and her gaze slid across that wide, straight expanse of powerful muscle and bone. 'It sounds familiar.'

'You?' It didn't seem possible. 'But you already had recognition before you started your business.'

His lips curved in what should have been a smile.

'To be recognisable as a face, or a body, plastered across the media in advertising campaigns isn't quite the same as genuine recognition.'

'Recognition for your achievements, you mean?'

Again that nod.

Was it naive to admit she'd never thought of the difference before? Raffaele Petri's phenomenal media presence had seemed the epitome of success. To be so watched, adored and admired…

It was as if he'd read her mind. 'Being known because

of how you look isn't an achievement.' His eyes held hers and phantom heat washed her scarred face. 'Being someone because of your actions, your success, is something else.'

Understanding stretched between them. An understanding she'd never before shared. It felt momentous. Lily sank back onto her seat, watching him avidly.

'Is that what drove you to build your business? The need to make your mark?' She admired him for that. It would have been easy to continue modelling. To move from that field where he was in such demand and strike out on his own must have taken grit as well as talent.

'Maybe. I wanted to take charge of my future. That's hard when you're dependent on the whims of advertisers and fashion gurus, likely to be out of style next year because they're hungry for a new face.'

She blinked, astounded that he shared such information. He wasn't a touchy-feely sort of guy. She'd seen him affable and relaxed but he could as easily intimidate with a look.

Was he too affected by the intimacy of the half-darkness, high above the city?

'I can't imagine you out of modelling work for long.' It wasn't just his staggering good looks. He had a magnetism Lily couldn't resist, no matter how she tried. And she'd tried. For over a month she'd fought the compulsion to watch him.

He laughed, the sound a soft ripple skating along her bare arms. 'It's a cutthroat business. Don't let the gloss fool you.'

'So you took to real estate as a safety net?' That was how he'd started his enterprise.

'You could say that. I was determined to make myself safe.'

'Safe?'

Again that quirk of the lips that should have been a smile, but which felt, in the dimness, like something else.

'I was born poor. It takes a lot of money to stop worrying you'll lose everything and end up in the gutter again.'

Lily nodded. She knew he didn't come from money. But the gutter? Was that just a figure of speech?

'Building my business meant I could choose my direction, doing things the way I want, not dependent on others.'

'I know what you mean.'

He sat back, and even in the semi-darkness she felt his piercing regard.

Lily held her breath, waiting for him to continue. He didn't. He looked perfectly relaxed, watching her. But he sat closer than in any meeting. There was nothing between them except a few scant inches of space.

Abruptly the elusive feeling of companionship dissipated.

The silence grew and Lily's lungs tightened with the effort to breathe normally, not gulp down huge draughts of warm air, scented with that man and spicy deliciousness she'd come to associate with him.

'What are you thinking?' she burst out when she couldn't bear the silence.

His mouth quirked up again and this time she spied amusement. 'I'm thinking how similar we are.'

He had to be kidding! They were galaxies apart.

'We're both loners.' He ticked the point off one finger. Lily watched, fascinated that he lumped himself with her there. Raffaele Petri was always surrounded by people. In the office he was the hub around which everyone revolved, eager to meet his needs. She'd seen enough media reports to know that out of the office he was surrounded by glamorous, beautiful people, drawing them like a magnet.

But how many is he close to?

The question had never occurred to her before.

'We both want the security of success.' Another tick. 'We both want to make our mark, rather than have the world judge us on how we look.'

Lily sucked in her cheeks on a hiss of shock, blinking at those knowing eyes. She'd never mentioned the problem she'd had since her teens—of people not seeing her, just her scarred face.

It stunned her that he'd picked up on that.

Why had she thought he wouldn't get it? Because he wasn't interested in anyone but himself? Yet he'd continually surprised her with what he knew about her.

Because he was so handsome?

For the first time it struck her that he carried a burden too—far easier, of course, since his looks must have opened doors. In a weird way they were linked—judged by people because of their faces—his utterly gorgeous and hers downright ugly.

Slowly Lily released her breath, and with it some of the tautness in her shoulders and neck.

She nodded. He'd put into words something she'd never admitted. That she still fought to be judged as someone other than the woman with the appallingly scarred face.

That was why, until now, she'd enjoyed working from home instead of in someone else's office. When people couldn't see her they treated her like anyone else—no pity or sneaking stares or embarrassment.

Working here in New York was the first time in years she'd begun to relax with others. Were the people here remarkable or did her hard-won confidence in her work mean she was less concerned with their initial reaction? Whatever the cause, she felt more relaxed and accepted than she'd expected. It irked to admit it but her forced move had been good for her.

'We've both set up our own businesses too. That's another point in common.' It didn't matter that his was a multinational empire and hers a fledgling company carrying brand-new debt. The principle was the same. 'Did your previous career help you get started?'

His laugh was short. 'Not in the beginning. I wasn't

taken seriously. I was a face, not a businessman. No one understood how single-minded I'd had to be to get where I was.'

'I suppose people think modelling is easy.' She had.

'Modelling?' He shifted in his seat, his head swinging up, and she had a curious feeling she'd missed something. 'Let's just say I paid my dues to climb out of the hole where I started life.' His face hardened. 'Getting investors to trust me with their assets was tough. Everyone expected me to fail.'

'But you didn't.'

'In the beginning, when I needed advice and investors, no one would touch me. Later it was different. People wanted a part of what I'd built, but by then I was used to working alone.' He shrugged. 'Maybe being forced to go solo was a good thing. It made me more determined to succeed and learn from my mistakes.'

'Did you make many? Mistakes?' Lily leaned forward, her hands clasped between her knees.

'Plenty. I had money, I'd been careful about saving, but I overextended myself with a project that ran into problems. It was touch-and-go for a while.'

Lily knew the feeling. 'But you succeeded.' Fervently she hoped she could too.

He lifted one hand, palm up, in a gesture that seemed wholly Italian. 'It was the only option I'd accept.'

Didn't that say it all? Raffaele Petri was a man who, as Pete said, made it his policy always to get what he wanted. Did she have the same determination to succeed?

'You make it sound easy.'

'Not easy. Straightforward. I refused to accept failure. I did whatever it took to succeed.'

Could she do that? She was trying. How hard she was trying!

Perhaps it was ridiculous to take solace from the example of the man who'd disrupted her plans, the one forcing her to work twice as hard as usual just to keep on top of her obligations. Yet she felt buoyed.

'Have you considered narrowing your market?' His query dragged her out of her reverie.

'Sorry?'

'Your market. It seems very broad. You're doing personnel security checks. You've taken a job for a small business plus some project for a planning authority. Then there's your work for me, which is in a different ballpark. I'm asking if you need to specialise and become the best at what you do instead of being all things to all people.'

Lily surveyed him with surprise. Instead of anger that she wasn't devoting all her efforts to his project, he was interested in her business? Offering advice? It was too good an opportunity to ignore.

'Specialising would cut off some lucrative income.' Like those security checks she didn't particularly enjoy.

'Lucrative long-term or short-term?'

She hadn't thought about it like that. 'Lucrative enough to pay the bills while I build my name in the areas I want.'

'And do you have a plan for the transition from doing everything to doing only what you want as your core business?'

Lily hesitated. Her business plan had been based on doing more of the same. General expansion rather than targeted. Her focus had been on building income to make the enterprise as secure as possible.

'I see.' He sat back.

So did she. 'There's a gap in my planning, isn't there?'

She didn't feel defensive. This shadowy version of Raffaele Petri, sitting easily with her in the garden, wasn't nearly as daunting as the one she worked with daily. She could almost pretend to forget her attraction to him. Despite her quickened pulse and the tingle of awareness, she felt easier with him than ever before. As if he were no longer a threat.

Amazing what a little moonlight could do. Or was it because his interest was in her work, not her?

'It sounds like you need to revisit your strategy. Unless you want to be stuck in a rut, tendering for every job, whether it interests you or not.'

Lily dragged her fingers through her hair, letting it slide away over her shoulder. 'I've had enough of that, working at things that don't interest me.'

Even in the moonlight she saw his eyebrows rise. 'Does that apply to what you're doing for me?'

Quickly Lily shook her head. 'No, I love that.' She paused, wondering if she sounded too eager. But he'd acknowledged she never ran to him seeking kudos. 'The projects are complex enough to be fascinating. I—' She paused. 'Signor P—'

'Raffaele. Or Raffa. Surely we've gone past formality.'

Lily wished his face wasn't half-shadowed. There was a note in his voice she couldn't recognise. It kicked her pulse into high gear.

Reluctantly she nodded. 'Raffaele.' She stumbled over his name. Not because she couldn't say it, but because it felt like an illicit pleasure on her tongue. As if she'd crossed some boundary. Heat spiked in her chest. 'Is there a chance you could…?'

'A chance I could…?' He leaned forward and she felt the waft of warm air as he exhaled. Lily blinked, overwhelmed by his sheer physical presence. The stark male beauty that even pale moonlight couldn't diminish. The challenging mind. The fizz of attraction.

Yet most appealing of all was the way he talked to her. He made her feel…important. As if she genuinely interested him.

Lily's gaze fell to those powerful hands at his knees. Her blood tingled as for one decadent moment she wondered how it would feel if he lifted a palm and put it on her bare flesh. A quiver of exultation coursed through her. Till sanity returned.

The very fact he was so close, discussing corporate planning of all things, proved he had no interest in her physically. It was her mind, her plans he was curious about.

She was glad. It was what she wanted, to be taken seriously as a businesswoman.

Yet Lily couldn't help wondering what it would be like, just once, to be desired by a man.

She gulped down a sudden restriction in her throat. She didn't do self-pity. Far better to focus on what she *could* get out of life.

'I wondered if you had any advice. About how or when to make that switch from taking every job to something more targeted.'

Her nerves stretched with the growing silence. But just when she'd decided she'd gone too far, he spoke.

Raffa watched Lily expound a point, gesturing, the light catching the small scar on the back of her hand. It caught the larger scar on her cheek too. But not even that detracted from her lit-from-within animation.

When she talked about her business it was with an enthusiasm most women reserved for a lover. An enthusiasm he found hard to resist.

True passion was rare.

How many would-be entrepreneurs had approached him to give them a start up? How many established businessmen had tried to entice him into a shared deal? He was adept at resisting, going his own way.

Yet here he was, caught up in Lily Nolan's enthusiasm for a solid, but nevertheless tiny enterprise.

Or, more accurately, caught up in watching her, enjoying the change from buttoned-up, defensive worker bee to a woman who even in this gloom shone with an inner glow. A woman who made him wonder what she'd do if he stretched his arm out and hauled her onto his lap.

Her effervescence was a turn-on. It was no hardship to discuss business plans with her. He'd been genuinely interested, but beyond that was an edge that had nothing to do with commerce and everything to do with the fact that for the first time in recent memory he found himself contemplating taking a lover.

Lily Nolan?

It was a crazy idea.

'When will that report on Bradshaw's Caribbean property be complete?'

She looked surprised at his question. Understandable given it had nothing to do with their discussion. 'Tomorrow. I've got one more thing to check in the morning.'

'Excellent. You can have ten days off when it's done. That will give you time to work through your other responsibilities.' He gestured to her now dormant laptop. The sooner she got on top of those, the sooner he could have her to himself. He needed her. For her expertise, he assured himself.

'Ten days? But I've only worked for you a short time.'

Raffa's mouth kicked up. Who complained about time off? 'Don't worry. I'm getting my money's worth from you and I intend to keep doing so. When you start back we'll be in a crucial stage of the project and I'll want you available twenty-four-seven.'

Slowly she nodded. 'Well, I *am* on the premises, so I'll be available.'

Raffa shook his head. 'We won't be in New York. We'll be in the Caribbean, on Bradshaw's home turf.'

She stilled, her eyes widening. 'We?'

'That's right. We. I want you where you can be most useful.'

This was a sensible business decision. It had nothing to

do with the tug of attraction he felt towards Lily Nolan. Almost nothing.

She opened her mouth, the same tight expression settling on her face that he'd become used to before tonight. It didn't bother him. Now he knew something of the vital, intriguing, oddly innocent woman behind the facade.

He looked forward to seeing more of that woman. To learning her secrets.

'And, before you object, this is a requirement, not a request. Finish what you have to. I don't want you bringing other work. I want you completely at my disposal.'

CHAPTER SIX

'THAT'S IT FOR NOW. Thanks, everyone.' Raffaele ended the video conference with a final word to Consuela in New York about a contract.

Lily eased back in her seat, stretching. She was tired, but good tired. Working with Raffaele was intense—satisfying, but a challenge to keep up. Just as well she'd been well prepared for the meeting.

He was a dynamic entrepreneur but his restless energy since they'd arrived on Bradshaw's island was electric. There must be a personal element to this. She sensed it in the grim twist of Raffaele's mouth when the other man was mentioned, and his insistence on breakneck speed, as if completion couldn't come fast enough. Yet even now he was cagey about the details of his plan, as if it were too important to share in full.

'Right. Time for a break.'

She looked up to find he'd shut the screen and was watching her. His stare made her feel abruptly *un*professional.

Lily worked hard *not* to think of him as a desirable man. But it was like trying to pretend the sun didn't shine out there on the white sand of this island paradise. The mere sight of his sinewy, powerful forearms, dark gold beneath rolled-up sleeves, made her stupid heart thud.

They were alone in his spacious bungalow, set a little apart from the other accommodation spread through the leafy resort gardens. The rest of the team were thousands of miles away in New York and Lily felt a flicker of guilt that she alone had travelled here with him. Even her smaller bungalow was gorgeous, with its plantation-style furnishings, four-poster bed and ocean views.

'Dinner at the poolside café, I think.'

Lily could imagine him there. With his burnished good looks and casual white cotton shirt and trousers, he'd be right at home amongst the bikini-clad beauties.

She averted her gaze, gathering her gear. 'Enjoy yourself. I'll start following up—'

'Later, Lily. It's time to eat.' That mellow voice trailed through her veins.

She fixed on a smile. 'I'll grab something in my room. I want to get this down while it's fresh.'

To her surprise he came to stand before her, crossing his arms and planting his feet wide, owning the space.

Her pulse danced that silly little jig. No matter how often she saw him, he still had the power to enthral her. She should be immune to Raffaele Petri. But since that night on his rooftop her defences were in tatters.

He'd taken time to advise her on her fledgling enterprise. She'd never had a mentor and eagerly soaked up his suggestions. He'd been kind, discussing her insignificant start-up company.

Who'd have thought Raffaele Petri could be kind?

There'd been more too. He'd told her about his own business. For the first time she saw her research in a wider context. It was exciting to feel part of something bigger than her own narrow goals. He'd made her feel valued, as if she *belonged*. It was rare and satisfying.

Above all was the heady sense he saw her not just as an employee but as a woman interesting in her own right. He made her feel he saw *her* as no one else did. She was human enough to want him to admire what he saw.

'That can wait. Food first. Leave your stuff here and collect it later.'

He was inviting her to eat with him? Excitement buzzed.

Or was that horror at the thought of sitting at the resort's most public venue beside the most gorgeous man on the planet? With all those beautiful people looking on?

Her shrinking stomach warned it was both.

'Thanks, Raffaele.' She paused, savouring his name. 'But I'd prefer to eat alone and get my thoughts together.'

'In your room?'

She nodded, scrambling up from the low seat.

To her consternation he didn't step away and she found herself toe to toe with him, close enough for the heat of his body to brand her. For that evocative scent of his to inveigle its way into her nostrils.

Awareness shuddered through her—real, alive, all-consuming.

The daunting truth was that she wanted him as a woman wanted a man. It was laughable. He'd been supportive and, yes, kind, but there was no way he'd ever—

'Hiding again, Lily?'

Her chin tipped up as if yanked on a string. She met gleaming eyes and read knowledge in them. Her breath froze and splintered in her lungs.

'I don't know what you're talking about.' He couldn't know how she felt about him. Could he?

Raffa scented her fear. He'd learned to recognise it early, a legacy of growing up in the rough end of a derelict neighbourhood. He wanted to tell her it was okay.

But it wasn't okay, not if what he suspected was right. His hands clenched as he strove not to reach for her. The impulse to reassure, to comfort was so unexpected and strong, it shocked him.

He'd been many things to many women.

But a comfort? Never.

Yet he persisted. His suspicion had grown so strong he'd found himself pondering it rather than his plans for Bradshaw. Nothing, he vowed, would deter him from justice for Gabriella. For her sake, and for Lily's, he needed to sort this so he could focus again.

'We've worked together long enough for me to be able

to read you, at least a little.' He'd never met anyone so self-contained. It made him itch to discover her secrets. 'I know you're scared.'

She froze. He sensed the tightening of her slim frame as her eyebrows rose. 'I don't know what you mean.'

He gave her full marks for bravado.

'You think I haven't noticed that you hide away?' He shook his head. 'You never go out. Ever. In New York you stayed in the office or in the guest suite. When other staff talk about what they did on the weekend or meet for a drink after work, you don't join in.' He'd been too absorbed in his plan for justice to realise at first how insular she was. But, once he did, it was glaringly obvious. Like the way she concealed herself behind that long hair.

'You *know* I don't have time for that.' She waved a hand dismissively. 'I'm working full-time for you and trying to keep my business afloat back home.'

True, but that wasn't the whole story.

'You've got time to eat with me. Here. Now.' He paused. 'Unless you're afraid of that too?'

'Too?' Lily shifted as if to step away but he blocked her exit.

'I saw you on the beach at dawn.' At her surprised look he shrugged. 'You're not the only early riser.'

Instantly suspicion, or was it fear, clouded those amber-brown eyes.

'You were staring out to sea, even waded knee-deep in the water a couple of times. But you didn't go in. Why was that? I could tell you were yearning to.'

She'd stood there in another long-sleeved shirt with cargo pants rolled up around her knees and it had struck him how she deliberately camouflaged that lithe, luscious body he'd seen in his garden.

He'd been about to approach her when he'd noticed her expression, illuminated in the peachy morning light. It was a look of such longing, such regret, it stirred discomfort. As if he'd intruded on something utterly personal.

The melancholy of that lone figure, arms crossed over her chest, just as now, had stayed with him all morning.

'I wasn't *yearning*. I was admiring. The view was spectacular.' She hitched a quick breath that betrayed discomfort, her gaze skittering away. 'Besides, I didn't bring a swimsuit.'

'You came to a Caribbean resort and didn't bring a swimsuit?' Disbelief dripped from each syllable.

Her chin jerked even higher. 'I don't own one.' She hurried on before he could interrupt. 'I'm here to work, not swim, remember?'

'I see.' She was finding excuses again. More than ever, he wanted to lay them bare.

'What do you see?' Anger vibrated in her voice and Raffa felt a little of his edginess ease. He preferred her angry to fearful or dejected. Watching her this morning, reading infinite sadness in that longing gaze, had felt like a sucker punch to the gut. He'd felt…lost, something he hadn't experienced since he was twelve and Gabriella had left him.

'That you're afraid of the water. Can't you swim?'

'Of course I can swim. I grew up on the coast. Learning to swim was compulsory.'

Raffa stared at her set features, reading the truth in her expression. Now they were getting somewhere.

He lifted his hand, gesturing to her scarred cheek. 'What happened? Was that from an accident in the water? Is that why you don't swim?'

Lily gasped and shifted back but she couldn't escape because of the couch behind her.

'Lily?'

'That's none of your business.' Her voice rose half an octave.

'Perhaps not. But it's time someone asked.' Clearly her

injury had affected more than her face. It was a crying shame that a woman so full of spark and energy should conceal herself.

Why was he making it his mission to interfere?

He was selfish to the core. Since when had he taken an altruistic interest in anyone?

'Just because you employ me doesn't give you a right to pry.'

Raffa said nothing, merely stood and waited.

He'd almost given up on an answer when the words burst from her. 'It wasn't a swimming accident. A jealous thug decided to make a point with a flask of acid.'

Raffa recoiled at the brutal words. He couldn't help but imagine the fiery burn on tender flesh, the howling pain. The shock and suffering. Nausea swirled in his belly and rose as bile in his throat. His heart pounded his ribs.

What sort of man attacked a defenceless woman?

Another like Robert Bradshaw.

Raffa's hands curled into fists, tension radiating up his arms to his shoulders and neck.

'Your boyfriend?' His words slid from between gritted teeth.

She shook her head, her long hair slipping around her cheeks. 'My best friend's. I was just in the wrong place at the wrong time, sitting beside her at the cinema. Rachel bore the brunt of it but my injuries kept me in and out of hospital for a long time while they tried to repair the damage.' Her voice was brittle.

It struck him how tough it must have been, not only badly injured, but in such a random way. How had she ever felt safe again?

He wanted to soothe her, haul her close and reassure her.

As if he had any experience of comforting a woman.

As if she'd accept his touch! She glared at him with the same distrust he'd once seen on a half-wild dog. As if she'd bite his hand if he came close.

'So why don't you swim?' There was something there, some reason she wouldn't go in the water. He'd seen it on her face in the dawn light. 'Is it the same reason you try to disappear?'

'Disappear? I'm here, aren't I?' Her voice told him he was on the right track. Defiance tinged with fear.

'Not all the time.' Did she even realise how often she tried to blend into the background? 'Sometimes, when you're passionate about a discussion or a new work direction, you forget to take a back seat. Then you're vibrant and persuasive and...*present*.' *He* always noticed her, but he also saw the way she tried not to attract attention. 'But it seems to me you're worried about being seen.'

She said nothing, yet he heard the snatch of indrawn air, saw the sudden lift of her breasts as her breathing turned shallow.

Her vulnerability made his chest clench.

'That's it, isn't it? The reason you wear those cover-up clothes.'

Her eyes narrowed to a gleam of amber fire. 'We can't all afford designer gear.'

'It's not about designer labels, Lily. You've got an attractive body yet you hide it as if you're ashamed. Did you even bring shorts or a sleeveless top here?'

Her silence said she hadn't. His suspicion grew to a certainty as so much became clear. Horror furrowed his gut at the implications.

'No summer clothes, no swimsuit, because you don't want anyone seeing you. You won't go in the water in case you attract attention. Even at dawn when you thought there was no one to see, you wouldn't risk it.' Her silent watchfulness told him he'd hit the truth. 'You want to take cover behind your drab clothes in the hope you won't be noticed.' Raffa was torn between incredulity and pity as he met that stubborn narrowed stare.

'It doesn't work that way, Lily.' His voice grated. He was

staggered at how much he felt for her. 'Don't you realise the more you try to hide, the more obvious you become? The more people watch and wonder? You think they don't see you hiding behind that long hair or those drab clothes? That they don't notice you avoiding them?'

'Who do you think you are to tell me what to wear or how to behave? If I want to wear my hair loose or wear long sleeves, that's my choice.' Her shimmering gaze scraped him from hairline to jaw. 'Even if it displeases a fashion expert like you.'

'And when it stops being a choice? When you deny yourself the pleasure of swimming because you're afraid, not of anything in the water, but of being seen?' Raffa tasted a dull, metallic tang on his tongue. 'That's not choice, Lily. That's when fear has taken over your life.'

The heel of her hand jammed into the centre of his chest, as if she could push him away. Or she needed an outlet for the emotions she'd bottled up so fiercely.

'Don't you *dare* lecture me!' Her voice was a gasp, her breathing too fast, too shallow. 'You have no idea what it's like.'

At the sight of her distress something turned over deep inside. He felt her quiver with the force of her emotions. How long had she dammed it all up? Energy radiated from her in sharp surges that zapped like electricity.

'Then tell me.' He clamped a palm over her hand, holding it to him, feeling the shudders rippling through her. He doubted she noticed.

She shook her head, her hair swirling silk-soft against his hand.

'Tell me, Lily.'

Finally her gaze meshed with his. Those eyes were like amber starbursts now, rimmed with honey-brown. Startling, unique, mesmerising.

'What do you want me to tell you? That for half my life people have looked at me as if I were a freak? They can't help but stare. And they talk to me slowly, in soft voices, as if they're so *sorry* for the way I look they think it's affected my ability to think. Then there are the ones who won't even look at me. They'll have a whole conversation staring at a point over my shoulder to avoid seeing the scar on my face.

'In one day I lost not just my face but my youth, my friend, my fearlessness. The bliss of being *normal*.'

She laughed, the sound off-key, tugging a chord in his belly. 'You have no idea of the jobs I had to give up because of the way people see me. A baker gave me work out of sympathy but lost customers because people didn't want me serving them. Perhaps it made them lose their appetite.'

Raffa tightened his hold, his jaw setting.

'The job in the property office where the other girls couldn't be comfortable working with someone who looked like me. Something about my presence was just too…unsettling.' Sarcasm laced her words and he couldn't blame her.

'But that's not the case now.'

'Sorry?' She looked up at him as if he spoke another language.

'However livid your scar once was, and however stupid some of your old work colleagues. That doesn't apply now.'

She snorted. 'You're going to tell me my scar has suddenly disappeared?'

'I'm telling you that, whatever it looks like, you're a different woman now to the one you were then. You're confident, capable and successful. You can stand up for yourself now. As for the scar—' He lifted his free hand and pushed her hair back behind her ear.

Instantly she stilled, the vibrant energy diminishing to a low-grade hum as if someone had flicked a switch.

Her breath, warm and sweet, feathered his face as he surveyed that taut skin. Raffa tried to imagine how angry it must once have looked, how shocking. But he'd grown so used to it he had trouble seeing it as anything but part of her.

'I've seen far worse,' he said finally.

With an audible snap she shut her mouth, wrenching her hand from his.

'I can't tell you how much better I feel after hearing that!'

Raffa's lips curved at her waspish response. He'd never met anyone so ready to attack in order to defend themselves. It had intrigued him from the first. 'I'm not being patronising, just truthful.'

'And this truth is meant to make my life easier, how?' She tilted her head in mock consideration, her hands going to her hips.

'Let me guess. I'll be so excited that the mighty Raffaele Petri has announced he's seen worse that I'll cut my hair, put on a bikini and spend the rest of my time here chatting up strangers. And, miraculously, no one will notice that one side of my face looks like something out of a horror movie.'

She thrust out her chin, invading his space. 'Get real, Raffaele. Would you touch a woman who looked like this? Of course you wouldn't.'

She opened her mouth for another jibe then shut it when he lifted his palm to the taut skin of her cheek. He heard a hiss and felt her whole body rise with her quick intake of breath. She stared up at him, eyes wide.

He moved his hand over warm skin, exploring, learning the contour of cheekbone and jaw, scar and unblemished skin that was petal-soft. Finally his thumb discovered the rapid tattoo of her pulse. So vital, so fascinating.

Her sweet fruit scent filled his nostrils as he leaned closer, surveying her brilliant eyes, drawn by the inexplicable sense of anticipation trembling between them.

Then, abruptly, she was gone, sliding away from his touch. A few angry strides and she was across the room, shoulders heaving.

He stood where she'd left him, oddly bereft.

What had just happened?

'You have no idea what my life has been like with this scar. Don't you dare tell me it's all okay. I don't need your condescension.'

Raffa was dazed by the emotions she'd evoked. Pity. Protectiveness. Arousal. Anger. And something else.

He'd been trying to help. And what did he get for his pains? That would teach him to try being altruistic!

'Of course, you're the only one in the world whose life has been affected by the way they look.' The words were out before he knew it. 'You need to get over yourself, Lily. That scar can't blight your whole life. Not unless you let it.'

Her gasp was loud in the silence. Once more her hands found her hips and her chin lifted imperiously, like a queen surveying her dominions. Or, given that kindling look, judging some insubordinate slave.

'Get *over* myself?' She shook her head, her stunned eyes never leaving his. 'I don't know what's more insulting. That you pretend I've somehow done this—' she gestured to her face '—to myself. Or that you're looking for sympathy because you've been judged on your looks. Sympathy from *me*?' Her tone said it all.

She was right. Raffa had no grounds to complain. Even if his looks had led him to places, to actions he regretted. He'd have done anything to escape grinding poverty and what he'd done…well, others would say he'd been supremely fortunate. Even if it meant he carried a taint that time couldn't erase.

He'd done what he had to and escaped more lightly than many. As for his looks—he might have been used, and even, some would say, abused, because of them. But he'd made his fortune with his face and emerged triumphant.

Yet in the dark recesses of his soul he acknowledged unexpected kinship with Lily and her problems. Both judged because of the way they appeared.

The difference was that she carried her scars on the outside. His were internal.

'You're absolutely right. I've no cause for complaint. I've got everything a man could want and more.' He didn't add that having everything money could buy didn't counteract the hollowness at the core of a world centred only on himself. The suspicion, too late, that such hollowness would eventually consume him.

'But believe me, Lily, if you don't make a change soon, you won't be able to. Either you let that scar define you or you make the life you want in spite of it.'

Raffa turned on his heel and strode to the door, willing down the tumultuous boil of feelings. He wasn't interested in emotion. He wasn't interested in scars, real or psychological. He was here for a single vital purpose. It was time he got on with it.

He needed to forget the murky...*feelings* Lily evoked and concentrate on Robert Bradshaw. Justice and revenge were much simpler.

CHAPTER SEVEN

NOTHING HELPED. LILY HAD paced her bungalow half the evening, reliving the conversation, coming up with scathing retorts, and still Raffaele's words scraped like a blade scratching flesh. Like the memory of acid on her cheek.

Work hadn't helped. Not that she'd done any work for *him*. She'd dragged out her laptop and spent hours on tasks for her business.

All night she'd worked, but no matter how busy she was, she couldn't stop his words in her brain. Or the fear, deep in her roiling belly, that he might be right. It had stopped her sleeping, despite her exhaustion.

These last years it should have been easier to face the world, especially since surgery had diminished the horror factor of her injury. Yet, perversely, each trip into town had become more difficult than the last. Travelling was a nightmare of self-consciousness, and forcing herself into that New York office every day...

Lily shook her head, hair sliding reassuringly across her cheeks. She'd had to face down panic attacks just to get through the door.

You think they don't see you hiding behind that long hair or those drab clothes?

She stilled. He'd all but accused her of being a coward. She who'd weathered such pain, such grief, and then had to face the unmistakable, if unspoken, blame of the whole community when *she'd* been the one to survive rather than Rachel. Vibrant, pretty, life-of-the-party Rachel, star of the swim squad, the debating team, academically gifted, on her way to stellar success in whatever field she chose.

Rachel, her best friend.

Lily gulped down a sob that shook her from her shoulders to her soles.

She didn't do self-pity. She didn't!

She'd faced medical treatments and long convalescence stoically when all her peers were enjoying themselves. Hadn't she forced herself to succeed, refusing to give up when one job after another failed? She'd been determined to stand on her own feet, not be a burden to her worried parents and protective brothers. She'd worked like a slave to establish her own business, carve success and security.

Security away from the world.

A continent away from her family and the last of her friends.

The air rushed from her chest as if she'd been stabbed in the lungs. She felt herself deflating, crumpling, her knees collapsing till she sagged onto the edge of the bed.

It hurt to breathe. Blackness clouded the edge of her vision like churning storm clouds. Spots of white burst around her as the world turned grey, then darker. Her head swam. Any second now the blackness would consume her.

Then, with a huge, juddering heave, her lungs opened up, drawing in air that seared all the way down her aching throat. The grey retreated. The room, with its pale furnishings and bright tropical accents, came into focus. Through the window she saw the golden bloom of dawn fringe the horizon, spreading across the water towards her.

Raffaele was right.

She was scared. More than scared—she was petrified. When had it happened?

She'd been so busy forcing herself to face the world, the need to find a job, build a career and be independent from her worried, loving parents. She hadn't noticed when wariness had gradually become withdrawal, independence had turned to isolation and the comfort of her own home had become a cage.

Reluctantly, each muscle protesting, she turned her head.

Across the bed lay strewn the items she'd tossed there last evening when her rage had been white-hot. A staff member from the resort boutique had brought them in glossy, silver-ribboned bags. Only one person could have sent them.

A broad-brimmed hat, a bright skirt of some soft fabric that slipped through her fingers like cool water. A sleeveless top sporting a designer label, a one-piece swimsuit and a long, loose gauzy cover-up, for wearing while lolling by the pool. There was even a pair of cute sandals with ribbons that tied around the ankles.

Each in her size.

Each worth more than she'd spend on clothes in a year.

Each mocking her.

Her fury had spiked at the idea of Raffaele ordering them, daring her to wear them.

As if it was any of his business what she wore.

Now they lay, taunting her, a challenge she couldn't ignore.

How had he known what she hadn't recognised in herself? It wasn't as if she were important to him, yet he'd taken time to see her as more than an employee. He'd seen her as an individual. As someone who counted. He'd forced her to understand herself clearly for the first time in years.

The pain of that self-knowledge tore at her.

Gritting her teeth, Lily reached out and touched the swimsuit. The fabric was soft, fluid and silky, frighteningly thin.

It gave nowhere to hide.

Raffa flicked water from his eyes, treading water. Five laps of the bay and his chest was on fire, his legs and arms like jelly. But exertion hadn't brought relief.

All night he'd been haunted by Lily's face when he'd told her to move on with her life, stop taking cover and ignore her scar.

His gut clenched, making him sink below the surface

till he kicked harder. Who was he to tell her how to live? How could he begin to imagine what it was like to be her?

Sometimes his arrogance appalled even himself.

He turned from the headland, back towards the bay, ready for another punishing lap, when a lone figure on the beach stopped him. A figure with pale limbs, long hair and a body clad in bronze. Dawn light caught each supple angle and sweet curve. It burnished the taut swimsuit that clung to Lily's delectable body.

Why had he ever thought it a good idea for her to bare herself?

Testosterone surged, weighting his body, tightening each muscle, turning his lungs into a furnace where each breath was an ache of pure heat.

She was unadorned. He tried to tell himself it was the simplicity of the picture she made that affected him. But he'd seen countless women—clothed, unclothed, in ball gowns and swimsuits, towels and wisps of nothing. None affected him like this.

He took in her ravaged cheek, lit by the morning sun as she shook her hair off her face. The movement was one of impatience, determination, and it made his heart jump.

His lips curved in a proud smile. He hadn't been sure she'd accept the gauntlet he'd thrown down. She could just as easily have nestled further into that protective shell, cutting herself off from the world. From him.

He admired her fierce determination. She was a worthy adversary.

Raffa reminded himself she wasn't an adversary, but an employee.

Except in the oldest contest of all, the struggle between male and female.

He couldn't ignore it any longer. For almost two months he'd pretended Lily Nolan was intriguing because of her prickly ways and quick mind. And her determination not to be cowed by his wealth or position. They were part of it, but not all. Denial only went so far, especially in a man who, after years of celibacy, of utter disinterest in sex, felt the sudden rush and roar of desire.

She waded out till the water was hip deep, her smile widening with each step. The glow on her face made him feel like a voyeur, watching an intensely private moment, yet he couldn't look away. He'd never seen her like this, so strong and free and elemental.

In a sinuous movement she lifted her hands over her head and dived. Raffa waited till he saw her begin a strong, easy stroke. Then he dragged in a rough breath and turned to the headland. He'd have to clamber over the rocks instead of sand to get out but she deserved her solitude.

Lily shivered as the warm sea breeze feathered her face, her bare neck and legs. Despite the blaze of sunshine she was chilled to the marrow, frozen by apprehension. She'd never felt more vulnerable since that first day out of hospital.

She'd chosen this chair by the poolside out of bravado, proving to herself she wasn't the coward Raffaele thought her.

But it seemed she was. Her joints felt as if they'd been welded solid with the effort it took to remain here, in full public view, and wearing so little.

'Can I join you?' The voice, like rich caramel, swirled around Lily. Beckoning warmth encircled her, coaxing taut muscles to ease just a little.

Something like relief fizzed in her veins.

He'd come.

She hadn't expected him to.

Or wanted him, she assured herself.

Slowly Lily turned. Raffaele Petri stood on the flag-stones, his back to the pool and the outdoor café/bar where guests gathered. Against the azure of the pool his gold-toned body, bare but for damp board shorts and a half-buttoned shirt, glowed. The sun gilded his tousled hair, but it was his eyes, deep-set and probing, that snagged her attention.

A flare of heat ran through her veins then dropped to eddy in her stomach.

She should be furious with him.

She *wanted* to be furious.

But she was grateful too. He'd ripped the blinkers from her eyes.

She shrugged, stiff muscles protesting. 'Sounds good. With you here they'll forget to look at me.'

More likely the other resort guests would wonder what the most beautiful man on the planet was doing with such an ugly woman. Beauty and the Beast.

She reminded herself she didn't care. That was her mantra as of dawn this morning. She'd given up worrying about the effect she had on others. Or she would, she assured herself, once she got used to being out in public. For now she'd pretend to ignore the prickle across her skin as the weight of so many curious eyes grazed her.

'They're too busy worrying about their suntans to pay attention to us.'

Lily stifled a snort of disbelief. No one could help but notice Raffaele. He hooked a chair close and sank into it, the fluid grace of his athletic body mesmerising.

Yet he wasn't at ease. The smile edging his lips wasn't his usual confident one. It looked lopsided, almost self-conscious.

The idea confused her. She snatched at it greedily, anything to distract herself from her surroundings.

Raffaele was utterly sure of himself. He was powerful, able to get what he wanted with the click of his fingers. Nor did a crisis faze him. She'd seen him work through unexpected and potentially calamitous developments in the office. He'd been unflappable, thriving on challenge.

'Espresso.' He nodded to the waiter who'd materialised

beside them. 'And...?' He looked questioningly at her empty glass.

'Another fruit juice, thank you, Charles.' She lifted her head to meet the waiter's eyes, feeling the sun warm her bare cheeks. In a fit of defiant energy she'd coiled her hair up, using every pin she possessed to secure it. No more covering her cheeks. No more concealment. It had sounded simple back in her bungalow, but here, where everyone passing could see her, she felt exposed.

'You're on first-name terms with the waiter?'

'You disapprove?' She closed her eyes, telling herself she enjoyed the feel of the sun on her face.

'Not at all. But a lot of people don't bother to discover the names of people who serve them.'

'I'm a researcher, remember. You'd be amazed how much I've found out from talking with the locals. But the fact is they're so friendly I enjoy getting to know them.' They'd made her feel welcome despite her nerves in a new place, meeting new people.

'Lily?'

She opened her eyes to find Raffaele leaning close. The blaze of those ocean-bright eyes did odd things to her breathing.

'Yes?'

He paused and she frowned, wondering at his unaccustomed hesitation.

'I apologise.'

Lily stared, watching his lips form the words but not believing the evidence of her eyes or her ears.

'Apologise?' Raffaele Petri? He might not be the ogre who'd once threatened to destroy her business. He might even be kind. But she'd never heard him admit regret.

The line of his mouth kinked in a brittle smile. 'Last night. What I said to you—'

'Don't.' She shook her head, again hyper-aware of the

warmth of the sun on her cheeks instead of the swish of her hair.

'You were right.' The words were thick in her throat, an admission of her own blindness. She should have seen the truth sooner. 'I *was* hiding.' It was the hardest admission she'd ever made.

He nodded, his gaze fixed on her face. A tremor ran through her, her fingers twitching with the almost unstoppable urge to wrench her hair down and conceal herself.

'I know. I wasn't apologising for that. But for the way I spoke to you. I'm sorry. I was angry, arrogant. I should have been more tactful.'

Lily's mouth sagged. No apology for what he'd done, just the way he'd done it. What must it be like to be so utterly sure of yourself?

But he wasn't. She read his wariness and regret. She'd swear that was doubt in his set features. The realisation tipped the world out of balance for the second time in less than twenty-four hours.

'What are you smiling about?' His brow furrowed.

'Nothing. Really.' She paused and dragged in a fortifying breath, watching the waiter place their drinks on the table then leave. 'I… Thank you. I think if you'd been kind I wouldn't have listened. You *made* me listen because you didn't mince your words.'

She owed him so much. Without pausing for second thoughts she reached out and touched him lightly on the back of the hand.

Instantly energy fizzed and crackled up her arm, prickling her skin and drawing the hairs on her nape upright.

Dismay wrenched at her insides. She had an immediate, overwhelming certainty that she'd gone too far. Not because he looked disapproving, but because of the dart and fizz of pleasure making her body come alive in a whole new way. She looked down, *willing* her fingers not to close around his. It took far too long for her hand to obey her brain, yanking back as if scalded.

Her eyes fluttered shut as she sucked in a horrified breath. How could such a little thing be so devastating?

'Lily?' That low voice hummed through every erogenous zone in her body. She had to get a grip. She was twenty-eight, not some teenager.

Except when it came to dealing with attractive men that was exactly how she felt: fourteen and flustered, gauche and totally inexperienced.

Lily snapped open her eyes, forcing herself to meet that stunning blue stare. 'I accept your apology. I hated the way you said it but I'm glad you did.' Her pent-up breath expelled in a whoosh. 'I can't believe I never saw it before.'

'Hey, don't beat yourself up. You're a remarkable woman. You've achieved so much. And, no, I don't just mean your work for me.' He gestured to her cheek. 'Coping with that would tax anyone. You've done superbly.'

'Why are you being so kind?'

'Kind?' His eyes rounded. 'I'm realistic. What you've built for yourself, the woman you are—that took guts and determination.'

He meant it. This wasn't like the well-meaning bonhomie of her family, whose exuberant praise for even the smallest achievements made her feel…not patronised… but as if perhaps those small achievements were the best she could ever do.

Guilt smote her. It wasn't like that, really. Her family had been on her side through the darkest days. She wouldn't have got through what she had without them. Of course they'd wanted to celebrate each small step forward. But eventually she'd become claustrophobic, encircled by their protectiveness.

Yet Raffaele's no-nonsense approach, his confrontational attitude, challenging her to rise above her fear, had made all the difference.

She cleared her throat. 'I could say the same about you. You've come a long way.'

Was it imagination or did the shutters come down on his expression? Strange. She'd never considered he had no-go territory. Raffaele seemed so confident and at ease.

A moment later the impression was gone. He lifted his coffee cup for a leisurely sip, leaning into his chair, one arm looped over the back. The pose stretched the gap of his half-open shirt, revealing a sprinkling of hair across his tightly muscled chest.

Lily blinked, cursing her inability to concentrate. This was the closest she'd ever been to a virile, attractive man in his prime and it tied her brain in knots.

A woman on the far side of the pool stumbled to a stop, staring, before recovering her poise and her dropped beach towel. The fact Lily wasn't the only one responding to Raffaele's stunning looks didn't make her feel better.

It made her feel…possessive. He was here with *her*, even if it was just their business connection and his concern for her welfare that linked them.

'That was another life.' His smile was brief but dazzling, yet Lily couldn't help feeling he used it to distract her.

He didn't want to talk about his past? She could relate to that. She opened her mouth to ask about his plans for this resort, if and when he acquired it from Robert Bradshaw, but he got in first.

'You'll need to be careful of the sun.' He gestured to the filmy caftan of bronze and golden brown she wore over her swimsuit. 'Delightful as that outfit is, there's no sun protection and your skin is like cream.'

Was that a compliment or an accusation? A reminder that she'd lived the last few years immured at home, using work as an excuse not to go out?

To Lily's amazement she felt heat creep under her skin. A heat that had nothing to do with the sunshine and everything to do with Raffaele Petri's heavy-lidded gaze on her body. It had been more than a decade since she'd blushed but that stare was unlike anything she'd ever experienced. Men didn't look at her that way. Ever.

'Where's the hat I ordered for you? You should at least be wearing that.'

It was a sign of her stress that she'd actually forgotten the clothes she wore had been bought by him.

Suddenly the slinky bronze swimsuit felt too clingy. And as for the gossamer-thin cover-up—its light-as-air delicacy against her arms and bare thighs now made her imagine another touch...the touch of trailing masculine fingers.

'I don't need a nanny, Raffaele.' She might have problems going out among people but she was twenty-eight, able to watch out for sunburn.

'Just as well.' His drawl rang alarm bells in some never-before-accessed part of her brain. 'Because I don't feel at all like a nanny.'

His expression jammed the breath in her lungs. Worse, it drew the heat that skimmed her body down into a spiralling vortex.

Lily clamped her hands on the arms of her chair, willing herself not to shift restlessly. But his look was making her feel...aroused. Aware. Awash with longing.

Her nipples tightened into buds and she crossed her arms, hoping she looked annoyed, anything but needy.

It would be excruciatingly awful if he realised how attracted she was. Enough to imagine she read sexual interest in his glance.

'That's another thing. I owe you for the clothes. I know you only sent them as a challenge, to dare me out of my comfort zone, but I have to pay you back.'

Once more his gaze skimmed over her, with the swift precision of a connoisseur. What did he see, apart from her blemished face? A too-pale body that held no allure when compared with the women he knew? Of course that was it. He'd even bought this outfit in shades of brown, surely a sign he saw her as a drab sparrow.

'And for the pleasure of seeing you in them.'

'Sorry?' The screech of her chair scraping back on the flagstones almost obliterated the sound of her shock-diminished voice. Her heart thrummed so hard against her ribs she felt light-headed.

'I said, I wanted to see you in them. You've got a lovely body, Lily. You should be proud of it.'

She shook her head.

'You've made your point about me being a recluse. You don't need to say things that aren't true.' He had no idea how cruel that was. How badly a woman who'd never had such a compliment in her life yearned for it to be real.

She'd spent half a lifetime being told that true beauty was on the inside. But some pathetic, juvenile part of her still longed to be thought pretty. Just once.

'You think I'm lying?' His dark eyebrows steepled together. 'You know me, Lily. I always get straight to the point. These days I tell the unvarnished truth instead of any easy lies.'

He leaned forward, closing the gap between them. His bluer than blue eyes pinioned her. 'You have a beautiful body, Lily, and I enjoy looking at you. *That's* the truth.'

CHAPTER EIGHT

RAFFA WATCHED HER stalk from the pool terrace, along the path through the gardens. Head up, shoulders back, long legs supple and strong, hips swaying in unconscious invitation. She was as alluring as any classically beautiful model he'd known.

More. There was nothing artificial about Lily. From those pert breasts to that searing golden-brown stare she was authentic.

Desirable.

Around the poolside heads turned to follow her progress. Raffa saw women lean close together, whispering, their expressions varying from sympathy to horror.

No doubt about it, Lily had been brave sitting here alone, without even a hat to conceal her scarred face.

But for every female shudder he caught more masculine stares. Some overt, some discreet, all fixed on the delectable sway of her body.

Raffa tried to analyse what it was about her that fired his libido. The swell of her hips? The ripe thrust of her breasts? The long, seductive curve of thigh and calf?

Maybe the way her voice turned to a throaty purr when she was annoyed. Or the curious mix of vulnerability and vivacity that kept him on his toes. Even her prickly defensiveness appealed, provoking him time and again to pursue the woman who tried to disguise herself.

For the first time he was attracted to a woman's mind, her thoughts and character, as well as her body.

Whatever this was, he'd passed the point of hoping it would go away. She'd stirred him out of sexual apathy so profoundly he felt wired, attuned to her as a predator to his prey. Her every shift of mood jangled his senses, under-mining his concentration on the vital deal he'd come here to close. He should be focused on Bradshaw, yet Lily was a distraction he couldn't ignore.

Worryingly, she also aroused dormant feelings—con-cern, protectiveness, caring. Feelings expunged the day his childhood ended. The day Gabriella had been found dead.

Raffa sank back in his seat, winded by the devastating simplicity of what he faced.

For the first time in his life there was no careful con-sideration of pros and cons, of benefits versus risks. Just untrammelled desire, simple and unprecedented.

That explained his less than impressive performance just now. No one hearing him would believe he'd once made a living out of sweet-talking women. He'd known how to pan-der to female fantasies, to become whatever they wanted for long enough to get what he in turn needed from them. He'd been smooth but never obvious. He'd made each one feel special. That had been his gift and his greatest asset.

The question was, had he completely lost his touch?

Raffa was lost in thought when a flash of colour caught his eye. A stream of dark gold as familiar as the reflection he saw in the mirror if ever he bothered to look. Colour as rich as ancient coins, hoarded for a king's pleasure, but instead of cold metal this was a ribbon burnished by the sun, cascading down a woman's back. It rippled in soft waves as she moved.

Emotion clutched his chest, digging talons deep into his heart, squeezing his lungs. His breath stopped on a harsh rasp. She moved again, slender arms pushing her hair over her shoulder in a gesture he'd known from infancy.

Gabriella.

Raffa opened his mouth till instinct, more primitive than logic, stopped him. To call out would break the magic.

He wanted to run to her. Pour out his apologies for not

behaving better, for not appreciating how lucky he was to have her. For driving her away in frustration that last night. He was twelve again and desperate. He felt grief and regret, shame and hope.

Till she moved again and the magic was lost.

It wasn't Gabriella.

Of course it wasn't. Gabriella was twenty-one years' dead. Yet for a moment she'd been vividly alive again. Raffa's heart sprinted in a sickening, uneven gallop, his lungs atrophied and he forced his fisted hands to loosen.

The young woman moved again, walking through the shallow end of the pool, and her walk wasn't Gabriella's. Her hair wasn't down to her waist and she was boyishly slim whereas Gabriella had been curvy.

One thing they had in common though. They were both in their teens. The girl was around fifteen or sixteen, much younger than the man helping her from the pool.

Raffa was turning away when his gaze sharpened. That wasn't her father taking her arm. He recognised the fleshy face and ham-like hands. Hands that lingered on her hips. *Robert Bradshaw.* The man he'd avoided since arriving. He had no interest in seeing him till he was ready to make his move. Making Bradshaw sweat, waiting for that moment, was a bonus.

But it wasn't the deal on Raffa's mind now. It was Gabriella and how Bradshaw had ushered her aboard his boat twenty-one years ago, an arm hovering near her waist as he offered champagne.

The next morning Gabriella was dead.

There was a crash and Raffa looked down to see glass splintered across the paving where he'd knocked his drink.

Bradshaw heard it too, his head snapping up. Seconds later he was patting the girl and murmuring in her ear before leaving her.

'Signor Petri. It's good to see you at last.' He lunged forward to shake hands but Raffa avoided the gesture, leaning down to collect broken glass.

'Leave that. It's what the staff are for.' The Englishman turned as a waiter hurried out with a brush and pan. 'About time! You should have been here instantly.'

'It's fine.' Raffa nodded to the waiter. 'My fault.'

Seconds later the glass was cleared and Bradshaw hefted himself into a chair. 'I've been wanting to catch up with you. We've a lot to discuss.' He waved expansively. 'Excellent idea to come here personally to see the resort before we close a deal. It's really something, isn't it?'

Behind his air of ease Raffa detected strain. Good. That was a start. Ideally Raffa would see him behind bars for the rest of his life but, as that wasn't possible, the revenge he'd planned would have to be enough.

'It's peaceful.' He saw Bradshaw frown, dismayed at Raffa's lack of praise. The man was no negotiator, letting his fear show.

'Come to my house and I'll see you get some action.' Bradshaw leaned in. 'Come to dinner. I'll throw a private party. I'm sure you'll enjoy it.'

Raffa was shaking his head before Bradshaw stopped speaking. 'I'm afraid not.' He didn't bother giving an excuse. Let him stew.

Bradshaw's smile grew guarded. 'Later in the week then. Let me know when you're free to discuss business. In the meantime, relax, enjoy.' He leaned close enough for Raffa to smell sweat and expensive aftershave.

'Would you like some female company to amuse you while you're here? It would be very discreet.' When Raffa didn't respond he continued, flicking a glance across the pool. 'A nice, fresh girl. Blonde, maybe? Or redhead? Just say the word.'

Nausea clutched Raffa's belly as he followed Bradshaw's leering gaze to the girl he'd seen earlier. His hands dug so tight into his chair's armrests he'd probably mark the metal like he wanted to mark Bradshaw's face. It was a miracle he held back, a miracle possible only because he knew Bradshaw would pay with everything he had and everything he'd ever wanted, once this deal went through.

'No,' Raffa croaked. 'Nothing. I'm here for peace and quiet.'

Abruptly he levered himself up, barely acknowledging the other man's babble about meeting soon for sundowners at his house.

Raffa nodded and strode away. He told himself his tactic to make Bradshaw sweat could only help negotiations. But the truth was he couldn't stomach being within spitting distance of the man. He didn't trust himself not to do him violence.

CHAPTER NINE

SEEING BRADSHAW LEFT a sour taste in Raffa's mouth. He wanted this wrapped up. But after more long distance discussions with his legal team, he acknowledged there were still matters to be sorted before he brought Bradshaw to his knees. The delay rankled, but at least it had the bonus of making Bradshaw even more desperate.

When Lily knocked on his villa door for their early evening meeting, relief hit like the smack of an ocean wave. Raffa needed distraction from his circling thoughts but more, he'd wondered if she'd show after what had passed between them.

He couldn't explain it but since seeing Bradshaw and that girl at the pool, Raffa had been unsettled, ridiculously on edge as emotions crowded close. Calm evaded him as if the thick skin he'd spent a lifetime nurturing had been scraped raw. He felt... He *felt*! And it wasn't just hatred of Bradshaw.

He told himself he needed the distraction of work.

Yet Lily looked anything but professional in the clothes he'd chosen. An aqua scoop-necked top and wraparound skirt in aqua with a swirl of gold that fluttered enticingly around her legs. She hesitated in the doorway, giving him time to drink her in and to stifle the urge to haul her close. His gaze dipped briefly, taking in the ankle ties on the sandals that accentuated her sexy calves.

An appreciative smile curled inside him, a smile he repressed. She was skittish enough already. 'You're here. Good. We've a lot to get through.'

Predictably, instead of stiffening at his tone, Lily seemed

reassured as she stepped over the threshold and onto the polished wood floor.

'This is for you.' She offered an envelope.

Her resignation? The idea tore his thoughts completely free of Bradshaw and business. His chest hollowed as he made himself reach for it, noting the way she relinquished it as soon as he grasped it.

Had he pushed her too far? She was like a porcupine, raising spiky quills if he got too near. Yet he knew she wanted him as much as he wanted her. If only he could entice her to let down her guard.

Mouth firm, Raffa tore open the envelope. 'Money?'

'For the clothes.' Her voice was as tight as her shoulders.

Briefly Raffa considered admitting it had been pure pleasure choosing clothes for her, ones that suited her and made the most of her delectable body. That if he'd had his way he wouldn't have stopped there. He'd have bought the ivory lace nightgown for starters. Just for the pleasure of seeing her in it, then peeling it away.

'Consider it a business perk.' He held the envelope out to her. 'I insisted on bringing you here.'

She shook her head. For once there was no accompanying ripple of brown silk around her shoulders. She'd pinned her hair up again. Pinned it so tight it was a wonder she didn't have a headache.

Definitely one for gestures, his *piccola istrice*. How sharp, he wondered, were her quills?

'I buy my own clothes.'

'Even if you didn't choose them?' If she'd had her way there'd have been more concealing shirts and baggy trousers.

'I accepted them, therefore I pay.' As she said it her hand rose to her neckline. A sign of nerves?

It struck him anew how difficult it must be for Lily to reveal herself like this. But he knew better than to show his thoughts, much less praise her courage.

'Fine.' He tossed the envelope onto the table where he'd drawn up two chairs. 'Now, let's get started. I want to go over every last detail. Nothing can be missed.'

As ever when they worked, time slid by unnoticed. Lily began to relax as Raffaele focused on business.

There were no kindling glances or personal comments. They were again boss and employee, or more precisely, colleagues. Raffaele recognised the expertise of his team and treated them with respect. Lily thrived on feeling appreciated.

'When are you meeting Robert Bradshaw?' They'd been at the resort two nights and she knew there'd been at least one invitation to dine at Bradshaw's house on the far side of the island.

'In good time.' Raffa's voice was brusque.

'But isn't that why you're here?' Raffaele had driven his team like the devil to prepare for this deal. He'd come here himself rather than delegate. 'You're deliberately delaying?'

One eyebrow rose. 'The time's not right. I'm waiting till he's heard confirmation his play for more capital has failed. Then he'll be more amenable to my terms.'

'What if it doesn't fail?'

'Oh, it will.' Raffa's eyes flashed with an expression that unsettled, until Lily reminded herself they were discussing Robert Bradshaw.

She had no sympathy for the Englishman. Born with wealth, he'd squandered his fortune through excess. His few attempts at running any of the businesses he'd inherited had ended disastrously and now he teetered on the brink of ruin. Not that you'd know it from his lavish lifestyle.

'You're turning the screw?'

Raffa leaned back, linking his hands behind his head. The movement emphasised the heavy breadth of muscled shoulders and taut biceps beneath his casual shirt. Lily dragged her gaze to the old deeds she'd unearthed. But her breath came in shallow little bursts. She didn't feel professional but dizzy and shamefully entranced.

How much longer could she pretend disinterest?

'I've shown my hand by coming here. That's enough. No point letting Bradshaw think he'll get everything he wants.' Venom dripped from Raffaele's tone as he said the Englishman's name, confirming her suspicion of bad blood between the men. Yet her searches had uncovered no link.

'He's desperate for a partner to put up cash to renovate the place. Even he recognises profits aren't what they could be and it's his last money-making asset.'

'So the longer he waits, the more desperate he becomes.'

'Unless he finds another partner. It's a calculated risk not to rush in. The resort is an appealing investment.'

Lily nodded. It was like Paradise. She wouldn't be surprised if at least one of the other companies she'd worked for, De Laurentis Enterprises, was interested.

'But he wants you because you've got the golden touch.' Raffaele's hotels were a byword for discreet luxury that appealed to the seriously wealthy who sought respite from the paparazzi. And who had deep, deep pockets.

'It seems a shame to change the place. It's wonderful as it is.' Her gaze drifted to the white curve of beach framed by lush gardens. To her surprise the bright sky had darkened to indigo, torches lighting the path through the trees. It was later than she'd thought.

'It needs updating to attract the clientele Bradshaw wants.'

'The way the poolside bar has been updated?' Lily pursed her lips. While the rest of the resort had a graceful if slightly worn charm with plantation shutters, airy rooms and individual bungalows, the bar was sleek, black-tiled and ostentatiously modern with vivid neon light displays and uncomfortable, trendy metal chairs.

Raffaele's lip curled. 'Bradshaw's one effort at updating the place. The man's got no sense. The clientele he wants to attract can fly to New York or elsewhere if they want urban modern. They'll come here for premium luxury and privacy. And to experience the Caribbean, its tastes and laid-back style.'

'So what would you do? How would you change it?'

'Reduce the number of bungalows for a start.' He responded almost before she'd finished speaking. 'Keep the best and get rid of the rest. People pay for the privilege of privacy. Remodel and upgrade everything. Each villa would have its own pool, spa, butler and chef. Put in a truly fabulous restaurant on the hill featuring a new twist on traditional local flavours and produce. Bring in the absolute best in everything. Improve...'

'What?' She leaned across the table.

Abruptly Raffaele shook his head. 'It doesn't matter. All that matters is getting Bradshaw to accept my offer.' His voice was harsh, his words clipped.

Lily sat back. It was stupid to feel rebuffed. She wouldn't be involved when Raffaele put his plans into action. He had other staff for that. But she'd been caught up in his enthusiasm. His energy had drawn her, making her want more.

There was no more. Not with Raffaele. Not unless it was legwork for some other project.

She swallowed, realising it wasn't even his vision for the resort that had held her spellbound. It was Raffaele. She'd never known a man so charismatic, so vital. If she reached out a hand towards him she knew she'd feel the buzz and zap of energy radiating from him.

Yet the desire to touch was more than that.

She wanted to touch him the way a woman touched her lover.

Lily stood. 'It's time I left.'

He stood when she did, his expression unreadable. 'There's no rush. I've ordered dinner to be served here.'

Dinner? With Raffaele?

Lily felt the punch of her heart against her ribs. She

imagined them sitting, drinking in the view, sipping wine and feasting on seafood as they relaxed in each other's company. He'd be charming and she'd be witty and insightful and when their gazes locked she'd read heat and hunger and—

'We've finished for the day, haven't we?' Her voice was scratchy. Better that than needy, she told herself. Heat crept up her throat at the thoughts she'd harboured. 'Unless there's something else you wanted me to do.' She made a production of gathering her gear.

'There is, as it happens.'

Her head snapped up as those deep cadences wrapped around her. 'Yes?'

'I want you to dine with me.'

Lily blinked. 'Why?'

'I want your company.'

Her fingers curled around her laptop. She felt out of her depth.

The look he gave her, grave yet knowing, sent a wobble from her chest all the way to her knees. It was the sort of look she'd imagined a man gave a woman he was interested in. It made her pulse flutter in her throat as if she'd swallowed a swarm of bright island butterflies.

Lily had never received such a look before.

She didn't know what to do with it.

Or with the hammering excitement within.

She swallowed hard. Clearly she was superimposing her secret cravings on him. Raffaele Petri had a host of beautiful women to choose from. It was laughable to think he could be attracted to her.

Beyond laughable. It was pathetic.

'It's time I went.' Before she made a fool of herself.

'You said that before.' He crossed his arms over his chest and it struck her for the first time that he stood between her and the door.

Lily spread clammy hands on the table, hoping its solidity would help penetrate the fog in her brain. Help her think straight and stop imagining things.

Except, when she looked up, Raffaele's blue eyes sparked with something that made her belly curl and her nipples bud against her bra. Her skin felt tight, as if the woman inside were bursting to escape.

'It's true. We've finished for the night.'

Slowly he shook his head, the movement accentuating the shadows beneath his high cheekbones.

'I sincerely hope not.' Was it imagination or was his voice thicker, his accent more pronounced? It ran through her veins like warm caramel.

Lily dragged her hands from the table as if its surface was electrified. A large hand snapped out and captured her wrist. Instantly she stilled, all except for the quiver reverberating from her tingling fingers up her arm and down to the soles of her feet.

'What do you want, Raffaele? What are you playing at?' Old habit came to the rescue and her chin jutted. She'd spent half a lifetime pretending to be impervious to hurt.

'What do you think I want?' It was the voice of her dreams, seductive, alluring and full of desire.

Impossible!

She yanked her hand free, stepping out of reach. Her breath sawed through searing lungs.

He was flirting. Sending her that half-lidded look that had turned a single photo into a multi-million-dollar success for a famous men's clothing company.

The impact of it in the flesh, on *her* flesh, was devastating.

'Stop it, Raffaele!' She was almost beyond caring that he might hear the hurt beneath her belligerence. She needed to get away. 'I don't…' She shook her head, wishing she hadn't made a point of pinning her hair up, wishing it could swish around her face, concealing an expression she feared must reveal the yearning in her soul.

'Don't what?'

Don't flirt. She didn't know how. Had no experience of it. Which made this game he played even more cruel.

'What are you afraid of, Lily?' His voice, rough suede, caressed her skin, drawing it to tingling life.

You.

Of you and everything you make me feel.

'I didn't think anything fazed you, Lily. You're so feisty, so focused.'

She cleared her throat to speak as he moved close enough for her to inhale the tantalising scent of warm male skin, salt spice and the sea. But determination wasn't enough. Not when she looked up into ocean-blue eyes. They burned with a heat that beckoned to every feminine instinct she'd spent fourteen years suppressing.

'Is it this you're afraid of?' His head lowered and warmth brushed her lips. The soft caress of perfectly sculpted lips. The fleeting, beckoning taste of Paradise as his tongue slicked the seam of her mouth.

Lily's eyelids flickered, weighted by the desire rolling through her, inexorably growing, expanding, clogging every sense. All she knew was the scent and taste of Raffaele, the heat of his breath on her lips, the pulse of longing throbbing within.

Air brushed her mouth as his lips left hers and for a heartbeat nothing moved. She didn't even breathe.

Lily forced her eyes open. Azure depths captured her and it was as if she'd ventured too far out to sea. Except she wasn't sinking, she was floating, buoyed by an anticipation so acute she felt she'd shatter if he didn't put an end to it and kiss her properly.

'I'm not afraid,' she lied.

She was terrified. Thrilled. Exultant. Curious.

Lily felt her hand settle against the muscled plane of his chest. Beneath her palm beat a steady pulse that seemed leisurely compared with her own wildly careering heartbeat.

He was *real*. Not the phantom lover of her dreams. His flesh was hotter than hers even through his shirt.

His chest rose under her touch, making her aware of the masculine power beneath the designer panache. The air of languid relaxation Raffaele so often adopted was a front, she realised, as sparks tickled her palm, racing up her arm. The man was all potent power.

But he was her boss. He was one of the most beautiful men on the planet, and she—

'Lily.' His voice was so deep she felt its reverberation in her belly. His hand was hard as it clamped her palm to his chest.

She shifted back. 'This is a mistake.'

He moved with her, his thigh brushing hers. Ripples coursed up her leg to the spot between her thighs where a different pulse beat—needy and quick.

'No mistake. Admit it, Lily. This feels *right*.'

His left hand captured her nape, long fingers spearing through her hair to hold her still as his head slanted down.

Time moved in infinitely slow seconds. Slow enough for her to realise that, despite his hold, she had only to turn her head or step back and she'd be free.

But she didn't move. It *did* feel right. More, it felt inevitable. Why pretend when for weeks she'd wondered what it would be like to kiss Raffaele?

His lips touched hers again, once, twice, before settling on her mouth, sealing her breath with his. For a moment he held utterly still. She absorbed the rich, warm scent of his skin, the delicious tang of him on her tongue, the long body hard up against hers, and the gentleness of his hand at the back of her head, cradling, tender...

Then those azure eyes closed, his head tilting as he delved between her parted lips. One swiping caress and sensation shuddered down her backbone and further, weakening her knees. They trembled as she clutched him, drawn by the slide of his mouth, his probing tongue and the waves of need, dark and intoxicating, that buffeted her.

His hand tightened on her skull, the angle of his mouth changed and the kiss grew harder, insistent, demanding. Raffaele drew her tongue between his lips, sucking, and a shot of adrenaline, of *something,* fired in her blood. The pulse between her legs quickened, her nipples against his chest so sensitive she almost cried out as each muffled breath abraded them against him. She was on fire, burning up in a heat he both kindled and promised to assuage.

Was it possible to climax just from kissing?

Lily slipped her hands up to clasp his face, framing hard bone and taut skin, learning sculpted contours as his tongue flicked hers, inviting her to join him, to give in.

A mighty shudder ran through her, a sigh that made no sound in the whirling ecstasy of the moment. A sigh of surrender as Lily let herself go and for the first time in her life kissed a man.

He'd guessed she'd be delicious. He'd expected fire beneath her guarded prickliness.

But still he wasn't prepared. Lily's slender body turned to flame against him, all eager passion and flagrant, hungry need. He felt her shake in his hold, her whole body trembling. But not with fear. Not when she kissed him back with such glorious abandon.

He couldn't get enough, clutching her greedily.

Tongue on tongue, lips against lips, heart to heart, soft belly to quickening arousal—she was all he'd hoped for and more. The scent of sweet pears vied with a tantalising hint of musk and she tasted…he couldn't describe her flavour, other than addictive.

Raffa drew her against his mouth and his groin. How long since he'd felt that urgent spiral of desire? That restless hunger to possess?

For years he'd been celibate, uninterested in women. Yet

Lily, with her shaking hands and clumsy kisses, turned him on more than any practised seductress.

She pressed in, her teeth mashing his lip. Her untutored eagerness was beguiling as nothing he'd ever experienced. Raffaele was used to women blasé about sex, who enjoyed it but were never surprised by it.

By contrast he sensed shock as well as delight in Lily's response. As if all this was new.

Would you touch a woman who looked like this?

Of course you wouldn't.

Her words slammed into him. And the memory of Lily's grave eyes as she'd said it, hurt dragging her mouth down.

In the midst of the maelstrom something inside him stilled, held its breath.

Instinct urged him to take advantage of her eagerness. But some damned part of his brain had begun working, sifting what she'd said, analysing the inexperience in her kisses and clutching hands.

It couldn't be.

No woman got to twenty-eight without being kissed.

His mind reeled. It was inconceivable to a man who'd lost count of his sexual partners well before he was out of his teens. Yet the small, still reasoning part of his brain acknowledged Lily kissed like a virgin.

Shock ground through his belly. Tangled threads of desire and guilt twisted into a jumbled knot that grew and grew till it pressed upon his chest, cramping his lungs, stopping his breath.

He reared back, panting, heart hurling itself against his ribs. He looked down at parted lips, plump and pink. Almost, he slammed his mouth back onto hers as the tide of wanting rose.

But he forced himself to think. To observe.

Her breathing was even more out of kilter than his, her eyes closed. On one side of her face was clear, flushed skin, soft as silk. On the other, the broad, taut brand of healed flesh. She'd called it ugly, something from a horror movie. To Raffa it had merely become part of her, like the way she wrinkled her nose when he said something she disagreed with. Or the glow in her eyes when she forgot to be cautious and revealed her natural ebullience.

Could it be true no man had got this close because of her scar?

Or maybe she'd been too defensive to let one near. That, he could believe.

Her eyes snapped open, searching with an intensity that made Raffa feel every one of his thirty-three tarnished years.

He could barely remember being a virgin. He'd never kissed one in his life.

As for taking one to bed, as he'd aimed to take Lily after a champagne supper—he shuddered, seeing the awed hope in her gaze. The innocence, for once unguarded.

She trusted him.

Raffa thought of the things he'd done to get where he was today, the seedy, *special* arrangements. He was sullied in ways Lily would never know. Ways that didn't show on the outside, but were there, a stain nothing could remove.

Aghast, he dropped his hands as a new thought needled.

Had he, at some unconscious level, understood Lily's innocence? Was he grasping for it as once, years ago, a jaded businesswoman had lusted after Raffa's innocence as much as his young body and fair face?

Bile rose in a gush. Acid filled his mouth, obliterating the taste of her, the beckoning, elusive flavour of innocent pleasure.

What had he ever known of innocent pleasure?

'Raffaele?' Her whisper tugged his libido and his conscience—two entities that had lain dormant for so long he'd thought he'd lost both. 'What is it?'

Caution clouded her desire. It happened so fast it confirmed everything he'd wondered about the hurt she'd endured in the past. She'd schooled herself to disappointment.

'You're right,' he croaked. 'Dining together is a bad idea.' He cleared his throat, forcing out the words. 'It's better if you leave.'

She spun away before he stopped talking, was out of the villa within seconds. But not before he saw hurt in her eyes. And the way her head rocked back as if he'd hit her.

Raffa stood where she'd left him, sucker-punched by an unseen blow to his belly at the pain he'd inflicted.

Worse, though, was the knowledge he couldn't fix this. He couldn't be the man Lily needed.

CHAPTER TEN

HOURS LATER, LILY still cringed when she thought of the frantic way she'd clung to Raffaele, begging for more.

One touch of his lips was all it had taken for every defence to collapse, laid waste by his caresses and her desperate hunger.

She'd been so needy she'd thought she'd explode with wanting. Another kiss like that and she'd probably have climaxed where she stood. It almost made the years of waiting worth it, to experience such incandescent pleasure.

Raffaele was a master of the sensual arts. No wonder he hadn't wanted to continue the experiment. She'd been gauchely overeager, lost to everything but the wonder of her first kiss.

Twenty-eight and kissed for the first time!

And the last, if tonight was any indicator.

Lily groaned and swung around to pace the darkened room. There was no danger of tripping over anything. She'd retraced her steps thousands of times in the last few hours, unable to settle while she was so awash with fury, frustration and embarrassment.

Why, oh, why had she let him dare her into taking a risk? Into believing after all these years things had changed and her scar didn't matter?

Had she *really* thought Raffaele was attracted to her? The kiss was all about curiosity on his part and she'd left herself wide open to hurt.

Her ribs seemed to contract around her frantically beating heart. She'd believed Raffaele different. Caring, despite his ruthless streak and patent expectation of always getting his own way. She'd never believed him cruel.

But what he'd done tonight…

Oh, get over it! You were only too eager to kiss the man. You can't blame him for pulling back. Just because you're besotted—

Lily slammed an iron bar across that thought. She was *not* going there. Not now. Not ever.

She was going to do what she always did. Pick herself up, dust herself off and get on with life. Bury herself in work. Strive to achieve.

Except she'd left her laptop in his villa and nothing, not even a tsunami, was going to propel her back there.

Her gaze went to the view beyond the window, the pale crescent of sand and dark glitter of water. There was one way she could expel this restless energy. Spinning on her heel, she crossed the room, reefing off her top and bra. Her skirt slithered to the floor and she stepped out of it, then her underwear, tugging pins from her hair. Naked, she grabbed the new swimsuit, obliterating any thought of the man who'd given it to her as she dragged it on. Of course he hadn't chosen it personally.

Moments later she was closing the door of her villa, breathing the sweet scent of blossom in the resort gardens and the tantalising saltiness of the sea. She took a step, only to slam to a halt as she saw something on her private patio.

Someone, not something.

In the starlight he looked impossibly tall as he vacated the chair and stood.

'How long have you been here?' The words were staccato beats, crashing through the silence. Adrenaline blasted her bloodstream, triggering heightened awareness. She registered the residual warmth of the flagstones beneath her bare feet, the throb of her pulse, the prickle as her flesh tightened, responding to Raffaele's nearness. And the lingering taste of him on her tongue, like a delicacy her memory refused to discard.

In the gloom she made out his characteristic shrug. 'A while. I thought you were asleep.'

Lily hadn't bothered with lights. She didn't want to face herself in the mirror. Darkness had been a refuge.

'I don't want you here.' The words scraped from the bottom of her bruised soul.

'I know.' His voice sounded curiously hollow.

'Then why are you here?' She jammed her hands on her hips, finding comfort in indignation.

'I wanted to make sure you were okay.'

'By sitting here in the dark?' She'd never heard anything so unlikely.

'I didn't want to leave you all alone. I felt…responsible.'

Ridiculous how that stung.

'I'm an adult, Raffaele.' She swallowed his name, hating that even now she loved the taste of it. Lily wanted to rage and curse at the power he had over her. It wasn't supposed to be this way. She was supposed to loathe him.

'There's no need to feel responsible. I look after myself.' For a moment she felt the weight of that drag at her shoulders. The years of being alone, dealing with everything solo. Then she straightened. 'Don't wait up for me. I'm going for a swim.'

One swift step and he blocked her path. 'At night?'

Lily angled her jaw, as if she could meet his eyes in the shadows.

'You're not my keeper. Now step aside. There's no need for this…' she waved her hand dismissively '…show of solicitude. Go away and concentrate on Robert Bradshaw. He's the reason you're here.'

She needed to remember that. Raffaele's focus was business. He was single-minded to the point of obsession with this project. She was a curiosity, a diversion.

'You can't swim now. It's too dangerous.' The words sounded as if they'd been ground out, like glass splintering beneath a twisting boot. 'What if you get a cramp and there's no one to help?'

A writhing, seething, lava-hot surge of anger shot through her, that he pretended to care. She sidestepped and stalked past.

Hard fingers shackled her wrist, pulling her up short.

'Let. Me. Go. Now.'

'Lily, listen to me, I—'

'No.' She swung around, staring up into features now illuminated by starlight, features as flagrantly gorgeous as ever. Lily felt the inevitable lift inside her chest, then the slow burn of shame that she couldn't, even now, eradicate the wanting.

'*You* listen, Raffaele. I may be different to the people you know. I may *look* different. But I deserve respect. I'm not some amusing freak, here to entertain you in your downtime. I—'

'*Per la Madonna!*' The low roar of his voice filled the air, his hand gripping hers. 'Don't talk like that.'

'Why not? It's the truth.'

A rush of words filled her ears, low, fluid, a non-stop litany of what had to be curses, though she couldn't understand the Italian. She'd never heard Raffaele sound so far from the savvy, self-contained entrepreneur she knew.

'You can't think that! It's not true.'

Abruptly weariness gathered her in. What was the point of listening to Raffaele excuse his behaviour?

'I'm not interested, Raffaele. Just go. Leave me be.'

'Lily. I swear it wasn't like that.'

'What was it like, then?' She knew she shouldn't ask. His answer would only rub salt in the wound but she couldn't stop herself.

'It was…unbelievable. Better than I'd ever—'

'No! Don't you *dare*!' Lily reefed her fingers from his, clapping her hands over her ears. 'Don't lie.' She spun away, stumbling down the sandy path towards the beach.

This time it wasn't his hand that stopped her. It was his whole arm, looping around her waist, hauling her back against his tall frame. Heat and muscle burned her back. But it was nothing to the fire roaring within.

'It's no lie.' His breath feathered her neck, stirring her hair. 'Kissing you was the best thing I've done in years.'

Lily shook her head. How was she supposed to stay strong when he used words like that to undo her? Despite her indignation, her knees wobbled. She was in danger of sagging against him.

Deliberately she snorted her disgust. 'Right. That's why you pulled away as if you'd been burned. Why you told me to leave.'

'I told you to leave because I realised you deserved better...than I can give you.'

Her bitter laugh tore the night. 'Better? You have to be kidding.' He kissed like a god. What could be better? 'You just didn't like the way I kissed you back. It reminded you that it was ugly Lily Nolan in your arms.'

Sibilants hissed against her ear as another burst of Italian washed around her, rougher this time. His arm at her waist turned hard as iron.

'Didn't like it? You have no idea.' Gone were the smooth cadences of his seductive voice. Instead it sounded like gravel dipped in burning tar. 'If I didn't like it would I react like this?'

He hauled her back so she was plastered against him. Hard thighs pressed into her and an enormous erection rose between the cheeks of her buttocks.

Lily swallowed convulsively, eyes popping, not just at the impossibility of his arousal, but the sheer size.

In this moment, with only the flimsy fabric of her swimsuit and his clothing between them, she felt her inexperience like a brand. The sensation of him jutting against her created a hollow ache between her legs. Even the liquid heat pooling there couldn't fill the void.

'Does it feel like I don't want you?' He ground against her. The slide of his arousal against her almost bare skin was unlike anything she'd ever known, the rough caress of his voice the most potently seductive sound she'd heard. 'Well, *cara*? Does it? You've been driving me crazy.' This time his lips touched her ear as he spoke, sending shivers of pleasure through her.

'I don't understand.'

'Don't you? You might be a virgin but you're not that innocent, Lily. You can *feel* how I want you.'

The shivers turned to a mighty trembling that racked her from head to toe. She wanted him so badly her skin felt too tight, as if she was going to burst out of it. Need and excitement warred with a lifetime's caution.

She was beyond denying her lack of experience. What was the point? It must be obvious.

'But you pushed me away.' Did he hear the hurt she tried to disguise?

'Of course I pushed you away. It wasn't right. You deserve someone better.'

Yet his arm clamped her to him. His body seared everywhere they touched, branding her. And that hard, swollen ridge against her backside… It took everything she had not to arch back, pressing into him.

'That's the second time you've said that,' she gasped. 'It still doesn't make sense.'

The sound of rough breathing filled her ears. His. Hers. The tumult of her pulse. Finally he spoke. 'You're an innocent. You deserve someone who can treasure that, turn your first time into something special.'

'You can't?' It didn't occur to Lily to play coy. Not with need battering her and Raffaele's breath, his body, his words, an enticement she'd given up trying to resist.

His laugh was short and sharp, off-key. He slid his arm across her stomach as if about to release her and Lily grabbed at it, holding on with both hands. His arm was sinewy, dusted with silky hair, every bit as gorgeous as it looked by daylight.

'I have no experience of innocence, Lily. I'm not the man for you.' There was finality in his words. They struck with the resonance of metal on stone.

'I don't believe you.' Releasing her hold on his arm, she twisted round, breasts to his ribs. He was so hot. So heavy against her belly. The weight of his erection made it hard to think. But she wanted him enough to ignore pride and self-preservation.

She slipped her hand, palm down, between them, curving it round his shaft. To her amazement it jumped in her hand as if it had a mind of its own. Her fingers flexed and tightened and she was rewarded with the sound of Raffaele's hiss of shock.

'Don't, Lily.' Hard fingers dug into her shoulders. 'You need someone special for your first time. That shouldn't be me. It shouldn't be anyone *like* me.'

Hands on her shoulders, he stepped back, creating distance. She felt his loss with a keening desperation.

'Don't go. I want—'

'I want too, but it's better this way. You'll find someone—'

'Don't talk rubbish. There won't be anyone else. There hasn't been and there won't ever be.' Not with her face.

For a long, aching moment she waited for his response but there was none.

Defeated, she pulled away so he had to release his hold or follow her. Of course he let her go.

Exhaustion consumed her. The nervous energy that had kept her wired for hours bled away. She'd never felt so weary.

'Just go, Raffaele. I've had enough. I can't follow your logic. You say you want me but you refuse to take me. You say my looks don't matter, but they do. You and I know they do.' Deliberately she lifted her face so what light there was spilled across her features. 'If they didn't you wouldn't hold back. You wouldn't pretend I could choose to make love with you then tell me I can't.'

Lily heard the defeat in her voice and knew she'd reached breaking point. Swiftly she turned, grabbing the door of her bungalow. 'I've never had that choice with any man and I never will.'

Just once, Lily wanted passion, even if only for a night. She wanted to feel as close as a woman could to a man, to experience physical pleasure at a man's hands. Not out of pity or kindness, but because he desired her as much as she did him.

As if that will ever happen.

Worse still, she wanted that with Raffaele. The man she feared she'd fallen for.

Her shoulders jumped as she bit back a silent sob.

The villa door opened easily and she felt sand under her feet as she stepped onto the cool tiles. But the door wouldn't shut behind her. She looked over her shoulder to find Raffaele blocking it, following her inside.

Desperation rose. 'Please go.' She couldn't stomach more conversation. 'I want to be alone.'

He pulled the door from her hand, closing it behind him with a quiet snick, trapping them in darkness.

'I can't—'

'Shh. It's okay.' Broad hands reached for her shoulders, drawing her to him, filling her with his spicy scent and that terrible, raw yearning.

'It's not okay.' Her voice hit a discordant note and he heard her fight back tears. 'Please, Raffaele. Please leave.'

Her pain tore Raffa's heart. He'd never heard Lily beg. He hated the sound of vulnerability—worse, of defeat. She was stronger than anyone he knew. He wrapped a hand around her back, the other plundering the silken softness of her hair as he held her close.

He breathed in the subtle sweet-as-fruit fragrance of her skin. He couldn't leave her like this, believing her looks had driven him away. It would only reinforce those negative feelings about her scar.

Raffa told himself he was here for Lily's sake. But he was selfish. He'd followed her because he couldn't walk away, despite knowing he wasn't the man she needed.

'I'm not going anywhere. You're stuck with me.'

'But you said…' Her voice was muffled, her lips caressing his collarbone, shooting sensation to his groin.

'What I said was right. I should go. But I can't. I want you too much.'

Later he'd regret this. Lily would too. But it was beyond him to turn back.

He'd never pretended to be a man of honour. Hadn't he spent his life pandering to excess and self-indulgence? Hadn't he built his fortune on the desire for pleasure? Sure, it had been about providing pleasure for others, but he wasn't spotless. He'd learned to grab what he wanted whenever and wherever temptation offered.

He wanted now.

How badly he wanted.

Bending at the knees, he slipped an arm beneath her legs, another around her back, and hiked her up in his arms. She was all sinuous, lissom curves and smooth, fragrant flesh. Her hair spilled over his bare arm and even that notched his need higher.

Her gasp was loud but it barely registered over the racing thud of his heartbeat as he headed for the bedroom. She'd left her shutters wide open and there was enough light to make out the bed.

His leg hit the mattress and he let himself fall, still cradling her, toppling together but twisting so she didn't take his full weight. Even so, the sensation of her half beneath him sent fire scudding through his body.

'You don't need to do this.' Her voice was half shock

and half bravado. Even in the gloom he made out the tight line of her jaw.

Something, a sensation he wasn't familiar with and couldn't identify, curled in on itself, burrowing through his chest. More than approval, more than pride or even protectiveness.

'You're wrong. I need to do exactly this. I tried not to take advantage, I really did. But I'm not cut out for self-denial.' Not surprising when he'd never tried denying himself anything he wanted, not since he'd worked and finagled his way out of poverty, setting his sights on a better life.

'But—'

Raffa stopped her words with his mouth, damming her protest. An instant later she was returning his kiss with a fervour that shattered his last attempt to hold back. The blaze of wanting consumed them, making her writhe beneath him. His thoughts sped to stripping her out of her swimsuit and impaling himself in her welcoming body as soon as possible.

She's a virgin.

Doesn't that mean anything to you?

The thought diverted his thoughts even as he dragged her shoulder strap down one arm, past the elbow she accommodatingly lifted, and off.

A second later her breast was in his hand, perfect, delectable. He lowered his head, licked a peaked nipple and felt her jerk high off the bed. Raffa stretched out his leg to capture both of hers before he lowered his head again to that stiff peak. He'd thought her taste addictive when he'd kissed her mouth, but this...this made him desperate.

'Please.' Her voice was a moan, her hands clutching him as he drew on her nipple, feeling her shift and buck beneath him.

His erection throbbed against her hip. Much more of this and he'd come before he even got naked.

Lily might be a virgin but she was all passionate woman, and a woman already on the brink.

Pride whispered that it was his seductive skills making her so desperate for release. Logic decreed long-term celibacy played its part.

Twenty-eight and virginal. The thought slowed his urgent touch. For him this surge of desire was remarkable, unique, after years of no interest in sex. But for Lily tonight had to be more. He had to make it perfect.

A man as tainted as he shouldn't be the one to introduce her to sex. But he'd do his damnedest to make it special for her.

Which meant tonight would be all about her.

He looped his fingers under her other shoulder strap and again she helped, eager to peel away the clingy fabric so both breasts were bare.

Her sigh of delight spurred him on as he held her in both hands, weighing those delectable breasts, sucking first one then the other, drawing pleasure from her till he thought he'd go mad from the effort of restraint.

The enticing scent of feminine arousal fogged his brain as he peeled her swimsuit down, over her arching ribs and soft belly, past the jut of her hip bones. His hand brushed the silk between her legs and she shuddered. So ready.

Yet Raffa took his time, rolling the fabric down her legs and away before acquainting himself with the arch of her instep, the slim circle of her ankle, the lush smoothness of her calf. When he kissed her knee and moved higher she sighed.

He followed the sound higher to the smooth flesh of her inner thigh, first one leg, then the other. They were trembling around him as he pushed them wider, jamming his shoulders against her as he opened her to him.

'Please,' she whispered in a purr of sound he knew would haunt his dreams from now on. 'I need you.'

His erection throbbed against the constriction of his

clothes. He wanted to rip his trousers away and thrust his way to release.

Which was why he made no move to undress. He didn't trust himself.

Inching higher, he felt her tension rise. There was something he wanted almost as much as to lose himself in her beautiful body. That was to taste the first orgasm she'd ever accepted from a man.

Lily whimpered as he kissed her there, her fingers tunnelling through his hair, her body restless. He'd barely settled at her centre, had merely taken one slow lick when he felt the fine tremor in her body turn to a judder of building ecstasy.

She cried his name in a hoarse gasp as she accepted the pleasure he gave her, returning it tenfold. Her deep quivers of delight, the tang of her in his mouth and the feel of her flexing, strong yet helpless, beneath him were gifts more precious than he expected. And the way she tugged him close, hands and legs pulling him in, enfolding him as if she couldn't bear to let go...

Had he felt this way before?

The answer was a resounding no.

With Lily he wasn't the cynical man of thirty-three who'd long ago lost interest in women, with their avarice and selfishness. Nor the kid who'd had his first taste of sex as a boy toy of a much older woman seeking diversion. He was someone new.

For years Raffa had used and been used. A commodity craved by women and advertisers who weren't interested in *him*. Never once had he felt as real, as honest, as with Lily.

He lay, centred on her, surrounded by her broken gasps, her trembling limbs and clutching hands, and discovered, to his amazement, it really did feel better to give than to receive. He *wanted* to please her.

Of course he wanted her for himself, but equally he

wanted to bask in her rapture as she learned delight in its many forms.

He lifted his hand, gently caressing her damp curls, and felt her jerk beneath his touch, still so sensitive.

How could he resist an invitation like that?

His expertise with women, his intimate, encyclopaedic knowledge of their bodies, wasn't something to be proud of. He'd acquired it as a necessary skill then later used it to get his own sexual satisfaction quickly. But tonight, as he turned that knowledge to seducing Lily, he was grateful for it. Every touch, every kiss, each slide of his body against hers, each murmured encouragement, had the sole purpose of making her first foray into sex memorable.

Gratification filled him with every sigh she uttered, every sob of delight, every climax. Till finally she lay, utterly spent.

His groin was on fire, his erection impossibly swollen, yet he pulled back.

Tonight was for her.

He couldn't quite believe it, but found himself moving to the side of the bed. Time to let her sleep.

'Don't go.'

'You're awake?' She lay so lax he'd assumed she was out for the count.

'How could I sleep?'

'Close your eyes. You'll sleep soon.' Raffa brushed her hair from her hot brow, feeling an unfamiliar wave of tenderness.

Surprisingly strong fingers caught his wrist. In the darkness he caught the glitter of her stare.

'We're not finished. I want *you*, Raffaele. I don't want to be a virgin anymore.'

Raffa couldn't remember denying himself anything he wanted and he wanted Lily with every fibre. But a decent man would leave her for the lover who, some day, would give her not just sex, but the relationship she deserved. A man nothing like himself.

Fingers shackled his other wrist as he made to move. He could break her hold, but her next words stopped him.

'I'm not a charity case, Raffaele. Don't make me feel like one.' There was just enough light for him to make out the movement of her throat as she swallowed. 'I thought you...wanted me too.'

Did she have any idea how close to the edge her words dragged him? Clearly not.

'Or was all this some elaborate attempt not to hurt my feelings?' Pride was in her stretched-thin voice, but pain too, and defiance.

'You've got a lot to learn about men, *tesoro*, if you think I don't want you.' He yanked her hand from his wrist and jammed it against his chest, where his heart galloped.

He caught the way her eyes widened, then she smiled, slow and wide, with the age-old power of a born seductress.

'Then show me.'

Her hands slipped to his trousers, one fumbling at the button and the other tugging the zip, till he had to rear back lest he lose himself there and then.

A moment later he stood beside the bed, drinking in the sight of her spreadeagled there, her hair a fathomless pool spilling out from her shoulders, her limbs pearly.

A man could only resist so much. He wrenched open the drawer of the bedside table, finding the packet of condoms thoughtfully provided for guests. After that everything blurred till he was naked and rolling on protection.

Then he was on her, flesh to flesh, bone and muscle against sweet femininity, and he was shaking as if he'd never done this before. As if it was his first time, not hers, and he was terrified of getting it wrong.

'This could be a little uncomfortable.' His guttural whisper was unrecognisable as he propped himself above her, taking his weight, holding steady at her entrance.

'You mean it could hurt.' Yet she laughed, as if she felt none of the strain weighing his every movement. 'It's okay. I won't break.'

Her hand slipped down, reaching for him, and instinctively he moved, knowing he couldn't last if she touched him now. The glide became a thrust which turned into a surge of power, taking him deep into close, slick space that opened around him, welcoming him.

There was no gasp of pain, no horror, just a moment of resistance then heaven.

Raffa's breath stalled. He tried to breathe, to calm the pulse storming in his blood, the sharp, rising pull of pleasure. Except Lily confounded him. She wrapped her arms about him, lifted her legs and clung on.

'Yes.' The hot sibilant branded his ear as she rubbed her cheek against his. 'Like that. Please.'

That was all it took for Raffaele Petri, renowned for his sexual expertise and stamina, versed in every carnal art and long past the age of impulsiveness, to buck hard against her, shattering with a roar of anguished delight till the world disappeared in a dizzying swirl.

CHAPTER ELEVEN

HE WASN'T SURE what woke him but for once in his life Raffa wasn't eager to get up. He lay, eyes closed, content to enjoy the comfort of lying here, replete.

Usually he was up straight away, diving into each day with a determination to meet every challenge and win. Today felt different. *He* felt different.

He stretched and immediately stilled, registering warm flesh beneath his arm, against his body. Feminine curves, fragrant and enticing.

Lily.

His eyes snapped open and he found himself staring into a serious, questioning gaze of glowing amber, flecked with brown.

Shock buffeted him.

He'd spent the night in Lily Nolan's bed.

He never spent the night with any woman. They got ideas about permanency and relationships, as if they'd shared more than sex.

Memories bombarded, vivid, intoxicating memories of Lily falling apart again and again. And of him, utterly out of control. Him expecting familiar sexual satisfaction and finding something beyond his wildest imaginings.

Raffa sucked in a breath and slid his hand back from the indent of her waist. It was only then he realised he'd clamped one thigh over hers in his sleep, caging her to him.

As if even in sleep he couldn't let her go.

The mighty erection prodding her belly reinforced that.

'You weren't expecting to see me, then.' Her voice was curiously flat, as if she'd ironed out all emotion. But he felt the sudden rigidity in her, saw the brightness dim in her eyes and the hint of a smile die on her lips.

So it started. The games women played. The emotional blackmail they employed.

Deliberately Raffa stilled in the act of drawing his leg away.

'I didn't expect to see anyone. I sleep alone.' There was a hard edge to his words. He resented explaining himself.

'Then you should have left last night. This is my bed. I didn't invite you here, if you remember.'

'I remember.' She'd infuriated him, worried him, turned what should have been simple sex into something complicated. He'd felt like some dastardly villain when he'd sent her away and she'd fled, drawing the scraps of her dignity behind her. Later, when she'd talked of being ugly and not desirable—he'd been torn between hunger and the fear he'd hurt her even more by taking what they both wanted.

She'd made him confront the dark truth at the core of himself, the sense of being tainted, too soiled to touch an innocent.

Yet he had. He'd given her a night of unabated delight. In the process he'd crossed so many boundaries he'd ventured into unfamiliar territory. A difficult, unpleasant place where feelings burgeoned in the pit of his belly. He felt edgy, like the first time he'd left the warren of familiar childhood streets, not knowing what threatened around the next corner.

Now she looked at him like something she'd tracked in on the bottom of her shoe.

'It's time you left. It's getting late.'

Raffa didn't like the memories her words evoked. It had been years, a lifetime ago, since a woman had shown him the door when his services were no longer required.

He felt a burst of that ancient resentment, as if he were a youth again, frustrated anger at himself for letting himself be used, even if it was his only way out of the hole he'd grown up in. Shame that he managed to find physical pleasure when honour dictated he should take none when money changed hands.

Raffa shoved the memories away. It was a place he didn't visit.

'Why?' he drawled, his voice harsh. 'You're ashamed to be seen letting me out of your villa so early in the morning?'

Her eyes widened. 'More like saving your reputation. I'm sure you'd rather not let it be known where you'd spent the night.'

On the words she lifted her hand and pushed her hair off her face, turning her head a fraction so the sunlight spilling across the bed slanted over her scarred cheek.

Instantly, as if a giant fist smashed into his solar plexus, Raffa's indignation disintegrated.

Even after last night, after he showed her again and again how beautiful she was, how much he craved her, Lily didn't believe it.

'You think your face will repel me?' His voice was a low growl. As if she'd let a tiger into her bedroom. His eyes glittered so fiercely Lily felt almost anxious.

There was nothing to be anxious about. She'd had the sort of night she'd never believed she'd experience, discovering intimacy with the only man who could tempt her to let down her guard. She'd loved every minute and would carry the memories for the rest of her days.

Now it was over. Last night's kindness was over. That was obvious the moment he opened his eyes and reeled back.

It was time to move on.

It wasn't as if she'd expected he'd want a *relationship* with her.

'I think it's a new day and it's time we ended this…' Lily didn't have a word to describe last night. Especially as they still lay naked together, his thigh imprisoning her hip and his shaft pressed against her stomach. She kept her hands tucked together in front of her, knuckles touching his chest when he breathed deep, locked together so she couldn't be tempted to reach out.

Yet inside her muscles clenched and released and clenched again, feeling the empty ache she'd never experienced before Raffaele had taught her to want him. She wanted him to fill that void, hold her close and take her to heaven. Being with him, sharing that ultimate intimacy had been mind-blowing.

'You say that because you're scared.'

'Scared?' She looked into narrowed eyes and felt herself fall into those blue depths. 'Of what?'

'That last night was real.'

He stopped the protest rising in her mouth when he lifted one palm to her face, flattening it over the taut, uneven flesh of her scar. Slowly he dragged his hand down, investigating from temple to chin in excruciating detail.

Lily's pulse jittered and danced within a body frozen in shock.

'Don't. There's no need.'

He shook his head and this time she thought she read a softening in that bright gaze.

'There's every need, Lily.' He leaned forward so his breath feathered her lips. As if on cue, her eyelids lowered in anticipation of his kiss. Even angry and hurt, she couldn't help responding.

What she hadn't expected was for him to kiss not her lips but her cheek. Her maimed, ugly cheek.

She reared back, pushing him away, but he was already there, lips skimming her temple, pressing her ravaged face. Not feather-light touches either. These were real, deliberate. She felt each caress as if branded. Everywhere from her cheekbone to her jaw, the corner of her mouth and out towards her ear. There wasn't a centimetre Raffaele didn't touch.

Lily's breath clogged. She couldn't twist away; his powerful body and hands held her still.

Pain built behind her ribs, rising in her throat to scratch the back of her mouth.

Finally, finally he lifted his head and the air rushed from her in an audible whoosh, collapsing lungs on fire till she drew in another breath, this one redolent of spice and musk and Raffaele.

It was too much. More than Lily could take. Moisture pricked the back of her eyes, her throat constricting.

On a surge of desperate energy she shoved him with both hands. She must have taken him by surprise because he fell back long enough for her to tug away, half-sitting, dragging her hair out from between them. She grabbed the sheet and—

'Stop running away.'

Lily stilled, closing her eyes as she sought something like calm.

'I'm not running. I just don't appreciate you pretending…'

'Pretending what? To be attracted to you? To not be fazed by the fact you've got a mark on your face?'

A mark! As if it were a mole or a smudge instead of a stonking great—

'Yes!' The word hissed from her as she rounded to face him. Gilded by the morning light, rumpled and angry and utterly gorgeous—the sight of him cleaved a shard of pain through her middle. 'I don't want you pretending anymore. Even though I appreciate what you did last night. Don't think I don't.'

She'd expected something hurried and perfunctory. Instead she'd been gifted with a night that dazzled her senses and made her poor heart ache even harder for something she couldn't have.

'You're a slow learner, Lily. How many times do I have to prove I don't give a damn for your scar?' He paused, his scrutiny so intense she felt it track over her. Then he shook his head. 'You're hiding behind that, aren't you? You're using that as an excuse.'

'I don't know what you're talking about.' Desperate, she swung away, shifting closer to the edge of the bed.

'It's easier to pretend it's your scar holding you back, than that you're holding yourself back from living. Because you're a coward.'

Lily froze. Even her heart seemed to stall.

What did this man want from her?

How many times did she have to prove herself?

She'd left her refuge and crossed the globe at his insistence. She'd worn the clothes he'd ordered. She'd swam for the first time in years. She'd sat out in public, baring her face and body to all those curious eyes. From the first there'd been something about him that dared her to live up to his expectations. As if he knew she was stronger than even she realised.

And now she'd given him her virginity—begged him to take it, abandoning herself utterly.

'You're pushing me away because you don't want to admit you want more from me.'

Lily squeezed her eyes shut, letting her head sink towards her chest.

How did he know? Was she so transparent?

'Why do you say that?' That croak of a voice wasn't her own.

'Because I feel the same.'

Stunned, Lily spun round. Raffaele's eyes were serious, his mouth grim. As if she got to *him* as he did her!

'I don't understand.'

His bark of laughter scratched like clawing fingernails up her spine. 'Neither do I. But I know this. I'm not ready to walk away from you, and I don't believe you're ready to do that either. This…attraction between us isn't anywhere near over.'

Lily frowned, hope and horror vying for supremacy. 'You don't sound thrilled about it.'

'It wasn't what I planned.'

Slowly she nodded. She understood having a plan and sticking with it. Goals, achievements, more goals. It was how she lived her life. Nice and orderly.

Until Raffaele had woken her in the middle of the night with that heartbreaker of a voice. Ever since, she'd been living out of her comfort zone.

And enjoying it, she realised. He'd dragged her, kicking and screaming, out of her refuge and into…life, with its risks and fears and triumphs. He hadn't treated her gently. He'd challenged and instinctively she'd responded.

A firm hand covered her fist where she still held her hair, caught in a long twist.

'Maybe it's time to let go a little. Do something unplanned and see where it leads.'

Was he talking to himself or her?

'I dare you,' he murmured.

'What? To have an affair?' She sounded so prim. So uptight. So unlike the woman who'd melted to his touch.

Raffaele leaned closer, his wide shoulders hemming her in. 'I don't care what you call it but I want more of it. Of you. Unless you're frightened.'

Of course she was frightened. Who knew what would happen if she gave in to her weakness for this man, not just for a night but longer?

A shimmy of heat flared in her stomach. Excitement. Desire. Greed.

And something else in the region of her heart. It couldn't really be love. Not after such a short time. Not for a man so patently not for her in the long-term.

But in the short-term…

'I'm not scared.' At least her voice didn't shake.

A smile lurked in the grooves at the corners of his mouth. 'Prove it. Now.'

Abruptly he released her and rolled onto his back, spreadeagled across the rumpled sheets. With languid grace he lifted his arms to rest his head on his hands.

He was unashamedly virile. Her gaze traced the dip and bulge of muscle and bone, the jut of his erection, the glint of golden hair and the flash of sapphire as he cast her a sideways glance.

'Put your hair up out of the way.'

Lily hated being ordered to do anything. Yet Raffaele's throaty growl was the most delicious thing she'd ever heard. And it told her what she felt was shared. Heat catapulted through her.

One-handed, she groped across the bedside table, finding a couple of hairpins. Seconds later her hair was pinned up haphazardly.

'And a condom. On the table.' The growl grew deeper.

She turned, saw an unopened foil packet in the litter and felt that throb of need again. Her hand was unsteady as she tore it open.

Who'd have thought twenty-four hours ago that she'd be doing this? Shocked laughter trembled on her lips, only to die as she turned back and saw Raffaele watching. He looked relaxed as a cat, sprawled in the sun, yet the atmosphere was taut with expectation.

She opened her mouth to say she'd never put on a condom before, then realised it was superfluous. Raffaele knew and was challenging her to deal with it.

Biting her cheek, she shuffled across the bed, bashful despite the sizzle in her blood. Kneeling over him, she concentrated on her task, diverted by the feel of him, silk over steel. Inevitably she fumbled, hearing his intake of breath.

'Did I hurt you?' An upwards glance caught his jaw clenched and nostrils flared as if in pain.

'Absolutely not. Just—' he paused to swallow '—finish what you're doing.'

This time, as she smoothed the sheath down, she watched his face and realised it was arousal creating that stark look on his face and turning the thighs beneath her to granite.

She, Lily Nolan, was seducing Raffaele Petri, luring him to the brink of control. He wanted her here, wanted her touch, even if it was a little clumsy. Wanted *her*.

Warmth spread through her body, like sunlight coursing through darkness.

Lily rose on her knees and shuffled forward. Still he didn't move, though the muscles in his arms and shoulders flexed. She hesitated, wishing he'd help her, give a suggestion, but of course there was none. This was about her taking charge. The notion was decadently tempting.

Lily held him, bracing one hand on the bed. A familiar hot spice scent filled her nostrils. His scent, she realised, not some bottled fragrance. It lured, beckoned, as if she wasn't already in his thrall.

Slowly she lowered herself till they touched. She caught fire in Raffaele's bluer than blue eyes and the quick throb of a pulse in his throat. Then, watching him watch her, she eased down, eyes widening at the slow, inexorable, amazing sense of him filling her.

It was like last night only different. Exquisite closeness, a fullness that seemed greater than the physical act of sex. It filled her heart, making her blink from an excess of emotion.

Lily felt the sun on her scarred cheek, saw her lover's gaze drink her in and the look in his eyes made her feel triumphant, special, even beautiful.

If she could bottle this moment she would. But already it was over, the breathless stillness giving way to restlessness as she moved against him, her eyelids flickering as flames licked inside her. Raffaele's hands went to her hips, steadying her when she quivered and hesitated, yet letting her set her own rhythm.

In the morning light she was fascinated to read the signs of his arousal. The clench of a muscle in his jaw, the way his chest heaved high, his stifled gasp when she changed her angle and his hips rose, driving them harder together.

Delight beckoned, but so did the idea of pleasing Raffaele, returning at least a little of the bliss he'd given her last night.

Planting hands on his shoulders, she leaned forward. His gaze riveted on the swing of her breasts, the gleam in his eyes as powerfully arousing as the sensation of their bodies sliding together in perfect harmony.

Lily grabbed one of his hands and planted it on her breast. Instantly his fingers moulded, kneading, not gently but enough to send pleasure rocketing through her. Her movements quickened, more staccato than smooth, but it didn't matter because Raffaele's thrusts kept pace, faster, stronger, more abrupt.

Again that fierce triumph filled her. This was something she could do for him. Lily snagged Raffaele's other hand, pressed it against her breast, holding his hands in place with both of hers.

His mouth sagged as he fought for air, the tendons in his neck standing proud. That big, strong body was trembling, on the brink, and it was more exciting than anything that had gone before.

Lily leaned down, holding his gaze. When she was so close she felt his breath hot on her lips she whispered, 'I want to watch you come, Raffaele.'

There was an instant of silence. His heavy-lidded eyes blinked wide then she felt it, the out-of-control buck of his body, the rushed surge inside her turning into a pulsating thrust that ignited the embers of her own climax. There was a muted growl that turned into a rolling roar. His hands kneaded her breasts, sending bolts of rapture from her nipples to her womb where the fire burst its bounds, devouring her as it devoured him.

Together they jerked and shook and shuddered and through it all she was lost in his azure gaze, reading awe that matched her own.

It was only as she collapsed, muscles failing in the wake of such a potent climax, that Raffaele shifted his grip, pulling her head down to his. He bestowed a kiss that tasted different to any they'd shared. It was slow and tender and, as she gave herself up to it, Lily realised the last of her defences had shattered.

CHAPTER TWELVE

RAFFA LOOKED ACROSS the wide veranda of the plantation house to the man he was here to meet.

The man he was here to ruin.

Triumph stirred. Soon Gabriella would be avenged.

Yet he found it difficult to relish the moment when he was distracted by guilt.

He'd made a mistake bringing Lily with him, despite her desire to see the place. He shouldn't have subjected her to Bradshaw. The man's first startled look at her face had morphed into distaste before he belatedly put on a smarmy smile of welcome and became excruciatingly over-solicitous.

It had made Raffa want to throttle him. But beside him Lily had merely stiffened, her face turning mask-like. Raffa knew her well enough now to realise that mask hid hurt but she wouldn't thank him for interfering.

'It's a lovely old house,' she murmured. 'I particularly like the full-length windows and shutters.'

Bradshaw smiled expansively and launched into a monologue about the property.

Its bones were beautiful but it had been let go. Paint peeled on the shutters and even from here Raffa could see blank spaces inside where furniture and paintings had been emptied from the sitting room.

If it had been *his* family home Raffa would have cherished it, not left it to crumble and fade.

The thought caught him up short.

What a joke. Raffa had inherited nothing except his face. And the family trait. Everyone in his old neighbourhood knew the Petri women were saints, suffering long and stoically. For the Petri men were renowned sinners, handsome rogues who enticed beautiful women into motherhood and occasionally matrimony, then abandoned them. Sordid— that was what they were.

No wonder he'd ended up as he had.

'Sorry?' He caught Bradshaw leaning forward in his seat, obviously repeating something.

'Mr Bradshaw was offering you a tour of the house.' Lily's voice had a husky edge that reminded him what they'd been doing just an hour ago.

Bradshaw was unable to hide his eagerness. 'Or perhaps we should go inside and get straight down to business. Leave the ladies to themselves.' His toothy grin widened as a woman wafted through the French doors onto the veranda as if on cue.

Raffa noted her studied pose, her sinuous walk, and felt recognition stir. Blonde, tanned and overdressed, she flashed a diamond bracelet and a come-hither smile.

Olga Antakova. One-time model and would-be trophy mistress.

'Raffa. It's been ages.' Her voice purred but her eyes were ice chips. No doubt she was remembering the way he'd bundled her out of his limo the night he'd found her there in nothing but a fur coat and aspirations to live as a pampered sex toy.

'Olga.' He inclined his head. 'This is Lily Nolan.' His voice was warm as he said Lily's name and the blonde's eyes widened.

'How do you do, Ms Antakova. Or should I call you Olga?' Lily shot him an impatient look as if wondering why he wasn't already off, closing the deal with Bradshaw.

Lily could be almost as single-minded as him. Raffa admired that. He enjoyed the way her mind worked, the unexpected depths she brought to any discussion. Almost as much as the way she all but purred her pleasure when he touched her.

He rose, telling himself it was stupid to delay here, feeling protective. He knew Lily could look after herself.

Deliberately he put down his glass and turned to the man he'd been pursuing for so long. It was time to put his offer on the table. 'Lead on, Bradshaw.'

Olga was speaking, reminiscing about an opulent society event where she'd played a starring role. Lily tuned out, realising all she had to do was murmur occasional encouragement.

She'd been nervous on the way across the island, wondering if she'd hold her own with Robert Bradshaw and his guests. Even knowing she looked her best in her new dress, she'd been daunted. Despite her growing confidence, she still didn't like meeting strangers and the thought of a crowd filled her with nerves. But she'd been determined not to hide away as she'd once have done. Besides, there were only two people here, and Raffaele was with her.

Should she be worried that made her so happy?

This...relationship was short-term, she knew that. Yet being with him, feeling valued as an equal and especially as a woman, gave her a new perspective and a new confidence.

Thanks to Raffaele for daring her to confront her fears. With him she was a woman capable of anything. Even bringing the sexiest, most powerful man she'd ever met to trembling desperation.

So what if Bradshaw averted his eyes from her face? As for Olga, she'd dismiss any woman who wasn't as glamorous as herself.

What concerned Lily was Raffaele. Behind the confident air she'd read deep-seated tension. Was this deal really so vital? Bizarrely she'd wanted to grab Raffaele's hand and reassure him. As if he weren't perfectly able to deal with a lightweight like Bradshaw.

'So, Raffa is your boss?' Olga didn't wait for her answer but kept talking. Obviously she couldn't conceive of Lily as his lover.

Lily shifted in her chair, imagining how she must look to the glamorous Russian, her damaged face in stark contrast to Raffaele's male beauty.

Then the twist of silver around her wrist caught her eye. Raffaele had presented her with the bangle to go with the dress she'd bought on impulse. It was simple yet elegant and she loved it. It felt like a talisman, reminding her how unexpectedly wonderful her world had become.

It was the first time anyone had bought her jewellery. The first time she'd felt comfortable adorning herself. It had felt momentous, a symbol of a bright new start.

But mostly she'd been thrilled by Raffaele's expression when he gave it to her. Not only approval but—

'You two work closely together?' Olga drained her glass and leaned back languidly. Yet there was nothing languid about her eyes. They were like a cat's, watchful, hungry.

'He must trust you to bring you here.' Olga lifted her hand to play with her tousled curls and the band of diamonds around her wrist sparkled in the sunlight. 'You must know if he's ready yet to do a deal with dear Robert.'

Was the woman really so naive as to expect her to betray a confidence?

Olga leaned forward, her voice dropping. 'Robert's been so reasonable. He even offered a forty-five per cent share of the resort.' She shook her head. 'If Raffa is interested he'd better move fast. Others are interested too.'

So that was the deal. A partnership.

Raffaele hadn't mentioned that. He didn't have partners. He delegated day-to-day management of individual enterprises but he was always the final authority.

Could he change to accommodate a partner?

More to the point, why would he? The resort was charming. But what made it so attractive he'd change the habit of a career and take a partner to get it?

'Well? Is he here to make a deal?' Olga's eagerness was obvious. Maybe she really cared for Bradshaw.

'Raffaele doesn't inform me of his plans.'

'That one keeps everything close to the chest.' Olga's mouth tightened and Lily was consumed with a need to know exactly what had been between Raffaele and the Russian woman. 'But you must have some idea?'

Did that wide-eyed look work with men? 'That's not something I can discuss. One of my conditions of employment is complete confidentiality.'

The other woman leaned back, surveying Lily speculatively.

'That's why you won't talk. You're in love with him, aren't you?'

'Sorry?' Lily gaped, horrified.

The blonde looked knowing. 'You're so protective, like a mother hen guarding her chick.' She laughed, the sound grating. 'As if that one needs your protection.'

Lily plonked her glass down, every muscle and sinew twanging with shock.

In love with Raffaele.

Olga had put into words the fear, the dreadful yearning hope that haunted Lily. She'd told herself it couldn't be true, but in her heart of hearts she hadn't been able to deny it.

'You have an excellent imagination to read that from the fact I won't discuss his business.' Lily was proud of her even tone.

'It's not just that. There's the way your eyes follow him when he's not looking. You eat him up.'

Denial stuck in Lily's throat. *Had* she made her feelings obvious? Sickening fear rose that maybe Raffaele had seen her stare at him like that. Except Olga had specified 'when he's not looking.'

Lily shrugged. 'He's the most attractive man I've ever seen. Why wouldn't I look? But, as for anything else? He's not my type.'

'Let's be frank. He's *every* woman's type. You'd have to be blind not to be attracted. And even if you *were* blind, he knows his way around women. He's had plenty of practice using those skills to get exactly what he wants.'

It was on the tip of Lily's tongue to say Olga wasn't in any position to throw stones, but she snapped her mouth shut. It was no secret Raffaele's life was littered with women.

Lily told herself she was grateful for all that experience. She had no one to compare him with but if she was destined to have just one lover, she'd lucked out with Raffaele. The way he made her feel...

That was when she realised what it was she read in Olga's sharp gaze. Jealousy.

'Raffaele rejected you, did he?'

Lily's words halted Raffa in the doorway.

He'd left Bradshaw ringing his lawyer since Raffa had given tomorrow as the deadline to agree to his terms. He'd cut the meeting short, not wanting to leave Lily with Olga Antakova. Unease had been a low thrum in his belly all through the meeting.

What he hadn't expected was to hear Lily take the Russian head-on.

'Reject *me*?' Olga's tone dripped ice. 'As if I'd give him the chance. I have more taste than to fall for a man like that.'

Raffa's lips twitched. No, Olga hadn't fallen for him, but she had tried to catch him the best way she could. And been furious when he'd spurned her. She represented everything he despised in the high gloss, low sincerity world he inhabited. Sex, affection, even friendship were tools to get what you wanted. Commodities. The woman was a million light years from Lily.

'A man like what? Raffaele is incredibly attractive.'

Call him shallow, but hearing Lily's words felt *good*. They kept him where he was, just out of sight.

Raffa was used to the hyperbole of the media, those 'sexiest man' tags, and to fawning women. Yet hearing Lily admit her attraction in her trademark husky voice had a surprisingly powerful effect. Despite their passionate affair she'd never verbalised it, except when she gasped his name in ecstasy.

'I prefer a man with more class.' Olga was giving her best aristocratic impersonation, as if born to diamonds and caviar.

Raffa took a step forward, ready to make his presence known, but Lily's words stopped him again.

'Class? If Raffaele doesn't have that, I don't know who does. He's savvy and successful but he's decent too. And kind. Not every successful businessman can say that.'

Decent? Kind?

Raffa had been called many things but never, to his knowledge, either of those. Formidable, driven, impatient— that was his current reputation, if you discounted the usual flummery about his looks. And before that? No, neither word fitted the younger him.

'You're attracted by his rough around the edges past?' Olga's voice was frosty. 'I prefer a gentleman.'

'By gentleman I assume you mean someone who never had to work for what he's got?' Lily's voice was even but the precise clip to her words gave her away. 'I'm more impressed by someone who's worked hard for what he has. I find that admirable.'

Her words shouldn't matter. Words had long ago lost any power over him. But Raffa felt his heart bash his rib cage in a double-time rhythm that snared his breath.

He'd never had anyone defend him.

Not since Gabriella.

It made him feel… He couldn't describe the hot turmoil

rising from his belly, clogging his chest and squeezing his throat. Emotion clawed his vitals.

'Oh, Raffa had to work. But not in the way you think.' Olga's tone was snide. 'I met someone who's sure she came across him when he was young, in Italy. You'd be surprised at—'

'Reminiscing, are you, ladies?' He strolled onto the veranda, watching Olga start.

He raised an eyebrow, but she said nothing. She dealt in poison, but wasn't brave enough for a frontal attack. Particularly since she hoped he would pour money in her lover's greedy hands.

He looked at Lily, reading anger in her gleaming eyes and taut frame. Raffa put his hand on her slender shoulder, enjoying the way she instantly eased closer.

'Olga says she knew someone who knew you in Italy.'

'Really?' He held the Russian's eyes. 'What was their name?'

She snapped her gaze away. 'No one important. She wasn't even sure it was you.'

Raffa said nothing. He'd be surprised if her acquaintance would come out publicly with her memories. Nor would it bother him if she did. He'd done what he had to escape poverty.

Yet he tasted bile.

He'd had enough of this place. Dealing with Bradshaw, staying his hand instead of grabbing the man and demanding he admit what he'd done to Gabriella was hard enough. Walking back to find Olga baiting Lily was even worse.

'Ready to go?' His hand tightened on her shoulder and she lifted her gaze to his.

'Absolutely.' She turned to the other woman. 'Goodbye, Olga.'

He slid his hand from Lily's shoulder and threaded his fingers through hers as they stepped onto the path.

She stiffened. 'You want them to know we're not just colleagues?' Lily's whisper was for his ears alone.

'Does it matter? I'm not ashamed of you, Lily. Or of us.' Though the thought surfaced that she'd be ashamed of him if she knew his past.

Lily squeezed his fingers and warmth filled him. She was passionate but outside the bedroom she never touched him.

Because she preferred privacy?

Or because she thought he wanted their liaison kept quiet? As if *she* were some shameful secret.

It was people like himself and Olga and Bradshaw who should be ashamed! Lily ought to be nothing but proud of herself.

Raffa disengaged his hand from Lily's and looped his arm around her shoulder, pulling her hard against his side. Her curves slid against him as they walked and once more that sense of rightness as he held her stifled other thoughts.

A swift turn of her head revealed stunning eyes, brown with an inner glow of amber. A hint of a smile tugged her lips and something in his chest rolled over, as if his heart belly-flopped against his lungs, squeezing the air out.

Raffa stopped, turning to face her.

She lifted her chin, eyebrows rising in question as she planted her hands on his chest.

Deliberately, aware they were in full view of the house, he lowered his head and touched his lips to Lily's. Her mouth opened, inviting him into a realm of sweet pleasure. Instantly any thought of the outside world, of proving a point, disappeared.

Only the knowledge there were better places to kiss her made him eventually pull back. Her eyes shone and her husky laugh urged him on as he clasped her hand and turned towards the resort.

By the time they'd followed the path through the gardens to his bungalow, Lily was breathless and his pulse strummed a quickened beat. Usually he enjoyed the view of the crescent beach and clear waters. Today it didn't register.

Digging for his key card, he tugged her to the door. Palm to wood, he pushed the door open and kept moving.

It was shadowy in the foyer but he read the gleam in Lily's eyes. Her breasts thrust out with each snatched breath.

'So, you find me incredibly attractive, do you?' Raffa strove for light-hearted but his voice emerged rough and urgent.

'You know I do.' Lily stared back. 'That's not news. You've known that for ages.'

Not ages. She'd concealed her feelings well behind her prickly exterior. His *piccola istrice*.

'What are you smiling at?' Her palms flattened on his chest, reigniting that slow-burning fire.

'Me.' He covered her hands with his, his smile fading. 'I can't believe how much I need you.' And not just sexually.

Her words earlier had affected him. Her praise of his character had echoed inside with every step they took back to the villa. Each word swelled inside him, taking up all the available space, clotting his brain, filling him with a pleasure as unfamiliar as it was intoxicating.

Raffa couldn't explain it. Didn't want to. All he wanted was an outlet for this…fullness, this feeling he was about to burst out of his skin. It had to be sexual. There was no other explanation.

One step and he backed her against the wall. Another and he was between her legs, his thigh pressing up. He watched the convulsive movement of her pale throat as she swallowed.

Releasing her hands, he cupped her breasts, revelling in the way they fitted his palms. Seconds later she was groaning, her head lolling against the wall as he rolled her nipples between his fingers.

Raffa bent to scrape his teeth along her bare flesh where

her shoulder curved up to that delectable slender neck. Another groan and she slumped into him, hands on his shoulders for support.

Teeth gritted in a feral smile, Raffa tugged at her dress, lifting it, yanking at her panties till they ripped and fell, leaving him in possession of downy softness. His fingers probed, finding liquid heat as her thighs clamped tight around him.

Urgent now, his need a compulsion he hadn't a hope of taming, he reefed at his trousers, wrenching them open, shoving fabric away till he was unencumbered, fully aroused and sliding against slick, delicate folds.

There. He grabbed her thigh and hooked it over his hip. Just…there and—

'Condom.'

At first Raffa didn't register the wisp of sound. Not till she said it again, a hoarse gasp that made him shudder into stillness just as he began a long, slow thrust into Paradise.

Heat surrounded him. Lush softness. Their laboured breathing. And within him that urgency, unlike anything he'd known, to possess, to claim, to brand Lily as his.

Air sawed from his burning lungs then in again as he managed shallow gasps.

He fought for control. His brain ordered him to withdraw, take the precautions he always did, protect them both. But his body was in full-scale mutiny. It wanted completion, now. Not just completion but to claim Lily rough and hard and completely.

Raffa winced as, finally, he withdrew. The sense of loss was so keen it knifed like a blade through his belly.

Dragging in oxygen, he bent and fumbled for his trousers. His hand met Lily's, already in his pocket.

'Here.' She pressed the packet into his hand.

Her eyes were like gems, he realised. Faceted, gleaming gems, with shards of honey-brown fire.

'Quickly.'

He didn't need encouragement, was already ripping it open with his teeth, extracting the condom and rolling it on.

Lily sighed as he grabbed her hips and plunged inside. Heat met heat and desire coiled tight. He tried to give himself time by focusing on her, watching her eyes flicker half closed and her ripe lips part. She keened his name in that raw, beautiful voice he knew he was the only man ever to hear and that was all it took to drag him over the edge. Raffa thrust hard and shuddered, desperate to capture that pinnacle and take her with him.

Or perhaps she took him, the waves of her climax breaking around him with the force of an ocean surge.

How long they stayed there, sagging against the wall, Raffa didn't know. It seemed hours before he had the strength to carry her to bed, collapsing with her in a tangle of slick, spent bodies.

Never had release been so cataclysmic.

Never once had he come near to forgetting protection.

Lily Nolan affected him as no woman ever had. Raffa realised that for the first time a woman had real power over him. Albeit a power she didn't realise she wielded.

He wanted to spurn the idea, tell himself it was impossible. Yet as sleep claimed him he gathered her close, revelling in the way she clung to him, and smiled.

CHAPTER THIRTEEN

How HAD HE ever thought Lily ordinary? Her eyes glowed and the late-afternoon light turned her sun-kissed hair to bronze. They lay side by side on the sand, spent from sex and swimming. The small beach he'd discovered beyond the resort was deserted and they'd made it theirs.

It was hard to believe just a few hours ago they'd been at Bradshaw's house. This felt a world away from his polluted presence.

'Olga called you Raffa. Were you close?' The sharpness in Lily's question took him by surprise. As did the realisation Lily had never once called him by the diminutive. Yet the way she said his name felt uniquely intimate.

'No. Never.' He covered her hand, hating the idea of Lily believing he'd been with the Russian. 'I met her on a photo shoot. Later she invited herself into my limo and tried to seduce me.'

Lily gaped and he had to repress a smile. 'You're not joking, are you?'

He shook his head.

'I suppose women throw themselves at you all the time.' What was she thinking? Even now sometimes, he found her hard to read.

'It's not always about me. Most of them want the lifestyle. Olga wanted money, not me.'

Lily nodded as she stroked a line from his damp collarbone down his chest. Her lips turned up in a smile that loosened something inside him. 'At least I'm upfront. You know I want your body.'

'Then we're equal,' he growled, drawing his hand over her breast, feeling that tug of satisfaction as her breath caught and her eyes dilated. She looked like a sea nymph, temptation for any man.

Desire stirred. But it didn't diminish that other sensation, the one he'd felt when they came back from Bradshaw's house. That strange fullness, as if just looking at Lily created feelings that crammed him to the brim.

Sex hadn't shifted it. Instead it had settled deep inside him, bone-deep. Raffa frowned, moving his hand down to clasp the curve of her waist.

'What's wrong?' She cupped his jaw, her brow crinkling with concern. Unlike other women, Lily really cared about him. It was distracting, disturbing. And it felt frighteningly good.

No one had cared about him since Gabriella. He found it hard to accept. He and Gabriella had been close as blood could make them. They'd clung to each other after their mother died, fighting the odds to stay together.

'Nothing.'

Wide eyes surveyed him. He could almost hear that analytical brain of hers whirring into gear. 'Was it something Olga said? About the work you used to do?'

If only it were that simple. 'Raffaele?' Lily leaned close and he inhaled the scent of sweet pears, saltwater and warm woman. The combination went to his head, the look in her eyes exacerbating that sensation of fullness, as if a king tide rose within him. 'What work did you do in Italy?'

Raffa hesitated, torn between a lifetime of keeping secrets and the compulsion to trust someone as he hadn't trusted since he was twelve. He'd felt unsettled, not himself, ever since taking Lily to visit Bradshaw.

Finally she dropped her gaze, and her hand. 'It's probably time we went back—'

'I had sex with women for money.'

The words throbbed into echoing silence, broken only by the soft shush of a wave and the squawk of a seabird.

Lily's head jerked up. 'No wonder you're so good at

it.' She stopped, eyes widening as if shocked at her words rather than his. 'You must have made a fortune.'

Lily's response was so unexpected he almost laughed. Except memories of those days were too bitter. 'Hardly a fortune. But enough to feed and clothe me and get me out of the slums.' He had to push out each word. This was something he'd never spoken of.

'I can't imagine real poverty.'

Raffa swallowed what he was going to say, that poverty could make you do terrible things, things you regretted.

'You don't mind?' He couldn't read her thoughts but nor could he see revulsion in her features. Then he realised what he'd asked. Was he seeking Lily's *approval*? His brow knotted.

'It's in the past. I have no right to mind.'

Yet Raffa found himself wanting—what? Absolution? Understanding? It didn't make sense.

'When I was eighteen I met a woman who knew someone that needed a model. The one they'd lined up was ill and they needed a replacement quickly.'

'That's how you started modelling?'

'Yes. Through one of my clients.' He used the word deliberately. Testing Lily's reaction?

Why was her response so important? Raffa lived his life pleasing himself, no one else. Yet he found his hand tight on her waist and his breathing shallow as he waited for her to speak.

'Did it take long to begin modelling full-time?'

'No. They liked my look. I had more work than I could handle.' His mouth twisted. He remembered their excitement at the combination of his looks and streetwise aura. As if growing up in the gutter was a bonus.

'So you were only doing...the other for a short time.'

Was that a blush?

'Long enough. I was almost fifteen when I began.'

'Almost fifteen?' If he'd wanted a reaction he'd got one.

Lily's voice rose, her fingers digging into the muscle of his upper arm as she levered herself up to a sitting position. 'That's…that's appalling!'

Something crumpled in Raffa's chest. He didn't bother moving but sank back onto the sand.

'That's child exploitation. Wasn't there anyone to protect you?'

It took a few seconds to digest that her outrage wasn't directed at him. 'I looked older.'

'It doesn't matter how old you looked. You were a kid.' He saw anger etched in Lily's features. Not because he'd prostituted himself, but because there'd been no one to stop him.

'They were bored and I was there. I spent a lot of time around the marina where the fancy yachts moored.'

Lily shook her head, her damp hair sliding across her shoulders. 'Where was your family?'

Raffa jackknifed up to sit beside her, resting his arms on bent knees. 'I had none.'

'I'm so sorry.' The hand on his arm was gentle and there was true regret in her voice.

He could grow addicted to Lily's empathy.

'It was a long time ago.' Yet the ache when he thought of Gabriella was real. 'Our father left when I was a baby. I have no idea if he's still alive. Our mother died when I was nine.'

'You said "our."'

Raffa fixed his gaze on a yacht out to sea, its sails pristine white against the bright water. He never spoke of this. Yet the compulsion to keep talking was strong. What could it hurt?

'My sister, Gabriella, died when I was twelve. After that I was taken to an orphanage but I kept running away. I spent most of my time on the streets.'

'They didn't treat you well?' She leaned closer, her warmth counteracting the chill in his bones as she pressed into his side.

'Well enough.'

'But?'

He looked down to find her gaze intent.

Ingrained caution warred with the desire to let go, relinquish the barrier he'd constructed around himself. Already Lily had breached it, making him experience feelings that defied logical description. It would be easy to distance himself as he always did, except he didn't want to.

'But I was looking for the man who killed my sister.' With the words came an easing inside, as if someone had slashed open thick cords binding his chest.

'Killed?' Shock filled her. She wrapped her hand tighter around Raffa's arm and leaned against his shoulder.

A mighty sigh racked him.

'My sister looked after me when our mother died, or tried to. I was a handful.' Lily heard self-reproach. 'She was patient, honest and *good*. I was wild and she was the one who reined me in. She took the place of our mother but I didn't make things easy for her.'

'What happened?'

'Gabriella took after our grandmother, who'd been an actress in France. She was beautiful. Stunning.'

Just like Raffaele. Lily had wondered how he came by his fair colouring. Even for a northern Italian it was surely unique.

'As long as I can remember Gabriella caught men's attention, but she never returned it. She was reserved. She never went out partying. She never even had a boyfriend.

'Men invited her out but she never accepted. Until that night. She'd met a man who invited her to a party on his boat and this time she went.'

'He was someone special?'

Lily felt Raffaele stiffen. 'No, she went because of me. I'd been hanging around with kids she didn't approve of and I'd been acting up, accusing her of being too strict.

We had a row.' He sucked in a deep breath. 'She was only eighteen herself and trying to manage a boy with the devil inside him. That night she'd had enough. One minute she was telling me why I shouldn't hang about with that crowd. The next she said she needed some adult conversation and she'd go to the party after all. She took off her apron, put on her shoes and headed out the door.'

Raffaele stared out to sea and Lily followed his gaze, knowing he didn't see the beautiful vista before them.

'I followed at a distance. I'd never seen her lose her temper like that and I was worried.' His voice hollowed. 'I should have stopped her.'

'What happened?' Lily needed to know but didn't want to hear.

'She went to the marina where the expensive cruisers were moored for the boat show. I saw her board one where there was a party—people and music and laughter. I figured I'd see her in the morning but she never came home.' A shudder ripped through him. 'Next day she was found floating in the sea. The coroner said there was alcohol and a cocktail of drugs in her system, including one used in date rape. She died of an overdose.'

Lily's breath hissed between her teeth. Horror prickled her skin, making each hair on her nape and arms stand to attention.

'It wasn't your fault.' Slowly she sat up, relinquishing her hold and turning to him. Raffaele swung round, his eyes locking on hers with such intensity she felt scorched. Such pain she read there. Such guilt.

'If it hadn't been for me she'd never have gone.' His voice ground low. 'Despite what the police said, she was an innocent. I knew Gabriella. She'd never been with a man, never had a drink with one before that night. He drugged her and she died.'

'You saw the man she met?'

Raffaele nodded. 'I told the police but they didn't believe me. I gave a description but they said there was no such person to be found.' He snorted. 'As if he'd stay. The cruiser had gone, but I kept looking year after year.'

'That's why you hung around the marina.' And had been spotted by those rich women who thought nothing of taking a young boy's innocence. Lily's stomach curdled. No wonder Raffaele didn't talk about his past. 'But you never saw him again.'

'Oh, yes, I did. Earlier this year.' Raffaele's voice was glacial, the set of his jaw aggressive. 'That's when I discovered his name—Robert Bradshaw.'

Lily goggled, struggling to take it in. 'The same Robert Bradshaw...?' But of course it was the same. The pieces fell into place, the reason Raffaele was so driven with this deal. She'd *known* there was something between the two men.

She read determination in Raffaele's harsh expression and a fierceness that stirred uneasiness.

'How can you want to work with him?'

'It's harder than I thought.' He inclined his head. 'I look at him and I want to wrap my fingers around his podgy throat and squeeze.'

Lily froze at the lethal intent in his voice.

'You can't be sure he's the one responsible for your sister's death. It might have been someone else on the boat.' She wasn't trying to defend him, but Raffaele's ferocity frightened her.

His head whipped around, his stare like the sheen of polished sapphires, cold and merciless.

'It was his boat. His party. He was the one lusting after Gabriella, I saw it in his face. Even if he wasn't the one to dope her, he was still responsible for her safety.'

Lily agreed. He'd invited Gabriella and should have looked after her. From what she'd seen of Robert Bradshaw, he didn't look after anyone but himself.

'So how can you work with him?'

Raffaele's lips turned up in a slow smile that looked...

carnivorous. 'It's worth it. As soon as this deal is done he'll be dead in the water, financially speaking.'

Lily shuddered at his word choice, her mind going to the image of a young woman, golden-haired like her brother, lifeless in the sea. An instant later she was on her feet, arms wrapped around her torso. Despite the balmy air she felt cold.

'You want revenge.'

'I think of it as justice.' He was at her shoulder, his eyes fixed on the distance. He looked as handsome as ever but the lines of that achingly beautiful face were forbidding, as if the man who'd made sweet love to her just an hour ago had been evicted by a stranger. Someone who knew violence and distrust, who'd been used and abused. Who was completely closed off.

Lily rubbed her hands up her chilled arms.

'How will becoming his partner get justice for your sister? Once you renovate the resort he'll profit from your investment and your experience. How is that punishment?'

Raffaele would turn the place into an ultra-exclusive, über-profitable retreat for the rich and famous. It was what he did. That was why Bradshaw was so desperate to bring Raffaele into the equation, holding off other interested parties.

Raffa's smile widened in a way that made her glad it was Bradshaw in his sights, not her.

'That's the beauty of it.' His voice, like velvet over honed steel, scraped her nerves. 'He's so caught up in anticipating a huge profit he can't see anything else.'

'What else is there to see?' Lily stepped in front of him, forcing him to focus on her. His eyes were bright, almost feverish, and their expression made her uneasy.

'Bradshaw is massively in debt.' Lily nodded. That was no secret. 'He's going to give me majority ownership of the whole island in return for money to cover his most pressing debts.'

'Olga said a forty-five per cent share.'

'That's what Bradshaw offered, not what I'll accept.'

They both knew Bradshaw would take Raffaele's terms. He was desperate.

'He'd lose control of the resort—'

'Not just the resort, the whole island.'

'But in return he can rely on you to upgrade the place and make it profitable in a way he can't.'

'So he thinks.' Raffaele's eyes gleamed.

'You can't do it?' Lily had never heard Raffaele doubt himself and it took her aback.

'Oh, I can do it. But why should I?'

Lily frowned. 'I don't follow. Surely that's the deal—that you invest and upgrade the place?'

'You'd think so, wouldn't you? Whereas, in fact, all I'm promising on paper is the cash to meet his immediate needs. That's already a substantial sum.'

'You're not tied in to upgrading the resort?'

He shook his head. 'No. Bradshaw just assumes I'll make it a priority because of the amount I'm spending to acquire it.'

'But you're in no hurry.'

Lily's breath escaped in a rush. It was on the tip of her tongue to ask what sort of businessman Bradshaw was, but she knew the answer. Her research had revealed a man of puffed-up self-importance who lived the good life but had no clue how to fund it apart from spending the inherited wealth others had accumulated.

'What are you going to do?'

'Once he's signed on the dotted line? Absolutely nothing.'

Lily frowned. 'What about your plans to improve the resort?' She'd heard the enthusiasm in his voice when he spoke of turning it into a truly special place to escape.

'Plans? I have no plans.' Seeing her confusion he went on. 'Oh, I've got ideas on what would make the place work.

It's a shame, really, when there's such potential here, but I've no intention of turning it into a profit-making venture while Bradshaw owns so much as a centimetre of sand here.'

'And you're ensuring he can't interest other investors to do that, by keeping the majority ownership yourself.'

He nodded. 'Not only that. The agreement I've given Bradshaw binds us both to seeking approval from the other before beginning any form of redevelopment.'

'So he's hamstrung. He'll have no saleable assets or income.' He wouldn't be able to sell his minority ownership nor could he start a new money-making venture himself.

She spun round, her gaze going to the headland at the end of the beach, beyond which the resort villas were scattered. What would happen to it? She imagined the buildings crumbling, vegetation taking over with no one to take care of them. For if Raffaele wasn't going to run the place for profit he wouldn't bother taking care of it.

Lily whipped around to face him as a thought lodged in her head. 'What about the staff?'

'What about them?'

'They rely on the resort for their work.'

He shrugged. 'They'll need to find something else.'

Lily looked beyond him to the gorgeous, deserted waters surrounding the island. 'There isn't anything else.'

'Then they'll move.' He frowned and bent to pick up their beach towels. 'There's always work elsewhere.'

'You can't mean that.'

Raffaele's frown became a scowl. 'Of course I mean it. My sole intention in buying this place is to destroy Bradshaw. I intend to see it through. There will be no resort on this island. No enterprise of any kind.'

Something plunged hard in Lily's belly. Her illusions falling and shattering?

She'd believed Raffaele a man she could admire. More, she'd thought herself in love with him. She'd suffered through the story of his murky past and terrible loss but now… Distress churned and she had to fight to stand straight, not bend double, nursing pain.

Lily thrust her hands onto her hips. 'Most of them have lived here for generations. They've brought up their children here. There's even a school.'

Raffaele's shoulders rose and fell. 'A little collateral damage. But don't worry, they'll be helped to relocate. It's no big deal.'

Collateral damage. The unimportant consequence of an action.

Lily knew collateral damage. That was what she'd been the day Tyson Grady had decided to make his ex-girlfriend pay for dumping him. He'd got what he wanted. Rachel never got the chance to go out with anyone else. She'd died as a result of the acid he'd thrown in her face. And Lily— well, Lily had suffered for being in the wrong place at the wrong time.

Bile rose in her throat, threatening to choke her. The sheer arrogance of these males with their feuds and their paybacks sickened her.

'No big deal? This is their *home!*' Her breath snagged in tight lungs. She met Raffaele's gaze and saw no softening, just fierce determination. 'Doesn't that mean anything to you?'

'They can make their home somewhere else. What matters is making sure Bradshaw gets his deserts. Ruining him financially isn't nearly enough. Just be thankful I'm stopping there and not taking the law into my own hands.' There was a flash of something dangerous in those blue eyes. A flash that sent a quiver of fear ricocheting through her.

Lily's hands fell to her sides. The fight went out of her. Bradshaw wasn't the only one to be duped, was he? Suddenly she felt cold, despite the warmth of the sun and the sand.

'I thought I knew you,' she whispered. 'I thought you were…' Her throat closed before she could blurt out any more.

She'd thought he'd risen above his pain and his past to become someone special. She'd thought him kind and caring because he'd helped her face her demons. Instead Raffaele Petri was every bit as hard and conscienceless as she'd first thought. How could she have been so wrong?

'Lily? Where are you going?'

She shoved out an arm to stop him when he stepped towards her. Then she was stumbling over the soft sand, clumsy in her haste to escape.

CHAPTER FOURTEEN

DANNAZIONE! TWELVE HOURS and still Raffa couldn't relax. He strode the path to the hill at the island's centre, needing an outlet for the furious energy that hadn't abated since yesterday and that scene with Lily.

Women!

One minute she was blinking up at him, sympathy in those glistening eyes. The next she was staring at him as if he were a monster.

Raffa's flesh crawled at the memory. He'd grown used to Lily's smiles. She'd even taken his part in the face of Olga's antagonism. He fought his own battles, but her defence had plucked at chords deep within, strumming feelings that still reverberated, refusing to disappear.

Bradshaw was the monster. Who knew how many women he'd abused?

Raffa broke through the trees to the summit. The ocean lay below him, awash with sunrise pinks and oranges. Bradshaw's crumbling mansion was lit in gold. In the other direction the resort lay sleeping.

Except someone else was up. A tiny figure crossed the white sand, wading into the water.

Lily. No one else swam at this hour. That was why he'd come inland.

He stilled, chest heaving. It wasn't exertion that made his heart crash. It was realising he'd come here to avoid her.

Raffa frowned. As a kid on the street he'd learned never to turn his back on the dangerous or the unpleasant.

If there was a problem, better to face it than hope it would magically resolve itself.

And she was a problem. Lily, the woman who'd unleashed worrying new forces, new *feelings*.

All night he'd wrestled with a disturbing desire to do something, say something, to banish her scowl so she'd smile at him like before.

How weak was that?

Was he going to stop his plan for retribution because some locals would be uprooted? They'd be better off on a larger island. Simple economics meant a bigger population attracted better services and job opportunities. He'd ensure they got help to relocate. Once they'd moved they'd probably thank him for the opportunities he'd provided.

This is their home! Lily's words echoed in his head.

She was too emotional. If there were problems with the relocation, he'd fix them. He wasn't like Bradshaw, using then discarding people.

Yet, annoyingly, doubt persisted. Just because he had no concept of home, was it possible he underestimated its importance?

Raffa folded his arms. It was sentimental twaddle.

He'd never had any attachment to 'home.' Even when his mother was alive, he'd rarely seen her as she struggled to support them. He'd been raised in a series of miserable rooms, each more rundown than the last. Home was where his sister was, not in cold concrete.

Yet the churning inside didn't ease.

It was like those early days, looking through windows to glimpse the secure, happy lives of other families, knowing they might as well live on another planet for all the similarity between them and him.

Lily made him feel like an outsider again.

He sucked in a breath, inhaling the scent of dew and foliage and flowers. That hint of sweetness reminded him of Lily's tantalising scent, understated yet seductive.

She'd inveigled her way into his life, not just his bed. The realisation welded his feet to the rocky ground.

Lily mattered.

He'd opened up to her, telling her things he never shared. He'd sweated on her reaction to his past then been relieved when, instead of turning away, she'd offered understanding. For the first time since Gabriella he'd had someone on his side. Someone who saw *him*, not just a face or a body. For that brief space he hadn't been alone. It had felt…good.

Raffa hefted another breath, eyes fixed on the tiny spot that was Lily, swimming in the bay.

He'd done more than open up. *He'd trusted her.* Despite the fact trust didn't come easily.

That was why he'd let her into his life. Why it hurt that she'd spurned him.

He'd waited last night for her to knock on his door, apologise for abandoning him and admit she'd been wrong.

He'd missed her.

Raffa's chest burned, his whole body was drawn tight. But worse was the raw ache right at his centre. An ache that echoed the loss he'd experienced when Gabriella died.

It didn't make sense. He'd only known Lily a few months. He felt protective after all she'd been through. He admired her brain and her sass and her indomitability. And her body. And her laugh.

And the husky way her voice broke when he stroked her supple body. And how she snuggled against him in her sleep. Because she wanted *him*, not his money or his reputation.

She cared. Which meant she'd see sense eventually. She was probably looking for a way to mend their argument right now. Maybe she was nervous about apologising. He knew he could be intimidating.

His pulse kicked at the thought.

In the distance Lily emerged from the water and crossed the beach towards her villa.

Raffa turned and started back down the path, his stride lengthening.

* * *

'Lily?' He pushed the door open and entered. The living room was empty, the shutters open to let in the breeze. Her laptop sat open on the coffee table beside a bag of liquorice. Raffa smiled. He'd watched Lily nibble the stuff when she was working hard, particularly if she was nervous.

Was she nervous about confronting him? Was that why she hadn't come to him?

As he crossed the room Raffa heard the shower. He was drawn by the thought of Lily, naked and glistening, of joining her and ending their argument with hot, satisfying sex.

He forced himself to turn away. This was about more than sex. He didn't know what this was between them, but he was determined to find out. And to find out, they had to talk.

Raffa frowned. Such thoughts were a foreign language, unfamiliar and difficult. Unease prickled between his shoulder blades. Did he really want to go there?

Restless, he stalked to the lounge, grabbing the laptop as he sat. Might as well see what updates Lily had done overnight. There'd be something—a nugget of information on the old plantation estate or some snippet about Bradshaw. The deal would be wrapped up in a few hours when Bradshaw signed. Yet still Lily insisted on working. Unless news of his scheme had changed all that. Suddenly he needed to know.

One tap and the screen came to life. Not a report, but an email.

Raffa was about to minimise the document when the title grabbed his attention.

Re: Island Deal—Urgent.

Maybe it was relevant after all. He scanned the text. It was brief. And it sent shockwaves through him.

Your report was excellent. More needed asap, especially on the counteroffer. What can you dig up? Cash bonus if you get me the info and we seal the deal, plus a week as my guest at the resort.
De Laurentis

Raffa gritted his teeth. De Laurentis. The savvy hotel developer who'd caught him out two years ago on that Greek deal. The one he'd outbid for the Seychelles property.

De Laurentis, asking Lily to provide information on a counteroffer for an island resort.

Raffa stared, the text on the screen blurring. There was a roaring in his ears, like the charge of a hundred motorcycles revving in his head. His belly contracted into a seething mass and pain radiated along his jawline as his teeth ground together.

De Laurentis.

And Lily.

Lily feeding De Laurentis information to rob Raffa of the deal with Bradshaw. Robbing him of his revenge.

'Raffaele?'

Lily hoisted the towel higher across her breasts. Her heart careered madly as wild hope rose.

He'd come.

All night she'd tossed and turned, wanting to go to him, wanting things to be as before. But she hadn't because what he planned was just plain wrong. If she went to his villa he'd seduce her with his beautiful body and rich voice and those big, clever hands. With the way he made her feel special.

She swallowed hard.

If she let him seduce her into acquiescence to his scheme she'd feel tainted, as if she'd betrayed the people who lived here. After all, it was her meticulous research that had got him here, poised to take over Bradshaw's business and close the resort.

But he'd come. He was ready to talk.

'Raffaele?' She loved saying his name. She loved—

He swung his head round, those bluer than blue eyes zeroing in and her buoyant lightness faded. It wasn't tenderness or understanding she read in his face. It was something that made her flesh pinch as if an army of venomous ants swarmed over her, nipping and stinging till she felt hot and distressed.

He shoved her laptop aside and stood.

Instantly she was aware of his superior height. Fury radiated from him as clearly as light from a bonfire.

'You've been busy.' His voice was soft. Not soft like a comfortable embrace but lethally soft, lifting the hair on the back of her neck.

'I've been for a swim.' She took a step forward, vowing not to be intimidated by the man she'd come to care for. He was angry because they took different views on his plans but they'd work through that. She'd already decided she needed to speak with him as soon as possible. Emerging to find him already here just made it easier.

'And you found time for work as well. What a busy woman you are.'

Despite her reassuring self-talk, Lily stopped short. She'd heard Raffaele demanding, angry, reassuring, even tender, but never sarcastic.

'You pay me to work.' It was a matter of pride that even though she was having an affair with the CEO, she still did her job.

'And so do others.'

Was that why he looked so grim?

'You know I've got other clients.'

'Not when I pay for your exclusive services.'

Lily's heart stilled then rushed into an uneven rhythm.

The way he said *exclusive services* made her think of something other than her research.

Heat scorched her breasts and throat. She wished she was fully dressed instead of draped in a towel, her wet hair slick down her back.

'The work is all but done. You said so yourself. My staff needed a hand on a project—'

'I pay for your time, end of story. I told you to clear your other work away.'

'I know but—'

'But nothing, Lily.' He stepped around the end of the lounge, stopping square in her personal space.

Normally that wouldn't matter. Normally she'd be reaching for him, eager to run her hands over his shoulders and into that thick hair, tugging his head down to hers.

But the current of energy running between them wasn't like that. This felt dark, troubling. Threatening.

Lily hitched her chin. 'What's the problem, Raffaele? All I've done is answer a few emails and—'

'And what?' It struck her that for the first time in ages there was not a hint of softening in his eyes. They looked hard and cold as rock crystal. 'And sold a report to my rival?'

'Sorry?'

'Don't play coy. I read the email. You're doing business with De Laurentis. You're selling him information, aren't you?'

Lily frowned. What had that project in Thailand to do with Raffaele? As far as she knew, he had no interests in that part of the world.

'I finalised a report for him weeks ago.'

'And now you're sending him inside information.' He leaned close, his breath brushing her lips. 'Have you forgotten the confidentiality clause in your contract? I can sue you for everything you've got and could ever earn if you betray me.'

Lily stared, reading nothing but antagonism and a thirst for blood, her blood, in that big, bold face.

Her throat scraped raw with the force of her indrawn breath.

'You think I've betrayed you?' Understanding dawned. 'You think I used the information you paid me to find and passed it to someone else.'

'Not just someone else. The only serious rival I've got. And not just the information you unearthed.' His voice was like the lash of a whip. 'I've shared things with you—my plans to take Bradshaw down. The fact I'm not going to give him what he wants—a profitable business he can leech off for the rest of his days. I *trusted* you.'

'You honestly think I betrayed that trust?' Lily's head jerked back as if he'd slapped her. 'You think I shared what you told me in confidence?'

She should be furious. Yet somehow all she felt was pain. Pain that he'd think so little of her. That shimmering joy she'd found with him had been an illusion, as insubstantial as a pool of water on a bed of sand.

'What else can I think? You're dealing information to my biggest rival. Or do you deny it's the same De Laurentis who made a name for himself with top class hotels in Italy? The one now investing in coastal resorts?'

'It's the same man, but—'

'But nothing!' As if hearing the way his voice had risen, he paused. When he spoke again his voice was slow, deliberate and barely above a whisper. 'I pay you an exorbitant salary. I expect discretion and loyalty.'

'I have been discreet and loyal.' The same discretion and loyalty she gave all her clients. Which was why she hadn't told Raffaele when she began working for him that she'd already committed to this job. De Laurentis deserved the same consideration Raffaele did. 'There's been no sharing of information.'

'You expect me to believe that? The man says he's desperate for information you can *dig up* on a counter-offer for this resort.' Raffaele didn't move yet seemed to swell, growing taller, more menacing. 'Well? Speak up.'

This was the man she'd fallen in love with.

The man she'd entrusted with her fragile hopes and dreams. The man she'd leaned on as she forced herself from hiding and into the world.

Hot tears spiked behind her eyes. Distress grabbed her throat and she had to work to find her voice. She laced her fingers together, squeezing.

'Despite how it looks, he's talking about another property. On another continent. I didn't tell you because I didn't see a conflict of interest at the time. They're completely separate. But, because of what's happened between you and me, I was about to write and tell him I can't work for him anymore.'

Lily had known that no matter what happened in the future, whether she worked for Raffaele or not, she couldn't work for his competitors.

'You expect me to believe that?'

Lily stared into that stony face, each beautiful line carved as if in granite. Into eyes that sliced through her. She'd swear she felt the cut right to the bone.

She'd turned herself inside out for Raffaele. He'd burst into her life and made her face her deepest fears head-on. He'd seduced her into believing the world could be an entrancing place, that *she* could be someone she'd never dreamed she could be.

He'd made her love him. And, worse, believe he might care for her, just a little.

And now, in one fell swoop, he'd smashed it all. The hopes, the joy, the trust.

That grim face held no doubt or tenderness. She'd made a monumental fool of herself. What had she been—a diversion? A curiosity? Reclusive and virginal and so naive. Someone a little different for a holiday fling.

Pain raked at her insides.

It wouldn't have hurt as much if he'd accused her of being unattractive. But he'd attacked her in the one place she'd always relied on. The one part of her life where she'd been strong and confident and sure of herself. Her professionalism. She'd believed in that when she'd believed in nothing else. And now he tried to smash that too.

'No, I don't expect you to believe it. I can see you've made up your mind, no matter what I say.' She hauled in oxygen and planted her hands on her hips. Somewhere, deep within, dreams were disintegrating, hopes vanishing. But one lesson Lily had learned well—to conceal hurt.

'There's nothing more to say, Raffaele. In the circumstances, I know you won't want me to work out my notice before I resign.'

Silence. Blankness on his features.

What had she expected? Second thoughts? An apology?

'You can resign tomorrow, *after* I close this deal. And know that if you try to pass any more information to De Laurentis in the meantime, my lawyers will make it their mission to destroy you.'

Silently Lily nodded. Words were beyond her. It took all her energy just to stand tall, bearing the weight of each lashing word.

He turned, glanced at the laptop, and she wondered if he was going to smash that too, or take it with him. Instead he strode to the door without looking back, confident in the knowledge no sane person would ignore his threat of legal action.

Clearly he expected simply to walk out of her life, dismissing all they'd shared. As if that, and she, meant nothing.

'You told me about your past.' Her voice was croaky but she knew he heard. 'The way you spoke made it sound like you felt...' She paused, searching for the right word. 'That you felt *diminished* because of what you'd done to get out of poverty.'

Raffaele stopped, his hand on the door. He didn't turn.

'It's not what you did for a living that taints you. It's the fact you haven't learned to trust anyone but yourself. Until you do you'll always be alone.'

She snatched a heavy breath.

'You made me trust you, Raffaele.' Lily almost choked on his name, but fought back despair. 'I hate that you've shattered that trust. But I intend to be stronger than you. I'm not going to let that destroy me. I'm going to get on with my life and not look back.'

For a heartbeat he stood unmoving, then without a word he dragged open the door and strode into the sunlight.

Had she really expected him to listen?

Lily stood in the centre of the room, rigid with shock. A forlorn, disbelieving part of her hoping he'd return when he calmed down.

He didn't return.

She stood so long, not daring to move lest the hurt inside break free and smash her into tiny pieces. But eventually her legs gave way and she staggered to the lounge.

Fifty minutes later she was on the motor launch heading for the next island. Two hours after that she was airborne, beginning the long trip away from Raffaele.

CHAPTER FIFTEEN

AT LAST IT was done. Bradshaw had signed the papers and Raffa was the majority owner of the island.

He should be crowing with delight, or at least smiling with satisfaction. Instead he felt a sense of anticlimax. As if this long-awaited victory wasn't everything he'd hoped for.

There'd been a moment of predictable, if shallow, pleasure when he'd refused Bradshaw's offer of a champagne toast to celebrate their partnership.

There'd been several minutes of gratification as he'd explained precisely why they would never work together. And the fact that he, Raffa, intended to ensure the island would never make a profit to support the man responsible for killing Gabriella.

Bradshaw had blustered and denied and finally pleaded, but the legal documents were watertight. He didn't have a leg to stand on.

Raffa had listened to Bradshaw ranting and threatening, and waited for the welcome surge of pleasure.

It didn't come. Instead he felt unsettled. Something gnawed at his gut. He and Consuela were almost back to the resort when he realised it was because justice, or vengeance, or whatever you named it, couldn't bring Gabriella back. The hole in his heart was still there, still raw. He'd failed her. If he'd been a better brother—

'My legs aren't as long as yours. Do you mind slowing a little?'

He glanced at Consuela, impeccable as ever in a severe charcoal suit. Interestingly, she didn't look like she'd just achieved a major victory either.

'Sorry. I was thinking.'

'Not happy thoughts. I assumed you'd be pleased.'

He shrugged and gestured for her to precede him where the path through the trees narrowed.

'I've got a few things on my mind.' Not just the unexpected sense of let-down but that scene this morning with Lily. His thoughts had circled back to her words time and again, even when signing the all-important contract.

'Something to do with Lily?'

Raffa's eyes fixed on the woman in front of him but she didn't look back, just kept walking.

'Why should it be to do with her?'

'Because when I arrived at the airport I saw her crossing the tarmac to board a plane.'

Raffa stumbled on the perfectly even surface of the path. 'Lily?' He'd only left her a short time ago. 'You're mistaken.'

Consuela stopped and turned. Her expression was neutral but there was something in her eyes he didn't recognise. 'I know Lily, remember? It was definitely her but she didn't see me. She looked...'

'What? How did she look?' Tension hummed through him, drawing him tight.

Consuela's mouth tightened. 'Let's just say that if the security staff hadn't stopped me I'd have gone over and given her a hug.' Her eyes narrowed and now he recognised her expression. Disapproval. Of him.

'But our flight isn't till tomorrow.' Why he said it he didn't know, except he was struggling to grasp the fact Lily had gone. He felt like someone had blasted a gaping hollow in his chest. He braced his feet wider.

It didn't make sense. He should be pleased to be rid of the woman who'd betrayed him. She'd saved him the necessity of travelling with a corporate spy.

Except ever since he'd accused her he'd felt *wrong*.

As if he were the one at fault.

As if he'd missed something.

As if he should have taken time to listen to her protests of innocence.

Doubt had beaten at him from the moment he'd left her but he hadn't let himself weaken and return. He'd had too much on his mind—his plan to exact justice on Bradshaw.

Now he felt as if he'd got his priorities wrong.

'Tell me. Who else was sniffing around this deal? Who else courted Bradshaw?'

Consuela's eyes widened but she rattled off names. Big leisure company consortiums. The ones he knew about.

'Anyone else? De Laurentis?'

'No, but Lily is the researcher. You should ask her.' One perfectly arched eyebrow rose. 'The last whisper I heard was that he had his sights on something in Asia. Thailand, I think.'

Raffa closed his eyes, a sick feeling dragging at his belly. He'd jumped so eagerly at the idea Lily had betrayed him. Had he *wanted* to believe it? Was it easier to believe the worst than try to live with the unsettling feelings she stirred? What did that say about him?

'Raffa! Are you okay? You look like you're going to keel over.'

He snapped his eyes open, finding no comfort in Consuela's concern.

'Speak to me. What's wrong?'

He lifted his face to the sunlight filtering through the trees. Way above was the wide blue arch of sky where Lily was flying away from him.

Realisation skewered him like an insect on a pin. It was an effort to draw breath and his voice, when he found it, was choked. 'I've just made the biggest mistake of my life.'

'So you'd call yourself a digital nomad, Ms Nolan? Working all around the globe? How do you find that?'

Lily smiled at the woman in the dark suit at the front of the audience. 'Lily, please.' She gripped the podium, not with horrible nerves as when she'd started her presentation, but because it was comfortable.

After visiting her family, joining the women's business breakfast group was the first thing she'd done on her return. She hadn't wanted to. She'd wanted to bury herself at home and stay there. Which was all the proof she needed that she *had* to do this.

She'd been shaking with nerves before each meeting, especially today, but came away each time feeling better than before. This was the first time she'd presented and initially it had been tough. Standing in front of all these people, sharing insights into her enterprise, was the test she'd set herself. Proof that she could and would be strong.

Which was a laugh, given how forlorn she felt. Only the determination to keep busy stopped her from curling up and weeping into her pillow. She wouldn't go back to the woman she'd been before Raffaele had forced her to change.

'Like anything, there are positives and negatives. I can work almost anywhere—'

'Just give me the chance to work on a tropical island,' someone said and there was a ripple of good-natured chuckles.

'It had a lot going for it.' Lily's smile grew fixed as an image of Raffaele filled her brain. The touch of his hands, the velvet tone of his voice, the bliss they'd shared, the sheer, dizzying delight.

And the abyss of pain.

She blinked and refocused.

'But it's still work, wherever I'm located, so access to a reliable network is vital. I couldn't risk long power outages, for instance, so I'd give storm season in the tropics a miss.' She forced a smile into her voice.

'And there are benefits to being in an office, face to face with colleagues. I'm currently looking into ways to make that happen regularly, so my team and I aren't always working in virtual isolation.'

'I'm afraid that's all we have time for this morning.' The MC made her way up to the podium, smiling.

Lily was returning her smile when a ripple of unease skated across her flesh, tugging her body to alert.

A whisper coursed through the room. Lily saw heads turn, not towards her as the MC thanked her and the audience applauded, but towards the back of the room.

Lily shook hands, said something suitable and widened her tight smile. But she didn't hear what the MC said about upcoming events. It was drowned by the thump of her pulse as slowly, with a feeling of inevitability, she lifted her gaze towards the rear exit.

Raffaele. Large as life and more gorgeous than she remembered.

Her knees loosened to wobbling jelly, making her grab the podium for support. A mere couple of months wasn't nearly long enough to get over him.

She'd known it was Raffaele from that first prickle of awareness, that familiar soaring sensation inside. Yet she hadn't believed it.

Fate, and Raffaele, couldn't be that cruel.

But it seemed they could.

The MC struggled to get the crowd's attention. But every woman had turned to watch Raffaele, suave and appallingly handsome in his trademark open-necked shirt, casual jacket and pale trousers that emphasised the length and strength of his powerful limbs. Lily's heart slammed her ribs in a stop-start beat that left her breathless.

His eyes met hers and she'd swear she heard a whoosh of flame as her body ignited.

Or was that her paper-thin defences? She wasn't ready to face him. She needed more time to look convincingly unaffected. Despair lashed her.

The MC said something, motioning her towards the side aisle of the auditorium.

Gaze still locked on Raffaele, Lily stepped away from

the podium, forcing her head up and shoulders back. She prayed she wouldn't stumble on those cotton-wool legs but refused to watch the ground. This was the man who'd used then discarded her like a piece of trash. She'd meet him eye to eye with no hint of weakness.

Vaguely she was aware of the audience watching, of excited whispers. But it was the whispers filling her head that nearly undid her. *Cara, tesoro,* and all those other Italian endearments he'd used in that deep velvet voice.

Lily told herself he'd used them deliberately to get what he wanted—the novelty of a twenty-eight-year-old virgin in his bed. Because if he'd meant any of them he'd have listened to her explanation, given her a chance. He'd have believed her.

She stopped close, staring into azure eyes that reminded her how he'd taken her to heaven. Ruthlessly she shut the memory down, licking her lips to moisten her parched mouth.

Instantly his gaze dropped to her mouth and her breath stalled. One look! That was all it took for him to turn her inside out all over again.

'I presume you want to talk with me?' Her voice was steely. She was amazed at how firm it sounded.

His eyes jerked up and she was surprised at how distracted he looked. How far from the determined, decisive CEO who'd ruthlessly cut her adrift.

For a moment he looked about to speak. Then he nodded and held open the door. The whispers grew to excited speculation as the door swung closed behind them.

'You've changed.' He hadn't meant to blurt it out but he was shocked.

Not by the way Lily had held the audience in the palm of her hand. He knew she was capable and a good communicator when genuinely interested in something.

Nor was it her new clothes that surprised him. She

looked good in slim-fitting trousers, heels and an amber silk top. More than good. He wanted nothing more than the freedom to run his hands over her body. Explore the satiny skin of her breasts and inner thighs that no silk could match. Let down her hair and tug her into him.

She swung her head round so their eyes met and there it was again, that punch to the gut. That frigid glitter. That total lack of welcome or warmth.

His belly tightened as terror tugged his vitals. It wasn't new. It had grown familiar since she'd gone. Yet he'd hoped for a glimmer of warmth.

'Of course I've changed. You taught me a lot.' Her mouth twisted and he felt searing pain. 'I learn from my mistakes.' Then the shutters came up.

She looked like a duchess surveying a beggar. Despite a lifetime pretending not to care, concealing emotions and revelling in the success and wealth he'd acquired, this time it mattered. It reminded him of his pedigree of poverty, his grubby past and every sordid encounter. Worse, it spoke of the way he'd mistreated her. Her disdain sliced to his soul, carving through the vast emptiness inside.

How had he thought he had a chance?

'Raffaele?' Her eyes rounded and for a fleeting moment her hand brushed his. The silver bangle on her wrist caught his eye and his heart pounded with excitement.

That touch, that moment of concern, and the fact she wore his gift, were all it took for hope to rise. Not because he really stood a chance, but because he had to try. He couldn't go on like this.

'We need to talk.' He quickened his pace, ushering her from the building. His hire car was parked at the kerb but she walked on when he would have opened the car door, her stride biting the pavement.

'Here.' It was a café. Not private. Not what he'd planned. But he'd take what he could get.

He followed her in, past empty tables and a display of

cakes. Lily hesitated before taking the furthest table, tucked into a corner. Raffa grabbed a seat, wondering if she realised she couldn't get away unless he moved. He doubted it. She looked distracted, her gaze skittering around the room.

There was silence till they'd ordered and received their coffees. Raffa took a sip and moved the cup away.

'Not up to your high standards?' Disapproval laced her tone.

'I'm not thirsty.' He had no idea how it tasted. His mouth was full of the metallic tang of fear. He leaned towards her. 'I'm sorry, Lily. So sorry.'

Her cup clattered back into its saucer, coffee spilling onto her hand.

Raffa heard her hiss of shock as he grabbed her wrist, pulling it towards him, reaching for a napkin at the same time to blot the hot liquid.

'Don't! I'm all right. I—'

Her words stopped when he lifted her hand, pressing his lips to the spot the liquid had seared. Raffa closed his eyes, a shudder of longing passing through him at the taste of Lily, as sweet and enticing as he remembered.

Pain battered his chest.

'I'm sorry. I can't apologise enough. I accused you of something I should have known you'd never do. I wronged you.' His lips moved against her skin, his eyes shut to block out the rejection he knew he'd see in her face.

He'd never thought himself a coward but he was now. He couldn't bear for her to send him away. His grip tightened on her slender wrist, turning her hand so he could plant a kiss on her palm.

She shivered. From horror? Distaste? Or pleasure?

Raffa forced his eyes open but kept them trained on that small, pale hand, noticing the tint of amber nail polish as her fingers curled over her palm.

His beautiful Lily. He'd feared she might withdraw into

her shell again but she was stronger than he gave her credit for. She'd emerged from her cocoon and nothing, not even a lout like him, would drive her back. He was proud of her.

'Why are you smiling?'

'Because you're even more beautiful than I remembered.'

Instantly she tugged her hand. But he was stronger and he'd use any advantage he had, even brute strength.

'Don't.' She sounded choked, not indifferent. 'You've had your fun. Just leave me alone.' Pain pierced at the hurt in her shadowed eyes and the crooked line of her mouth.

'You think I'm here for *amusement*?' Raffa stared. 'There's nothing amusing about my feelings, *tesoro*.'

'Don't talk like that.' Again she tried to free her hand and failed. 'I know it was…diverting to have a woman so different.' Her voice was a rushed whisper. 'But that's in the past. You can't make a fool of me like that again.'

Holding her wrist, he felt her pulse beat a runaway rhythm almost as fast as his own.

'I know you think you can't believe me after the way I rejected you.' He swallowed a knot of guilt and pain at the memory. 'But one thing you must understand. I was never *amused* by you. You were never a *diversion*. You were the most frighteningly real thing to happen to me in as long as I can remember.'

Raffa clasped her hand in both of his. 'No one else has made me feel the way you do.'

To his despair she shook her head, her mouth a mutinous line. 'You didn't feel anything. You turned on me. If you'd really felt anything for me—'

'Oh, I feel, *piccola istrice*. See how much.' He pushed her hand against his chest, spreading her fingers wide over the place where his heart crashed. 'I feel so much I'm terrified you'll turn me away without a hearing. Or that after hearing me out you'll say you're not interested.'

She blinked, an arrested expression in her eyes. 'Not interested in what?'

He shook his head. 'First I need to apologise properly and explain—'

'Not interested in what?'

This wasn't going as planned. He'd worked out what he needed to say, how he'd say it, and she was turning it all on its head. Turning *him* inside out.

'In me.'

Time stretched out like a bungee cord yanked almost to breaking point.

'I've already had you.'

Raffa couldn't prevent the grunt of pain her words dragged out. His chance was slipping away and he couldn't stop it. Panic nudged closer.

'I'm not talking about sex.' The way she shot a glance over his shoulder at the café behind him told him his voice had risen but he didn't care.

'If you're not talking about sex, what then?'

He swallowed, his mouth dry with fear. Had he ever, in his life, laid himself so bare? It went against every instinct of self-preservation to put himself in anyone's power.

'In me. Body and soul. Heart and mind.' He felt her shiver and hurried on before she could stop him. 'I love you, Lily.'

To his horror he saw her eyes well. He reached out and cupped her cheek, brushing dampness from the corner of her eye with his thumb.

'Don't cry, Lily. Please.' It felt as if she'd wrenched his heart out.

'What do you expect me to do when you say something like that?'

He swiped his thumb over her lush lips, feeling them quiver. 'I *want* you to say yes. That you'll stay with me.'

'I can't think when you do that.'

'Good.' His heart soared at the news. For once he did the

decent thing and pulled back. But he stayed close enough to see how the amber at the centre of her irises glowed as if with an inner fire. Always that had been a sign of Lily's pleasure, or excitement. Or emotion.

'How can you love me? You acted like you hated me that morning.'

'And I've regretted it ever since. I couldn't even concentrate on the deal with Bradshaw because I was too busy regretting my behaviour.'

Her forehead crinkled. 'Then why did you? If you loved me—'

Raffa captured her other hand, holding them both tight. 'It won't seem sensible to someone as logical as you, but feeling the way I do—' he swallowed '—loving you, petrified me. I've never loved anyone except my sister and mother. With you I feel *more*. I care about you, Lily. About making you realise how special you are. About your happiness.'

She opened her mouth and he pressed a finger to her warm lips. 'I trusted you with things I've never spoken about to any other person. I felt drawn to you in ways I didn't understand and it terrified me. I think that's part of the reason I reacted so violently to the possibility of you betraying me. It was easier to push you away than put myself on the line and ask you to love me back.' He drew a slow breath, redolent of coffee and sweet pears and warm female flesh.

'I was frightened you'd reject me.'

Reluctantly he dropped his hand from her mouth. He'd run out of words. Which meant facing her judgement. Desperately he tried to read her thoughts, but Raffaele was stuck on her trembling mouth.

'How many women have rejected you, Raffaele?' Her voice was a thick whisper.

Instantly he was defensive. 'Those women in the past don't count. They didn't know or want me. They wanted my money or my body.' He paused. 'Except I suppose they do matter. Why would you want a man who—?'

Lily tugged her hand free and pressed her palm to his mouth. 'Stop right there.'

She smelled so good, like the dreams that had plagued his sleep since she left. He slicked out his tongue, tasting her, and her hand jerked back.

'I don't care about the women in your past.' Was it really possible?

'Then what do you care about?' Was that a softening in her expression?

'Why would you fall in love with me? It's not sensible.'

'I think it's the most sensible thing I've done in my life. Fall for a woman who's generous, beautiful, sexy, honest, and challenges me to be a better man. I've even rethought my plan for the resort because of you.'

To his horror that beautiful mouth wobbled again. 'How am I supposed to resist you when you're so…?'

'In love?' For the first time since he'd arrived he felt his heart lift. 'Desperate? Ready to do anything?'

'Honest.' She shook her head. 'If you really do feel…'

'I do. I love you, Lily. I've been falling for you since the night you seduced me long-distance with that sexy voice.'

Her eyes widened but a smile fluttered at the corners of her mouth. That smile was like warmth on a freezing winter night.

'I've been falling for you since we sat on your rooftop and you listened to me talk about my hopes and dreams. You were so understanding.'

Raffa stilled, all his senses focused on Lily and the words she'd just used.

'Falling for me?' Was it possible after what he'd done?

She nodded and a flush crept up her throat. 'I've been in love with you for ages.' Her whisper all but stopped his heart. Unfamiliar heat prickled the back of his eyes.

'Raffaele?' She put her hand to his cheek. 'Are you all right?'

He cleared his throat. 'I honestly don't know. I've never felt like this.' At least he knew what this feeling of fullness was, of fear and hope. 'I've never loved anyone like this.'

Her mouth widened into the most beautiful smile he'd ever seen. 'Neither have I.'

For the first time in his life he was lost for words. But not for long. Old shame and new regret hadn't quite died. 'I don't deserve you.'

'Nonsense. You're the best thing that's ever happened to me.' Amber fire sparked in her gaze as if challenging him to disagree. 'By far the best thing.' She paused. 'But I have a question. What is it you call me—*picc*…?'

Raffa grinned. He couldn't help it. He'd never believed such happiness existed. Even the prospect of facing his beloved's wrath when she learned he'd been calling her his little porcupine couldn't dim his smile.

'Why don't we go somewhere more private so I can explain?'

'Why don't we?' Lily placed her hand in his and he knew he was the luckiest man in the world.

EPILOGUE

LILY SMOOTHED HER palms down the scarlet silk skirt of her halter neck dress. Her sexy matching sandals slowed her walk to a sinuous, hip-tilting gait.

The outfit had seemed perfect in the resort boutique but she couldn't help having second thoughts. Maybe something a little less obvious would have been better.

'Lily!' She turned to see Pete from the New York office waving a glass from beyond the pool. 'Great party.'

Beside him Consuela, resplendent in a caftan of blue and purple, chatted with the resort's head butler who, with the rest of the staff, had been given this weekend off.

The island was in carnival, all work done by staff brought in for the duration as everyone involved in redeveloping the resort enjoyed a well-deserved party before the opening next week.

Calypso music filled the air and laughing children wove between the adults before jumping into the pool with the maximum possible splashes. Lily laughed too. Raffaele had done something special here. She was proud of him.

After Robert Bradshaw heard what Raffaele intended for the island it had been easy to persuade him to take cash for the rest of his claim to it. According to Raffaele, that meant after he paid off his debts he'd have enough to support himself on the equivalent of a modest wage for a couple of years. More than enough time for him to find an honest job. Though Lily couldn't imagine him working.

Now the island was a shared enterprise. The resort workers whose families had lived here for generations were the principal owners and Raffaele a minority shareholder. It had been a staggeringly generous gesture but it made everyone happy, not least Raffaele, who seemed to think he had to atone for his past.

Lily didn't care about his past, so long as she could help him make his future all it should be.

She wove through the party towards the new restaurant. There was Raffaele in conversation with the head chef. Lily slipped her hand under Raffaele's arm.

Every doubt she'd had about her dress dissolved as he turned and took her in from head to toe. The gleam in his eyes told her everything she needed to know but he said it anyway. 'You look gorgeous.'

His lips were gentle on hers but she felt the way he held himself in check, because she felt the same. When he lifted his head his smile was just for her.

'You'll have to excuse me, Henry,' Raffaele said to the chef. 'There's somewhere else I need to be.'

'Sure.' Henry grinned. 'I'll see you later.'

Raffaele made to pull her closer, but Lily stepped back, threading their fingers together. 'Not here.'

Eyebrows raised, he followed her, patiently waiting as they left the celebration behind and finally emerged on the path behind their private beach. Through the trees stood the shell of what would be their sometime home. Raffaele had offered to relocate to Australia but Lily had refused, for now happy to move wherever business took them.

'What is it, my love?' His voice, that rich-as-caramel caress, wove its magic and she melted into him.

'There's something I need to know.'

'Hmm?' He dipped his head to nibble her neck and Lily's head lolled back, warmth filling her. But still nerves prickled her nape.

She'd planned her words carefully, but they were fading from her brain. Raffaele had the power to undo her.

'I want to know if you'll marry me.' The words shot out before his sensual assault stopped thought.

He stilled. Eyes brighter than the heavens met hers. They

were questioning, stunned. 'You want to make an honest man of me?' The hint of humour couldn't hide his doubts.

'You're already an honest man.' He didn't speak of it but she knew he still felt guilty over his past. Lily threaded her hands through his thick golden hair and pulled his head down. 'You're the only man for me, Raffaele. I want to be with you always.' She watched him swallow hard. 'Unless marriage makes you uncomfortable.'

'No!' He wrapped his arm around her waist, his other hand warm at the back of her neck. 'If you really believe it would work—'

'I *know* it will work.'

'Well, then.' He pressed a tender kiss to her lips. 'We both know I rely on your advice on all important projects.'

'Is that a yes?' Lily's heart skipped.

'You think I'd let you go now?' He shook his head. 'I may have a lot to learn about relationships and feelings but I'm not crazy. Of course it's yes. I want to spend my life with you, *piccola istrice*.'

'I am *not* your little porcupine.' She pushed his shoulders in mock outrage, enjoying how he pulled her close so she felt his muscled body through the thin silk.

'No? But I so enjoy soothing you—' his big hand traced fire down her breast '—till you let down your guard.'

Lily sighed. 'Sounds like a lifetime's project.'

His lazy smile stole her heart all over again. It was brighter than the sunrise and warmed her to the core of her being. 'That's the plan. And I've never looked forward to anything more.'

* * * * *

WANT ME, COWBOY

MAISEY YATES

One

November 1, 2018
Location: Copper Ridge, Oregon

WIFE WANTED—

Rich rancher, not given to socializing. Wants a wife who will not try to change me. Must be tolerant of moods, reported lack of sensitivity and the tendency to take off for a few days' time in the mountains. Will expect meals cooked. Also, probably a kid or two. Exact number to be negotiated. Beard is nonnegotiable.

November 5, 2018
Revised draft for approval by 11/6

WIFE WANTED—

~~Rich rancher, not given to socializing.~~ Successful rancher searching for a wife who enjoys rural living. ~~Wants a wife who will not try to change me. Must be tolerant of moods, reported lack of sensitivity, and the tendency to take off for a few days' time in the mountains.~~ Though happy with my life, it has begun to feel lonely, and I would like someone to enhance my satisfaction with what I have already. I enjoy extended camping trips and prefer the mountains to a night on the town. ~~Will expect meals cooked. Also, probably a kid or two. Exact number to be negotiated. Beard is nonnegotiable. I~~ I'm looking for a traditional family life, and a wife and children to share it with.

"This is awful."

Poppy Sinclair looked up from her desk, her eyes colliding with her boss's angry gray stare. He was holding a printout of the personal ad she'd revised for him and shaking it at her like she was a dog and it was a newspaper.

"The *original* was awful," she responded curtly, turning her focus back to her computer.

"But it was all true."

"Lead with being less of an asshole."

"I *am* an asshole," Isaiah said, clearly unconcerned with that fact.

He was at peace with himself. Which she admired on some level. Isaiah was Isaiah, and he made no apologies for that fact. But his attitude would be a problem if the man wanted to find a wife. Because very few other people were at peace with him just as he was.

"I would never say I want to—" he frowned "'—enhance my enjoyment.' What the hell, Poppy?"

Poppy had known Isaiah since she was eighteen years old. She was used to his moods. His complete lack of subtlety. His gruffness.

But somehow, she'd never managed to get used to *him*. As a man.

This grumpy, rough, bearded man who was like a brick wall. Or like one of those mountains he'd disappear into for days at a time.

Every time she saw him, it felt as if he'd stolen the air right from her lungs. It was more than just being handsome—though he was. A lot of men were handsome. His brother Joshua was handsome, and a whole lot easier to get along with.

Isaiah was… Well, he was her very particular brand of catnip. He made everything in her sit up, purr…and want to be stroked.

Even when he was in full hermit mode.

People—and interacting with them—were decidedly not his thing. It was one reason Poppy had always been an asset to him in his work life. It was her job to sit and take notes during meetings…and report her read on the room to him after. He was a brilliant businessman, and fantastic with numbers. But people… not so much.

As evidenced by the ad. Of course, the very fact that he was placing an ad to find a wife was both contradicting to that point—suddenly, he wanted a wife!— and also, somehow, firmly in affirmation of it. He was placing an ad to find her.

The whole situation was Joshua's fault. Well, probably Devlin and Joshua combined, in fairness.

Isaiah's brothers had been happy bachelors until a

couple of years ago when Devlin had married their sister Faith's best friend, Mia.

Then, Joshua had been the next to succumb to matrimony, a victim of their father's harebrained scheme. The patriarch of the Grayson family had put an ad in a national newspaper looking for a wife for his son. In retaliation, Joshua had placed an ad of his own, looking for an unsuitable wife that would teach his father not to meddle.

It all backfired. Or...front fired. Either way, Joshua had ended up married to Danielle, and was now happily settled with her and her infant half brother who both of them were raising as their son.

It was after their wedding that Isaiah had formed his plan.

The wedding had—he had explained to Poppy at work one morning—clarified a few things for him. He believed in marriage as a valuable institution, one that he wanted to be part of. He wanted stability. He wanted children. But he didn't have any inclination toward love.

He didn't have to tell her why.

She *knew* why.

Rosalind.

But she wouldn't speak her foster sister's name out loud, and neither would he. But she remembered. The awful, awful fallout of Rosalind's betrayal.

His pain. Poppy's own conflicted feelings.

It was easy to remember her conflicted feelings, since she still had them.

He was staring at her now, those slate eyes hard and glinting with an energy she couldn't quite pin down. And with coldness, a coldness that hadn't been there before Rosalind. A coldness that told her and any other woman—loud and clear—that his heart was unavailable.

That didn't mean her own heart didn't twist every time he walked into the room. Every time he leaned closer to her—like he was doing now—and she got a hint of the scent of him. Rugged and pine-laden and basically lumberjack porn for her senses.

He was a contradiction, from his cowboy hat down to his boots. A numbers guy who loved the outdoors and was built like he belonged outside doing hard labor.

Dear God, he was problematic.

He made her dizzy. Those broad shoulders, shoulders she wanted to grab on to. Lean waist and hips— hips she wanted to wrap her legs around. And his forearms…all hard muscle. She wanted to lick them.

He turned her into a being made of sensual frustration, and no one else did that. Ever. Sadly, she seemed to have no effect on him at all.

"I'm not trying to mislead anyone," he said.

"Right. But you *are* trying to entice someone." The very thought made her stomach twist into a knot. But jealousy was pointless. If Isaiah wanted her…well, he would have wanted her by now.

He straightened, moving away from her and walking across the office. She nearly sagged with relief. "My money should do that." As if that solved every potential issue.

She bit back a weary sigh. "Would you like someone who was maybe…interested in who you are as a person?"

She knew that was a stupid question to ask of Isaiah Grayson. But she was his friend, as well as his employee. So it was kind of…her duty to work through this with him. Even if she didn't want him to do this at all.

And she didn't want him to find anyone.

Wow. Some friend she was.

But then, having…complex feelings for one's friend made emotional altruism tricky.

"As you pointed out," he said, his tone dry, "I'm an asshole."

"You were actually the one who said that. I said you *sounded* like one."

He waved his hand. "Either way, I'm not going to win Miss Congeniality in the pageant, and we both know that. Fine with me if somebody wants to get hitched and spend my money."

She sighed heavily, ignoring the fact that her heart felt an awful lot like paper that had been crumpled up into a tight, mutilated ball. "Why do you even *want* a wife, Isaiah?"

"I explained that to you already. Joshua is settled. Devlin is settled."

"Yes, they are. So why now?"

"I always imagined I would get married," he said simply. "I never intended to spend my whole life single."

"Is your biological clock ticking?" she asked drily.

"In a way," he said. "Again, it all comes back to logic. I'm close to my family, to my brothers. They'll have children sooner rather than later. Joshua and Danielle already have a son. Cousins should be close in age. It just makes sense."

She bit the inside of her cheek. "So you…just think you can decide it's time and then make it happen?"

"Yes. And I think Joshua's experience proves you can make anything work as long as you have a common goal. It *can* be like math."

She graduated from biting her cheek to her tongue. Isaiah was a numbers guy unto his soul. "Uh-huh."

She refused to offer even a pat agreement because she just thought he was wrong. Not that she knew much of anything about relationships of…any kind really.

She'd been shuffled around so many foster homes as a child, and it wasn't until she was in high school that she'd had a couple years of stability with one family. Which was where she'd met Rosalind, the one foster sibling Poppy was still in touch with. They'd shared a room and talked about a future where they were more than wards of the state.

In the years since, Poppy felt like she'd carved out a decent life for herself. But still, it wasn't like she'd ever had any romantic relationships to speak of.

Pining after your boss didn't count.

"The only aspect of going out and hooking up I like is the hooking up," he said.

She wanted to punch him for that unnecessary addition to the conversation. She sucked her cheek in and bit the inside of it too. "Great."

"When you think about it, making a relationship a transaction is smart. Marriage is a legal agreement. But you don't just get sex. You get the benefit of having your household kept, children…"

"Right. Children." She'd ignored his first mention of them, but… She pressed her hands to her stomach unconsciously. Then, she dropped them quickly.

She should not be thinking about Isaiah and children or the fact that he intended to have them with another woman.

Confused feelings was a cop-out. And it was hard to deny the truth when she was steeped in this kind of reaction to him, to his presence, to his plan, to his talk about children.

The fact of the matter was, she was tragically in love with him. And he'd never once seen her the way she saw him.

She'd met him through Rosalind. When Poppy had turned eighteen, she'd found herself released from her foster home with nowhere to go. Everything she owned was in an old canvas tote that a foster mom had given her years ago.

Rosalind had been the only person Poppy could think to call. The foster sister she'd bonded with in her last few years in care. She'd always kept in touch with Rosalind, even when Rosalind had moved to Seattle and got work.

Even when she'd started dating a wonderful man she couldn't say enough good things about.

She was the only lifeline Poppy had, and she'd reached for her. And Rosalind had come through. She'd had Poppy come to Rosalind's apartment, and then she'd arranged for a job interview with her boyfriend, who needed an assistant for a construction firm he was with.

In one afternoon, Poppy had found a place to live, gotten a job and lost her heart.

Of course, she had lost it, immediately and—in the fullness of time it had become clear—irrevocably, to the one man who was off-limits.

Her boss. Her foster sister's boyfriend. Isaiah Grayson.

Though his status as her boss had lasted longer than his status as Rosalind's boyfriend. He'd become her fiancé. And then after, her ex.

Poppy had lived with a divided heart for so long. Even after Isaiah and Rosalind's split, Poppy was able to care for them both. Though she never, ever spoke to Rosalind in Isaiah's presence, or even mentioned her.

Rosalind didn't have the same embargo on mentions of Isaiah. But in fairness, Rosalind was the one who had cheated on him, cost him a major business deal and nearly ruined his start-up company and—by extension—nearly ruined his relationship with his business partner, who was also his brother.

So.

Poppy had loved him while he'd dated another woman. Loved him while he nursed a broken heart because of said other woman. Loved him when he disavowed love completely. And now she would have to love him while she interviewed potential candidates to be his wife.

She was wretched.

He had said the word *sex* in front of her like it wouldn't do anything to her body. Had talked about children like it wouldn't make her...yearn.

Men were idiots. But this one might well be their king.

"Put the unrevised ad in the paper."

She shook her head. "I'm not doing that."

"I could fire you." He leaned in closer and her breath caught. "For insubordination."

Her heart tumbled around erratically, and she wished she could blame it on anger. Annoyance. But she knew that wasn't it.

She forced herself to rally. "If you haven't fired me yet, you're never going to. And anyway," she said, narrowing her tone so that the words would hit him with a point, "I'm the one who has to interview your prospective brides. Which makes this my endeavor in many ways. I'm the one who's going to have to weed through your choices. So I would like the ad to go out that I think has the best chance of giving me less crap to sort through."

He looked up at her, and much to her surprise seemed to be considering what she said. "That is true. You will be doing the interviews."

She felt like she'd been stabbed. She was going to be interviewing Isaiah's potential wife. The man she had been in love with since she was a teenage idiot, and was still in love with now that she was an idiot in her late twenties.

There were a whole host of reasons she'd never, ever let on about her feelings for him, Rosalind and his feelings on love aside.

She loved her job. She loved Isaiah's family, who she'd gotten to know well over the past decade, and who were the closest thing she had to a family of her own.

Plus, loving him was just…easy to dismiss. She wasn't the type of girl who could have something like that. Not Poppy Sinclair whose mother had disappeared when she was two years old and left her with a father who forgot to feed her.

Her life was changing though, slowly.

She was living well beyond what she had ever imagined would be possible for her. Gray Bear Construction was thriving; the merger between Jonathan Bear and the Graysons' company a couple of years ago was more successful than they'd imagined it could be.

And every employee on every level had reaped the benefits.

She was also living in the small town of Copper Ridge, Oregon, which was a bit strange for a girl from Seattle, but she did like it. It had a different pace. But that meant there was less opportunity for a social life. There were fewer people to interact with. By default she, and the other folks in town, ended up spending a lot of their free time with the people they worked with every day. There was nothing wrong with that. She loved Faith, and she had begun getting close to Joshua's wife recently. But it was just... Mostly there wasn't enough of a break from Isaiah on any given day.

But then, she also didn't enforce one. Didn't take one. She supposed she couldn't really blame the small-town location when the likely culprit of the entire situation was *her*.

"Place whatever ad you need to," he said, his tone abrupt. "When you meet the right woman, you'll know."

"I'll know," she echoed lamely.

"Yes. Nobody knows me better than you do, Poppy. I have faith that you'll pick the right wife for me."

With those awful words still ringing in the room, Isaiah left her there, sitting at her desk, feeling numb and ill used.

The fact of the matter was, she probably *could* pick him a perfect wife. Someone who would facilitate his life, and give him space when he needed it. Someone who was beautiful and fabulous in bed.

Yes, she knew exactly what Isaiah Grayson would think made a woman the perfect wife for him.

The sad thing was, Poppy didn't possess very many of those qualities herself.

And what she so desperately wanted was for Isaiah's perfect wife to be *her*.

But dreams were for other women. They always had been. Which meant some other woman was going to end up with Poppy's dream.

While she played matchmaker to the whole affair.

Two

"I put an ad in the paper."

"For?" Isaiah's brother Joshua looked up from his computer and stared at him like he was waiting to hear the answers to the mystery of the universe.

Joshua, Isaiah and their younger sister, Faith, were sitting in the waiting area of their office, enjoying their early-morning coffee. Or maybe enjoying was overstating it. The three of them were trying to find a state of consciousness.

"A wife."

Faith spat her coffee back into her cup. "What?"

"I placed an ad in the paper to help me find a wife," he repeated.

Honestly, he couldn't understand why she was having such a large reaction to the news. After all, that was how Joshua had found his wife, Danielle.

"You can't be serious," Joshua said.

"I expected you of all people to be supportive."

"Why *me*?"

"Because that's how you met Danielle. Or you have you forgotten?"

"I have not forgotten how I met my wife. However, I didn't put an ad out there seriously thinking I was going to find someone to marry. I was trying to prove to dad that *his* ad was a stupid idea."

"But it turned out it wasn't a stupid idea," Isaiah said. "I want to get married. I figured this was a hassle-free way of finding a wife."

Faith stared at him, dumbfounded. "You can't be serious."

"I'm serious."

The door to the office opened, and Poppy walked in wearing a cheerful, polka-dotted dress, her dark hair swept back into a bun, a few curls around her face.

"Please tell me my brother is joking," Faith said. "And that he didn't actually put an ad in the paper to find a wife."

Poppy looked from him back to Faith. "He doesn't joke, you know that."

"And you know that he put an ad in the paper for a wife?" Joshua asked.

"Of course I know," Poppy responded. "Who do you think is doing the interviews?"

That earned him two slack-jawed looks.

"Who else is going to do it?" Isaiah asked.

"You're not even doing the interview for your own wife?" Faith asked.

"I trust Poppy implicitly. If I didn't, she wouldn't be my assistant."

"Of all the… You are insane." Faith stormed out of the room. Joshua continued to sit and sip his coffee.

"No comment?" Isaiah asked.

"Oh, I have plenty. But I know you well enough to know that making them won't change a damn thing.

So I'm keeping my thoughts to myself. However," he said, collecting his computer and his coffee, "I do have to go to work now."

That left both Isaiah and Poppy standing in the room by themselves. She wasn't looking at him; she was staring off down the hall, her expression unreadable. She had a delicate profile, dark, sweeping eyelashes and a fascinating curve to her lips. Her neck was long and elegant, and the way her dress shaped around her full breasts was definitely a pleasing sight.

He clenched his teeth. He didn't make a habit of looking at Poppy that way. But she was pretty. He had always thought so.

Even back when he'd been with Rosalind he'd thought there was something…indefinable about Poppy. Special.

She made him feel… He didn't know. A little more grounded. Or maybe it was just because she treated him differently than most people did.

Either way, she was irreplaceable to him. In the running of his business, Poppy was his barometer. The way he got the best read on a situation. She did his detail work flawlessly. Handled everything he didn't like so he could focus on what he was good at.

She was absolutely, 100 percent, the most important asset to him at the company.

He would have to tell her that sometime. Maybe buy her another pearl necklace. Though, last time he'd done that she had gotten angry at him. But she wore it. She was wearing it today, in fact.

"They're right," she said finally.

"About?"

"The fact that you're insane."

"I think I'm sane enough."

"Of course you do. Actually—" she let out a long, slow breath "—I don't think you're insane. But, I don't think this is a good idea."

"Why?"

"This is really how you want to find a wife? In a way that's this…impersonal?"

"What are my other options? I have to meet someone new, go through the process of dating… She'll expect a courtship of some kind. We'll have to figure out what we have in common, what we don't have in common. This way, it's all out in the open. That's more straightforward."

"Maybe you deserve better than that," she said, her tone uncharacteristically gentle.

"Maybe this is better for *me*."

She shook her head. "I don't know about that."

"When it comes to matters of business, there's no one I trust more than you. But you're going to have to trust that I know what will work best in my own life."

"It's not what I want for you."

A strange current arced between them when she spoke those words, a spark in her brown eyes catching on something inside him.

"I appreciate your concern."

"Yes," she echoed. "My concern."

"We have work to do. And you have wife applications to sort through."

"Right," she said.

"Preference will be given to blondes," he said.

Poppy blinked and then reached up slowly, touching her own dark hair. "Of course."

And then she turned and walked out of the room.

* * *

Isaiah hadn't expected to receive quite so many responses to his ad. Perhaps, in the end, Poppy had been right about her particular tactic with the wording. It had certainly netted what felt to him to be a record number of responses.

Though he didn't actually know how many women had responded to his brother's personal ad.

He felt only slightly competitive about it, seeing as it would be almost impossible to do a direct comparison between his and Joshua's efforts. Their father had placed an ad first, making Joshua sound undoubtedly even nicer than Poppy had made Isaiah sound.

Thereafter, Joshua had placed his own ad, which had offered a fake marriage and hefty compensation.

Isaiah imagined that a great many more women would respond to that.

But he didn't need quantity. He just needed quality.

And he believed that existed.

It had occurred to him at Joshua and Danielle's wedding that there was no reason a match couldn't be like math. He believed in marriage; it was romance he had gone off of.

Or rather, the kind of romance he had experience with.

Obviously, he couldn't dispute the existence of love. His parents were in love, after all. Forty years of marriage hadn't seemed to do anything to dampen that. But then, he was not like his mother. And he wasn't like his father. Both of them were warm people. *Compassionate*. And those things seemed to come easily to them.

Isaiah was a black-and-white man living in a world

filled with shades of gray. He didn't care for those shades, and he didn't like to acknowledge them.

But he wasn't an irrational man. Not at all.

Yet he'd been irrational once. Five years with Rosalind and they had been the best of his life. At least, he had thought so at the time.

Then she had betrayed him, and nearly destroyed everything.

Or rather, he had.

Which was all he had needed to learn about what happened to him and his instincts under the influence of love.

He'd been in his twenties then, and it had been easy to ignore the idea that his particular set of practices when it came to relationships meant he would be spending his life without a partner. But now he was in his thirties, and that reality was much more difficult to ignore. When he'd had to think about the future, he hadn't liked the idea of what he was signing himself up for.

So, he had decided to change it. That was the logical thing to do when you found yourself unhappy with where you were, after all. A change of circumstances was not beyond his reach. And so, he was reaching out to grab it.

Which was why Poppy was currently on interview number three with one of the respondents to his ad. Isaiah had insisted that anyone responding to the ad come directly to Copper Ridge to be interviewed. Anyone who didn't take the ad seriously enough to put in a personal appearance was not worthy of consideration, in his opinion.

He leaned back in his chair, looking at the neat expanse of desk in front of him. Everything was in its place in his office, as it always was. As it should be. And soon, everything in his personal life would be in place too.

Across the hall, the door to Poppy's office opened and a tall, willowy blonde walked out. She was definitely his type in the physical sense, and the physical mattered quite a bit. Emotionally, he might be a bit detached, but physically, everything was functioning. Quite well, thank you.

In his marriage-math equation, sex was an important factor.

He intended to be faithful to his wife. There was really no point in making a lifelong commitment without fidelity.

Because of that, it stood to reason that he should make sure he chose in accordance with his typical physical type.

By the time he finished that thought process the woman was gone, and Poppy appeared a moment later. She was glaring down the hall, looking both disheveled and generally irritated. He had learned to recognize her moods with unerring accuracy. Mostly because it was often a matter of survival. Poppy was one of the few people on earth who wasn't intimidated by him. He should be annoyed by that. She was his employee, and ought to be a bit more deferential than she was.

He didn't want her to be, though. He liked Poppy. And that was a rarity in his world. He didn't like very many people. Because most people were idiots.

But not her.

Though, she looked a little bit like she wanted to kill him at the moment. When her stormy, dark eyes connected with his across the space, he had the fleeting thought that a lesser man would jump up and run away, leaving his boots behind.

Isaiah was not that man.

He was happy to meet her. Steel-capped toe to pointy-toed stiletto.

"She was stupid," Poppy pronounced.

He lifted a brow. "Did you give her an IQ test?"

"I'm not talking about her intelligence," Poppy said, looking fierce. "Though, the argument could be made that any woman responding to this ad…"

"Are you about to cast aspersions on my desirability?"

"No," she said. "I cast those last week, if you recall. It would just be tiresome to cast them again."

"Why is she stupid?" he pressed.

"Because she has no real concept of what you need. You're a busy man, and you live in a rural…area. You're not going to be taking her out to galas every night. And I know she thought that because you're a rich man galas were going to be part of the deal. But I explained to her that you only go to a certain number of business-oriented events a year, and that you do so grudgingly. That anyone hanging on your arm at such a thing would need to be polished, smiling, and, in general, making up for you."

He spent a moment deciding if he should be offended by that or not. He decided not to be. Because she was right. He knew his strengths and his limitations.

"She didn't seem very happy about those details. And that is why I'm saying she's stupid. She wants to take this…job, essentially. A job that is a life sentence. And she wants it to be about her."

He frowned. "Obviously, this marriage is not going to be completely about me. I am talking about a *marriage* and not a position at the company." Though, he supposed he could see why she would be thinking in those terms. He had placed an ad with strict requirements. And he supposed, as a starting point, it *was* about him.

"Is that true, Isaiah? Because I kind of doubt it. You don't want a woman who's going to inconvenience you."

"I'm not buying a car," he said.

"Aren't you?" She narrowed her eyes, her expression mean.

"No. I realize that."

"You're basically making an arranged marriage for yourself."

"Consider it advanced online dating," he said. "With a more direct goal."

"You're having your assistant choose a wife for you." She enunciated each word as if he didn't understand what he'd asked of her.

Her delicate brows locked together, and her mouth pulled into a pout. Though, she would undoubtedly punch him if he called it a pout.

In a physical sense, Poppy was not his type at all. She was not tall, or particularly leggy, though she did often wear high heels with her 1950s housewife dresses. She was petite, but still curvy, her hair dark and curly, and usually pulled back in a loose, artfully pinned bun that allowed tendrils to slowly make their escape over the course of the day.

She was pretty, in spite of the fact that she wasn't the type of woman he would normally gravitate toward.

He wasn't sure why he was just now noticing that. Perhaps it was the way the light was filtering through the window now. Falling across her delicately curved face. Her mahogany skin with a bit of rose color bleeding across her cheeks. In this instance, he had a feeling the color was because she was angry. But, it was lovely nonetheless.

Her lips were full—pouty or not—and the same rose color as her cheeks.

"I don't understand your point," he said, stopping his visual perusal of her.

"I'm just saying you're taking about as much of a personal interest in finding a wife as someone who was buying a car."

He did not point out that if he were buying a car, he would take it for a test drive, and that he had not suggested doing anything half so crass with any of the women who'd come to be interviewed.

"How many more women are you seeing today?" he asked, deciding to bypass her little show of indignation.

"Three more," she said.

There was something in the set of her jaw, in the rather stubborn, mulish look on her face that almost made him want to ask a question about what was bothering her.

But only almost.

"Has my sister sent through cost estimates for her latest design?" he asked.

Poppy blinked. "What?"

"Faith. Has she sent through her cost estimates? I'm going to end up correcting them anyway, but I like to see what she starts with."

"I'm well aware of the process, Isaiah," Poppy said.

"I'm just surprised that you moved on from wife interviews to your sister's next design."

"Why would you be surprised by that? The designs are important. They are, in fact, why I am a billionaire."

"Yes. I know," Poppy said. "Faith's talent is a big reason why we're all doing well. Believe me, I respect the work. However, the subject change seems a bit abrupt."

"It *is* a workday."

Deep brown eyes narrowed in his direction. "You're really something else, do you know that?"

He did. He always had. The fact that she felt the need to question him on it didn't make much sense to him.

"Yes," he responded.

Poppy stamped.

She stamped her high-heel-clad foot like they were in a black-and-white movie.

"No, she hasn't sent it through," Poppy said.

"You just stomped your foot at me."

She flung her arms wide. "Because you were just being an idiot at me."

"I don't understand you," he said.

"I don't need you to understand me." Her brow furrowed.

"But you *do* need me to sign your paychecks," he pointed out. "I'm your boss."

Then, all the color drained from her cheeks. "Right. Of course. I do need that. Because you're my boss."

"I am."

"Just my boss."

"I've been your boss for the past decade," he pointed out, not quite sure why she was being so spiky.

"Yes," she said. "You have been my boss for the past decade."

Then, she turned on her heel and walked back into her office, shutting the door firmly behind her.

And Isaiah went back to his desk.

He had work to do. Which was why he had given Poppy the task of picking him a wife. But before he chased Faith down for those estimates, he was going to need some caffeine. He sent a quick text to that effect to Poppy.

There was a quick flash of three dots at the bottom of the message box, then they disappeared.

It popped up again, and disappeared again. Then finally there was a simple: of course.

He could only hope that when he got his coffee it wasn't poisoned.

Three hours and three women later, Poppy was wishing she had gone with her original instinct and sent the middle finger emoji to Isaiah in response to his request for coffee.

This was too much. It would be crazy for anyone to have their assistant pick their wife—a harebrained scheme that no self-respecting personal assistant should have to cope with. But for her especially, it was a strange kind of emotional torture. She had to ask each woman questions about their compatibility with Isaiah. And then, she had to talk to them about Isaiah. Who she knew better than she knew any other man on the face of the earth. Who she knew possibly better than she knew anyone else. And all the while his words rang in her ears.

I'm your boss.

She was his *employee*.

And that was how he saw her. It shouldn't surprise her that no-nonsense, rigid Isaiah thought of her primarily as his employee. She thought of him as her friend.

Her best friend. Practically family.

Except for the part of her that was in love with him and had sex dreams about him sometimes.

Though, were she to take an afternoon nap today, her only dreams about Isaiah would involve her sticking a pen through his chest.

Well, maybe not his chest. That would be fatal. Maybe his arm. But then, that would get ink and blood on his shirt. She would have to unbutton it and take it off him…

Okay. Maybe she was capable of having both dreams at the same time.

"Kittens are my hard line," the sixth blonde of the day was saying to her. All the blondes were starting to run together like boxes of dye in the hair care aisle.

"I…" Poppy blinked, trying to get a handle on what that meant. "Like… Sexually… Or?"

The woman wrinkled her nose. "I mean, I need to be able to have a kitten. That's nonnegotiable."

Poppy was trying to imagine Isaiah Grayson with a kitten living in his house. He had barn cats. And he had myriad horses and animals at his ranch, but he did not have a kitten. Though, because he already had so many animals, it was likely that he would be okay with one more.

"I will… Make a note of that."

"Oh," the woman continued. "I can also tie a cherry stem into a knot with my tongue."

Poppy closed her eyes and prayed for the strength to not run out of the room and hit Isaiah over the head with a wastebasket. "I assume I should mark that down under special skills."

"Men like that," the woman said.

Well, maybe that was why Poppy had such bad luck with men. She couldn't do party tricks with her tongue. In fairness, she'd never tried.

"Good to know," Poppy continued.

Poppy curled her hands into fists and tried to keep herself from… She didn't even know what. Screaming. Running from the room.

One of these women who she interviewed today might very well be the woman Isaiah Grayson slept with for the rest of his life. The last woman he ever slept with. The one who made him completely and totally unavailable to Poppy forever.

The one who finally killed her fantasy stone-cold.

She had known that going in. She had. But suddenly it hit her with more vivid force.

I am your boss.

Her boss. Her boss. He was her boss. Not her friend. Not her lover. Never her lover.

Maybe he didn't see his future wife as a new car he was buying. But he basically saw Poppy as a stapler. Efficient and useful only when needed.

"Well, I will be in touch," Poppy stated crisply.

"Why are *you* interviewing all the women? Is this like a sister wives thing?"

Poppy almost choked. "No. I am Mr. Grayson's assistant. Not his wife."

"I wouldn't mind that," Lola continued. "It's always

seemed efficient to me. Somebody to share the work-load of kids and housework. Well, and sex."

"Not. His. Wife." Poppy said that through clenched teeth.

"He should consider that."

She tightened her hold on her pen, and was surprised she didn't end up snapping it in half. "Me as his wife?"

"Sister wives."

"I'll make a note," Poppy said drily.

Her breath exited her body in a rush when Lola finally left, and Poppy's head was swimming with rage.

She had thought she could do this. She had been wrong. She had been an idiot.

I am your boss.

He was her boss. Because she worked for him. Because she had worked for him for ten years. Ten years.

Why had she kept this job for so long? She had job experience. She also had a nest egg. The money was good, she couldn't argue that, but she could also go get comparable pay at a large company in a city, and she now had the experience to do that. She didn't have to stay isolated here in Copper Ridge. She didn't have to stay with a man who didn't appreciate her.

She didn't have to stay trapped in this endless hell of wanting something she was never going to have.

No one was keeping her here. Nothing was keeping her here.

Nothing except the ridiculous idea that Isaiah had feelings for her that went beyond that of his assistant.

Friends could be friends in different cities. They didn't have to live in each other's pockets. Even if he had misspoken and he did see them as friends—and really, now that she was taking some breaths, she imagined that was closer to the truth—it was no excuse to continue to expose herself to him for twelve hours a day.

He was her business life. He was her social life. He was her fantasy life. That was too much for one man. Too much.

She walked into his office, breathing hard, and he looked up from his computer screen, his gray eyes assessing. He made her blood run hotter. Made her hands shake and her stomach turn over. She wanted him. Even now. She wanted to launch herself across the empty space and fling herself into his arms.

No. It had to stop.

"I quit," she said, the words tumbling out of her mouth in a glorious triumph.

But then they hit.

Hit him, hit her. And she knew she could take them back. Maybe she should.

No. She shouldn't.

"You *quit*?"

"It should not be in my job description to find you a wife. This is ludicrous. I just spent the last twenty minutes talking to a woman who was trying to get me to add the fact that she could tie a cherry stem into a knot with her tongue onto that ridiculous, awful form of yours underneath her '*skills*.'"

He frowned. "Well, that is a skill that might have interesting applications…"

"I know that," she said. "But why am I sitting around having a discussion with a woman that is obviously about your penis?"

Her cheeks heated, and her hands shook. She could

not believe she had just… Talked about his penis. In front of him.

"I didn't realize that would be a problem."

"Of course you didn't. Because you don't realize *anything*. You don't care about anything except the bottom line. That's all you ever see. You want a wife to help run your home. To help organize your life. By those standards *I* have been your damned wife for the past ten years, Isaiah Grayson. Isn't that what you're after? A personal assistant for your house. A *me* clone who can cook your dinner and…and…do wife things."

He frowned, leaning back in his chair.

He didn't speak, so she just kept going. "I quit," she repeated. "And you have to find your own wife. I'm not working with you anymore. I'm not dealing with you anymore. You said you were my boss. Well, you're not now. Not anymore."

"Poppy," he said, his large, masculine hands pressing flat on his desk as he pushed himself into a standing position. She looked away from his hands. They were as problematic as the rest of him. "Be reasonable."

"No! I'm not going to be reasonable. This situation is so unreasonable it isn't remotely fair of you to ask me to be reasonable within it."

They just stayed there for a moment, regarding each other, and then she slowly turned away, her breath coming in slow, harsh bursts.

"Wait," he said.

She stopped, but she didn't turn. She could feel his stare, resting right between her shoulder blades, digging in between them. "You're right. What I am looking for is a personal version of you. I hadn't thought about it that way until just now. But I am looking for a PA. In all areas of my life."

An odd sensation crept up the back of her neck, goose bumps breaking out over her arms. Still, she fought the urge to turn.

"Poppy," he said slowly. "I think you should marry me."

Three

When Poppy turned around to face him, her expression was still. Placid. He wasn't good at reading most people, but he knew Poppy. She was expressive. She had a bright smile and a stormy frown, and the absence of either was…concerning.

"Excuse me?"

"You said yourself that what I need is someone like you. I agree. I've never been a man who aims for second best. So why would I aim for second best in this instance? You're the best personal assistant I've ever had."

"I doubt you had a personal assistant before you had me," she said.

"That's irrelevant," he said, waving a hand. "I like the way we work together. I don't see why we couldn't make it something more. We're good partners, Poppy."

Finally, her face moved. But only just the slightest bit. "We're good partners," she echoed, the words hollow.

"Yes," he confirmed. "We are. We always have been.

You've managed to make seamless transitions at every turn. From when we worked at a larger construction firm, to when we were starting our own. When we expanded, to when we merged with Jonathan Bear. You've followed me every step of the way, and I've been successful in part because of the confidence I have that you're handling all the details that I need you to."

"And you think I could just… Do that at your house too?"

"Yes," he said simply.

"There's one little problem," Poppy said, her cheeks suddenly turning a dark pink. She stood there just staring for a moment, and the color in her face deepened. It took her a long while to speak. "The problem being that a wife doesn't just manage your kitchen. *That* is a housekeeper."

"I'm aware of that."

"A wife is supposed to…" She looked down, a pink blush continuing to bleed over her dark skin. "You don't feel that way about me."

"Feel what way? You know my desire to get married has nothing to do with love and romance."

"Sex." The word was like a mini explosion in the room. "Being a wife does have something to do with sex."

She was right about that, and when he had made his impromptu proposal a moment earlier, he hadn't been thinking of that. But now that he was…

He took a leisurely visual tour of her, similar to the one he had taken earlier. But this time, he didn't just appreciate her beauty in an abstract sense. This time, he allowed it to be a slightly more heated exploration.

Her skin looked smooth. He had noticed how lovely

it was earlier. But there was more than that. Her breasts looked about the right size to fit neatly into his hands, and she had an extremely enticing curve to her hips. Her skirts were never short enough to show very much of her leg, but she had nice ankles.

He could easily imagine getting down on his knees and taking those high heels off her feet. And biting one of her ankles.

That worked for him.

"I don't think that's going to be a problem," he said.

Poppy's mouth dropped open and then snapped shut. "We've never even... We've never even kissed, Isaiah. We've never even almost kissed."

"Yes. Because you're my assistant."

"Your assistant. And you're my foster sister's ex-fiancé."

Isaiah gritted his teeth, an involuntary spike of anger elevating his blood pressure. Poppy knew better than to talk about Rosalind. And hell, she had nothing to do with Poppy. Not in his mind, not anymore.

Yes, she was the reason Poppy had come to work for him in the first place, but Poppy had been with him for so long her presence wasn't connected with the other woman in any way.

He wasn't heartbroken. He never had been, not really. He was angry. She'd made a fool of him. She'd caused him to take his focus off his business. She'd nearly destroyed not only his work, but his brother's. And what would eventually be their sister's too.

All of it, all the success they had now had nearly been taken out by his own idiocy. By the single time he'd allowed his heart to control him.

He would never do that again.

"Rosalind doesn't have anything to do with this," he said.

"She's in my life," Poppy pointed out.

"That's a detail we can discuss later." Or not at all. He didn't see why they were coming close to discussing it now.

"You don't want to marry me," Poppy said.

"Are you questioning my decision-making, Poppy? How long have you known me? If there's one thing I'm not, it's an indecisive man. And I think you know that."

"You're a dick," Poppy said in exasperation. "How dare you... Have me interviewing these women all day... And then... Is this some kind of sick test?"

"You threatened to quit. I don't *want* you to quit. I would rather have you in all of my life than in none of my life."

"I didn't threaten to quit our friendship."

"I mostly see you at work," he said.

"And you value what I do at work more than what you get out of our friendship, is that it?"

That was another question he didn't know how to answer. Because he had a feeling the honest answer would earn him a spiked heel to the forehead. "I'm not sure how the two are separate," he said, thinking he was being quite diplomatic. "Considering we spend most of our time together at work, and my enjoyment of your company often dovetails with the fact that you're so efficient."

Poppy let out a howl that would not have been out of place coming from an enraged chipmunk. "You are... You are..."

Well, if her objection to the marriage was that they had never kissed, and never almost kissed, and he didn't want to hear her talk anymore—and all those things were true—he could only see one solution to the entire situation.

He made his way over to where Poppy was standing like a brittle rose and wrapped his arms around her waist. He dragged her to him, holding her in place as he stared down at her.

"Consider this your almost-kiss," he said.

Her brown eyes went wide, and she stared up at him, her soft lips falling open.

And then his heart was suddenly beating faster, the unsettled feeling in his gut transforming into something else. Heat. Desire. He had never looked at Poppy this way, ever.

And now he wondered if that had been deliberate. Now he wondered if he had been purposefully ignoring how beautiful she was because of all the reasons she had just mentioned for why they shouldn't get married.

The fact she was his assistant. The fact that she was Rosalind's foster sister.

"Isaiah…"

He moved one hand up to cup her cheek and brought his face down closer to hers. She smelled delicate, like flowers and uncertainty. And he found himself drawn to her even more.

"And this will be your kiss."

He brought his lips down onto hers, expecting… He didn't know what.

Usually, sexual attraction was a straightforward thing for him. That was one of the many things he liked about sex. There was no guesswork. It was honest. There was never anything shocking about it. If he saw a woman he thought was beautiful, he approached her. He never wondered if he would enjoy kissing her. Because he always wanted to kiss her before he did. But Poppy…

In the split second before their mouths touched, he wondered. Wondered what it would be like to kiss this woman he had known for so long. Who he had seen as essential to his life, but never as a sexual person.

And then, all his thoughts burned away. Because she tasted better than anything he could remember and her lips just felt right.

It felt equally right to slide his fingertips along the edge of her soft jawline and tilt her face up farther so he could angle his head in deep and gain access. It felt equally right to wrap both arms around her waist and press her body as tightly to his as he possibly could. To feel the soft swell of her breasts against his chest.

And he waited, for a moment, to see if she was going to stick her claws into him. To see if she was going to pull away or resist.

She did neither. Instead, she sighed, slowly, softly. Sweetly. She opened her mouth to his.

He took advantage of that, sliding his tongue between her lips and taking a taste.

He felt it, straight down to his cock, a lightning bolt of pleasure he'd had no idea was coming.

Suddenly, he was in the middle of a violent storm when only a moment ago the sky had been clear.

He had never experienced anything like it. The idea that Poppy—this woman who had been a constant in his world—was a hidden temptress rocked him down to his soul. He had no idea such a thing was possible.

In his world, chemistry had always been both

straightforward and instant. That it could simply exist beneath the surface like this seemed impossible.

And yet, it appeared there was chemistry between himself and Poppy that had been dormant all this time.

Her soft hands were suddenly pressed against his face, holding on to him as she returned his kiss with surprising enthusiasm.

Her enthusiasm might be surprising, but he was damn well going to take advantage of it.

Because if chemistry was her concern, then he was more than happy to demolish her worry here and now.

He reversed their positions, turning so her back was to his desk, and then he walked her backward before sliding one arm beneath her ass and picking her up, depositing her on top of the desk. He bent down to continue kissing her, taking advantage of her shock to step between her legs.

Or maybe he wasn't taking advantage of anything. Maybe none of this was calculated as he would like to pretend that it was. Maybe it was just necessary. Maybe now that their lips had touched there was just no going back.

And hell, why should they? If she couldn't deny the chemistry between them... If it went to its natural conclusion...she had no reason to refuse his proposal.

He slid one hand down her thigh, toward her knee, and then lifted that leg, hooking it over his hip as he drew her forward and pressed himself against her.

Thank God for the fullness of her skirt, because it was easy to make a space for himself right there between her legs. He was so hard it hurt.

He was a thirty-six-year-old man who had a hell

of a lot more self-control now than he'd ever had, and yet, he felt more out of control than he could ever remember being before.

That did not add up. It was bad math.

And right now, he didn't care.

Slowly, he slid his other hand up and cupped her breast. He had been right. It was exactly the right size to fill his palm. He squeezed her gently, and Poppy let out a hoarse groan, then wrenched her mouth away from his.

Her eyes were full of hurt. Full of tears.

"Don't," she said, wiggling away from him.

"What?" he asked, drawing a deep breath and trying to gain control over himself.

Stopping was the last thing he wanted to do. He wanted to strip that dress off her, marvel at every inch of uncovered skin. Kiss every inch of it. He wanted her twisting and begging underneath him. He wanted to sink into her and lose himself. Wanted to make her lose herself too.

Poppy.

His friend. His assistant.

"How dare you?" she asked. "How dare you try to manipulate me with… wth *sex.* You're my friend, Isaiah. I trusted you. You're just…trying to control me the way you control everything in your life."

"That isn't true," he said. It wasn't. It might have started out as…not a manipulation, but an attempt to prove something to both of them.

But eventually, he had just been swept up in all this. In her. In the heat between them.

"I think it is. You… I quit."

And then she turned and walked out of the room,

leaving him standing there, rejected for the first time in a good long while.

And it bothered him more than he would have ever imagined.

Poppy was steeped in misery by the time she crawled onto the couch in her pajamas that evening.

Her little house down by the ocean was usually a great comfort to her. A representation of security that she had never imagined someone like her could possess.

Now, nothing felt like a refuge. Nothing at all. This whole town felt like a prison.

Her bars were Isaiah Grayson.

That had to stop.

She really was going to quit.

She swallowed, feeling sick to her stomach. She was going to quit and sell this house and move away. She would talk to him sometimes, but mostly she had to let the connection go.

She didn't mean to him what he did to her. Not just in a romantic way. Isaiah didn't... He didn't understand. He didn't feel for people the way that other people felt.

And he had used the attraction she felt for him against her. Her deepest, darkest secret.

There was no way a woman without a strong, pre-existing attraction would have ever responded to him the way she had.

It had been revealing. Though, now she wondered if it had actually been revealing at all, or if he had just always known.

Had he known—all this time—how much she wanted him? And had he been…laughing at her?

No. Not laughing. He wouldn't do that. He wasn't cruel, not at all. But had he been waiting until it was of some use to him? Maybe.

She wailed and dragged a blanket down from the back of the couch, pulling it over herself and curling into a ball.

She had kissed Isaiah Grayson today.

More than kissed. He had… He had touched her.

He had *proposed* to her.

And, whether it was a manipulation or not, she had felt…

He had been hard. Right there between her legs, he had been turned on.

But then, he was a man, and there were a great many men who could get hard for blowup dolls. So. It wasn't like it was that amazing.

Except, something about it felt kind of amazing.

She closed her eyes. Isaiah. He was… He was absolutely everything to her.

She could marry him. She could keep another woman from marrying him.

Great. And then you can be married to somebody who doesn't love you at all. Who sees you as a convenience.

She laughed aloud at that thought. Yes. Some of that sounded terrible. But… She had spent most of her life in foster care. She had lived with a whole lot of people who didn't love her. And some of them had found her to be inconvenient. So that would put marrying Isaiah several steps above some of the living situations she'd had as a kid.

Then there was Rosalind. Tall, blond Rosalind who was very clearly Isaiah's type. While Poppy was...not.

How would she ever...cope with that? With the inevitable comparisons?

He hates her. He doesn't hate you.

Well. That was true. Rosalind had always gone after what she wanted. She had devastated Isaiah in the process. So much so that it had even hurt Poppy at the time. Because as much as she wanted to be with Isaiah, she didn't want him to be hurt.

And then, Rosalind had gone on to her billionaire. The man she was still with. She traveled around the world and hosted dinner parties and did all these things that had been beyond their wildest fantasies when they were growing up.

Rosalind wasn't afraid of taking something just for herself. And she didn't worry at all about someone else's feelings.

Sometimes, that was a negative. But right about now... Poppy was tempted—more than a little bit tempted—to be like Rosalind.

To go after her fantasy and damn the feelings and the consequences. She could have him. As her husband. She could have him...kissing her. She could have him naked.

She could be *his*.

She had been his friend and his assistant for ten years. But she'd never been his in the way she wanted to be.

He'd been her friend and her boss.

He'd never been hers.

Had anyone ever been hers?

Rosalind certainly cared about Poppy, in her own

way. If she didn't, she wouldn't have bailed Poppy out when she was in need. But Rosalind's life was very much about her. She and Poppy kept in touch, but that communication was largely driven by Poppy.

That was...it for her as far as family went. Except for the Graysons.

And if she married Isaiah...they really would be her family.

There was a firm, steady knock on her door. Three times. She knew exactly who it was.

It was like thinking about him had conjured him up.

She wasn't sure she was ready to face him.

She looked down. She was wearing a T-shirt and no bra. She was definitely not ready to face him. Still, she got up off the couch and padded over to the door. Because she couldn't *not*...

She couldn't not see him. Not right now. Not when all her thoughts and feelings were jumbled up like this. Maybe she would look at him and get a clear answer. Maybe she would look at him and think, *No, I still need to quit.*

Or maybe...

She knew she was tempting herself. Tempting him.

She hoped she was tempting him.

She scowled and grabbed hold of her blanket, wrapping it tightly around her shoulders before she made her way to the door. She wrenched it open. "What are you doing here?"

"I came to talk sense into you."

"You can't," she said, knowing she sounded like a bratty kid and not caring at all.

"Why not?"

"Because I am an insensible female." She whirled

around and walked back into her small kitchen, and Isaiah followed her, closing the front door behind him.

She turned to face him again, and her heart caught in her throat. He was gorgeous. Those cold, clear gray eyes, his sculpted cheekbones, the beard that made him more approachable. Because without it, she had a feeling he would be too pretty. And his lips...

She had kissed those lips.

He was just staring at her.

"I'm emotional."

He said nothing to that.

"I might actually throw myself onto the ground at any moment in a serious display of said emotion, and you won't like it at all. So you should probably leave."

Those gray eyes were level with hers, sparking heat within her, stoking a deep ache of desire inside her stomach.

"Reconsider." His voice was low and enticing, and made her want to agree to whatever commandment he issued.

"Quitting or marrying you?" She took a step back from him. She couldn't be trusted to be too close to him. Couldn't be trusted to keep her hands to herself. To keep from flinging herself at him—either to beat him or kiss him she didn't know.

"Both. Either."

Just when she thought he couldn't make it worse.

"That's not exactly the world's most compelling proposal."

"I already know that my proposal wasn't all that compelling. You made it clear."

"I mean, I've heard of bosses offering to give a

raise to keep an employee from leaving. But offering marriage…"

"That's not the only reason I asked you to marry me," he said.

She made a scoffing sound. "You could've fooled me."

"I'm not trying to fool you," he said.

Her heart twisted. This was one of the things she liked about Isaiah. It was tempting to focus on his rather grumpy exterior, and when she did that, the question of why she loved him became a lot more muddled. Because he was hot? A lot of men were hot. That wasn't it. There was something incredibly endearing about the fact that he said what he meant. He didn't play games. It simply wasn't in him. He was a man who didn't manipulate. And that made her accusation from earlier feel…wrong.

Manipulation wasn't really the right way to look at it. But he was used to being in charge. Unquestioned.

And he would do whatever he needed to do to get his way, that much she knew.

"Did you take the kiss as far as you did because you wanted to prove something to me?"

"No," he said. "I kissed you to try and prove something to *me*. Because you're right. If we were going to get married, then an attraction would have to be there."

"Yes," she said, her throat dry.

"I can honestly say that I never thought about you that way."

She felt like she'd just been stabbed through the chest with a kitchen knife. "Right," she said, instead of letting out the groan of pain that she was tempted to issue.

"We definitely have chemistry," he said. "I was genuinely caught off guard by it. I assume it was the same for you."

She blinked. He really had no idea? Did he really not know that her response to him wasn't sudden or random?

No. She could see that he didn't.

Isaiah often seemed insensitive because he simply didn't bother to blunt his statements to make them palatable for other people. Because he either didn't understand or care what people found offensive. Which meant, if backed into a corner about whether or not he had been using the kiss against her, he would have told her.

"I'm sorry," she said.

Now he looked genuinely confused. "You're apologizing to me. Why?"

"I'm apologizing to you because I assumed the worst about you. And that wasn't fair. You're not underhanded. You're not always sweet or cuddly or sensitive. But you're not underhanded."

"You like me," he pointed out.

He looked smug about that.

"Obviously. I wouldn't have put up with you for the past ten years. Good paying job or not. But then, I assume you like me too. At least to a degree."

"We're a smart match," he said. "I don't think you can deny that."

"Just a few hours ago you were thinking that one of those bottle blondes was your smart match. You can see why I'm not exactly thrilled by your sudden proposal to me."

"Are you in love with someone else?"

The idea was laughable. She hadn't even been on a date in...

She wasn't counting. It was too depressing.

"No," she said, her throat tightening. "But is it so wrong to want the possibility of love?"

"I think love is good for the right kind of people. Though my observation is that people mostly settle into a partnership anyway. The healthiest marriage is a partnership."

"Love is also kind of a thing."

He waved a hand. "Passion fades. But the way you support one another... That's what matters. That's what I've seen with my parents."

She stared at him for a long moment. He was right in front of her, asking for marriage, and she still felt like he was standing on the other side of a wall. Like she couldn't quite reach him. "And you're just...never going to love anyone."

"I *have* loved someone," he said simply.

There was something so incredibly painful about that truth. That he had loved someone. And she had used the one shot he was willing to give. It wasn't fair. That Rosalind had gotten his love. If Poppy would have had it, she would have preserved it. Held it close. Done anything to keep it for always.

But she would never get that chance. Because her vivacious older foster sister had gotten it first. And Rosalind hadn't appreciated what she'd had in him.

It was difficult to be angry at Rosalind over what had happened. Particularly when her and Isaiah being together had been painful for Poppy anyway. But right now... Right now, she was angry.

Because whole parts of Isaiah were closed off to Poppy because of the heartbreak he'd endured.

Or maybe that was silly. Maybe it was just going to take a very special woman to make him fall in love. And she wasn't that woman.

Well, on the plus side, if you don't marry him, you'll give him a chance to find that woman.

She clenched her teeth, closing her eyes against the pain. She didn't think she could handle that. It was one terrible thing to think about watching him marry another woman. But it was another, even worse thing to think about him falling in love with someone else. If she were good and selfless, pure and true, she supposed that's what she would want for him.

But she wasn't, and she didn't. Because if he fell in love, that would mean she wasn't going to get what she wanted. She would lose her chance at love. At least, the love she wanted.

How did it benefit her to be that selfless? It just didn't.

"I'll think about it," she said.

Four

"I'm not leaving here until I close this deal," he said.

"I'm not a business deal waiting to happen, Isaiah."

He took a step toward her, and she felt her resolve begin to weaken. And then, she questioned why she was even fighting this at all.

He was the one driving this train. He always was.

Because she loved him.

Because he was her boss.

Because he possessed the ability to remain somewhat detached, and she absolutely did not.

She could watch him trying to calculate his next move. She could see that it was difficult for him to think of this as something other than a business deal.

No, she supposed that what Isaiah was proposing *was* a business deal. With sex.

"You can't actually be serious," she said.

"I'm always serious."

"I get that you think you can get married and make it not about…*feelings*. But it's… I can't get over the sex thing, Isaiah. I can't."

There were many reasons for that, not the least of

which being her own inexperience. But she was not going to have that discussion with him.

"The kiss was good." He said it like that solved everything. Like it should somehow deal with all of her concerns.

"A kiss isn't sex," she said lamely. As if pointing out one of the most obvious things in the world would fix this situation.

"Do you think it's going to be a problem?"

"I think it's going to be weird."

Weird was maybe the wrong word. Terrifying.

Able to rip her entire heart straight out of her chest.

"You're fixating," he said simply. "Let's put a pin in the sex."

"You can't put a pin in the sex," she protested.

"Why can't I put a pin in the sex?"

"Because," she said, waving her hand in a broad gesture. "The sex is like the eight-hundred-pound gorilla in the room. In lingerie. It will not be ignored. It will not be…pinned."

"Put a pin in it," he reiterated. "Let's talk about everything else that a marriage between the two of us could offer you."

She sputtered. "Could offer *me*?"

"Yes. Of course, I don't expect you to enter into an arrangement that benefits only me. So far, I haven't presented you with one compelling reason why marriage between the two of us would be beneficial to you."

"And you think that's my issue?"

"I think it's one issue. My family loves you. I appreciate that. Because I'm very close to my family. Anyone I marry will have to get along with my family. You already do. I feel like you love my family…"

She closed her eyes. Yes. She did love the Grayson family. She loved them so much. They were the only real, functional family she had ever seen in existence. They were the reason she believed that kind of thing existed outside the land of sitcoms. If it weren't for them, she would have no frame of reference for that kind of normalcy. A couple who had been together all those years. Adult children that loved their parents enough to try to please them. To come back home and visit. Siblings who worked together to build a business. Who cared for each other.

Loud, boisterous holiday celebrations that were warm and inviting. That included her.

Yes, the Grayson family was a big, fat carrot in all of this.

But what Isaiah didn't seem to understand was that he was the biggest carrot of all.

An inescapably sexual thought, and she had been asked to put a pin in the sex. But with Isaiah she could never just set the sex aside.

"You love my ranch," he said. "You love to come out and ride the horses. Imagine. You would already be sleeping there on weekends. It would be easy to get up and go for a ride."

"I love my house," she protested.

"My ranch is better," he said.

She wanted to punch him for that. Except, it was true.

His gorgeous modern ranch house with both rustic and modern details, flawlessly designed by his sister, was a feat of architectural engineering and design. There was not a single negative thing she could say about the place.

Set up in the mountains, with a gorgeous barn and

horses and all kinds of things that young, daydreamer Poppy would have given her right arm to visit, much less inhabit.

He had horses. And he'd taught her to ride a year earlier.

"And I assume you want children."

She felt like the wind had been knocked out of her. "I thought we weren't going to talk about sex."

"We're not talking about sex. We're talking about children."

"Didn't your parents tell you where babies come from?"

His mouth flattened into a grim line. "I will admit there was something I missed when I was thinking of finding a wife through an ad."

She rolled her eyes. "Really?"

"Yes. I thought about myself. I thought about the fact that I wanted children in the abstract. But I did not think about what kind of mother I wanted my children to have. You would be a wonderful mother."

She blinked rapidly, fighting against the sting of sudden tears. "Why would you think that?"

"I know you. I've watched the way you took care of me and my business for the last ten years. The way you handle everything. The details in my professional life, Joshua and Faith's, as well. I've seen you with Joshua's son."

"I was basically raised by wolves," she pointed out. "I don't know anything about families."

"I think that will make you an even better mother. You know exactly what not to do."

She huffed out a laugh. "Disappearing into a heroin haze is a good thing to avoid. That much I know."

"You know more than that," he said. "You're good with people. You're good at anticipating what they want, what they need. You're organized. You're efficient."

"You make me sound like an app, Isaiah."

"You're warm and…and sometimes sweet. Though, not to me."

"You wouldn't like me if I were sweet," she pointed out.

"No. I wouldn't. But that's the other thing. You know how to stand up to me." The sincerity on his face nearly killed her. "We would be good together."

He sounded so certain. And she felt on the opposite side of the world from certain.

This was too much. It really was. Too close to everything she had ever dreamed about—without one essential ingredient. Except… When had she really ever been allowed to dream?

She had watched so many other people achieve their dreams. While she'd barely allowed herself to imagine…

A life with Isaiah.

Children.

A family of her own.

Isaiah had simply been off-limits in her head all this time. It had made working with him easier. It had made being his friend less risky.

But he was offering her fantasy.

How could she refuse?

"Your parents can't know it's fake," she said.

"Are you agreeing?"

She blinked rapidly, trying to keep her tears back. "They can't know," she repeated.

"It's not fake," he said simply. "We'll have a real marriage."

"They can't know about the ad. They can't know that you just... Are hiring me for a new position. Okay?"

"Poppy..."

"They can't know you're not in love with me."

She would die. She would die of shame. If his wonderful, amazing parents who only ever wanted the best for their children, who most certainly wanted deep abiding love for Isaiah, were to know this marriage was an arrangement.

"It's not going to come up," he said.

"Good. It can't." Desperation clawed at her, and she wasn't really sure what she was desperate for. For him to agree. For him to say he had feelings for her. For him to kiss her. "Or it's off."

"Agreed."

"Agreed."

For a moment she thought he *was* going to kiss her again. She wasn't sure she could handle that. So instead, she stuck her hand out and stood there, staring at him. He frowned but took her offered hand, shaking it slowly.

Getting engaged in her pajamas and ending it with a handshake was not the romantic story she would need to tell his family.

He released his hold on her hand, and she thought he was going to walk away. But instead, he reached out and pulled her forward, capturing her mouth with his after all, a flood of sensation washing over her.

And then, as quickly as it began, the kiss ended.

"No. It's not going to be a problem," he said.

She expected him to leave then. He was supposed

to leave. But instead, he dipped his head and kissed her again.

She felt dizzy. And she wanted to keep on kissing him. This couldn't be happening. It shouldn't be happening.

But they were engaged. So maybe this had to happen.

She didn't know this man, she realized as he let out a feral growl and backed her up against her wall. This was not the cool, logical friend she had spent all these years getting to know. This was…

Well, this was Isaiah as a man.

She had always known he was a man. Of course she had. If she hadn't, she wouldn't have been in love with him. Wouldn't have had so many fantasies about him. But she hadn't *really* known. Not like this. She hadn't known what it would be like to be the woman he wanted. Hadn't had any idea just how hot-blooded a man as detached and cool as he was on a day-to-day basis could be when sex was involved.

Sex.

She supposed now was the time to bring up her little secret.

But maybe this was just a kiss, maybe they weren't going to have sex.

He angled his head then, taking the kiss deeper. Making it more intense. And then he reached down and gripped the hem of her T-shirt, pulling it up over her head.

She didn't have a bra on underneath, and she was left completely exposed. Her nipples went tight as he looked at her, as those familiar gray eyes, so cold and rational most of the time, went hot.

He stared at her, his eyes glittering. "How did I not know?"

"How did you not know what?" Her teeth chattered when she asked the question.

Only then did she realize she was afraid this would expose her. Because while she could handle keeping her love for Isaiah in a little corner of her heart while she had access to his body—while she claimed ownership of him, rather than allowing some other woman to have him—she could not handle him knowing how she felt.

She'd had her love rejected too many times in her life. She would never subject herself to that again. Ever.

"How did I not know how beautiful you were?" He was absolutely serious, his sculpted face looking as if it was carved from rock.

She reached out, dragged her fingertips over his face. Over the coarse hair of his beard.

She could touch him now. Like this.

The kiss in his office had been so abrupt, so shocking, that while she had enjoyed it, she hadn't fully been able to process all that it meant. All the changes that came with it.

She didn't touch Isaiah like this. She didn't touch him ever.

And now... She finally could.

She frowned and leaned forward, pressing her lips slowly against his. They were warm, and firm, and she couldn't remember anything in the world feeling this wonderful.

Slowly, ever so slowly, she traced the outline of his bottom lip with her tongue.

She was tasting him.

Ten years of fantasies, vague and half-realized, and they had led here. To this. To him.

She slid her hands back, pushing them through his hair as she moved forward, pressing her bare breasts to his chest, still covered by the T-shirt he was wearing.

She didn't want anything between them. Nothing at all.

Suddenly, pride didn't matter.

She pulled away from him for a moment, and his eyes went straight down to her breasts again.

That would be her salvation. The fact that he was a man. That he was more invested in breasts than in feelings.

He was never going to see how she felt. Never going to see the love shining from her eyes, as long as he was looking at her body. And in this, in sex, she had the freedom to express everything she felt.

She was going to.

Oh, she was going to.

She wrapped her arms around his neck and pushed forward again, claiming his mouth, pouring everything, every fantasy, into that moment.

He growled, his arm wrapping around her waist like a steel band, the other one going down to her thighs as he lifted her up off the ground, pulling her against him. She wrapped her legs around his waist and didn't protest at all when he carried them both from the kitchen back toward her bedroom.

She knew exactly where this was going.

But it was time.

If she were totally, completely honest with herself, she knew why she hadn't done this before.

She was waiting for him.

She always had been.

A foolish, humiliating truth that she had never allowed herself to face until now. But it made pausing for consideration pointless.

She was going to marry him.

She was going to be with him.

There was nothing to think about.

There was a small, fragile bubble of joy in her chest, something she had never allowed herself to feel before. And it was growing inside her now.

She could have this. She could have him.

She squeaked when he dropped her down onto the bed and wrenched his shirt up over his head. She lay back, looking at him, taking in the fine, sculpted angles of his body. His chest was covered with just the right amount of dark hair, extending in a line down the center of his abs, disappearing beneath the waistband of his jeans.

She was exceptionally interested in that. And, for the first time, she hoped she was going to have those questions answered. That her curiosity would be satisfied.

He moved his hands to his belt buckle and reality began to whisper in her ear as he worked through the loops.

She didn't know why reality had showed up. It was her knee-jerk reaction to good things, she supposed.

In her life, nothing stayed good for long. Not for her. Only other girls got what they wanted.

The fact of the matter was, she wasn't his second choice after her much more beautiful foster sister.

She wasn't even his tenth choice.

She had come somewhere down the line of she-didn't-even-want-to-know-how-many bar hookups and the women who had been in her office earlier today.

On the list of women he might marry, Poppy was below placing an ad as a solution.

That was how much of a last resort she was.

At least this time you're a resort at all. Does it really matter if you're the last one?

In many ways, it didn't. Not at all.

Because she wanted to be chosen, even if she was chosen last.

He slowly lowered the zipper on his jeans and all of her thoughts evaporated.

Saved by the slow tug of his underwear, revealing a line of muscle that was almost obscene and a shadow of dark hair before he drew the fabric down farther and exposed himself completely, pushing his pants and underwear all the way to the floor.

She tried not to stare openmouthed. She had never seen a naked man in person before. And she had never counted on seeing Isaiah naked. Had dreamed about it, yes. Had fantasized about it, sure. But, she had never really imagined that it might happen.

"Now it's your turn," he said, his voice husky. Affected.

"I…"

She was too nervous. She couldn't make her hands move. Couldn't find the dexterity to pull her pajama pants down. And, as skills went, taking off pajama pants was a pretty easy one.

He took pity on her. He leaned forward, cupping her chin and kissing her, bringing himself down onto the bed beside her and pressing his large, warm palm between her shoulder blades, sliding his hand down the line of her back, just beneath the waistband of those pajamas. His hand was hot and enticing on her ass, and she arched her hips forward, his erection brushing against the apex of her thighs.

She gasped, and he kissed her, delving deep as he did, bringing his other hand around to cup her breast, his thumb sliding over her nipple, drawing it into an impossibly tight bud.

She pressed her hands against his chest, and just stared at them for a moment. Then she looked up at his face and back down at her hands.

She was touching his bare chest.

Isaiah.

It was undeniable.

He was looking down at her, his dark brows locked together, his expression as serious as it ever was, and it was just...*him*.

She slid her hands downward, watching as they traveled. Her mouth went dry when she touched those ab muscles, when her hands went down farther. She paused, holding out her index finger and tracing the indention that ran diagonally across his body, straight toward that place where he was most male.

She avoided touching him there.

She didn't know *how*.

But then, he took hold of her hand, curved his fingers around it and guided her right toward his erection.

She held back a gasp as he encouraged her to curl her fingers around his thick length.

He was so hot. Hot and soft and hard all at once. Then she looked back up, meeting his eyes, and suddenly, it wasn't so scary. Because Isaiah—a man who was not terribly affected by anything at all in the world, who seemed so confident in his ability to control everything around him—looked absolutely at a loss.

His forehead had relaxed, his eyes fluttering closed, his lips going slack. His head fell back. She squeezed him, and a groan rumbled in his chest.

Right now, she had the control, the power.

Probably for the first and only time in their entire relationship.

She had never felt anything like this before. Not ever.

A pulse began to beat between her legs, need swamping her. She felt hollow there, the slickness a telltale sign of just how much she wanted him too. But she didn't feel embarrassed about it. It didn't make her feel vulnerable. They were equals in this. It felt...exhilarating. Exciting. Right here in her little bed, it felt safe. To want him as much as she did.

How could it not, when he wanted her too?

Experimentally, she pumped her hand along his length, and he growled.

He was beautiful.

Everything she'd ever wanted. She knew he'd been made for her. This man who had captured her heart, her fantasies, from the moment she'd first met him.

But she didn't have time to think about all of that, because she found herself flipped onto her back, with Isaiah looming over her. In an easy movement, he reached between them and yanked off her pants and underwear.

He made space for himself between her legs, gripping his arousal and pressing it through her slick folds, the intimacy of the action taking her breath away, and then the intense, white-hot pleasure that assaulted her when he hit that perfect spot cleared her mind of anything and everything.

He did it again, and then released his hold on himself, flexing his hips against her. She gasped, grabbing his shoulders and digging her fingers into his skin.

His face was a study in concentration, and he cupped her breast, teasing her nipple as he continued to flex his hips back and forth across that sensitive bundle of nerves.

Something gathered low in her stomach, that hollow sensation between her legs growing keener...

And he didn't stop. He kept at it, teasing her nipple, and moving his hips in a maddening rhythm.

The tension within her increased, further and further until it suddenly snapped. She gasped as her climax overtook her, and he captured that sound of pleasure with his mouth, before drawing back and pressing the himself into the entrance of her body. And then, before she had a chance to tense up, he pressed forward.

The shocking, tearing sensation made her cry out in pain.

Isaiah's eyes clashed with hers.

"What the hell?"

Five

Isaiah was trying to form words, but he was completely overtaken by the feel of her around his body. She was so tight. So wet. And he couldn't do anything but press his hips forward and sink even deeper into her in spite of the fact that she had cried out with obvious pain only a second before.

He should stop. But she was kissing him again. She was holding him against her as she moved her hips in invitation. As her movements physically begged him to stay with her.

Poppy was a virgin.

He should stop.

He *couldn't* stop.

He couldn't remember when that had ever happened to him before. He didn't know if it ever had. He was all about control. It was necessary for a man like him. He had to override his emotions, his needs.

Right now.

But she was holding him so tight. She felt…so good. He had only intended to give her a kiss before he left.

And he *had* intended to go. But he'd been caught up...
in her. Not in triumph over the fact that he had convinced her to marry him.

No, he had been caught up in *her*.

In the wonder of kissing her. Uncovering her. Exploring her in a way he had never imagined he might.

But he'd had no idea—none at all—that she was
this inexperienced.

Poppy was brash. She gave as good as she got. She
didn't shy away from anything. And she hadn't shied
away from this either.

She still wasn't.

Her hands traveled down to cup his ass, and she
tugged at him, as if urging him on.

"Isaiah," she whispered. "Isaiah, please."

And he had no choice but to oblige.

He moved inside her, slowly at first, torturing them
both, and trying to make things more comfortable for
her.

He had no idea how he was supposed to have sex
with a damned virgin. He never had before.

He had a type. And Poppy was against that type in
every single way.

But it seemed to be working just fine for him now.

She pressed her fingertips to his cheek, then pulled
him down toward her mouth. She kissed him. Slow
and sweet, and he forgot to have control.

He would apologize later. For going too fast. Too
hard. But she kept making these sounds. Like she
wanted it. Like she liked it. She wrapped her legs
around his hips and urged him on, like she needed it.
And he couldn't slow down. Couldn't stop. Couldn't
make it better, even if he should.

He should make her come at least three more times before he took his own pleasure, but he didn't have the willpower. Not at all.

His pleasure overtook him, squeezing down on his windpipe, feeling like jaws to his throat, and he couldn't pull back. Not now. When his orgasm overtook him, all he could hear was the roar of his own blood in his ears, the pounding of his heartbeat. And then Poppy arched beneath him, her nails in his shoulders probably near to drawing blood as she let out a deep, intense cry, her internal muscles flexing around him.

He jerked forward, spilling inside her before he withdrew and rolled over onto his back. He was breathing hard, unable to speak. Unable to think.

"Poppy…"

"I don't want to talk about it," she said, crawling beneath a blanket beside him, covering herself up. She suddenly looked very small, and he was forced to sit there and do the math on their age difference. It wasn't that big. Well, eight years. But he had never thought about what that might mean.

Of course, he had never known her to have a serious relationship. But then, he had only had the one, and he had certainly been having sex.

"We should talk about it."

"Why?" Her eyes were large and full of an emotion he couldn't grab hold of. But it echoed in him, and it felt a lot like pain. "There's really nothing to talk about. You know that my… My childhood was terrible. And I don't see why we have to go over all the different issues *that* might've given me."

"So you've been avoiding this."

It suddenly made sense why she had been so fixated on the sex aspect of his proposal. He'd been with a lot of women. So he had taken for granted that sex would be sex.

Of course, he had been wrong. He looked down at her, all vulnerable and curled into a ball. He kissed her forehead.

It hadn't just been sex. And of course poor Poppy had no reference at all for what sex would be like anyway.

"I'm sorry," he said.

"Don't be sorry. But I... I need to be alone."

That didn't sit well with him. The idea of leaving her like this.

"Please," she said.

He had no idea how to handle a woman in this state. Didn't know how to...

He usually wasn't frustrated by his difficulty connecting with people. He had a life that suited him. Family and friends who understood him. Who he knew well enough to understand.

Usually, he understood Poppy. But this was uncharted territory for the two of them, and he was at a loss for the right thing to do.

"If you really need that."

She nodded. "I do."

He got up, slowly gathering his clothes and walking out of the bedroom. He paused in her living room, holding those clothes in his hands. Then he dropped them. He lay down on her couch, which he was far too tall for, and pulled a blanket over himself.

There. She could be alone. In her room. And tomorrow they would talk. And put together details for their upcoming wedding.

He closed his eyes, and he tried not to think about what it had felt like to slide inside her.

But that was all he thought about.

Over and over again, until he finally fell asleep.

Poppy's eyes opened wide at three in the morning. She padded out into the hall, feeling disoriented. She was naked. Because she'd had sex with Isaiah last night.

And then she had sent him away.

Because... She didn't know why. She hated herself? She hated him? And everything good that could possibly happen to her?

She'd panicked. That was the only real explanation for her reaction.

She had felt stripped and vulnerable. She had wanted—needed—time to get a hold of herself.

Though, considering how she felt this morning, there probably wasn't enough time in the entire world for her to collect herself.

She had asked him to leave. And he'd left.

Of course he had.

She cared for that man with a passion, but he was not sensitive. Not in the least. Not even a little bit.

You asked him to go. What do you want from him?

It was silly to want anything but exactly what she had asked for. She knew it.

She padded out toward the living room. She needed something. A mindless TV show. A stiff drink. But she wasn't going to be able to go back to sleep.

When she walked into the living room, her heart jumped into her throat. Because there was a man-shaped something lying on her couch.

Well, it wasn't just man-shaped. It *was* a man. Isaiah. Who had never left.

Who was defying her expectations again.

He'd been covered by a blanket, she was pretty sure, considering the fact that there was a blanket on the floor bunched up next to him. But he was still naked, sprawled out on her couch and now uncovered. He was...

Even in the dim light she could see just how incredible he was. Long limbs, strong muscles. So hard. Like he was carved from granite.

He was in many ways a mystery to her, even though she knew him as well as she knew anyone. If not better.

He was brilliant with numbers. His investments, his money management, was a huge part of what made Gray Bear Construction a success. He wasn't charismatic Joshua with an easy grin, good with PR and an expert way with people. He wasn't the fresh-faced wunderkind like Faith, taking the architecture world by storm with designs that outstripped her age and experience. Faith was a rare and unique talent. And Jonathan Bear was the hardest worker she had ever met.

And yet, Isaiah's work was what kept the company moving. He was the reason they stayed solvent. The reason that everything he had ever been involved with had been a success in one way or another.

But he was no pale, soft, indoor man. No. He was rugged. He loved spending time outdoors. Seemed to thrive on it. The moment work was through, Isaiah was out on his ranch. It amazed her that he had ever managed to live in Seattle. Though, even then, he had been hiking on the weekends, mountain biking and staying in cabins outside the city whenever he got the chance.

She supposed in many ways that was consistent enough. The one thing he didn't seem to have a perfect handle on was people. Otherwise, he was a genius.

But he had stayed with her.

In spite of the fact that she had asked him not to. She wasn't sure if that was an incredible amount of intuition on his part or if it was simply him being a stubborn ass.

"Are you just going to stand there staring at me?"

She jumped. "I didn't know you were awake."

"I wasn't."

"You knew I was looking at you," she said, shrinking in on herself slightly, wishing she had something to cover up her body.

Isaiah, for his part, looked completely unconcerned. He lifted his arms and clasped his hands, putting them behind his head. "Are you ready to talk?"

"I thought it was the woman who was supposed to be all needy and wanting to talk."

"Traditionally. Maybe. But this isn't normal for me. And I'm damn sure this isn't normal for you. You know, on account of the fact that you've never done this before."

"I said I didn't want to talk about my hymenal status."

"Okay."

He didn't say anything. The silence between them seemed to balloon, expand, becoming very, very uncomfortable.

"It wasn't a big deal," she said. "I mean, in that I wasn't waiting for anything in particular. I was always waiting for somebody to care about me. Always. But then, when I left home… When I got my job with you…" She artfully left out any mention of Rosalind.

"That was when I finally felt like I fit. And there just wasn't room for anything else. I didn't want there to be. I didn't need there to be."

"But now, with me, you suddenly changed your mind?"

She shifted, covering herself with her hand as she clenched her thighs more tightly together. "It's not that I changed my mind. I didn't have a specific No Sex Rule. I just hadn't met a man I trust, and I trust you and…and I got carried away."

"And that's never happened to you before," he said, keeping his tone measured and even. The way he handled people when he was irritated but trying not to show it. She knew him well enough to be familiar with that reaction.

"No," she admitted. Because there was no point in not telling him.

"You wanted this," he said, pushing into a sitting position. "You wanted it, didn't you?"

"Yes," she said. "I don't know how you could doubt that."

"Because you've never wanted to do this before. And then suddenly… You did. Poppy, I knew I was coercing you into marriage, but I didn't want to coerce you into bed."

"You didn't. We're engaged now anyway and… It was always going to be you," she blurted out and then quickly tried to backtrack. "Maybe it was never going to happen for me if I didn't trust and know the person. But I've never had an easy time with trusting. With you, it just kind of…happened."

"Sex?"

"Trust."

"Come here."

"There?"

He reached out and took hold of her wrist, and then he tugged her forward, bringing her down onto his lap in an elegant tumble. "Yes."

He was naked. She was naked. She was sitting on his lap. It should feel ridiculous. Or wrong somehow. This sudden change.

But it didn't feel strange. It felt good.

He felt good.

"I'm staying," he said.

"I asked you to leave," she pointed out.

"You didn't really want me to."

"You can't know that," she said, feeling stubborn.

It really wasn't fair. Because she *had* wanted him to stay.

"Normally, I would say that's true. But I know you. And I knew that you didn't really want me to leave you alone *alone*."

"You knew that?"

"Yes, even I knew that," he said.

She lifted her hand, let it hover over his chest. Then he took hold of it and pressed it down, over his heart. She could feel it thundering beneath her palm.

"I guess you can stay," she whispered.

"I'm too tall for this couch," he pointed out.

"Well, you can sleep on the floor."

That was when she found herself being lifted into the air as Isaiah stood. "I think I'll go back to your bed."

She swallowed, her heart in her throat, her body trembling. Were they really going to… Again?

"It's not a very comfortable bed," she said weakly.

"I think I can handle it."

Then he kissed her, and he kept on kissing her until they were back in her room.

Whatever desire she had to protect herself, to withdraw from him, was gone completely.

For the first time in her life, she was living her dream in Isaiah's arms. She wasn't going to keep herself from it.

Six

Poppy was not happy when he insisted they drive to work together the next day.

But it was foolish for them to go separately. He was already at her house. She was clearly resisting him taking over every aspect of the situation, and he could understand that. But it didn't mean he could allow for impracticality.

Still, she threw him out of the bedroom, closed herself in and didn't emerge until it was about five minutes to the time they were meant to be there.

She was back in her uniform. A bright red skirt that fell down to her knees and a crisp, white top that she had tucked in. Matching red earrings and shoes added to the very Poppy look.

"Faith and Joshua are going to have questions," she said, her tone brittle as she got into the passenger seat of his sports car.

"So what? We're engaged."

"We're going to have to figure out a story. And… We're going to have to tell your parents. Your parents are not going to be happy if they're the last to know."

"We don't have to tell my siblings we're engaged."

"Oh, you just figure we can tell them we knocked boots and leave it at that?" Her tone told him she didn't actually think that was a good idea.

"Or not tell them anything. It's not like either of them keep me apprised of their sexual exploits."

"Well, Joshua is married and Faith is your little sister."

"And?"

"You are an endless frustration."

So was she, but he had a feeling if he pointed that out at the moment it wouldn't end well for him.

This wasn't a real argument. He'd already won. She was here with him, regardless of her protestations. He'd risk her wrath when it was actually necessary.

"Jonathan will not be in today, if that helps. At least, he's not planning on it as far as I know."

She made a noise halfway between a snort and clearing her throat. "The idea of dealing with Jonathan bothers me a lot less than dealing with your siblings."

"Well. We have to deal with them eventually. There's no reason to wait. It's not going to get less uncomfortable. I could probably make an argument for the fact that the longer we wait the more uncomfortable we'll get."

"You know. If you could be just slightly less practical sometimes, it would make us mere mortals feel a whole lot better."

"What do you mean?"

"Everything is black-and-white to you. Everything is…easy." She looked like she actually meant that.

"That isn't true," he said. "Things are easy for me when I can line them out. When I can make categories and columns, so whenever I can do that, I do it. Life has variables. Too many. If you turn it into math, there's one answer. If the answer makes sense, go with that."

"But life *isn't* math," she said. "There's not one answer. We could hide this from everyone until we feel like not hiding it. We could have driven separate cars."

"Hiding it is illogical."

"Not when you're a woman who just lost her virginity and you're a little embarrassed and don't necessarily want everyone to know."

"You know," he said, his tone dry, "you don't have to walk in and announce that you just lost your virginity."

"I am aware of that," she snapped. She tapped her fingernails on the armrest of the passenger door. "You know. You're a pretty terrible cowboy. What with the sports car."

"I have a truck for the ranch. But I also have money. So driving multiple cars is my prerogative."

She made a scoffing sound. And she didn't speak to him for the rest of the drive over.

For his part, Isaiah wasn't bothered by her mood. After she had come to speak to him in the early hours of the morning, he had taken her back to bed where he had kept her up for the rest of the night. She had responded to every touch, every kiss.

She might be angry at him, but she wanted him. And that would sustain them when nothing else would.

The whole plan was genius, really.

Now that they'd discovered this attraction between them, she really was the perfect wife for him. He liked her. She would be a fantastic mother. She was an amazing partner, and he already knew it. And then there was this…this heat.

It was more than he'd imagined getting out of a relationship.

So he could handle moments of spikiness in the name of all they had going for them.

They drove through the main street of town in silence, and Isaiah took stock of how the place looked, altered for Christmas. All the little shops adorned with strings of white lights and evergreen boughs.

It made him wonder about Poppy's life growing up. About the Christmases she might have had.

"Did you celebrate Christmas when you were a child?" he asked.

"What?"

"The Christmas decorations made me wonder. We did. Just...very normal Christmases. Like movies. A tree, family. Gifts and a dry turkey."

She laughed. "I have a hard time believing your mother ever made a dry turkey."

"My grandma made dry turkey," he said. "She died when I was in high school. But before then..."

"It sounds lovely," Poppy said. "Down to the dry turkey. I had some very nice Christmases. But there was never a routine. I also had years where there was no celebration. I don't have...very strong feelings about Christmas, actually. I don't have years of tradition to make into something special."

When they pulled into the office just outside of town, he parked, and Poppy wasted no time in getting out of the car and striding toward the building. Like she was trying to outrun appearing with him.

He shook his head and got out of the car, following behind her. Not rushing.

If she wanted to play a game, she was welcome to it. But she was the one who was bothered. Not him.

He walked into the craftsman-style building behind her, and directly into the front seating area, where his sister, Faith, was curled on a chair with her feet underneath her and a cup of coffee beside her.

Joshua was sitting in a chair across from her, his legs propped up on the coffee table.

"Are you having car trouble?" Faith directed that question at Poppy.

Poppy looked from Isaiah to Joshua and then to Faith. And he could sense when she'd made a decision. Her shoulders squared, her whole body became as stiff as a board, as if she were bracing herself.

She took a deep breath.

"No," she said. "I drove over with your brother because I had sex with him last night."

Then she swept out of the room and stomped down the hall toward her office. He heard the door slam decisively behind her.

Two heads swiveled toward him, wide eyes on his face.

"What?" his sister asked.

"I don't think she could have made it any clearer," he said, walking over to the coffeepot and pouring himself a cup.

"You had sex with Poppy," Joshua confirmed.

"Yes," Isaiah responded, not bothering to look at his brother.

"You... *You.* And Poppy."

"Yes," he said again.

"Why do I know this?" Faith asked, covering her ears.

"I didn't know she was going to make a pronouncement," Isaiah said. He felt a smile tug at his lips. "Though, she was kind of mad at me. So. I feel like this is her way of getting back at me for saying the change in our relationship was simple."

Faith's eyes bugged out. "You told her that it was simple. The whole thing. The two of you... *friends...* *Poppy*, an employee of the past ten years... *Sleeping together.*" Faith was sputtering.

"It was good sex, Faith," he commented.

Faith's look contorted into one of abject horror, and she withdrew into her chair.

"There's more," Isaiah said. "I'm getting married to her."

"You are... *marrying Poppy*?" Now Faith was just getting shrill.

"Yes."

"You don't have to marry someone just because you have sex with them," Joshua pointed out.

"I'm aware of that, but you know I want to get married. And considering she and I have chemistry, I figured we might as well get married."

"But... Poppy?" Joshua asked.

"Why *not* Poppy?"

"Are you in love with her?" Faith asked.

"I care about her more than I care about almost anyone."

"You didn't answer my question," Faith said.

"Did no one respond to your ad?" Joshua was clearly happy to skip over questions about feelings.

Isaiah nodded. "Several women did. Poppy interviewed six of them yesterday."

Joshua looked like he wanted to say something that he bit back. "And you didn't like any of them?"

"I didn't meet any of them."

"So," Faith said slowly, "yesterday you had her interviewing women to marry you. And then last night you…hooked up with her."

"You're skipping a step. Yesterday afternoon she accused me of looking for a wife who was basically an assistant. For my life. And that was when I realized… She's actually the one I'm looking for."

"That is… The least romantic thing I've ever heard," Faith said.

"Romance is not a requirement for me."

"What about Poppy?"

He lifted a shoulder. "She could have said no."

"Could she have?" Faith asked. "I mean, no offense, Isaiah, but it's difficult to say no to you when you get something in your head."

"You don't want to hear this," Isaiah said, "but particularly after last night, I can say confidently that Poppy and I suit each other just fine."

"You're right," Faith said, "I don't want to hear it." She stood up, grabbing her coffee and heading back toward her office.

"I hope you know what you're doing," Joshua said slowly.

Isaiah looked over at his brother. "What about any of this doesn't look like I know what I'm doing?"

"Getting engaged to Poppy?" Joshua asked.

"You like Poppy," Isaiah pointed out.

"I do," Joshua said. "That's my concern. She's not like you. Your feelings are on a pretty deep freeze, Isaiah. I shouldn't have to tell you that."

"I don't know that I agree with you," he said.

"What's your stance on falling in love?"

"I've done it, and I'm not interested in doing it again."

"Has Poppy ever been in love before?" Joshua pressed.

Isaiah absolutely knew the answer to this question, not that it was any of his brother's business how he knew it. "No."

"Maybe she wants to be. And I imagine she wants her husband to love her."

"Poppy wants to be able to trust someone. She knows she can trust me. I know I can trust her. You can't get much better than that."

"I know you're anti-love… But what Danielle and I have…"

"What you and Danielle have is statistically improbable. There's no way you should have been able to place an ad in the paper for someone who is the antithesis of everything you should need in your life and fall madly in love with her. Additionally, I don't want that. I want stability."

"And my life looks terribly unstable to you?" Joshua asked.

"No. It doesn't. You forget, I was in a relationship for five years with a woman who turned out to be nothing like what I thought she was."

"You're still hung up on Rosalind?"

Isaiah shook his head. "Not at all. But I learned from my mistakes, Joshua. And the lesson there is that you can't actually trust those kinds of feelings. They blind you to reality."

"So you think I'm blind to reality?"

"And I hope it never bites your ass."

"What about Mom and Dad?"

"It's different," he said.

"How?"

"It's different for you too," Isaiah said. "I don't read people like you do. You know how to charm people. You know how to sense what they're feeling. How to turn the emotional tide of a room. I don't know how to do that. I have to trust my head because my heart doesn't give me a whole lot. What works for you isn't going to work for me."

"Just don't hurt her."

"I won't."

But then, Isaiah suddenly wasn't so sure. She was already hurt. Or at least, annoyed with him. And he wasn't quite sure what he was supposed to do about it.

He walked back toward Poppy's office and opened the door without knocking. She was sitting in her chair at her desk, not looking at anything in particular, and most definitely fuming.

"That was an unexpected little stunt," he said.

"You're not in charge of this," she pointed out. "If we are going to get married, it's a partnership. You don't get to manipulate me. You're not my boss in our marriage."

His lips twitched. "I could be your boss in the bedroom."

The color in her cheeks darkened. "I will allow that. However, in real life…"

"I get it."

He walked toward her and lowered himself to his knees in front of her, taking her chin in his hand. "I promise, I'm not trying to be a dick."

"Really?" He felt her tremble slightly beneath his touch.

He frowned. "I never try to be. I just am sometimes."

"Right."

"Joshua and Faith know. I mean, they already knew about the ad, and there was no way I was getting it by them that this wasn't related to that in some way."

"What did they say?"

"Joshua wants to make sure I don't hurt you."

She huffed a laugh. "Well. I'm team Joshua on that one."

"When do you want to tell my parents?" he asked. "We have our monthly dinner in three weeks."

"Let's...wait until then," she said.

"You want to wait that long?"

"Yes," she said. "I'm not...ready."

He would give her that. He knew that sometimes Poppy found interactions with family difficult. He'd always attributed that to her upbringing. "I understand. In the meantime, I want you to move your things into my house."

"But what about *my* house?" she asked.

"Obviously, you're coming to live on my ranch."

"No sex until we get married." The words came out fast and desperate.

He frowned. "We've already had sex. Several times."

"And that was...good. To establish our connection. It's established. And I want to wait now."

"Okay," he said.

She blinked. "Good."

He didn't think she'd hold to that. But Poppy was obviously trying to gain a sense of power here, and he was happy to give it to her.

Of course, that didn't mean he wouldn't try to se-duce her.

Seven

Poppy didn't have time to think much about her decision over the next few days. Isaiah had a moving company take all of her things to his house, and before she knew it, she was settling into a routine that was different from anything she had ever imagined she'd be part of.

They went to work together. They spent all day on the job, being very much the same Poppy and Isaiah they'd always been. But then they went home together.

And sexual tension seemed to light their every interaction on fire. She swore she could feel his body heat from across the room.

He had given her a room, her own space. But she could tell he was confused by her abstinence edict.

Even she was wondering why she was torturing herself.

Being with him physically was wonderful. But she felt completely overwhelmed by him.

She'd spent ten years secretly pining for him. Then in one moment, he'd decided he wanted something different, something more, and they'd been on their way to it. Isaiah had snapped his fingers and changed her world, and she didn't recognize even one part of it anymore.

Not even the ceiling she saw every morning when she opened her eyes.

She had to figure out a way to have power in this relationship. She was the one who was in love, and that meant she was at a disadvantage already. He was the one who got to keep his house. He was the one with the family she would become a part of.

She had to do something to hold on to her sanity.

It was hard to resist him though. So terribly hard.

When she felt lonely and scared at night, worrying for the future in a bedroom that was just down the hall from his, she wished—like that first night—that he would do a little less respecting of her commandments. That he would at least try to tempt her away from her resolve. Because if he did, she was sure it would fail.

But he didn't. So it was up to her to hang on to that edict.

No matter what.

Even when they had to behave like a normal couple for his parents' sakes.

And she was dreading the dinner at his parents' house tonight. With all of her soul.

Dreading having to tell a vague story about how they had suddenly realized their feelings for each other and were now making it official.

The fact that it was a farce hurt too badly.

But tonight they would actually discuss setting a wedding date.

A wedding date.

She squeezed her eyes shut for a moment, and then looked up at the gorgeous, custom-made cabinets in Isaiah's expansive kitchen. Maybe she should have a glass of wine before dinner. Or four. To calm her nerves.

She was already dressed and ready to go, but Isaiah had been out taking care of his horses, and she was still waiting for him to finish showering.

Part of her wished she could have simply joined him. But she'd made an edict and she should be able to stick to it.

She wondered if there was any point in preserving a sanity that was so frazzled as it was. Probably not.

Isaiah appeared a moment later, barefoot, in a pair of dark jeans with a button-up shirt. He was wearing his cowboy hat, looking sexy and disreputable, and exactly like the kind of guy who had been tailor-made for her from her deepest fantasies.

Or, maybe it was just that *he* was her fantasy.

Then he reached into his pocket and pulled out a black velvet box.

"No," she said.

He held it up. "No?"

"I didn't… I didn't know you were going to…"

"You have to have a ring before we see my parents."

"But then I'm going to walk in with a ring and they're going to know." As excuses went, it was a weak one. They were going to inform his parents of their engagement anyway.

They were engaged.

It was so strange. She didn't feel engaged to him.

Maybe because you won't sleep with him?

No. Because he doesn't love me.

She had a snotty response at the ready for her internal critic. Because really.

"They won't know you're engaged to me. And even so, were not trying to make it a surprise. We're just telling them in person."

The ring inside the box was stunning. Ornately designed, rather than a simple solitaire.

"It's vintage," he said. "It was part of a museum collection, on display in Washington, DC. I saw it online and I contacted the owner."

"You bought a vintage ring out of a museum." It wasn't a question so much as a recitation of what he'd just said.

"It was a privately owned collection." As if that explained it. "What?" he asked, frowning after she hadn't spoken for a few moments. "You don't look happy."

She didn't know how to describe what she was feeling. It was the strangest little dream come true. Something she would never have even given a thought to. Ever. She never thought about what kind of engagement ring she might want. And if she had, she would have asked for something small, and from the mall. Not from…*a museum collection.*

"I know how much you like vintage. And I know you don't like some of the issues surrounding the diamond trade."

She had gone on a small tirade in the office after seeing the movie *Blood Diamond* a few years ago. Just once. It wasn't like it was a cause she talked about regularly. "You…listened to that?"

"Yes," he responded.

Sometimes she wondered if everybody misunderstood him, including her. If no one knew just how deeply he held on to each moment. To people. Remembering a detail like that wasn't the mark of an unemotional man. It seemed…remarkably sentimental for him to remember such a small thing about her. Especially something that—at the time—wouldn't have been relevant to him.

She saw Isaiah as such a stark guy. A man who didn't engage in anything unnecessary. Or hold on to anything he didn't need to hold on to.

But that was obviously just what he showed the world. What he showed her.

It wasn't all of him.

It was so easy to think of him as cold, emotionless. He would be the first person to say a relationship could be a math equation for him, after all.

But remembering her feelings on diamonds wasn't math. It was personal.

There was no other man on earth—no other person on earth—who understood her the way Isaiah Grayson did.

She hadn't realized it until this moment. She'd made a lot of accusations about him being oblivious, but she was just as guilty.

And now…

She wanted to wear his ring. The ring he'd chosen for her with such thought and…well, extravagance. Because who had ever given her that kind of thought before? No one.

And certainly no one had ever been so extravagant for her.

Only him.

Only ever him.

He walked over to where she was sitting and took

the ring out of the box, sliding it onto her finger. He didn't get down on one knee. But then, that didn't surprise her.

More to the point, it didn't matter.

The ring itself didn't even matter. It was the thought. It was the man.

Her man.

It was how much she wanted it that scared her. That was the real problem. She wanted to wear his ring more than she wanted anything in the world.

And she was going to take it.

"Are you ready to go to dinner?"

She swallowed hard, looking down at the perfect, sparkly rock on her finger.

"Yes," she said. "I'm ready."

Isaiah felt a sense of calm and completion when they pulled into his parents' house that night. The small, modest farmhouse looked the same as it ever did, the yellow porch light cheery in the dim evening. It was always funny to him that no matter how successful Devlin, Joshua, Faith or Isaiah became, his parents refused to allow their children to buy them a new house. Or even to upgrade the old one at all.

They were perfectly happy with what they had.

He envied that feeling of being content. Being so certain what home was.

He liked his house, but he didn't yet feel the need to stop changing his circumstances. He wasn't settled.

He imagined that this new step forward with Poppy would change that. Though, he would like it if she dropped the sex embargo.

He wasn't quite sure why she was so bound by it,

though she had said something about white weddings and how she was a traditional girl at heart, even though he didn't believe any of it since she had happily jumped into bed with him a few weeks earlier.

It was strange. He'd spent ten years not having sex with Poppy. But now that they'd done it a few times, it was damn near impossible to wait ten days, much less however long it was going to be until their wedding. He was fairly confident she wouldn't stick to her proclamation that whole time, though. At least, he had been confident until nearly three weeks had passed without her knocking on his bedroom door.

But then, Poppy had been a twenty-eight-year-old virgin. Her commitment to celibacy was much greater than his own. He might have spent years abstaining from relationships, but he had not abstained from sex.

They got out of the car, and she started to charge ahead of him, as she had done on the way into the office that first morning after they'd made love. He was not going to allow that this time.

He caught up with her, wrapping his arm around her waist. "If you walk into my parents' living room and announce that we had sex I may have to punish you."

She turned her head sharply, her eyes wide. "Punish me? What sort of caveman proclamation is that?"

"Exactly the kind a bratty girl like you needs if you're plotting evil."

"I'm *not* plotting evil," she said, her cheeks turning pink.

He examined her expression closely. Knowing Poppy like he did, he could read her better than he could read just about anyone else. She was annoyed with him. They certainly weren't back on the same footing they had been.

But she wanted him. She couldn't hide that, even now, standing in front of his parents' home.

"But you're a little bit intrigued about what I might do," he whispered.

She wiggled against him, and he could tell she absolutely, grudgingly was intrigued. "Not at all."

"You're a liar."

"You have a bad habit of pointing that out." She sounded crabby about that.

"I don't see the point of lies. In the end, they don't make anything less uncomfortable."

"Most people find small lies a great comfort," she disagreed.

"I don't," he said, a hot rock lodging itself in his chest. "I don't allow lies on any level, Poppy. That, you do have to know about me."

He'd already been in a relationship with a woman who had lied to him. And he hadn't questioned it. Because he'd imagined that love was somehow the same as having two-way trust.

"I won't lie to you," she said softly, brushing her fingertips over his lips.

Instantly, he felt himself getting hard. She hadn't touched him in the weeks since he'd spent the night in her bed. But now was not the time.

He nodded once, and then tightened his hold on her as they continued to walk up the porch. Then he knocked.

"Why do you knock at your parents' house?"

"I don't live here."

The door opened, and his mother appeared, looking between the two of them, her eyes searching.

"Isaiah? Poppy."

"Hi," Poppy said, not moving away from his hold.

"Hi, Mom," Isaiah said.

"I imagine you have something to tell us," his mom said, stepping away from the door.

Isaiah led Poppy into the cozy room. His father was sitting in his favorite chair, a picture of the life he'd had growing up still intact. The feeling it gave him… It was the kind of life he wanted.

"We have something to tell you," Isaiah said.

Then the front door opened again and his brother Devlin and his wife, Mia, who was heavily pregnant, walked into the room.

"We brought chips," Mia said, stopping cold when she saw Isaiah and Poppy standing together.

"Yay for chips," Poppy said.

Then Joshua, Danielle and baby Riley came in, and with the exception of Faith, the entire audience was present.

"Do you want to wait for Faith?" his mom asked.

"No," Isaiah said. "Poppy and I are engaged."

His mother and father stared at them, and then his mother smiled. "That's wonderful!" She closed the distance between them and pulled him in for a hug.

She did the same to Poppy, who was shrinking slightly next to him, like she was her wilting namesake.

His father made his way over to them and extended his hand; Isaiah shook it. "A good decision," his dad said, looking at Poppy. And then, he hugged her, kissing her on the cheek. "Welcome to the family, Poppy."

Poppy made a sound that was somewhere between a gasp and a sob, but she stayed rooted next to his side.

This was what he wanted. This feeling. There was warmth here. And it was easy. There was closeness.

And now that he had Poppy, it was perfect.

Poppy didn't know how she made it through dinner. The food tasted like glue, which was ridiculous, since Nancy Grayson made the best food, and it always tasted like heaven. But Poppy had a feeling that her taste buds were defective, along with her very soul. She felt…wonderful and awful. All at once.

The Graysons were such an amazing family, and she loved Isaiah's parents. But they thought Isaiah and Poppy were in love. They thought Isaiah had finally shared his heart with someone.

And he didn't understand their assumptions. He thought they wanted marriage for him. A traditional family. But that wasn't really what they wanted.

They wanted his happiness.

And Isaiah was still… He was still in the same place he had always been, emotionally. Unwilling to open up. Unwilling to take a risk because it was so difficult. They thought she'd changed him, and she hadn't.

She was…enabling him.

She was enabling him and it was terrible.

After dinner, Poppy helped Nancy clear the dishes away.

"Poppy," she said. "Can I talk to you?"

Poppy shifted. "Of course."

"I've always known you would be perfect for him," Nancy said. "But I'm hesitant to push Isaiah into anything because he just digs in. They're all like that to a degree… But he's the biggest puzzle. He always has been. Since he was a boy. Either angry and very emotional, or seemingly emotionless. I've always known that wasn't true. People often find him detached, but I think it's because he cares so much."

Poppy agreed, and it went right along with what she'd been thinking when he'd given her the ring. That there were hidden spaces in him he didn't show anyone. And that had to be out of protection. Which showed that he did feel. He felt an awful lot.

"He's a good man," Nancy continued. "And I think he'll be a good husband to you. I'm just so glad you're going to be the one to be his wife, because you are exactly what he needs. You always have been."

"I don't… He's not difficult." Poppy looked down at her hands, her throat getting tight. "He's one of the most special people I know."

Nancy reached out and squeezed Poppy's hands. "That's all any mother wants the wife of her son to think."

Poppy felt even more terrible. Like a fraud. Yes, she would love Isaiah with everything she had, but she wasn't sure she was helping him at all.

"I have something for you," Nancy said. "Come with me."

She led Poppy back to the master bedroom, the only room in the house Poppy had never gone into. Nancy walked across the old wooden floor and the threadbare braided rug on top, moving to a highboy dresser and opening up a jewelry box.

"I have my mother's wedding band here. I know that you like…old-fashioned things. It didn't seem right for Danielle. And I know Faith won't want it. You're the one it was waiting for." Nancy turned, holding it out to Poppy.

Poppy swallowed hard. "Thank you," she said. "I'll save it until the... Until the wedding."

"It can stay here, for safekeeping, if you want."

"If you could," Poppy said. "But I want to wear it. Once Isaiah and I are married." Married. She was going to marry Isaiah. "Thank you."

Nancy gave Poppy another hug, and Poppy felt like her heart was splintering. "I know that your own mother won't be at the wedding," Mrs. Grayson said. "But we won't make a bride's side and a groom's side. It's just going to be our family. You're our family now, Poppy. You're not alone."

"Thank you," Poppy said, barely able to speak.

She walked back out into the living room on numb feet to find Isaiah standing by the front door with his hat on. "Are you ready to go?" he asked.

"Yes," she said.

She got another round of hugs from the entire family, each one adding weight to her already burdened conscience.

When they got out, they made their way back to the car, and as soon as he closed the door behind them, Poppy's insides broke apart.

They pulled out of the driveway, and a tear slid down her cheeks, and she turned her face away from him to keep him from seeing.

"I can't do this."

Eight

"What?"

"I can't do this," she said, feeling panic rising inside her now. "I'm sorry. But your parents think that I've... transformed you in some way. That I'm healing you. And instead, I'm enabling you to keep on doing that thing you love to do, where you run away from emotion and make everything about..."

"Maybe I just don't feel it," he said. "Maybe I'm not running from anything because there isn't anything there for me to run from. Why would you think differently?"

"Because you loved Rosalind..."

"Maybe. Or maybe I didn't. You're trying to make it seem like I feel things the exact same way other people do, and that isn't fair. I don't."

"I'm not trying to. It's just that your parents think—"

"I don't give a damn what my parents think. You were the one who wanted them to believe this was a normal kind of courtship. I don't care either way."

"Of course you don't."

"This is ridiculous, Poppy. You can't pull out of our agreement now that everybody knows."

"I could," she said. "I could, and I could quit. Like I was going to do."

"Because you would find it so easy to leave me?"

"No!"

"You're doing this because you feel guilty? I don't believe it. I think you're running away. You accuse me of not dealing with my feelings. But you were a twenty-eight-year-old virgin. You've refused to let me touch you in the time since we first made love, and now that you've had to endure hugs from my entire family suddenly you're trying to escape like a feral cat."

"I am not a feral cat." The comparison was unflattering.

And a little bit too close to the truth.

"I think you are. I think you're fine as long as somebody leaves a can of tuna for you out by the Dumpster, but the minute they try to bring you in the house you're all claws and teeth."

"No one has ever left me a can of tuna by a Dumpster." If he wanted claws, she was on the verge of giving them to him. This entire conversation was getting ridiculous.

"This isn't over." He started to drive them back toward his house.

"It is," she protested.

"No."

"Take me back to *my* house," she insisted.

"My house *is* your house. You agreed to marry me."

"And now I'm *un*agreeing," she insisted.

"And I think you're full of shit," he said, his tone so sharp it could have easily sliced right through her. "I think you're a hypocrite. Going on about what I need to do. Worrying about my emotional health when your own is in a much worse place."

She huffed, clenching her hands into fists and looking away from him. She said nothing for the rest of the drive, and then when they pulled up to the house, Isaiah was out of the car much quicker than she was, moving over to her side and pulling open the door. Then he reached into the car, unbuckled her and literally lifted her out as though she were a child. Holding her in his arms, he carried her up the steps toward the house.

"What the hell are you doing?" she shouted.

"What I should have done weeks ago."

"Making the transformation from man to caveman complete?"

He slid his hand down toward her ass and heat rioted through her. Even now, when she should be made of nothing but rage, she responded to him. Dammit.

"Making you remember why we're doing this."

"For your convenience," she hissed.

"Because I can't want another woman," he said, his voice rough, his eyes blazing. "Not now. And we both know you don't want another man."

She made a poor show of kicking her feet slightly as he carried her inside. She could unman him if she wanted to, but she wouldn't. And they both knew it.

"You can't do this," she protested weakly. "It violates all manner of HR rules."

"Too bad for you that I own the company. I *am* HR."

"I'm going to organize an ethics committee," she groused.

"This is personal business. The company has nothing to do with it."

"Is it? I think it's business for you, period, like everything else."

"It's personal," he ground out, "because I've been inside you. Don't you dare pretend that isn't true. Though it all makes sense to me now. Why you wanted me to stay away from you for the past few weeks."

"Because I'm just not that into you?" she asked as he carried her up the stairs.

"No. Because you're *too* into it."

She froze, ice gathering at the center of her chest. She didn't want him to know. He had been so clueless up until this point.

"You're afraid that I'll be able to convince you to stay because the sex is so good."

Okay. Well, he was a little bit onto it. But not really.

Just a little bit off base, was her Isaiah.

"You're in charge of everything," she said. "I didn't think it would hurt you to have to wait."

"I don't play games."

"Sadly for you, the rest of the world does. We play games when we need to. We play games to protect ourselves. We play games because it's a lot more palatable than wandering around making proclamations like you do."

"I don't understand games," he said. He flung open the door to his bedroom and walked them both inside. "But I understand this." He claimed her mouth. And she should have... She should have told him no. Because of course he would have stopped. But she didn't.

Instead, she let him consume her.

Then she began to consume him back. She wanted him. That was the problem. As much as everything that had happened back at the Grayson house terrified her, she wanted him.

Terrified. That wasn't the word she had used before. Isaiah was the one who had said she was afraid. And maybe she was. But she didn't know what to do about it.

It was like the time she had gone to live with a couple who hadn't been expecting a little girl as young as she was. They had been surprised, and clearly, their house hadn't been ready for a boisterous six-year-old. There had been a list of things she wasn't allowed to touch. And so she had lived in that house for all of three weeks, afraid to leave feet print on the carpet, afraid of touching breakable objects. Afraid that somehow she was going to destroy the beautiful place she found herself in simply because of who she was.

Because she was the wrong fit.

That was what it had felt like at the Graysons' tonight. Like she was surrounded by all this lovely, wonderful love, and somehow, it just wasn't for her. Wasn't to be.

There was more to it than that, of course, but that was the *real* reason she was freaking out, and she knew it.

But it didn't make her *wrong*.

It also didn't make her want to stop what was happening with Isaiah right now.

She was lonely. She had been a neglected child, and then she had lived in boisterous houses full of lots of children, which could sometimes feel equally lonely. She had never had a close romantic relationship as an adult. She was making friends in Copper Ridge, but moving around as often as she had made it difficult for her to have close lifelong friends. Isaiah was that friend, essentially.

And being close to him like this was a balm for a wound that ran very, very deep.

"You think this is fake?" he asked, his voice like gravel.

He bent down in front of her, grabbing hold of her skirt and drawing it down her legs without bothering to take off her shoes. Her shirt went next.

"Sit down," he commanded, and her legs were far too weak to disobey him. He looked up at her, those gray eyes intent on hers. "Take your bra off for me."

With shaking hands, she found herself obeying him.

"I imagine you're going to report me to HR for this too." The smile that curved his lips told her he didn't much care.

"I might," she responded, sliding her bra down her arms and throwing it onto the floor.

"Well, then I might have to keep you trapped here so you can't tell anyone."

"This is a major infraction."

"Maybe. But then again. I am the boss. I suppose I could choose to reprimand you for such behavior."

"I… I suppose you could."

"You're being a very bad girl," he said, hooking his fingers in the waistband of her panties and pulling them down to her knees. "Very bad."

Panic skittered in her stomach, and she had no idea how to respond. To Isaiah being like this, so playful. To him being like this and also staring at her right where he was staring at her.

"You need to remember who the boss is," he said, moving his hands around her lower back and sliding them down to cup her ass. Then he jerked her forward, and she gasped as he pressed a kiss to the inside of her thigh.

Then he went higher, and higher still, while she trembled.

She couldn't believe he was about to do this. She wanted him to. But she was also scared. Self-conscious. Excited. It was a whole lot of things.

But then, everything with Isaiah was a lot.

He squeezed her with both hands and then moved his focus to her center, his tongue sliding through her slick folds. She clapped her hand over her mouth to keep from making an extremely embarrassing noise, but she had a feeling he could still hear it, muffled or not.

Because he chuckled.

Isaiah, who was often humorless, chuckled with his mouth where it was, and his filthy intentions were obvious even to her.

And then he started to show her what he meant by punishment. He teased her with his tongue, with his fingers, with his mouth. He scraped her inner thigh with the edge of his teeth before returning his attention to where she was most needy for him. But every time she got close he would back off. He would move somewhere else. Kiss her stomach, her wrist, her hand. He would take his attention off of exactly where she needed him.

"Please," she begged.

"Bad girls don't get to come," he said, the edge in his voice sharp like a knife.

Those words just about pushed her over the edge all on their own.

"I thought you said you didn't play games," she choked out.

"Let me rephrase that," he said, looking up at her, a wicked smile curving his mouth. "I only play games in the bedroom."

He pressed two fingers into her before laughing at her again with his tongue, taking her all the way to the edge again before backing off. He knew her body better than she did, knew exactly where to touch her, and where not to. Knew the exact pressure and speed. How to rev her up and bring her back.

He was evil, and in that moment, she felt like she hated him as much as she had ever loved him.

"Tell me what you want," he said.

"You *know*."

"I do," he responded. "But you have to tell me."

"You're mean," she panted.

"I'm a very, very mean man," he agreed, sounding unrepentant as he slid one finger back through her folds. Tormenting. Teasing. "And you like it."

"I don't," she insisted.

"You do. Which is your real problem with all of this. You want me. And you want this. Even though you know you probably shouldn't."

"Well, what about you?" she asked, breathing hard. "You want it too. Or you wouldn't be trying so hard to convince me to go through with this marriage. Maybe *you* should beg."

"I'm on my knees," he said. "Isn't that like begging?"

"That's not—"

But she was cut off because his lips connected with that most sensitive part of her again. She could do nothing but feel.

She was so wet, so ready for him, so very hollow and achy that she couldn't stand for him to continue. It was going to kill her.

Or she was going to kill him. One of the two.

"Tell me," he whispered in her ear. "Tell me what you want."

"You," she said.

"Me?"

"You. Inside me. Please."

She didn't have to ask him twice.

Instead, she found herself being lifted up, brought down onto the bed, sitting astride him. He maneuvered her so her slick entrance was poised just above his hardness. And then he thrust up, inside her.

She gasped.

"You want to be in charge? Go ahead."

It was a challenge. And it gave her anything but control, when she was so desperate for him, when each move over him betrayed just how desperate she was.

He knew it too. The bastard.

But she couldn't stop, because she was so close, and now that she was on top she could...

Stars exploded behind her eyes, her internal muscles pulsing, her entire body shaking as her orgasm rocked her. All it had taken was a couple of times rocking back and forth, just a couple of times applying pressure where it was needed.

He growled, flipping her over and pinning her hands above her head. "You were just a bit too easy on me."

He kissed her then, and it was like a beast had been unleashed inside him. He was rough and untamed, and his response called up desire inside her again much sooner than she would have thought possible.

But it was Isaiah.

And with him, she had a feeling it would always be like this.

Always?

She pushed that mocking question aside.

She wasn't going to think about anything beyond this, right now.

She wasn't going to think about what she had told him before he carried her upstairs. About what she believed she deserved or didn't, about what she believed was possible and wasn't.

She was just going to feel.

This time, when the wave broke over her, he was swept up in it too, letting out a hoarse growl as he found his own release.

And when it was over, she didn't have the strength to get up. Didn't have the strength to walk away from him.

Tomorrow. Tomorrow would sort itself out.

Maybe for now she could hang on to the fantasy.

Poppy woke up in the middle of the night, curled around Isaiah's body. Something strange had woken her, and it wasn't the fact that she was sharing a bed with Isaiah.

It wasn't the fact that her resolve had weakened quite so badly last night.

There was something else.

She couldn't think what, or why it had woken her out of a dead sleep. She rolled away from him and padded into the bathroom that was just off his bedroom. She stood there for a moment staring at the mirror, at the woman looking back at her. Who was disheveled and had raccoon eyes because she hadn't taken her makeup off before allowing Isaiah to rock her world last night.

And then it suddenly hit her.

Because she was standing in a bathroom and staring at the mirror, and it felt like a strange kind of déjà vu.

It was the middle of the month. And she absolutely should've started her period by now.

She was two days late.

And she and Isaiah hadn't used a condom.

"No," she whispered.

It was too coincidental.

She went back into the bedroom and dressed as quickly and quietly as possible. And then she grabbed her purse and went downstairs.

She had to know.

She wouldn't sleep until she did. There were a few twenty-four-hour places in Tolowa, and she was going over there right now.

And that was how, at five in the morning in a public restroom, Poppy Sinclair's life changed forever.

Nine

When Isaiah woke up the next morning, Poppy wasn't in bed with him. He was irritated, but he imagined she was still trying to hold on to some semblance of control with her little game.

She was going to end up agreeing to marry him. He was fairly confident in that. But what he'd said about her being like a stray cat, he'd meant. She might not like the comparison, but it was true enough. Now that he wanted to domesticate her, she was preparing to run.

But her common sense would prevail. It didn't benefit her *not* to marry him.

And she couldn't deny the chemistry between them. He wasn't being egotistical about that. What they had between them was explosive. It *couldn't* be denied.

When he got downstairs, he saw Poppy sitting at the kitchen table. She was dressed in the same outfit she'd been wearing last night, and she was staring straight ahead, her eyes fixed on her clenched fists.

"Good morning," he said.

"No, it isn't," she responded. She looked up at him, and then she frowned. "Could you put a shirt on?"

He looked down at his bare chest. He was only wearing a pair of jeans. "No."

"I feel like this is a conversation we should have with your shirt on." She kept her gaze focused on the wall behind him.

He crossed his arms over his chest. "I've decided I like the conversations I have with you without my shirt better."

"I'm not joking around, Isaiah."

"Then you don't have time for me to go get a shirt. What's going on?"

"I'm pregnant." She looked like she was delivering the news of a death to him.

"That's…" He let the words wash over him, took a moment to turn them over and analyze what they made him feel. He felt…calm. "That's good," he said.

"Is it?" Poppy looked borderline hysterical.

"Yes," he said, feeling completely confident and certain now. "We both want children."

It was sooner than he'd anticipated, of course, but he wanted children. And…there was something relieving about it. It made this marriage agreement feel much more final. Made it feel like more of a done deal.

Poppy was his.

He'd spent last night in bed with her working to affirm that.

A pregnancy just made it that much more final.

"I broke up with you last night," she pointed out.

"Yes, you did a very good impression of a woman who was broken up with me. Particularly when you cried out my name during your… Was it your third or fourth orgasm?"

"That has nothing to do with whether or not we should be together. Whether or not we should get married."

"Well, now there's no question about whether or not we're getting married. You're having my baby."

"This is not 1953. That is not a good enough reason to get married."

He frowned. "I disagree."

"I'm not going to just jump into marriage with you."

"You're being unreasonable. You were more than willing to jump into marriage with me when you agreed to my proposal. Now suddenly when we're having a child you can't *jump into* anything? You continually *jump into* my bed, Poppy, so you can't claim we don't have the necessary ingredients to make a marriage work."

"Do you love me?" There was a challenge in her eyes, a stubborn set to her chin.

"I care very much about you," he responded.

It was the truth. The honest truth. She was one of the most important people in his life.

"But you're not in love with me."

"I already told you—"

"Yes. You're not going to do love. Well, you know what? I've decided that it feels fake if we're not in love."

"The fact that you're pregnant with my child indicates it's real enough."

"You don't understand. You don't understand anything."

"You sound like a sixteen-year-old girl having an argument with her parents. You would rather have some idealistic concept that may never actually happen than make a family with me?"

"I would rather... I would rather none of this was happening."

It felt like a slap, and he didn't know why.

That she didn't want him. Didn't seem to want the baby. He couldn't sort out the feeling it gave him. The sharp, stabbing sensation right around the area of his heart.

But he could reason through it. He was right, and her hysterics didn't change that.

There was an order to things. An order of operations, like math. That didn't change based on how people felt.

He understood...nothing right now. Nothing happening inside him, or outside him.

But he knew what was right. And he knew he could count on his brain.

It was the surest thing. The most certain.

So he went with that.

"But it is happening," he said, his voice tight. "You are far too practical to discard something real for some silly fantasy."

Her face drained of color. "So it's a *fantasy* that someone could love me."

"That isn't what I meant. It's a fantasy that you're going to find someone else who can take care of you like I can. Who is also the father of your child. Who can make you come the way that I do."

"Maybe it's just easy for me. You don't know. Neither do I. I've only had the one lover."

That kicked up the fire and heat in his stomach, and

he shoved it back down because this was not about what he felt. Not about what his body wanted.

"Trust me," he bit out. "It's never this good."

"I can't do this." She pressed a balled-up fist to her eyes.

"That's too bad," he said. "Because you will."

Resolve strengthened in him like iron. She was upset. But there was only one logical way forward. It was the only thing that made sense. And he was not going to let her take a different route. He just wasn't.

"I don't have to, Isaiah."

"You want your child growing up like you did? Being shuffled between homes?"

She looked like he'd hit her. "Foster care is not the same as sharing custody, and you know that. Don't you dare compare the two. I would have been thrilled to have two involved parents, even if I did have to change houses on the weekends. I didn't have that, and I never have had that. Don't talk about things you don't understand."

"I understand well enough. You're being selfish."

"I'm being *reasonable*!"

Reasonable.

Reasonable to her was them not being together. Reasonable to her was shoving him out of her life now that he'd realized just how essential she was.

"How is it reasonable to deny your child a chance at a family?" he asked. "All of us. Together. At my parents' house for dinners. Aunts and uncles and cousins. How is it unreasonable for me to want to share that with you instead of keeping my life and yours separate?"

"Isaiah…"

He was right, though. And what he wanted wasn't really about what he wanted. It was about logic.

And he wasn't above being heavy-handed to prove that point.

"If you don't marry me, I'm going to pursue full custody of our child," he said, the words landing heavily in the room.

Her head popped up. "You what?"

"And believe me, I'll get it. I have money. I have a family to back me up. I can make this very difficult for you. I don't want to, Poppy. That's not my goal. But I will have my way."

The look on her face, the abject betrayal, almost made him feel something like regret. Almost.

"I thought you were my friend," she said. "I thought you cared about me."

"I do. Which is why I'm prepared to do this. The best thing. The right thing. I'm not going to allow you to hurt our child in the name of friendship. How is that friendship?"

"Caring about someone doesn't just mean running them over until they do what you want. Friendship and caring goes both ways." She pressed her hand to her chest. "What I feel—*what I want*—has to matter."

"I know what you *should* want," he insisted.

If she would only listen. If she could, she'd understand what he was doing. In the end, it would be better if they were together. There was no scenario where their being apart would work, and if he had to play hardball to get her there, he damn well would.

"That isn't how wanting works. It's not how feelings work." She stood up, and she lifted her fist and slammed it down onto his chest. "It's not how any of this works, you robot."

He drew back, shock assaulting him. Poppy was one of the only people who had never looked at him that way before. Poppy had always taken pains to try to understand him.

"I'm a robot because I want to make sure my child has a family?" he asked, keeping his voice low.

"Because you don't care about what I want."

"I *want* you to want what *I* want," he said, holding her fist against his chest where she had hit him. "I want for this to work. How is that not feeling?"

"Because it isn't the *right feeling.*"

Those words were like a whip cracking over his insides.

He had *never* had the right feelings. He already knew that. But with Poppy his feelings hadn't ever felt wrong before. *He* hadn't felt wrong before.

She'd been safe. Always.

But not now. Not now he'd started to care.

"I'm sorry," he said, his voice low. "I'm sorry I can't open up my chest and rearrange everything for you. I'm sorry that you agreed to be engaged to me, and then I didn't transform into a different man."

"I never said that's what I wanted."

"It *is* what you wanted. You wanted being with me to look like being with someone else. And you know what? If you weren't pregnant, I might've been able to let you walk away. But it's too late now. This is happening. The wedding is not off."

"The wedding *is* off," she insisted.

"Look at me," he said, his voice low, fierce. "Look

at me and tell me if you think I was joking about taking custody."

Her eyes widened, her lips going slack. "I've always cared about you," she said, her voice shaking. "I've always tried to understand you. But I think maybe I was just pretending there was a heart in your chest when there never was."

"You can fling all the insults you want at me. If I'm really heartless, I don't see how you think that's going to make a difference."

Then she let out a frustrated cry and turned and fled the room, leaving him standing there feeling hollowed out.

Wishing that he was exactly what she had accused him of being.

But if he were heartless, then her words—her rejection—wouldn't feel like a knife through his chest.

If he were a robot, he wouldn't care that he couldn't find a way to order his feelings exactly to her liking.

But he did care.

He just had no idea what to do about it.

Ten

Ultimately, it wasn't Isaiah's threats that had her agreeing to his proposal.

It was what he'd said about family.

She was angry that it had gotten inside her head. That it had wormed its way into her heart.

No. Angry was an understatement.

She was *livid*.

She was also doing exactly what he had asked her to do.

The date for their wedding was now Christmas Eve. Of all the ridiculous things. Though, she supposed that would give her a much stronger association with the holiday than she'd had before.

His family was thrilled.

Poppy was not.

And she was still sleeping in her own room.

After that lapse when she had tried to break things off with him a week earlier, she had decided that she really, *really* needed Isaiah not to touch her for a while.

For his part, he was seething around the house with an intensity that she could feel.

But he hadn't tried to change her mind.

Which was good. Because the fact of the matter was he *would* be able to change her mind. With very little effort.

And besides the tension at home, she was involved in things that made her break out in hives.

Literally.

She had been itchy for three days. The stress of trying to plan a wedding that felt like a death march was starting to get to her.

The fact that she was going wedding-dress shopping with Isaiah's mother and sister was only making matters worse.

And yet, here she was, at Something New, the little bridal boutique in Gold Valley, awaiting the arrival of Nancy and Faith.

The little town was even more heavily decorated for the holidays than Copper Ridge. The red brick buildings were lined with lights, wreaths with crimson bows on every door.

She had opted to drive her own car because she had a feeling she was going to need the distance.

She sighed heavily as she walked into the store, the bell above the door signaling her arrival. A bright, pretty young woman behind the counter perked up.

"Hi," she said. "I'm Celia."

"Hi," Poppy said uncomfortably. "I have an appointment to try on dresses."

"You must be Poppy," she said.

"I am," Poppy said, looking down at her hands. At the ring that shone brightly against her dark skin. "I'm getting married."

"Congratulations," Celia said, as though the inane announcement wasn't that inane at all.

"I'm just waiting for…" The words died on her lips. Her future mother-in-law and sister-in-law. That was who she was waiting for.

Isaiah's family really would be her family. She knew that. It was why she'd said yes to this wedding. And somehow it hadn't fully sunk in yet. She wondered if it ever would.

The door opened a few moments later and Faith and Nancy came in, both grinning widely.

"I'm so excited," Faith said.

Poppy shot her an incredulous look that she hoped Nancy would miss. Faith of all people should not be that excited. She knew Isaiah was only marrying Poppy because of the ad.

Of course, no one knew that Isaiah was also marrying her because she was pregnant.

"So exciting," Poppy echoed, aware that it sounded hollow and lacking in excitement. She was a great assistant, but she was a lousy actress.

Celia ushered them through endless aisles of dresses and gave them instructions on how to choose preferred styles.

"When you're ready," Celia said, "just turn the dresses out and leave them on the rack. I'll bring them to you in the dressing room."

Poppy wandered through her size, idly touching a few of the dresses, but not committing to anything. Meanwhile, Faith and Nancy were selecting styles left and right.

She saw one that caught her eye. It looked as though it was off the shoulder with long sleeves that came to a point over the top of her hand and loops that would go over her middle finger. It was understated, sedate. Very Grace Kelly, which was right in Poppy's wheelhouse. The heavy, white satin was unadorned, with a deep sheen to it that looked expensive.

She glanced at the price tag. *Incredibly* expensive.

It was somewhat surprising that there was such an upscale shop in the small community of Gold Valley, but then the place had become something of a destination for brides who wanted to make a day of dress shopping, and the cute atmosphere of the little gold rush town, with its good food and unique shops, made for an ideal girls' day out.

"Don't worry about that," Nancy said.

"I can't not worry about it," Poppy said, looking back at the price.

"Isaiah is going to pay for all of it," Nancy said. "And he made sure I was here to reinforce that."

"I know it's silly to be worked up about it," Poppy said. "Considering he signs my paychecks. But the thing is… I don't necessarily want to just take everything from him. I don't want him to think that…"

"That you're marrying him for his money?" Faith asked.

"Kind of," Poppy said.

"He isn't going to think that," Nancy said with authority. "He knows you."

"Yes," Poppy said slowly. "I just…" She looked at them both helplessly. "He's not in love with me," she said. Faith knew, and there was no reason that Poppy's future mother-in-law shouldn't know too. She'd thought she wanted to keep it a secret, but she couldn't

bear it anymore, not with the woman she was accepting as family.

"I love him," Poppy said. "I want to make that clear.
I love him, and I told him not to let on that this was…a
convenient marriage. For my pride. But I can't lie to
you." She directed that part to his mother. "I can't
lie to you and have you think that I reached him or
changed him in a way that I haven't. He still thinks
this marriage is the height of practicality. And he's
happy to throw money at it like he's happy to throw
money at any of his problems. He's not paying for
this wedding because he cares what I look like in the
wedding dress."

She swallowed hard. "He's paying for it because he
thinks that making me his wife is going to somehow
magically simplify his life."

Nancy frowned. "You love him."

"I do."

"You've loved him for a long time, haven't you?"

Poppy looked down. She could see Faith shift uncomfortably out of the corner of her eye.

"Yes," Poppy confirmed. "I've loved him ever since
I met him. He's a wonderful person. I can see underneath all of the… Isaiah. Or maybe that's not the right
way of putting it. I don't even have to see under it. I love
who he is. And that…not everybody can see just how
wonderful he is. It makes it like a secret. My secret."

"I'm not upset with you," Nancy said, taking hold of
the wedding dress Poppy was looking at and turning it
outward. "I'm not upset with you at all. You love him,
and he came barreling at you with all of the intensity
that he has, I imagine, and demanded that you marry
him because he decided it was logical, am I right?"

"Very."

"I don't see what woman in your position could have resisted."

If only his mother knew just how little Poppy had resisted. Just how much she wasn't resisting him...

"I should have told him no."

"Does he know that you love him?" Faith asked.

"No," Poppy said.

And she knew she didn't have to tell either of them to keep it a secret. Because they just would.

"Maybe you should tell him," Faith pointed out.

Poppy bit back a smart remark about the fact that Faith was single, and had been for as long as Poppy had known her, and Faith maybe didn't have any clue about dealing with unrequited love.

"Love isn't important to him," Poppy said. "He *likes* me. He thinks that's enough."

Nancy shook her head. "I hope he more than likes you. Otherwise that's going to be a cold marriage bed."

Faith made a squeaking sound. "Mom. Please."

"What? Marriage is long, sweetheart. And sometimes you get distant. Sometimes you get irritated with each other. In those times all you've got is the spark."

Faith slightly receded into one of the dress racks. "Please don't tell me any more about your spark."

"You should be grateful we have it," Nancy said pointedly at her daughter. "It's what I want for you in your marriage, whenever you get married. And it's certainly what I want for Poppy and Isaiah."

Poppy felt her skin flushing. "We're covered there."

"Well, that is a relief."

She wasn't going to tell them about the baby. Not now. She was just going to try on wedding dresses.

Which was what they did.

For the next two hours, Poppy tried on wedding dresses. And it all came down to The One. The long-sleeved beauty with the scary price tag and the perfect train that fanned out behind her like a dream.

Celia found a veil and pinned it into Poppy's dark hair. It was long, extending past the train with a little row of rhinestones along the edge, adding a hint of mist and glitter.

She looked at herself in the mirror, and she found herself completely overwhelmed with emotion.

She was glowing.

There, underneath the lights in the boutique, the white dress contrasted perfectly with her skin tone. She looked like a princess. She felt like one.

And she had...

She looked behind her and saw Nancy and Faith, their eyes full of tears, their hands clasped in front of them.

She had a family who cared about this. Who was here watching her try on dresses.

Who cared for her. For her happiness.

Maybe Isaiah didn't love her, but she loved him. And... His mother and sister loved her. And that offered Poppy more than she had ever imagined she might have.

It was enough. It would be.

Nancy came up behind Poppy and put a hand on Poppy's shoulder. "This is the one. Let him buy it for you. Believe me, he'll cause enough trouble over the course of a lifetime with him that you won't feel bad about spending his money this way."

Poppy laughed, then wiped at a tear that fell down her cheek. "I suppose that's true."

"I'm going to try to keep from hammering advice at you," Nancy said. "But I do have to say this. Love is an amazing thing. It's an inexhaustible resource. I've been married a long time. And over the course of that many decades with someone, there are a lot of stages. Ebbs and flows. But if you keep on giving love, as much as you have, you won't run out. Give it even when it's not flowing to you. Give it when you don't feel like it. If you can do that… That's the best use of love that I can think of. It doesn't mean it's always easy. But it's something you won't regret. Love is a gift. When you have it, choosing to give it is the most powerful thing you can do."

Poppy looked back at her reflection. She was going to be a bride. And more than that, she was going to be Isaiah's wife. He had very clear ideas about what he wanted and didn't want from that relationship. He had very definite thoughts on what he felt and didn't feel.

She had to make a decision about that. About what she was going to let it mean to her.

The problem was, she had spent a lot of years wanting love. Needing love. From parents who were unable to give it for whatever reason. Because they were either too captivated by drugs, or too lost in the struggle of life. She had decided, after that kind of childhood, after the long years of being shuffled between foster homes, that she didn't want to expose herself to that kind of pain again.

Which was exactly what Isaiah was doing.

He was holding himself back. Holding his love back because he'd been hurt before. And somehow... somehow she'd judged that. As if she was different. As if she was well-adjusted and he was wrong.

But that wasn't true.

It was a perfect circle of self-protection. One that was the reason why she had nearly broken the engagement off a week ago. Why she was holding herself back from him now.

And they would never stop.

Not until one of them took a step outside that self-created box.

She could blame her parents. She could blame the handful of foster families who hadn't been able to care for her the way she had needed them to. She could blame the ones who had. The ones she had loved deeply, but whom she had ultimately had to leave, which had caused its own kind of pain.

She could blame the fact that Isaiah had been unavailable to her for all those years. That he had belonged to Rosalind, and somehow that had put him off-limits.

But blame didn't matter. The reasons didn't really matter.

The only thing that mattered was whether or not she was going to change her life.

No one could do it for her.

And if she waited for Isaiah to be the first to take that step, then she would wait forever.

His mother was right. Love was a gift, and you could either hoard it, keep it close to your chest where it wouldn't do a thing for anyone, or you could give it.

Giving her love was the only thing that could possibly open up that door between them. If she wanted him to love her, wanted him to find the faith to love her, she'd have to be the first one to stop protecting herself.

Poppy would have to open up her arms. Stop holding them in front of her, defensive and closed off.

Which was the real problem. Really, it had been all along.

That deeply rooted feeling of unrequited love that she'd had for Isaiah had been incredibly important to her. It had kept her safe. It had kept her from going after anyone else. It had kept her insulated.

But she couldn't continue that now.

Not if she wanted a hope at happiness. Not if she wanted even the smallest chance of a relationship with him.

Someone was going to have to budge first. And she could be bitter about the fact that it had to be her, but there was no point to that.

It was simple.

This wasn't about right or wrong or who should have to give more or less. Who should have to be brave.

She could see that she should.

And if she loved him… Well. She had to care more for him and less for her own comfort.

"I think I might need to give a little bit more love," Poppy said softly.

"If my son doesn't give back to you everything that you deserve, Poppy, you had better believe that I will scar him myself."

"I do believe it," Poppy said.

And if nothing else, what she had learned in that moment was invaluable.

Somebody was in her corner.

And not only had she heard Nancy say it, Poppy believed it. She couldn't remember the last time that had been true.

This was family.

It was so much better than she had ever imagined it could be.

Eleven

It was late, and Isaiah was working in his home office. His eyes were starting to get gritty, but he wasn't going to his room until he was ready to pass out. It was the only way he could get any sleep at all these days.

Lying in bed knowing she was just down the hall and he couldn't have her was torture. Distance and exhaustion were the only things he could do to combat the restlessness.

He looked up, catching his reflection in the window, along with the reflection of the lamp on his desk.

It was dark out. So dark he couldn't see anything. But he knew the view well. The mountains and hills that were outside that window. A view he had carefully curated after growing tired of the gray landscape of Seattle.

Poppy had been out shopping all day, and he hadn't seen her since she'd left that morning. But he had been thinking about her.

It was strange. The way his feelings for her were affected. A borderline obsession with a woman who should feel commonplace to him in many ways. She had been a part of his office furniture for the past decade.

Except, she'd always been more than that.

Yes. That was true. She always had been.

She was remarkable, smart and funny. Funny in a way he could never really manage to be. More than once, he had wished he could capture that sweetness and hold it to himself just for a little while.

Not that she was saccharine. No. She had no issues taking strips off his hide when it was necessary.

She was also so damn sexy he couldn't think of anything else, and she was starting to drive him insane.

He didn't have any practice with restraint. Over the years, he had been involved mostly in casual hookups, and the great thing about those was they could absolutely happen on his schedule. If the woman didn't matter, then all that was needed was time spent in an appropriate location, and a woman—any woman— would eventually indicate she was available.

But now, he was at the point where not just any woman would do. He needed Poppy.

She was still withholding herself from him, and he supposed he could understand. What with the fact that he had made threats to take her child away if she didn't fall in line. It was entirely possible he wasn't her favorite person at the moment.

That bothered him.

He wasn't very many people's favorite person. But Poppy liked him. At least, she had always seemed to. And now, he had found a very unique way of messing that up.

He'd had a lot of friendships not go the distance. Admittedly, this was quite the most creative way he'd had one dissolve. Proposing, getting that same friend pregnant, and then forcing her to marry him.

Not that he was *forcing* her. Not *really*. He was simply giving her a set of incredibly unpleasant options. And forcing her to choose the one she found the least unpleasant.

He supposed he could take some small measure of comfort in the fact that he wasn't the *least* pleasant option.

But then, that had more to do with the baby than with him.

He sighed heavily.

He'd never felt this way about a woman before. The strange sense of constant urgency. To be with her. To fix things with her. The fact that she was angry with him actively bothered him even when she wasn't in the room displaying that anger.

He could feel it.

He could actually feel someone else's emotion. Stronger than his own.

If he wasn't so fed up, he might marvel at that.

He didn't know what was happening to him.

He was obsessing about the desire. Fixated on it. Because that he understood. Sex, he understood.

This need to tear down all the walls inside him so that he could...

He didn't know.

Be closer to her? Have her feel him, his emotions, so difficult and hard to explain, as keenly as he felt hers?

They'd been friends for ten years. Now they were lovers.

His feelings were like nothing he'd ever felt for a friend or a lover.

The door opened behind him, and he didn't have to turn to see that it was Poppy standing in the doorway. She was wearing her favorite red coat that had a high collar and a tightly belted waist, flaring out at her hips. Her hands were stuffed in her pockets, her eyes cast downward.

"How was your day?"

Her voice was so soft it startled him. He turned. "Good. I wish it were over."

"Still working?"

"Yes. Faith is interested in taking on a couple more projects. I'm just trying to make sure everything balances out."

"I chose a wedding dress."

He had half expected her to say that she had chosen a burlap sack. Or nothing at all. As a form of protest.

"I'm glad to hear it," he said, not quite sure what she wanted him to say. Not quite sure where this was leading at all.

"I've missed you."

The words landed softly, then seemed to sing down deep into his heart. "I've seen you every day for the past week."

"That isn't what I meant." A small crease appeared between her brows as she stared at him. "I'm not going to say I miss the way we used to be. Because I don't. I like so much of what we have now better. Except…we don't have it right now. Because I haven't let you get close to me. I haven't let you touch me."

She pushed away from the door jamb and walked slowly toward him. His eyes were drawn downward, to the wicked, black stilettos on her feet. And to her bare legs. Which was odd, because she was wearing a coat as if she had been outside in the cold, and he would have thought she would have something to cover her skin.

"I've missed you touching me," she said, her voice growing husky. "I've missed touching you."

She lifted her hands, working the button at the top of her coat, and then the next, followed by the next. It exposed a V of brown skin, the soft, plump curve of her breasts. And a hint of bright yellow lace.

She made it to the belt, working the fabric through the loop and letting the coat fall open before she undid the button behind it, and the next button, and the next. Until she revealed that she had nothing on beneath the coat but transparent yellow lace. Some sort of top that scooped low around her full breasts and ended above her belly button, showing hints of dark skin through the pattern, the darker shadows of her nipples.

The panties were tiny. They covered almost nothing, and he was pleased with that. She left the heels on, making her legs look impossibly long, shapely and exactly what he wanted wrapped around him.

"What did I do to deserve this?" he asked.

It wasn't a game. Not a leading question. He genuinely wanted to know.

"Nothing," she said. She took a step toward him, lifted the delicate high heel up off the ground and pressed her knee into the empty space on the chair, just beside his thigh.

She gripped the back of the chair, leaning forward. "You haven't done anything at all to deserve this. But I want it. I'm not sure why I shouldn't have it. I think... I think this is a mess." Her tongue darted out, slid over her lips, and he felt the action like a slow lick. "*We* are a mess. We have been. For a long time. Together. Apart. But I'd rather be a mess with you than just a mess who lives in your house and wears your ring. I'd rather be a mess with you inside of me. We're going to get married. I'm having your baby. We're going to have to be a family. And I don't know how to…fix us. I don't know how to repair the broken spaces inside of us. I don't know if it's possible. But nothing is going to be fixed, nothing at all if we're just strangers existing in the same space. If I'm still just your personal assistant when I'm at work."

"What are you going to be when you're at work?"

"Your personal assistant. And your fiancée. And later, your wife. We can't separate these things. Not anymore. We can't separate ourselves."

She pressed her fingertips against his cheek and dragged her hand back, sliding her thumb over his lower lip. "I'm so tired of being lonely. Feeling like… nobody belongs to me. That I don't belong to anyone."

Those words echoed inside him, and they touched something raw. Something painful. He felt… He felt as if they could be words that were coming out of his own mouth. As if she was putting voice to his own pain, a pain he had never before realized was there.

"I want you," she said.

He reached out, bracing his hands on her hips, marveling at the erotic sight of that contrast. His paler hand over the deep rich color of her skin.

A contrast. And still a match.

Deep and sexual and perfect.

He leaned forward and pressed a kiss to her breast, to the bare skin just above the edge of lace. And she gasped, letting her head fall back. It was the most erotic sight. Perfect and indulgent, and something he wanted to hold on to and turn away from with matching intensity.

He wanted her to make him whole. He wanted to find the thing that she was talking about. That depth. That sense of belonging.

Of not being alone.

Of being understood.

He had never even made that a goal. Not even when he'd been with Rosalind. He'd never imagined that a woman might…understand him. He didn't quite understand himself. No one ever had.

He was different. That was all he knew.

He didn't know how to show things the way other people did. Didn't know how to read what was happening right in front of him sometimes.

Was more interested in the black-and-white numbers on a page than the full-color scene in front of him.

He couldn't change it. Didn't know if he would even if he could. His differences were what had made him successful. Made him who he was. But there were very few people willing to put up with that, with him.

But Poppy always had.

She had always been there. She had never—except for the day when she'd hit him in the chest and called him a robot—she had never acted like him being different was even a problem.

Maybe she was the one who could finally reach him. Maybe she was the one he could hold on to.

"I want you," he said, repeating her words back to her.

"I'm here," she said, tilting his face up, her dark eyes luminous and beautiful as she stared down at him. "I'm giving myself to you." She leaned forward, her lips a whisper from his. "Can I be yours, Isaiah?"

"You already are."

He closed the distance between them and claimed her mouth with his.

It was like a storm had exploded. He pulled her onto his lap, wrapping his arms around her tightly as he kissed her. As he lost himself in her. He wanted there to be nothing between them. Not the T-shirt and jeans he was wearing, not even the beautiful lace that barely covered her curves.

Nothing.

Nothing but her.

A smile curved his lips. She could maybe keep the shoes. Yes, he would love for her to have those shoes on when he draped her legs over his shoulders and thrust deep inside her.

"I want you so much," he said. The words were torn from him. Coming from somewhere deep and real that he wasn't normally in touch with. "I think I might die if I don't have you."

"I've been in front of you for ten years," she whispered, kissing the spot right next to his mouth, kissing his cheek. "Why now?"

Because he had seen her. Because she had finally kissed him. Because…

"I don't see the world the way everyone else does," he whispered. "I know that. Sometimes it takes an act of God for me to really notice what's happening in front of me. To pull me out of that space in my head. I like it there. Because everything makes sense. And I put people in their place, so I can navigate the day with everything just where I expect it. I can never totally do that with you, Poppy. You always occupied more spaces than you were supposed to.

"I hired you, but you were never only my assistant.

You became my friend. And then, you wouldn't stay there either. I put control above everything else. I always have. It's the only way to… For me to make the world work. If I go in knowing exactly what to expect, knowing what everything is. What everyone is. And that's how I didn't see. But then…the minute our lips touched, I knew. I knew, and I can't go back to knowing anything different."

"You like blondes," she pointed out.

"I don't," he responded.

"Rosalind was blonde," Poppy said, brazenly speaking the name she usually avoided at all costs. "And there have been a string of them ever since."

"I told you. I like certainty. Blondes are women I'm attracted to. At least, that was an easy way to think of it. I like to bring order to the world in any way I can."

"And that kept you from looking at me?"

He searched her face, trying to get an idea of what she was thinking. He searched himself, because he didn't know the answer. She was beautiful, and the fact that he hadn't been obsessed with her like this for the past decade was destined to remain a mystery to him.

"Maybe."

She touched his face, sliding her palms back, holding him. "You are not difficult," she said. "Not to me. I like you. All of you."

"No," he responded, shaking his head. "You… You put up with me, I'm sure. And I compensate for the ways that I'm difficult by…"

"No, Isaiah. I like all of you. I always have. There's no putting up with anything."

He hadn't realized how much words like that might mean. Until they poured through him like sunshine dipping down into a low, dark valley. Flooding him with light and warmth.

When he'd been younger, he'd had a kind of boundless certainty in his worldview. But as he'd gotten older—as he'd realized that the way he saw things, the way he perceived interactions and emotions, was often different from the other people involved—he'd started questioning himself.

The older he'd gotten the more he'd realized. How difficult people found it to be his friend. How hard he found it sometimes to carry on a conversation another person wanted to have when he just wanted to charge straight to the point.

How much his brother Joshua carried for him, with his lightning-quick response times and his way with words.

Which had made him wonder how much his parents had modified for him back before he'd realized he needed modification at all.

And with that realization came the worry. About how much of a burden he might be.

But not to Poppy.

He reached up and wrapped his fingers around her slender wrists, holding her hands against his face. He looked at her. Just looked. He didn't have words to respond to what she had said.

He didn't have words.

He had nothing but his desire for her, twisting in his gut, taking him over. Control was the linchpin in his life. It was essential to him. But not now. Now, only Poppy was essential. He wanted her to keep touching him.

Control could wait. It could be set aside for now.

Because letting go so he could hold on to this—to her—was much more important.

It was necessary.

He slid her hands back, draping her arms over his shoulders so she was closer to him, so she was holding on to him. Then he cradled her face, dragging her mouth to his, claiming her, deep and hard and long. Pouring everything that he felt, everything he couldn't say, into this kiss. Into this moment.

He pulled away, sliding his thumb across her lower lip, watching as heat and desire clouded her dark eyes. He could see her surrender to the same need that was roaring through him.

"I always have control," he mumbled, pressing a kiss to her neck, another, and then traveling down to her collarbone. "Always."

He pressed his hand firmly to the small of her back, holding her against him as he stood from the chair, then lowered them both down onto the floor.

He reached behind her and tugged at the top she was wearing. He didn't manage to get hold of the snaps, and he tore the straps, the elastic popping free, the cups falling away from her breasts.

He didn't have to tell her he was out of control. She knew. He could see it. In the heat and fire burning in her dark eyes, and in the subtle curve of her full lips.

She knew that he was out of control, for her. And she liked it.

His efficient, organized Poppy had a wild side. At least, she did with him.

Only for him.

Suddenly, the fact that she had never been with another man before meant everything. This was his.

She was his.

And it mattered.

More than he would have ever thought it could. He had never given thought to something like that before. He didn't know why he did now. Except… Poppy.

Poppy, who had always been there.

She was a phenomenon. Someone he couldn't understand, someone he wasn't sure he wanted to understand. He didn't mind her staying mysterious. An enigma he got to hold in his arms. As long as this burning bright glory remained.

If he stopped to think, she might disappear. This moment might vanish completely, and he couldn't bear that.

She tore at his clothes too, wrenching them away from his body, making quick work of his shirt before turning her attention to his pants.

As she undressed him, he finished with her clothes, capturing her nipple in his mouth, sucking it in deep. Tasting her. Relishing the feel of her, that velvet skin under his tongue. The taste of her.

It wasn't enough. It never would be. Nothing ever would be.

He felt like his skin was hypersensitized, and that feeling ran all the way beneath his skin, deeper. Making him feel…

Making him *feel*.

He pressed his face into the curve of her neck, kissing her there, licking her. She whimpered and shifted beneath him, wrapping her fingers around his thick length, squeezing him. He let his head fall back, a hoarse groan on his lips.

"Not like that," he rasped. "I need to… No, Poppy. I need you."

"But you have me." She looked innocent. Far too innocent for the moment.

She stroked him, sliding her fingers up and down his length. Then she reached forward, planting her free hand in the center of his chest and pushing him backward slightly. He didn't have to give. He chose to. Because he wanted to see what she would do. He was far too captivated by what might be brewing beneath the surface.

Her breasts were completely bare for him. And then she leaned forward, wrapping her lips around the head of his erection, sliding down slowly as she took all of him into her mouth.

He gritted his teeth, her name a curse on his lips as he grabbed hold of her dark curls and held on tightly while she pleasured him with her mouth. He was transfixed by the sight of her. By the way she moved, unpracticed but earnest. By the way she made him feel.

"Have you ever done this before?" He forced the words out through his constricted throat.

The answer to that question shouldn't matter. It was a question he never should have asked. He'd never cared before, if one of his partners had other lovers. He would have said he preferred a woman with experience.

Not with Poppy. The idea of another man touching her made him insane.

She licked him from base to tip like a lollipop, and then looked up at him. "No."

He swore, letting his head fall back as she took him in deep again.

"Does that matter to you?" she asked, angling her head and licking him.

"Don't stop," he growled.

"Does it matter, Isaiah?" she repeated. "Do you want to be the only man I've ever touched like this? Do you want to know you that you're the only man I've ever seen naked?"

His stomach tightened, impossibly. And he was sure he was going to go right over the edge as her husky, erotic words rolled over him.

"Yes," he bit out.

"Why?"

"Because I want you to be mine," he said, his tone hard. "Only mine."

"I said I was yours," she responded, stoking the length of him with her hand as she spoke. "You're the only man I've ever wanted like this."

His breath hissed out through his teeth. "Me?"

"The only one. From the time you hired me when I was eighteen. I could never… I wanted to date other men. But I just couldn't. I didn't want them. Isaiah, I only wanted you."

Her dark eyes were so earnest as she made the confession, so sincere. That look touched him, all the way down. Even to those places he normally felt were closed off.

She kissed his stomach, up higher to his chest, and then captured his lips again.

"I want you," she said. "Please."

She didn't have to ask twice. He lowered her onto her back and slipped his fingers beneath the waistband of those electric yellow panties, sliding his fingers through her slick folds slowly, slowly, drawing out all that slick wetness, drawing out her pleasure. Until she was whimpering and bucking beneath him. Until she was begging him.

Then he slipped one finger deep inside her, watched as her release found her. As it washed over her like a wave. It was the most beautiful thing he'd ever seen.

But it wasn't enough.

He pulled her panties off and threw them onto the floor, positioning himself between her thighs, pressing himself to the entrance of her body and thrusting in, rough and decisive. Claiming her. Showing her exactly who she belonged to.

Just as he belonged to her.

He lost himself completely, wrapped in her, consumed by her. That familiar scent, vanilla and spice, some perfume Poppy had always worn, mingling with something new. Sweat. Desire. Skin.

What they had been collided with what they were now.

He gripped her hips, thrust into her, deep and hard, relishing her cry of pleasure as he claimed her. Over and over again.

She arched underneath him, crying out his name, her fingernails digging into his skin as her internal muscles pulsed around him.

And he let go. He came on a growl, feral and unrestrained, pleasure like fire over his skin, in his gut.

And when it was over, he could only hold her. He couldn't speak. Couldn't move. Didn't want to.

He looked down at her, and she smiled. Then she pressed her fingers to his lips.

He grabbed her wrist, kissed her palm. "Come to bed with me," he said.

"Okay."

Twelve

At three in the morning, Isaiah decided that they needed something to eat. Poppy sat on the counter wearing nothing but his T-shirt, watching as he fried eggs and bacon.

She wondered if this was…her life now. She could hardly believe it. And yet, she didn't want to believe anything different.

She ached just looking at this man.

He was so…him. Undeniably. So intense and serious, and yet now, there was something almost boyish about him with his dark hair falling into his eyes, his expression one of concentration as he flipped the eggs in the pan flawlessly without breaking a yolk.

But then, he was shirtless, wearing a pair of low-slung gray sweatpants that seemed perilously close to falling off. His back was broad and muscular, and she enjoyed the play of those muscles while he cooked.

Just that one moment, that one expression on his face, could come close to being called boyish. The rest of him was all man.

He served up the eggs and bacon onto a plate, and he handed Poppy hers, then set his on the counter beside her. He braced himself on the counter, watching her expectantly.

"Do you often have midnight snacks?" she asked.

"No," he said. "But then, tonight isn't exactly routine. Eat."

"Are you trying to fortify me so we can have sex again?"

His lips curved upward. "Undoubtedly."

"This bacon is tainted with ulterior motives," she said, happily taking a bite.

"You seem very sad about that."

"I am." She looked down, then back up, a bubble of happiness blooming in her chest.

"I wanted to make sure you were taken care of," he said, his voice suddenly serious. "Do you feel okay?"

"Yes," she said, confused for a moment.

"No...nausea, or anything like that?"

Right. Because of the baby. So he wasn't only concerned about her. She fought off a small bit of disappointment.

"I feel fine," she said.

"Good," he said.

"Because if I had morning sickness I'd have to miss work?" she asked, not quite certain why she was goading him.

"No. Because if you were sick it would upset me to see you like that."

Suddenly, she felt achingly vulnerable sitting here like this with him.

Isaiah.

She was having his baby. She'd just spent the past

couple of hours having wild sex with him. And now she just felt...so acutely aware of who she was. With her hair loose and curly, falling into her face that was free of makeup. Without her structured dresses and killer high heels.

She was just Poppy Sinclair, the same Poppy Sinclair who'd bounced from home to home all through her childhood. Who had never found a family who wanted her forever.

Her throat ached, raw and dry.

His large hand cupped her chin, tilted her face upward. "What's wrong?"

Her heart twisted. That show of caring from him made the vulnerability seem like it might not be so bad. Except...even when he was being nice, it hurt.

She definitely liked a little bit of opposition in her life, and Isaiah was always around to provide that. Either because of her unrequited feelings, or because he was such an obstinate, hardheaded man.

Somehow, all of that was easier than...feeling. It was all part of remaining closed off.

This...opening up was hard, but she had expected that. She hadn't expected it to be painful even when nothing bad was happening.

"I was just thinking," she said.

"About?"

"Nothing specifically," she said.

Just about who she was, and why it was almost ludicrous that she was here now. With him. With so many beautiful things right within her reach.

A family. A husband. A baby.

Passion.

Love.

"You can tell me," he said, his gray eyes searching.

"Why do you *want* me to tell you?" she pressed.

"Because you're mine. Anything that is bothering you… Give it to me. I want to…help. Listen."

"Isaiah…" Her eyes burned.

"Did I make you cry?" He looked genuinely concerned by that. He lifted his hand, brushed his thumb beneath the corner of her eye, wiping away a tear she hadn't realized was there.

"You didn't," she said. She swallowed hard. "I was just… It's stupid."

"Nothing is stupid if it makes you cry."

"I was thinking, while I was sitting here watching you take care of me, that I don't remember what it's like to have someone care for me like this. Because… I'm not sure anyone ever really has. People definitely showed me kindness throughout my life—I'm not saying they didn't. There were so many families and houses. They blur together. I used to remember everyone's names, but now the earlier homes are fading into a blur. Even the people who were kind.

"I remember there was a family… They were going to take me to the fair. And I'd never been before. I was so excited, Isaiah. So excited I could hardly contain myself. We were going to ride a Ferris wheel, and I was going to have cotton candy. I'd never had it before." She took another bite of her bacon and found swallowing difficult.

"The next day, that family found out that the birth mother of a sibling group they were fostering had given birth to another baby. Child services wanted to arrange to have the baby brought in right away. And…that required they move me. The baby had to be with her half siblings. It was right. It made sense."

"You didn't get to go to the fair."

She blinked and shook her head. A tear rolled down her cheek, and she laughed. "It's stupid to still be upset about it. I've been to the fair. I've had cotton candy. But I just… I can remember. How it hurt. How it felt like the world was ending. Worse, I think, is that feeling that nothing in the world is ever stable. That at any moment the rug is going to be pulled out from underneath me. That everything good is just going to vanish. Well, like cotton candy once it hits your tongue."

"I want to take care of you," he said, looking at her, his gray eyes fierce. "Always."

"Don't make promises you can't keep," she said, her stomach churning.

"Don't you trust me?"

She wanted to. But he didn't love her. And if they didn't share love, she wasn't sure what the bond was supposed to be. They had one. She didn't doubt that. And she loved him more than ever.

They would have the baby.

Once they were married it would feel better. It would feel more secure.

"I don't know if you can…understand. But… You've been one of the most constant people I've ever had in my life. Rosalind and I don't see each other very often, but she made sure I was taken care of. She didn't forget me. She's my family. And you… You're my family too."

"If you want to invite Rosalind to the wedding you can," he said.

She blinked. Stunned, because usually any mention of Rosalind's name earned her nothing but stony silence or barely suppressed rage. "She can come to our…wedding?"

"She matters to you," Isaiah said. "And what happened between the two of us isn't important anymore."

"It isn't?" Hope bloomed in her heart, fragile and new, like a tiny bud trying to find its way in early spring. "But she…broke your heart," Poppy finished.

"But now I have you. The rest doesn't matter."

It wasn't the declaration she wanted, but it was something. Better than the promise of a fair or cotton candy or anything like it.

And she wanted to hope.

So she did.

And she leaned forward and kissed him. With each pass of his lips over hers, she let go of a little more of the weight she carried and held on to him a little bit tighter.

Thirteen

Isaiah had actually taken a lunch break, which wasn't like him, and then it had turned into a rather long lunch. In fact, he had been out of the office for almost two hours, and Poppy couldn't remember the last time he had done that in the middle of the day. She was almost sure he never had, unless he'd taken her with him because it was a working lunch and he had needed somebody to handle the details.

It made her edgy to have him acting out of character.

At least, that's what she told herself. In reality, she just felt a little edgy having him out of her sight. Like he might disappear completely if she couldn't keep tabs on him. Like everything that had happened between them might be imaginary after all.

She tried to relax her face, to keep her concern from showing. Even though there was no one there to see it. It was just… The situation made her feel tense all over. And she shouldn't. Last night had been…

She had never experienced anything like it. Never before, and the only way she would again was if…

If they actually got married.

If everything actually worked out.

She placed her hand lightly on her stomach and sent up a small prayer. She just didn't want to lose any of this.

She'd never had so much.

She sighed and stood up from her desk. She needed some coffee. Something to clear her head. Something to make her feel less like a crazy lady who needed to keep a visual on her fiancé at all times.

Of course, she *was* a crazy lady who wanted a visual on her fiancé at all times, but, it would be nice if she could pretend otherwise.

Then the door to her office opened and she turned and saw Isaiah standing there in the same black T-shirt and jeans he'd been wearing when he left. But his arm was behind his back, and his expression was...

She didn't think she had ever seen an expression like that on his face before.

"What are you doing?" she asked.

"I went out looking for something for you," he said, his expression serious. "It was harder to find than I thought it would be."

"Because you didn't know what to get me?"

"No. Because it turns out I had no idea where to find what I was looking for."

She frowned. "What's behind your back?"

"Roses would have been easy," he said, and then he moved his hand and she saw a flash of pink. He held out something that was shaped like a bouquet but was absolutely not.

She stood there and just...stared for a moment.

Another diamond ring wouldn't have affected her as deeply as this gesture.

Seemingly simple and inexpensive.

To her…it was priceless.

"Cotton candy," she breathed.

"I just wanted to find you some to have with lunch." He frowned. "But now of course it isn't lunchtime anymore."

Isaiah in his most intense state, with his dark brows and heavy beard, holding the pinkest, fluffiest candy in the world, was her new favorite, absurd sight.

She held back a giggle. "Where did you go to get this?"

"There's a family fun center in Tolowa that has it, funnily enough."

"You drove all the way to… Isaiah." She took hold of the cotton candy, then wrenched it from his hand and set it on her desk before wrapping her arms around his neck and kissing him.

"It's going to melt," he said against her lips.

"Cotton candy doesn't melt."

"It shrinks," he pointed out.

"I love cotton candy, don't get me wrong. But I'd rather eat you," she returned.

"I worked hard for that."

She laughed and reached behind her, grabbing hold of the cotton candy and taking a bite, the sugar coating her lips and her tongue. Then she kissed Isaiah again, a sugary, sweet kiss that she hoped expressed some of what she felt.

But not all of it.

Because she hadn't told him.

She was afraid to.

Last night had been a big step of faith, approaching him and giving herself to him like that. It had been her *showing* him what was in her heart. But she knew that wasn't enough. Not really. She needed to say it too.

It had to be said.

She cupped his face and kissed him one more time, examining the lines by his gray eyes, the weathered, rugged look his beard gave him, that sharp, perfect nose and his lips… Lips she was convinced had been made just for her.

Other women had kissed them. She'd seen them do it. But it didn't matter. Because those lips weren't for those women. They were for her. They softened for her. Smiled for her. Only she reached those parts of Isaiah, and she had been the only one for a long time.

And yes, Rosalind had reached something in him Poppy hadn't managed to reach, but if she could do all these other things to him, if she could make him lose control, make him hunt all over creation for cotton candy, then maybe in the future…

It didn't matter. What might happen and what might not. There was only one thing that was certain. And that was how she felt.

She'd loved him for so long. Through so many things. Growing his business, enduring a heartbreak. Long hours, late nights. Fighting. Laughing. Making love.

She'd loved him through all of that.

And she'd love him forever.

Not telling him…worrying about what might happen was just more self-protection, and she was done with that.

"I love you," she said.

He went stiff beneath her touch, but she truly hadn't expected a different reaction. It was going to take him time. She didn't expect a response from him right away; she didn't even want one.

"I've always loved you," she said. "In the beginning, even when you were with Rosalind. And it felt like a horrible betrayal. But I wanted you. And I burned with jealousy. I wanted to have your intensity directed at me. And then when she... The fact that she got to be the only one to ever have it... It's not fair.

"I want it. I love you, Isaiah. I've loved you for ten years, I'll love you for ten more. For all my years. You're everything I could ever want. A fantasy I didn't even know I could create. And I just... I love you. I loved you before we kissed. Before we made love. Before you proposed to me and before I was pregnant. I just...love you."

His expression hadn't changed. It was a wall. Impenetrable and flat. His mouth was set into a grim line, his entire body stiff.

"Poppy..."

"Don't. Don't look at me like you pity me. Like I'm a puppy that you have to kick. I've spent too much of my life being pitied, Isaiah, and I don't want to be pitied by you."

"You have me," he said. "I promise that."

"You don't love me," she said.

"I can't," he said.

She shook her head, pain lancing her heart. "You won't."

"In the end, does it make a difference?"

"In the end, I suppose it doesn't make a difference, but on the journey there, it makes all the difference.

Can't means there's nothing... Nothing on heaven or earth that could make you change. Won't means you're choosing this. You're choosing to hold on to past hurts, to pain. You're choosing to hold on to another woman instead of holding on to me. You accused me of clinging to a fantasy—of wanting a man who might love me, instead of taking the man who was right in front of me. But what you're doing is worse. You're hanging on to the ghosts of the past rather than hanging on to something real. I think you could love me. I think you might. But you have it buried so far down, underneath all this protection..."

"You don't understand," he said, turning away from her and pushing his fingers through his hair. "You don't understand," he repeated, this time more measured. "It's easy for you. You don't have that disconnect. That time it takes to translate someone's facial expression, what the words beneath their words are, and what it all means. Rosalind was the clumsiest liar, the clumsiest cheat in the entire world, and I didn't know. Because she said she loved me, and so I believed it."

Poppy let out a harsh, wounded breath. "And you don't believe me?"

"I didn't say that."

"But that's what it is. You don't trust me. If you trusted me, then this wouldn't be an issue."

"No," he said. "That isn't true. I felt like a tool when everything happened with Rosalind. She broke places in me I hadn't realized were there to be broken. I don't think you can possibly understand what it's like to be blindsided like that."

Her vision went fuzzy around the edges, her heart pounding so hard she thought she might faint.

"You don't… I just told you one small piece of what it was like to grow up like I did. How anticipating what might happen tomorrow was dangerous because you might be in a whole new house with a bunch of strangers the next day. My life was never in my control. Ever. It was dangerous to be comfortable, dangerous to care. There was a system, there were reasons, but when I was a child all I knew was that I was being uprooted. Again and again."

"I'm sorry. I didn't mean…"

"We've all been hurt. No one gives us a choice about that. But what are you going to do about it? What is the problem? Say it out loud. Tell me. So that you have to hear for yourself how ridiculous this all is."

"It changed something in me," he said. "And I can't… I can't change it back."

"You *won't*. You're a coward, Isaiah Grayson. You're running. From what you feel. From what you *could* feel. You talk about these things you can't do, these things you can't feel. These things you can't understand. But you understand things other people never will. The way you see numbers, the way you fit it all together—that's a miracle. And if your brain worked like everyone else's, then you wouldn't be that person. You wouldn't be the man I love. I don't want you to change who you are. Don't you understand that? That's not what I'm asking for. I'm asking for you to hold on to me instead of her."

He took a step back, shaking his head slowly. "Poppy…"

"Where's my big, scary, decisive boss? My stubborn friend who doesn't back down? Or is this request terrifying because I'm asking for something that's not in your head? Something that's in your heart?"

Her own heart was breaking, splintering into a thousand pieces and falling apart inside her chest. She thought she might die from this.

She hadn't expected him to be able to give her a response today, but she hadn't known he was going to launch into an outright denial of his ability to ever, ever love her.

"Maybe I don't have a heart," he said, his voice hard. "Maybe I'm a robot, like you said."

"I don't think that's true. And I shouldn't have said that in the first place."

"But maybe you were closer to the truth than you want to believe. Maybe you don't love me like I am, Poppy. Maybe you just see things in me that aren't there, and you love those. But they aren't real."

She shook her head, fighting back tears. "I don't think that's true. I've been with you for a decade, Isaiah." She looked at his face, that wonderful, familiar face. That man who was destroying everything they'd found.

She wanted to hit him, rage at him. "I *know you*. I know you care. I've watched you with your family. I've watched you work hard to build this business with Joshua and Faith, to take it to the next level with the merger. You work so hard, and that's not…empty. Everything you've done to support Faith in her dream of being an architect…"

"It's her talent. I can't take the credit."

"Without you, the money wouldn't flow and that would be the end of it. You're the main artery, and you give it everything. You might not express how you care the way other people do, but you express it in a real, tangible way." He didn't move. Didn't change his expression. "You can love, Isaiah. And other people love you."

He said nothing. Not for a long moment.

"I would never take our child from you," he said finally.

"What?"

"I won't take our child from you. Forcing you to marry me was a mistake. This is a mistake, Poppy."

She felt like that little girl who had been promised a carnival, only to wake up in the morning and have her bags packed again.

The disappointment even came complete with cotton candy.

"You don't want to marry me?"

"I was forcing it," he said. "Because in my mind I had decided that was best, and so because I decided it, it had to be true. But... It's not right. I won't do that to you."

"How dare you? How dare you dump me and try to act like it's for my own good? After I tell you that I love you? Forcing me to marry you was bad enough, but at least then you were acting out of complete emotional ignorance."

"I'm always acting out of emotional ignorance," he said. "Don't say you accept all of me and then act surprised by that."

"Yeah, but sometimes you're just full of shit, Isaiah. And you hide behind those walls. You hide behind that brain. You try to outwit and outreason everything, but life is not a chess game. It's not math. None of this is. Your actions least of all. Because if you added up everything you've said and done over the past few weeks, you would know that the answer equaled love. You would know that the answer is that we should be together. You would know that you finally have what you want and *you're giving it away*.

"So don't try to tell me you're being logical. Don't try to talk to me like I'm a hysterical female asking something ridiculous of you. You're the one who's scared. You're the one who's hysterical. You can stand there with a blank look on your face and pretend that somehow makes you rational, but you aren't. You can try to lie to me. You can try to lie to yourself. But I don't believe it. I refuse."

She took a deep breath. "And I quit. I really do quit this time. I'm not going to be here for your convenience. I'm not going to be here to keep your life running smoothly, to give you what you want when you want it while I don't get my needs met in return. If you want to let me go, then you have to let me go."

She picked up the cotton candy. "But I'm taking this." She picked up her coat also, and started to walk past him and out of the room. Then she stopped. "I'll be in touch with you about the baby. And I will pay you back for the wedding dress if I can't return it. Please tell… Please tell your mom that I'm sorry. No. Tell them you're sorry. Tell them you're sorry that you let a woman who could never really love you ruin your chance with one who already does."

And then she walked out of the office, down the hall, past Joshua's open door and his questioning expression, through the lobby area, where Faith was sitting curled up in a chair staring down at a computer.

"Goodbye," Poppy said, her voice small and pained.

"What's going on?" Faith asked.

"I quit," Poppy said. "And the wedding is off. And… I think my heart is breaking. But I don't know what else to do."

Poppy found herself standing outside the door, waiting for a whole new life to start.

And, like so many times before, she wasn't confident that there would be anything good in that new life.

She took a breath. No. There would be something good. This time, there was the certainty of that.

She was going to be a mother.

Strangely, out of all this heartbreak, all this brokenness, came a chance at a kind of redemption she had never really let herself believe in.

She was going to be a mother.

It would be her only real chance at having a good mother-daughter relationship. And yes, she would be on the other side of it. But she would give her child the best of herself.

A sad smile touched her lips. Even without meaning to, Isaiah had given her a chance at love. It just hadn't been the kind of love she'd been hoping for.

But…it was still a gift.

And she was going to cling to it with everything she had.

Fourteen

Isaiah wasn't a man given to excessive drinking, but tonight he was considering it.

By the time he had gotten home from work, Poppy had cleared out her things. He supposed he should have gone after her. Should have left early. But he had been…

He had been frozen.

He had gone through the motions all day, trying to process what had happened.

One thing kept echoing in his head, and it wasn't that she loved him, though that had wrapped itself around his heart and was currently battering at him, making him feel as though his insides had been kicked with a steel-toed boot.

Or maybe just a stiletto.

No, the thing that kept going through his mind was what she'd said about his excuses.

He had known even as he said it out loud that he didn't really believe all the things he'd said. It wasn't true that he couldn't love her.

She had asked if he didn't trust her. And that wasn't the problem either.

He didn't trust himself.

Emotion was like a foreign language to him. One he had to put in effort to learn so he could understand the people around him. His childhood had been a minefield of navigating friendships he could never quite make gel, and high school and college had been a lot of him trying to date and inadvertently breaking hearts when he missed connections that others saw.

It was never that he didn't feel. It was just that his feelings were in another language.

And he often didn't know how to bridge the gap.

And the intensity of what he felt now was so sharp, so intense that his natural inclination was to deny it completely. To shut it down. To shut it off. It was what he often did. When he thought of those parts of himself he couldn't reach…

He chose to make them unreachable.

It was easier to navigate those difficult situations with others if he wasn't also dealing with his own feelings. And so he'd learned. Push it down. Rationalize the situation.

Emotion was something he could feel, hear, taste and smell. Something that overtook him completely. Something that became so raw and intense he wanted to cut it off completely.

But with her… He couldn't.

When he was making love with her, at least there was a place for all those feelings to go. A way for them to be expressed. There was something he could do with them. With that roaring in his blood, that sharp slice to his senses.

How could he give that to someone else? How could he... How could he trust himself to treat those emotions the way that they needed to be treated?

He really wanted a drink. But honestly, the explosion of alcohol with his tenuous control was likely a bad idea. Still, he was considering it.

There was a heavy knock on his front door and Isaiah frowned, going down the stairs toward the entry.

Maybe it was Poppy.

He jerked the door open and was met by his brother Joshua.

"What are you doing here?" Isaiah asked.

"I talked to Faith." Joshua shoved his hands in his pockets. "She said Poppy quit."

"Yes," Isaiah said. He turned away from his brother and walked toward the kitchen. He was going to need that drink.

"What did you do?"

"You assume I did something?" he asked.

Isaiah's anger rang a little bit hollow, considering he knew that it was his fault. Joshua just stared at him.

Bastard.

Was he so predictably destructive in his interpersonal relationships?

Yes.

He knew the answer to that without thinking.

"I released her from her obligation," Isaiah said. "She was the one who chose to leave."

"You released her from her obligation? What the hell does that mean?"

"It means I was forcing her to marry me, and then I decided not to." He sounded ridiculous. Which in and of itself was ridiculous, since *he* never was.

His brother pinched the bridge of his nose. "Start at the beginning."

"She's pregnant," Isaiah said.

Joshua froze. "She's…"

"She's pregnant," Isaiah repeated.

"How…"

"You know exactly how."

"I thought the two of you had an arrangement. Meaning I figured you weren't going to go…losing control," Joshua said.

"We had something like an arrangement. But it turned out we were very compatible. Physically."

"Yes," Joshua said, "I understood what you meant by compatible."

"Well, how was I supposed to know? You were just standing there staring at me." He rubbed his hand over his face. "We were engaged, she tried to break it off. Then she found out she was pregnant. I told her she had to marry me or I would pursue full custody—"

"Every woman's fantasy proposal. I hope you filmed it so you'll always have a memory of that special moment."

Isaiah ignored his brother. "It was practical. But then…then she wanted things I couldn't give, and I realized that maybe forcing a woman to marry me wasn't the best idea."

"And she's in love with you."

Isaiah sighed heavily. "Yes."

"And you said you couldn't love her back so she left?"

"No," he said. "I said I couldn't love her and I told her I wouldn't force her to marry me. And then she left."

"You're the one who rejected her," Joshua said.

"I don't know how to do this," Isaiah said, his voice rough. "I don't know how to give her what she wants while…while making sure I don't…"

He didn't want to say it because it sounded weak, and he'd never considered himself weak. But he was afraid of being hurt, and if that wasn't weakness, he didn't know what was.

"You can't," Joshua said simply, reading his mind. "Loving someone means loving them at the expense of your own emotional safety. Sorry. There's not another alternative."

"I can't do that."

"Because one woman hurt you?"

"You don't understand," Isaiah said. "It has nothing to do with being hurt once. Rosalind didn't just hurt me, she made a fool out of me. She highlighted every single thing that I've struggled with all my life and showed me how inadequate I am. Not with words. She doesn't even know what she did."

He took a deep breath and continued, "Connecting with people has always been hard for me. Not you, not the family. You all…know how to talk to me. Know how to deal with me. But other people? It's not easy, Joshua. But with her I thought I finally had something. I let my guard down, and I quit worrying. I quit worrying about whether or not I understood everything and just…was with someone for a while. But what I thought was happening wasn't the truth. Everything that should've been obvious was right in front of me."

"But that's not your relationship with Poppy. And it isn't going to be. She's not going to change into something else just because you admit that you're in love with her."

"Poppy is different," Isaiah said. "Whatever I thought I felt then, this is different."

"You love her. And if you don't admit that, Isaiah? Maybe you won't feel it quite so keenly, but you won't have her. You're going to...live in a separate place from the woman you love?"

"I won't be a good father anyway," Isaiah said.

"Why do you think that?"

"How am I going to be a good father when I can't... What am I going to teach a kid about relationships and people? I'm not wired like everyone else."

"And maybe your child won't be either. Or maybe my child will be different, and he'll need his uncle's help. Any of our children could need someone there with him who understands. You're not alone. You're not the only person who feels the way that you do."

Isaiah had never thought about that. About the fact that his own experiences might be valuable to someone else.

"But Poppy..."

"Knows you and loves you. She doesn't want you to be someone else."

Isaiah cleared his throat. "I accused her of that."

"Because she demanded you pull your head out of your ass and admit that you love her?"

"Yes," he admitted.

"Being alone is the refuge of cowards, Isaiah, and you're a lot of things, but I never thought you were a coward. I understand trying to avoid being hurt again. After everything I went through with my ex, I didn't want anything to do with a wife or another baby. But now I have Danielle. I have both a wife and a son. And I'm glad I didn't let grief be the deciding factor in my life. Because, let me tell you something, that's easy. It's easy to let the hard things ruin you. It's a hell of a lot braver to decide they don't get to control you."

"It hurts to breathe," Isaiah said, his voice rough. "When I look at her."

"If you aren't with her, it'll still hurt to breathe. She just won't be beside you."

"I didn't want a wife so I could be in love," Isaiah said. "I wanted one to make my life easier."

"You don't add another person to your life to make it easier. Other people only make things harder, and you should have a better understanding of that than most. You accept another person into your life because you can't live without them. Because easy isn't the most important thing anymore. She is. That's love. And it's bigger than fear. It has to be, because love itself is so damned scary."

"Why does anyone do it?" Isaiah asked.

"You do it when you don't have a choice anymore. I almost let Danielle walk away from me. I almost ruined the best thing I'd ever been given because of fear. And you tell me why a smart man would do that? Why does fear get to be the biggest emotion? Why can't love win?"

Isaiah stood there, feeling like something had shifted under his feet.

He couldn't outrun emotion. Even when he suppressed it, there was an emotion that was winning: fear.

He'd never realized that, never understood it, until now.

"Think about it," Joshua said.

Then he turned and walked out of the house, leaving Isaiah alone with his obviously flawed thinking.

He loved Poppy.

To his bones. To his soul.

He couldn't breathe for the pain of it, and he had no idea what the hell he was supposed to do with the damned fear that gnawed at his gut.

This had all started with an ad for a wife. With the most dispassionate idea any man had ever hatched.

Him, divorcing himself from feeling and figuring out a way to make his life look like he wanted it to look. To make it look like his parents' lives. His idea of home.

Only now he realized he'd left out the most important thing.

Love.

It was strange how his idea of what he wanted his life to be had changed. He had wanted to get married. He had wanted a wife. And he'd found a way to secure that.

But now he just wanted *Poppy*.

Whether they were married or not, whether or not they had perfect, domestic bliss and Sunday dinners just like his parents, whether they were in a little farmhouse or his monstrosity of a place... It didn't matter. If she was there.

Wherever Poppy was...that was his home.

And if he didn't have her, he would never have a home.

He could get that drink now. Stop the pain in his chest from spreading further, dull the impending realization of what he'd done. To himself. To his life. But he had to feel it. He had to.

He braced himself against the wall and lowered his head, pain starting in his stomach, twisting and turning its way up into his chest. Like a shard of glass had been wedged into the center of his ribs and was pushed in deeper with each breath.

He'd never lost love before.

He'd had wounded pride. Damaged trust.

But he'd never had a broken heart.

Until now.

And he'd done it to himself.

Poppy had offered him all he needed in the world, and he'd been too afraid to take it.

Poppy had lived a whole life filled with heartbreak. With being let down. He'd promised to take care of her, and then he hadn't. He was just another person who'd let her down. Another person who hadn't loved her like she should have been loved.

He should have loved her more than he loved himself.

He clenched his hand into a fist. He was done with this. With this self-protection. He didn't want it anymore.

He wanted Poppy.

Now. Always.

More than safety. More than breathing.

But he'd broken her trust. She'd already loved and lost so many people in her life, had been let down by parades of people who should have done better, and there was no logical reason for her to forgive him.

He just had to hope that love would be stronger than fear.

Fifteen

Poppy was a study in misery.

She had taken all her easily moved things and gone back to her house.

She wasn't going to flee the town. She loved her house, and she didn't really have anywhere else to go at the moment. No, she was going to have to sort that out, but later.

She wasn't entirely sure what she wanted. Where she would go.

She would have to find another job.

She could, she knew that. She had amply marketable skills. It was just that… It would mean well and truly closing the door on the Isaiah chapter of her life. Possibly the longest chapter she even had.

So many people had cycled in and out of her life. There had been a few constants, and the Graysons had been some of her most cherished friends. It hurt. Losing him like this. Losing them. But this was just how life went for her. And there was nothing she could do about it. She was always, forever at the mercy of people who simply couldn't…

She swallowed hard.

There was no real furniture left in her house after she'd moved to Isaiah's ranch. She had gathered a duffel bag full of clothes and a sleeping bag. She curled up in the sleeping bag on the floor in the corner of her bedroom and grabbed her cell phone.

There was one person she really owed a phone call.

She dialed her foster sister's number and waited.

"Hello?"

"I hope it's not too late," Poppy said, rolling to her side and looking out the window at the inky black sky.

It had the audacity to look normal out there. Clear and crisp like it was just a typical December night and not a night where her world had crashed down around her.

"Of course not. Jason and I were just getting ready to go out. But that can wait. What's going on?"

"Oh. Nothing... Everything."

"What's going on?" Rosalind repeated, her voice getting serious. "You haven't called in a couple of months."

"Neither have you," Poppy pointed out.

"I know. I'm sorry. I've never been very good at keeping in touch. But that doesn't mean I don't like hearing from you."

"I'm pregnant," Poppy blurted out.

The pause on the other end was telling. But when Rosalind finally did speak, her voice was shot through with excitement. "Poppy, congratulations. I'm so happy for you."

"I'm single," she said as a follow-up.

"Well, I figured you would have altered your announcement slightly if you weren't."

"I don't know what I'm going to do." She pulled her knees up and tucked her head down, holding her misery to her chest.

"If you need money or a place to stay… You know you can always come and stay with me and Jason."

Poppy did know that. Maybe that was even why she had called Rosalind. Because knowing that she had a place with her foster sister made her feel slightly less rootless.

She wouldn't need to use it. At least, she *shouldn't* need to use it. But knowing that Rosalind was there for her helped.

Right now, with the only other anchor in her life removed and casting her mostly adrift, Rosalind was more important than ever.

"Isaiah isn't being a terror about it, is he?" Rosalind asked.

"Not… Not the way you mean," Poppy said slowly. "It's Isaiah's baby."

The silence stretched even longer this time. *"Isaiah?"*

"Yes," Poppy said. "And I know… I know that's… I'm sorry."

"Why are you apologizing to me?" Rosalind sounded genuinely mystified.

"Because he's your…your ex. And I know I don't have a lot of experience with family, but you're the closest thing I have to a sister, and I know you don't… go dating your sister's ex-boyfriends."

"Well. Yes. I suppose so. But he's my *ex*. From a long time ago. And I'm with someone else now. I've moved on. Obviously, so has he. Why would you keep yourself from something you want just because…just because it's something other people might not think was okay? If you love him…"

Poppy realized that the guilt she felt was related to the fact that her feelings for Isaiah had most definitely originated when Isaiah had not been Rosalind's ex.

"I've had feelings for him for a long time," Poppy said quietly. "A really long time."

"Don't tell me you feel bad about that, Poppy," Rosalind said.

"I do," Poppy said. "He was your boyfriend. And you got me a job with him. In that whole time…"

"You didn't *do* anything. It's not like you went after him when were together."

"No."

"I'm the cheater in that relationship." Rosalind sighed heavily. "I didn't handle things right with Isaiah back then. I cheated on him, and I shouldn't have. I should have been strong enough to break things off with him without being unfaithful. But I wasn't."

They'd never talked about this before. The subject of Isaiah had always been too difficult for Poppy. She'd been so angry that Rosalind had hurt him, and then so resentful that her betrayal had claimed such a huge part of his heart.

But Poppy had never really considered…how Rosalind's past might have informed what she'd done.

And considering happiness had made Poppy act a lot like a feral cat, she should have.

"He was the first person who treated me really well, and I felt guilty about it," Rosalind continued. "But gratitude isn't love. And what I felt for him was gratitude. When I met Jason, my whole world kind of turned over, and what I felt for him was something else. Something I had never experienced before.

"I caused a lot of trouble for Isaiah, and I feel bad about it. But you certainly shouldn't feel guilty over having feelings for him. You should... You should be with him. He's a great guy, Poppy. I mean, not for me. He's too serious and just...not *right* for me. But you've known him in a serious way even longer than I have, and if you think he's the guy for you..."

"We were engaged," Poppy said. "But he broke it off."

"What?"

"It's a long story." Poppy laughed. "A very Isaiah story, really. We got engaged. Then we slept together. Then I broke up with him. Then I got pregnant. Then we slept together again. Then we kind of...got back engaged... But then he...broke up with me because I told him I was in love with him."

"We really need to not have so much time between phone calls," Rosalind said. "Okay. So... You being in love with him...scared him?"

"Yes," Poppy said slowly.

She wasn't going to bring up Rosalind's part in the issues between Poppy and Isaiah. Mostly because Poppy didn't actually believe they were a significant part. Not specifically. The issues that Isaiah had with love and feelings were definitely on him.

"And you're just going to...let him walk away from what you have?"

"There's nothing I can do to stop him. He said he doesn't love me. He said he doesn't... He doesn't want a relationship like that. There's nothing I can do to change how he feels."

"What did you do when he said that?"

"I yelled at him. And then… I left."

"If I was in love with a guy, I would camp out on his doorstep. I would make him miserable."

"I have some pride, Rosalind."

"I don't," Rosalind said. "I'm a crazy bitch when it comes to love. I mean, I blew up a really good thing to chase after Jason."

"This is… It's different."

"But you love him."

"How many times can I be expected to care for someone and lose them? You know. Better than anyone, you understand what growing up was like for me. For us. People were always just…shuffling us around on a whim. And I just… I can't handle it. Not anymore."

"There's a really big difference between now and then," Rosalind pointed out. "We are not kids. This is what I realized, though a little bit late with Isaiah. I wasn't a child. I didn't have to go along. I had a choice. Child services and foster families and toxic parents don't get to run our lives anymore, Poppy. We are in charge now. You're your own caseworker. You are the one who gets to decide what kind of life you want to have. Who you want to live with. What you'll settle for and what you won't. You don't have to wait for someone to rescue you or accept it when someone says they can't be with you."

"I kind of do. He said…"

"What's the worst that could happen if you fight for him one more time? Just one more?"

Poppy huffed out a laugh. "I'll die of humiliation."

"You won't," Rosalind said. "I guarantee you, humiliation isn't fatal. If humiliation were fatal, I would have died twice before Jason and I actually got married. At *least*. I was insecure and clingy, and a lot of it was because of how our relationship started, which was my own fault. My fear of getting him dirty and losing him dirty, that kind of thing. But…now we've been married for five years, and…none of that matters. Now all that matters is that we love each other. That we have each other. Everything else is just a story we tell and laugh about."

"You know Isaiah. He was very certain."

"I don't actually know Isaiah as well as you do. But you're going to have a baby with him. And… Whether or not you get him in the end, don't you think what you want is worth fighting for? Not for the sake of the baby, or anything like that. But for you. Have you ever fought for *you* before, Poppy?"

She had started to. When Isaiah had broken things off. But…

She didn't know if she really had.

Maybe Rosalind was right. Maybe she needed to face this head-on. Again.

Because nobody controlled the show but her. Nobody told her when to be done except for her.

And pride shouldn't have the last word.

"I love you," Poppy said. "I hope you *know* that. I know we're different. But you've been family to me. And… You're responsible for some of the best things I have in life."

"Well, I'm going to feel guilty if Isaiah breaks your heart."

"Even if he does… I'll be glad he was in my life for as long as he was. I love him. And…being able to love someone like this is a gift. One I don't think I fully appreciated. With our background, just being able to admit my love without fear, without holding back... That's something. It's special. It's kind of a miracle."

"It really is," Rosalind said. "I had a rocky road to Jason. I had a rocky road to love, but Poppy, it's so worth it in the end. I promise you."

"I just hope Isaiah realizes how special it is. How amazing it is. His parents always loved him. He grew up in one house. He...doesn't know that not everyone has someone to love them."

"He might have had all of that, Poppy, but he's never had you. Don't sell yourself short."

Poppy tried to breathe around the emotion swelling in her chest. "If it all works out, you're invited to the wedding," Poppy said decisively.

"Are you sure?"

"Of course. You're my family. And the family I've created is the most important thing I have."

"Good," Rosalind said. "Then go fight for the rest of it."

Poppy would do that. She absolutely would.

Isaiah didn't know for sure that he would find Poppy at her house. He could only hope that he would.

If not, he would have to launch a search of the entire town, which everyone was going to find unpleasant. Because he would be getting in faces and asking for access to confidential records. And while he was confident that ultimately he would get his way, he would rather not cut a swath of rage and destruction through the community that he tried to do business in.

But, desperate times.

He felt like he was made entirely of feelings. His

skin hurt from it. His heart felt bruised. And he needed to… He needed to find Poppy and tell her.

He needed to find her and he needed to fix this.

It was 6:00 a.m., and he had two cups of coffee in his hand when he pounded on the door of her house with the toe of his boot.

It took a couple of minutes, but the door finally opened and revealed Poppy, who was standing there in baggy pajama pants with polar bears on them, and a plain shirt. Her hair was exceptionally large and sticking out at all angles, one curl hanging in her face. And she looked…

Not altogether very happy to see him.

"What are you doing here?"

"I brought you coffee."

"Yesterday you brought me cotton candy, and you were still a dick. So explain to me why I should be compelled by the coffee." She crossed her arms and treated him to a hard glare.

"I need to talk to you."

"Well, that works, because I need to talk to you too. Though, I was not going to talk to you at six in the morning."

"Were you asleep?"

"Obviously. It's six in the morning." Then her shoulders slumped and she sighed, backing away from the door. "No. I wasn't sleeping."

He found himself relieved by that.

"I couldn't sleep at all," she continued. "Because I kept thinking about you. You asshole."

He found that extraordinarily cheering.

"I couldn't sleep either," he said.

"Well, of course not. You lost your assistant. And

you had to get your own coffee as a result. Life is truly caving in around you, Isaiah."

"That isn't why I couldn't sleep," he said. "I talked to my brother last night."

"Which one?"

"Joshua. Who was not terribly impressed with me, I have to say."

"Well, I'm not sure who could be terribly impressed with you right at the moment."

She wasn't letting him off easy. And that was all right. He didn't need it to be easy. He just needed to fix it.

"I do feel," he said, his voice coming out so rough it was like a stranger's. "I feel a lot. All the time. It's just easier when I don't. So I'm very good at pushing down my emotions. And I'm very good at separating feelings from a moment. That way I have time to analyze what I feel later, instead of being reactionary."

"Because being reactionary is bad?"

"Yes. Especially when… When I might have read a situation wrong. And I do that a lot, Poppy. I'm a perfectionist. I don't like being wrong."

"This is not news to me," she said.

"I know. You've also known me long enough that you seem to know how to read me. And I… I'm pretty good at reading you too. But sometimes I don't get it right. Feelings are different for me. But it doesn't mean I don't have them. It does mean that sometimes I'm wrong about what's happening. And… I hate that. I hate it more than anything. I hate feeling like everything is okay and finding out it isn't. I hate feeling like something is wrong only to find out that it's not."

"You know everyone makes those mistakes," she

said gently. "Nobody gets it completely right all the time."

"I do know that," he said. "But I get it wrong more often than most. I've always struggled with that. I've found ways to make it easier. I use organization. My interest in numbers. Having an assistant who helps me with the things I'm not so great at. All of those things have made it easier for me to have a life that functions simply. They've made it so I don't have to risk myself. So I don't have to be hurt.

"But I'm finding that they have not enabled me to have a full life. Poppy, I don't just want easy. That was a mistake I made when I asked you to find me a wife. I thought I wanted a wife so I could feel the sense of completeness in my personal life that I did my professional life. But what I didn't realize was that things felt complete in my professional life because I was with you every day."

He took a step toward her, wanting to touch her. With everything he had.

"I had you in that perfect space I created for you. And I got to be with you all the time," he continued. "Yours was one of the first faces I saw every morning. And you were always one of the last people I saw before I went home. There was a rightness to that. And I attributed it to…the fact that you were efficient. The fact that you were organized. The fact that I liked you. But it was more than that. And it always has been. It isn't that I didn't think of you when I decided to put an ad in the paper for a wife. You were actually the reason I did it. It's just that… I'm an idiot."

He paused and watched her expression.

"Are you waiting for me to argue with you?" She blinked. "I'm not going to."

"I'm not waiting for you to argue. I just want you to… I want you to see that I mean this. I want you to understand that I didn't do it on purpose. There's just so many layers of protection inside me, and it takes me days sometimes to sort out what's happening in my own chest.

"You are right. I hated it because it wasn't in my head. I hated it because it all comes from that part of me that I find difficult. The part that I feel holds me back. It is amazing to have a brother like Joshua. Someone who's a PR expert. Who seems to navigate rooms and facial expressions and changes in mood seamlessly. I've had you by my side for that. To say the right thing in a meeting when I didn't. To give me your rundown on how something actually went so that I didn't have to."

"I already told you it's not hard for me to do that for you. The way you are doesn't bother me. It's just you. It's not like there's this separate piece of you that has these challenges and then there's you. It's all you. And I could never separate it out. I wouldn't even want to. Isaiah, you're perfect the way you are. Whether there is a label for this or not. Whether it's a disorder or it isn't. It doesn't matter to me. It's all you."

"I bet you resented it a little bit yesterday."

"You hurt me. You hurt me really badly. But I still think you're the best man I know. I still… Isaiah, I love you. You saying terrible things to me one day is not going to undo ten years of loving you."

The relief washing through him felt unlike anything he'd ever experienced before. He wanted to drop to his knees. He wanted to kiss her. Hold her. He wanted to unlock himself and let everything he felt pour out.

Why wasn't he doing that? Why was he standing there stiff as a board when that wasn't at all what he felt?

So he did.

He dropped down to his knees and he wrapped his arms around her, pressing his face against her stomach. Against Poppy and the life that was growing inside her.

"I love you," he whispered. "Poppy, I love you."

He looked up at her, and she was staring down at him, bewildered, as he continued, "I just... I was so afraid to let myself feel it. To let myself want this. To let myself have it. I can't help but see myself as an emotional burden. When I think of everything you do for me... I think of you having to do that in our lives, and it doesn't feel fair. It feels like you deserve someone easier. Someone better. Someone you don't have to act as a translator for."

"I've had a long time to fall in love with other men, Isaiah. But you are the one I love. You. And I already told you that I don't see you and then the way you process emotion. It's all you. The man I love. All your traits, they can't be separated. I don't want them to be. You're not my project. You... You have no idea what you give to me. Because I've never told you. I talked with Rosalind last night."

"You did?"

"Yes." Poppy crouched down, so that they were eye to eye. "She told me I needed to fight for you. That we are not foster children anymore, and I can't live like someone else is in control of my destiny. And she's right. Whether or not you showed up at my house this morning, we were going to talk. Because I was going to come find you. And I was going to tell you again that I love you."

"I'm a lot of work," he said, his voice getting rough.

"I don't care. It's my privilege to have the freedom to work at it. No one is going to come and take me away and move me to a different place. No one is controlling what I do but me. If I choose to work at this, if I choose to love you, then that's my choice.

"And it's worth it. You mean everything to me. You hired me when I was an eighteen-year-old girl who had no job experience, who had barely been in one place for a year at a time. You introduced me to your family, and watching them showed me how love can function in those kinds of relationships. Your family showed me the way people can treat each other. The way you can fight and still care. The way you can make mistakes and still love."

"That's my family. It isn't me."

"I haven't gotten to you yet." She grabbed hold of his chin, her brown eyes steady on his. "You've told me how difficult it is for you to navigate people. But you still do it. You are so loyal to the people in your life. Including me.

"I watched the way you cared for Rosalind. Part of that was hiring me, simply because it meant something to her. Part of that was caring for her, and yes, in the end you felt like you made a mistake, like she made a fool out of you, but you showed that you had the capacity to care deeply.

"You have been the most constant steady presence in my life for the past decade. You've shown me what it means to be loyal. You took me with you to every job, every position. Every start-up. You committed to me in a way that no one else in my life ever has. And I don't know if you can possibly understand what that means for a foster kid who's had more houses than she can count."

Poppy stroked his face, her heart thundering hard, her whole body trembling. She continued, "You can't minimize the fact that you taught me that people can care that deeply. That they might show it in different ways, but that doesn't mean they don't care.

"I *do* know you have feelings, Isaiah. Because your actions show them. You are consistent month to month, year to year. It doesn't matter whether I misinterpret your reaction in the moment. You're always in it for the long haul. And that seems like a miracle to me." Her voice got thick, her eyes shiny. "You are not a trial, Isaiah Grayson. You are the greatest gift I've ever been given. And loving you is part of that gift."

The words washed over him, a balm for his soul. For his heart.

"I was afraid," he said. "Not just of being too much for you—" the words cut his throat "—but of losing you. I wish I were that altruistic. But I'm not. I was afraid because what I feel for you is so deep... I don't know what I would do if I lost you. If I... If I ruined it because of... Because of how I am."

"I *love* how you are." Poppy's voice was fierce. "It's up to me to tell you when something is wrong, to tell you when it's right. It doesn't matter how the rest of the world sees things, Isaiah. It matters how *we* see things. Here. Between us.

"Normal doesn't matter. Neither of us is normal. You're going to have to deal with my baggage. With the fact that I'm afraid I don't know how to be a mother because I never had one of my own. With the fact that sometimes my first instinct is to protect myself instead of fighting for what I feel. And I'm going to have to learn your way of communicating. That's love for everyone. Sometimes I'll be a bigger burden. And sometimes you will be. But we'll have each other. And that's so much better than being apart."

"I think I've loved you for a very long time. But it felt necessary to block it out. But once I touched you… Once I touched you, Poppy, I couldn't deny it. I can't keep you or my feelings for you in a box, and that terrifies me. You terrify me. But in a good way."

She lifted her hand, tracing a line down the side of his face. "The only thing that terrifies me is a life without you."

"Will you marry me? This time I'm asking. Not because you're pregnant. Not because I want a wife. Because I want you."

"I will marry you," she said. "Not for your family. Not in spite of you, but because of you. Because I love you."

"I might be bad when it comes to dealing with emotion, but I know right now I'm the happiest man in the world."

His heart felt like it might burst, and he didn't hide from it. Didn't push it aside. He opened himself up and embraced all of it.

"There will have to be some ground rules," Poppy said, smiling impishly.

"Ground rules?"

"Yes. Lines between our personal and professional lives. For example, at home, I'm not making the coffee."

"That's a sacrifice I'm willing to make."

"Good. But that won't be the only one."

He wrapped his arms around her and pulled them both into a standing position, Poppy cradled against his chest. "Why don't I take you into your bedroom and show you exactly what sorts of sacrifices I'm prepared to make."

"I don't have a bed in there," she protested as he carried her back toward her room. "There's just a sleeping bag."

"I think I can work with that."

And he did.

Epilogue

December 24, 2018

WIFE FOUND—

Antisocial mountain man/businessman Isaiah Grayson married his assistant, his best friend and his other half, Poppy Sinclair, on Christmas Eve.

She'll give him a child or two, exact number to be negotiated. And has vowed to be as tolerant of his mood as he is of hers. Because that's how love works.

She is willing to stay with him in sickness and in health, in a mountain cabin or at a fancy gala. As long as she is with him. For as long as they both shall live.

She's happy for him to keep the beard.

They opted to have a small, family wedding on a mountain.

The fact that Poppy was able to have a family wedding made her heart feel like it was so full it might burst. The Grayson clan was all in attendance, standing in the snow, along with Rosalind and her husband.

Poppy peeked out from around the tree she was hiding behind and looked at Isaiah, who was standing next to Pastor John Thompson. The backdrop of evergreens capped with snow was breathtaking, but not as breathtaking as the man himself.

He wasn't wearing a suit. He was wearing a black coat, white button-up shirt and black jeans. He also had on his black cowboy hat. He hadn't shaved.

But that was what she wanted.

Him.

Not some polished version, but the man she loved.

This would be her new Christmas tradition. She would think of her wedding. Of their love. Of how her whole life had changed because of Isaiah Grayson.

For her part, Poppy had on her very perfect dress and was holding a bouquet of dark red roses.

She smiled. It was the fantasy wedding she hadn't even known she wanted.

But then, she supposed that was because she hadn't known who the groom might be.

But this was perfectly them. Remote, and yet surrounded by the people they loved most.

There was no music, just the deep silence of the forest, the sound of branches moving whenever there was a slight breeze. And Poppy came out from behind the tree when it felt like it was time.

She walked through the snow, her eyes never leaving Isaiah's. She felt like she might have been walking down a very long aisle toward him for the past ten years. And that each and every one of those years had been necessary to bring them to this moment.

Isaiah didn't feel things the way other people did. He felt them deeper. It took longer to get there, but she knew that now she had his heart, she would have it forever.

She trusted it. Wholly and completely.

Just like she trusted him.

He reached out and took her hand, and the two of them stood across from each other, love flooding Poppy's heart.

"I told you an ad was a good idea," he whispered after they'd taken their vows and the pastor had told him to kiss the bride.

"What are you talking about?"

"It's the reason I finally realized what was in front of me the whole time."

"I think we would have found our way without the ad."

"No. We needed the ad."

"So you can be right?" she asked, holding back a smile.

He grinned. "I'm always right."

"Oh, really? Well then, what do you think is going to happen next?"

He kissed her again, deep and hard and long. "I think we're going to live happily-ever-after."

He was right. As always.

* * * * *